K.I.A.

ALEXANDER CHARALAMBIDES

ISBN **978-0954729257**

Standard Edition

Published by Byzantion Books

Created with Vellum

I WAS THIRTEEN WHEN I FIRST SUSPECTED MY PARENTS were not who they said they were.

It was the morning before my birthday party. I remember watching the dawn, since I couldn't sleep the night before. I think it was the first time I'd ever seen it.

It wasn't nerves; don't get the wrong idea about me. I'd been bedridden for two weeks before that, my back was too sore to just lie there, so I wandered around the attic for hours. It wasn't anything I hadn't done before, just the latest link in a chain of passing illnesses; muscle aches, lethargy, depression.

Let's start with the basics; you are a tulpa; a cognitive device to facilitate faster, more rational thought, recall and decision-making.

Yes, I'm aware that the westernized name for the concept is based on a mistranslation. Essentially, you're here to serve as an undetectable diary, one that can't be read or stolen, and hopefully, through practice, help me to keep a clear head. However, in order to do that, you need to know my objectives, and to understand them, you need more context.

I've been heavily medicated for as long as I can remember, but the morning I just told you about is the first time I made the decision to stop taking that medication.

I wasn't smart about it. Halfway through the "party" my parents pulled me aside, and asked me why they found my pills buried in their potted plant. The conversation didn't go well.

This was the point when I started to suspect them; there was no crying or shouting; they cycled through their arguments until I told them that the medicine made me feel worse, not better, and they shut themselves in their room.

I could hear them whispering to each other. Steadily, cautiously.

Their absence was more than enough to kill the mood;

most of the guests were parents, part of a school and local community for people with special needs children. They came out of obligation, and left without other adults to complain to.

At the time, I was still gullible.

They called my "uncle".

His name is Jonathan Cooper, he's tall, always straight backed, and almost always smells slightly of cheap, store brand mint chewing gum, although I've never seen him chew any.

He's my social worker. I've known him for as long as I can remember, and he's the whole reason you're here.

My life is not exciting. That's not to say that it's uneventful, but events tend to follow a predictable sequence of illness, apathy, school trouble. I'm sure you can see the reciprocal relationship between the three, not that you've ever been ill, but Jonathan, every time he got the chance, could break that cycle.

We never did anything special together; we would just talk. He's one of the few; no, the only person I know capable of listening. Not that I'm known for my talkativeness. He must be quite patient, too.

I think this is already the most I've ever said to anyone at once, so let me get to the point; I'm older now, and smarter. I've never wanted to be a part of someone's deception, and I've never been able to shake the feeling that I'm living my life in a cage.

Two years ago, to the day, was the last time I saw social worker Jonathan Cooper. He handed me a photograph of us with some of his co-workers, on the day I was adopted. I asked him when our next meeting would be, and he wouldn't tell me.

He said, "Things are changing, Hildegard. Maybe not for the better." He's the only person who ever used my full name.

I stayed in touch with him. Usually by text or email. It wasn't perfect, but I could always reach him if I needed someone to talk to, and even if he was busy he'd always get back to me.

Except it's been two months since I heard from him.

After that, I worked up the courage to stop taking the pills.

It didn't happen all at once, it took a while to find the best hiding places and disposal methods. It didn't help that the pills came from unmarked bottles from my adoption agency, either. A few weeks ago I took them to a pharmacist, and they couldn't tell me what they were.

That was when I knew this was more than paranoia.

I nearly ended up in the back of a police car, and I sat in front of the principal more than once. None of that matters now, because it was worth it.

I'm thinking clearly. No part of me hurts. I can stay awake through the afternoon.

A few weeks after that, I started getting out of the house. I went to visit my old orphanage. It's not far. They had records, lots of records, but no one recognized Cooper in the photo. They didn't know any of the other men in it, either.

"Things are changing. Maybe not for the better."

I can't be sure what he meant on our last meeting, two years ago. Did he want me to stay safe and forget him, or be smart and find him?

I think, or at least, I hope, that he knew me well enough to know which one I'll choose.

So I'm going to run away from home.

Don't get the wrong idea. I'm not the sort of person who has pictures of Paris on their wall, and I have no intention of hitch-hiking anywhere. I'm not interested in "romantic" or "exotic" journeys, and I don't need to find myself, whatever that means.

That's why you're here. If we're going to find Cooper, and find out why my life has been the way it's been, we have to be careful. So you and I, we're going to take things slowly. We're going to get all the information we need, and most importantly, we're going to do whatever else it takes.

Right now, that entails projecting the illusion of normalcy. Not very liberating, but absolutely necessary.

"Hildegard!"

My foster parents only use my full name as part of their intimidation attempts. The layout of the house makes it necessary for them to shout to be heard up here in the attic.

Don't get the wrong idea; it's spacious, warm and sanitary. They don't have the imagination to abuse me.

They're shouting to remind me of an appointment they made for me. I don't need reminding, and now they'll think that I'm leaving because of them.

I lift myself out of my chair, the one I've been sitting in since I created you. It isn't comfortable, it never has been. It helps me think. Maybe one day I'll point it out the window instead of at the wall.

I hate the way the stairs creak. I'm not heavy, but it feels wrong to let someone know I'm coming.

"Do you want to be late?" One of them looks up at me, arms fastened around the lowest bannister. "Got everything you need?"

"Yes." I'm not going to tell you their names, they're not important. One is very tall, has little hair, and is usually staring into a book. The other is short, nosy, and usually smells like flour.

"Want me to drive you?"

"I prefer to walk." I've already eaten. I'm hydrated. I have running shoes, ID, and some money, all in a small bag on the table where I'd left them.

"Sure?" She asks, crumbs falling to the breakfast table. "I'm going that way later." A glance at the other. "I could pick you up when you're done." I look at my watch. It's a stout plastic box with a digital face. I mention it because it's a lot like you, and it should give you a good idea of my priorities. The other reason I mention the watch is that it's almost time to leave; my appointment is with the family doctor at the local hospital. About half an hour's walk.

"Well, okay." She looks at me like I just stepped on her toe as I check the contents of my duffel. "If you change your mind-" she holds up a hand to her ear in a gesture that might be an imitation of a phone "-give me a call." Everything's accounted for.

"When you get back, Hildegard." He looks up from his book. "We'll have another discussion about your educational future."

"There's nothing to discuss," I tell him, and he goes back to his book. The fact that I already know my future won't stop him from bringing it up later.

My hand's on the doorknob, and I can feel the dry summer air through the keyhole.

"H, I know you hate the idea of a military academy." She's still sitting at the table, looking down into her empty plate. Her hand is resting on her husband's. "But it's a full scholarship, Truman is so much better than anything we could afford for you, and it's so accommodating for people like you and registration ends tomorrow, so-"

The door creaks open, and the smell of baking concrete

outside slithers under my nose. I'm not in the mood to argue, so I close the door behind me before they can get up.

My head clears once I leave the house. Probably because I spent so long tranquilized there.

The neighborhood isn't much better, but there are places I can go if I'm not ready for home, or if school's too much. I haven't used them much since I stopped taking the pills, but I'll never forget them. The trees near the senior center, the hollow sculpture in the park, even the row of spotless pastel dumpsters outside the school gym.

I'm not going to tell you the name of the neighborhood, since it's not important to our mission or in general.

The hospital itself is more what you would expect from something called a clinic. From the outside, most of what you see is glass, chrome, and those long banners and square signs that read like redundant advertisements. There isn't much call for the messier part of medical care here, since accident and crime rates are almost non-existent.

They know me here. I've visited many times, and I can tell by the way the woman at the desk runs off, she was expecting my guardians to come with me.

They like to sit in on the diagnoses and gently nod their heads.

She talks into her phone, glances down at her appointments, sees I made one under my own name, and gives me the usual platitudes and broad estimates.

There are benches here, flanked by the sort of potted plants you'd find in airports or funeral homes, but I don't feel like sitting, firstly, out of principle, but secondly, and more importantly, because I have questions.

I've always been taken to the same doctor, so is he in on it?

Does he meet with my foster parents before and after my checkups? Probably won't get the chance to find out what he knows, and luckily it doesn't matter that much: Going undetected is our priority.

So I try to avoid my usual glare, and I stand by reception until the woman behind the desk tells me where I need to be.

Dr. Caulder's office, just below the single rooms and above the children's ward.

The path there's flanked by the usual suspects, rubbing their hands and scanning pamphlets. I think I might be the only person with a legitimate medical issue to ever visit.

It does feel strange, coming here without an escort, like any moment someone will walk up to me and shout that I'm not allowed to be here. They might be right; I'm not technically sick anymore. As far as I know, anyway.

Caulder gives me his practiced smile the moment after I enter. He doesn't do a very good job. I think he remembers me.

"Ah, back again, Ms.-" He runs his hands through a stack of papers.

"Hildegard."

"All right, then, Hildegard-" He slides over on his desk chair "-please have a seat." I take a seat as Caulder opens one drawer after another, and in moments his hands are full of diagnostic tools. "So," he says, turning back to me, "this is the first time we've talked about things without your parents-"

"Guardians."

"All right, guardians." He's always been one of those doctors impressed by their own bedside manner. "Now, which of your-" he pauses to look down at what's probably a very long list. "-symptoms in particular would you like to discuss? Your medication should be taking care of most of them, if you'd like a prescription for something specific, I'll see what I can do, but-" He looks up at me, maybe in the eye. I look down at the floor. His voice sounds honest, but in some of the scenarios I'm imagining, Dr. Caulder plays an important role.

"My medication."

"Yes?" he asks.

"It didn't come from you, did it?" Obvious, but it doesn't hurt to make sure.

"No, no," he looks down at his papers again. "Did your guardians really not discuss things with you?"

"No," I say. "Tell me where it came from."

"Well, as I have it here-" he scans the page "-it was a series of government prescriptions; your adoption agency-" he flinches a little at "adoption", everyone does "-recommended them to your guardians; I have to assume they were accurate."

"So you never knew what they were?"

"No, Hildegard." He looks up from his papers. "I did ask them, many times to tell me, but all I could do for you was to prescribe as conservatively as possible to avoid your treatments interacting, so-" He turns in his chair, and puts his papers away. "-you've had some sort of medical event, I assume." On the way here, I put some thought into the phrasing that might have the most impact on a health care professional.

"I'm cured," I tell him. He looks me up and down for a moment.

"You can't be cured; your symptoms were chronic, most without any obvious cause, so-"

"Read them out," I tell him. He doesn't argue, he just pulls more papers, ancient, coffee-stained printouts, from under his desk.

"Well, most of them were related, but the chronic pain,

the fatigue, they're all-"

"Gone."

"And the slowed metabolism, low body temperature?" He spins around to his discarded pile of diagnostic instruments. "I have to check this." He jabs a thermometer at me.

"You don't need to take my temperature. The fact that I walked here, from my house, should be enough."

"Well, all right." He leans back in his chair, the list of symptoms still in his hands. "Everything physical. What about your prosopagnosia?"

"Still there."

"Yes." He places the charts back into his desk. "I suppose you'd be seeing the world quite differently without it, but that's not what I want to focus on." I think he eyes the door for a second. "You stopped taking whatever your guardians were giving you."

From what I can tell, Dr. Caulder is not a part of this, whatever "this" turns out to be. I think he may also be a good person, but even if he isn't, he's still a responsible doctor. There are some things he has to tell my "guardians."

"No. My symptoms stopped while I was still taking them."

He knows that doesn't add up. I'll give him credit for not being gullible.

"Well-" He's not going to argue. Good. "-I'd still like to run some tests, if that's okay, nothing invasive, you remember what we discussed last time?"

"Whole Genome Sequencing."

"Yes, yes, now, it might seem scary-" he's back in child-comforting mode. "-but it doesn't mean a thing about who you are, and it can help us figure out where some of your problems-" He realizes there's a problem with his script, "-where, uh, some of them might have gone, it takes some time, but-"

My phone rings. Only three people have my number; my guidance counselor, who has never used it, my guardians, and Cooper.

"Go ahead, Hildegard. I don't have another appointment for a few hours."

Each one of them has a different ringtone; a series of beeps with just enough variation in pitch, tone and speed for me to tell them apart. I edited them myself.

"Hello." I've never understood why people answer the phone like someone's knocked on their door, but people expect something, and you have to make some noise so that people know you've picked up the phone.

"Where are you? Your father and I-" the rest is platitudes. I wait for an appropriate moment to insert myself.

"I'm in my appointment with Dr. Caulder."

"Oh, all right." Concision is not in her nature. "Well, I just thought you'd like to know, some people from Truman Academy called, they-"

"Remind me, what's that?" I know what Truman is, but obviously she needs reminding on how much I care.

"The school. The one you got the scholarship for? Registration's nearly over."

"So?" I ask, as Caulder taps out something on his computer.

"Well, they just called to ask about you, and I told them you weren't home; they ended up asking a lot of questions about how you were, where you were; I think they just wanted to know if you were coming."

"And what did you tell them?"

"Well." She sighs over the phone. "I don't know what your plan is, so I couldn't tell them."

The house won't be fun tonight, not that it usually is. I put the phone to my chest.

"You said the sequencing takes a long time?" I ask the doctor.

"Uh, yes, but, I mean, comparatively speaking, our new facilities and networking with other clinics, running the results through government records-"

"How long?" I ask again. He glances down at his watch.

"I could have the results by morning if you were to stay overnight-" I put the phone back to my ear.

"Dr. Caulder says he wants to keep me overnight for observation. I'll be back tomorrow."

"Oh, all right, I'll tell your father-" I hang up, and put the phone back in my pocket.

"I'll have everything prepared in around a half-hour." He stands up from his chair, still typing.

The door swings open, and he guides me out into the corridor. "We'll just take a cheek swab, and that'll be it for today. We should have a room open if you'd rather stay here until the results?"

"That's fine." I tell him. I'll sleep through this academy registration period in one of the hospital's single rooms, and be rested enough to decide on tomorrow's first step. The doctor is almost certainly innocent, but he never seemed in on it. The only thing I've learned about him is how malleable he seems.

❄

Tuesday

Coop says I have to write more in my diary.

Went to the doctor today. He said I am pretty sick, but we already knew.

New mom and dad talked to him for a long time, and I

wasn't allowed to see, so I waited with Coop out in the hall. We played strangers. It was fun.

Later they said I had to keep all my pills and maybe get new different ones.

❄

The room is comfortable. It's always been like that. Not sure how long I slept.

Probably hours. Looking under the blinds, it's dark.

Have I spent more time here than in the attic at home? I thought the plastic plants and beige curtains might somehow give me a panic attack, or just be reminders of something I'd rather forget. Maybe all the time I spent here wasn't so bad.

The digital clock at my bedside reads four hours, thirty two minutes, ante meridian. I slept quite easily, but something at the back of my mind eased me awake three minutes ago.

It reminds of a photograph I took once.

The clock, I mean. One of high school's first efforts to "motivate me to include myself." It was angled as if I were lying in bed, with my digital clock and open window in the same shot. I thought it was good.

It probably wasn't, I didn't know anything about photography at the time, and I still don't. There was some discussion among the judges, apparently.

Eventually I got the "special prize" which existed in a void unrelated to first, second or third. I didn't win, no one involved had any illusions about that, but they asked me to stagger up on stage anyway, so that everyone could see how special I was, and how generous the faculty were.

What is it about lying awake in bed that brings back bad memories?

It's not gone. The feeling on the back of my neck. Like I

know I left my window open on a cold day. I did something wrong, made some sort of important mistake.

My legs twitch, so I get out of bed, swallow the warm remains of my water bottle, and try to calm down. It's nerves, it has to be. Once the sequencing is over, and Dr. Caulder confirms I'm fine, I'm going to leave everything I've ever known.

It's not, though. I've been dealing with that for weeks.

There's more to life than this. More than most people would ever know. And if there isn't, you and I will have to make it for ourselves.

Light sweeps under the curtains. Through the building, I hear the vibrations of a heavy engine, coming slowly to a stop. There's another beam of light, and then a third, rolling under the curtains, around my room, and then rumbling still.

I try, as subtly as I can, to open a gap between the curtain and the edge of the window.

Jeeps. Hummers. I don't know what they're called, but a pack of heavy, squat, black vehicles sit crowded around the back entrance. The angle's too steep to tell much about them, but there are men crowded around the door. One of them talks to a doctor, while the rest pour silently in.

It looks like they have guns.

I snatch up my phone from the bedside table. No bars.

Can I use something In this room? Don't think so. I can't call for help, and I definitely can't fight them. I have to escape.

There's no reason for them to be here for me, or for them to hurt me, but as the thought crosses my mind, I hear a shout, and, running back over to the window, I can see the doctor, his hands in plastic cuffs.

They drag him away, kicking and shouting, a black bag over his head.

I know the hospital's layout pretty well, at least on this floor.

I can find my way back to the doctor's office or down to the lobby easily. There are plenty of stairwells and elevators, as well as hiding places like toilets, closets and offices that are probably empty.

The door to my room is new, well-oiled, so it slides open without a sound. Still no sign of the men, whoever they are, in the corridor outside. I can hear something, though. Shouting, maybe, from a long way away; someone's definitely upset about something.

Standing in the middle of the overnight wards is probably a bad idea. There aren't very many emergencies near here, but this is still a hospital, and this is probably the most open floor.

I make for the closest stairwell, 3B, and try to step as quietly as I can. Things might be easier on some of these patients with gowns; my shoes are bound to make more noise. I might have to get rid of them unless I can find something to wrap them in.

There's a crash, and the sound of breaking glass. Couldn't be more than two floors down. They're coming from the ground floor, up.

That should have been obvious. I must be panicking. Is this what it's like? Not enjoying it so far.

I could go back, see if I could find somewhere to hide in the overnight wards, but there are only two floors above that, and I wouldn't have enough time to escape before they started to come down again, I have to go ahead, and I have to do it before they come to me.

The stairwell's bright and clean, like always, and through the glass of the outside wall I can see the silhouettes of more heavy black vehicles, growling in the lot.

Halfway down, I stop. There's a cart here full of cleaning supplies, with no janitor to be found.

Mops, water, some chemical sprays. Probably useless. There's a pair of heavy duty cleaning gloves under the biggest mop, so I take them and put them on as fast as I can.

I know this spot, there are a few corridors we always used to take from Caulder's office to where I would spent the night, and as I round the corner I see what I'm looking for.

A dirty brown door, hanging slightly open. Inside, apart from shelves stocked with heavy duty cleaning supplies, is a boring gray oblong. A fuse box.

I test the gloves for a moment, wringing my hands, making a fist.

Realistically, there's no way for me to know if they'll protect me, but if I'm committed to being realistic then I would've given up already.

I reach into the box, and start pulling out as many wires as I can see. There are sparks for a second, then a far off crash, and darkness. It might not be the advantage I need, but at least I tried.

I ditch the gloves among the piles of soap, and step back out into the darkened hospital. Obviously, I can't see in the dark; at least, not as well as I could normally, but neither can they. Unless they all have night vision goggles, which I wouldn't rule out. In either case, what I really need now is a flashlight.

I can still see where I'm going, mostly. It's bright outside, almost a full moon, and as I take another step forward, beams of light jump onto the wall to my right, and for a second I see silent shadows with raised, gesturing hands.

The next stairwell is too far. I need somewhere to hide.

The closest room is the children's ward, so I step as quietly as I can through the opening. There are still a few patients here; most have just woken up from the power cut. There are more shadows on the wall, and light streams in from both sides of the ward. I can hear the rush of heavy footsteps in time.

I flatten against the wall by the door, and slide, as quietly as I can, under the bed.

All I can see are flashlight beams, dancing around the room, illuminating different scenes for moments at a time. Most kids get a second or two of crying before they're cuffed, gagged, and on the floor.

I think a girl sees me, crawling along the ground. For just a second, our eyes meet, but a gloved hand catches her by the ankle, and drags her away, her eyes closed as tight as she can make them.

Two men kneel by her body, turning her face back and forth under a flashlight as they secure the plastic cuffs around her shaking wrists.

Another beam of light plays across them. Their uniforms are black, and heavy with pouches. Their faces are hidden behind plastic respirators, and tubes coil around their shoulders like snakes. There's a patch on their shoulders, a two-masted ship in profile, sitting perfectly straight on a calm sea.

The lights roll away as the men heave the girl and the other children upright. One of them gives more hand signals and they stalk, single file, out the door.

This is not a bunch of criminals. This is some kind of professional operation. They might even work for the government. I should feel scared, but I don't anymore.

In the empty children's ward, I have time to think. I always knew something was happening behind the scenes. The possibility had occurred to me that I was just a paranoid schizophrenic.

I'm certain it's never been more reassuring to be hunted

by anonymous kidnap squads.

Now that particular epiphany's been dealt with, it's time to focus more on my current situation. The flashlights have faded, along with the rustle of equipment and weapons. If I'm going to move, it has to be now. There are a few ways down to ground level, but only one has a good view, so I pick myself up from under the bed, and go on my way as quietly as I can.

The corridors, dark and deserted, are surprisingly recognizable, and the window by the stairwell lets in just enough moonlight for me to skirt the edge.

The situation out front is pretty similar to all the other angles I've seen, crowds of big, brick shaped cars, with one key difference. Further back, near the road, are police cruisers, just sitting there, lights flashing. I think I can even make out a few officers leaning on the hoods of their cars, trying to get a better view of what's going on in here.

There's a creak behind me, and the beam of a flashlight sweeps over my back.

They'll be here in seconds, the stairwell and corridors to my left and right are empty; my hand runs over the window's catch, and it slides open. I stand outside, in the cold, balancing on a gutter, and try to close the window as quietly as I can.

Pressing my back to the outside of the hospital's walls, I can just hear the men go by. I'm not high enough to be seriously injured, but falling now would probably really hurt. I don't know if it's my balance or the wind, but something nudges me. My hand shoots out, grabs a drain pipe, and I'm steady again.

My breath starts to come back. Slowly. I used to get nausea looking out windows higher than my bedroom.

I can see flashlight beams, lots of them. Now my eyes are adjusted to the dark, there are slivers of light shining from every window on every floor. I have nowhere to go, but for the moment, I'm in comparatively little danger, so I just watch, to confirm my suspicions.

Some lights are linear; they move up to the top, and then down. Some seem to do circuits of the same floor, while others go up and down between floor two and floor four. There are a few irregularities; lights around the clinic entrance, probably leading the people they've "arrested" into custody. The police don't seem to be involved, except as spectators.

This pattern is an intelligent one, I'm pretty certain of that. Finding a flaw should just be a question of working out what the pattern is for, shouldn't it?

They probably told the local police otherwise, but they're almost certainly here to capture someone, hopefully not me. If I was in charge of this, I'd just call in a bomb threat, probably of a really specific kind, and be there to offer the police help when they realize they don't have the people or equipment to deal with it.

It wouldn't be hard; around here the police don't deal with much other than parking tickets and speeders.

I'm not sure how that can help me, but there is something else; the ambulance bay. I can just see the tip of the ramp from here, and since it leads out into the road, there are exactly zero vehicles around it, police or otherwise. If I can get there, I won't even have to involve the police; I could walk home.

They can't be that stupid. Whoever's directing the search pattern is smart, but would they really leave the ambulance bay under guarded as a trap?

I don't know, but I can't stop now after coming this far.

Stepping back through the window into the hospital's cold corridor, I can see the route I need to take.

The soldiers, if that's what they are, have gone up, and from the pattern I saw outside, there should be no one between me and freedom.

Ahead's the next stairwell, completely dark, and around the final corner, I can see the door to the garage. I've never been in there. Actually, I have. A few times. I just wasn't conscious.

It should be easy to choose to open this door, but my hand, an inch from the handle, is hesitating. It's the same feeling from before, a cold breath on my neck, but there's nowhere else to go.

I wrap my hand around the handle, and ease the door open as quietly as I can.

Kneeling against the open door, I can hear voices, but not clearly enough to tell what they're saying.

The garage is crowded, though; too many footsteps.

From here, I can see about half the room. The ramp leading down to the ambulance, the open gate, and some piles of stretchers and medical supplies. It's completely dark, apart from the distant rays of street lights filtering in past the ambulance. Somewhere on the wall I can't see is a light source, and since I hear but don't see people, I'm going to assume that's where they're standing.

I test the floor; it changes from plastic tile to concrete at the threshold. Not really ideal. I lay flat on the ground, and try to crawl, as slowly as possible, on elbows and knees. The railings on the ramp to the ambulance, combined with the darkness, should keep me hidden, as long as the people in here keep talking, I might even be able to listen in.

It feels as if my heart should be beating out of my chest, whatever that means, but to be honest, I think I'd prefer that. What it actually feels like, as the ambulance inches closer, is freezing to death in a blizzard. Each time my heart beats, there's a second of suspense as I wait for the next one.

I can't stand up. It's too low, they'll see me. I'll have to crawl all the way.

"All teams, reporting in for the fifth sweep."

"And?"

"Still nothing."

I want to turn on my side, watch them, but I can see enough in my peripheral vision. Five men, standing in a group, one holds a small light, strapped to the forest of pouches and armor on his chest. The others peer into a variety of equipment, propped up on black plastic legs or resting on piles of bags and boxes.

The ambulance's tire is by my hand. The back of my neck hasn't stopped itching.

It's getting worse, in fact.

"It may be time to consider the possibility we were misinformed. Should've brought dogs."

"Sir?"

I'm under the ambulance now. Five feet to go. I turn on my side, to watch them.

"She's not here. How is she not here?"

Leaning against the far rail is a man with the proportions of a spider monkey, equipment hanging off him like autumn leaves on a tree. He's looking right at me.

The door I'd left ajar creaks, and the stairwell behind me groans. Above me, I can feel the ambulance humming. I have no room to look back, but I can hear something heavy step into the room.

"Anything?" He doesn't take his eyes off me as he asks the question. I don't hear a response. He shakes his head, and speaks into something at the collar of his armor. "All teams, this is Giant 1, we're aborting. Blue and green escort Giant 2 back to base. Red are with me, we'll be appeasing the locals, over."

I can hear a chorus of assents through the radio, and as all their backs are turned, I crawl as fast as I can through the distance that separates the ambulance from the road.

I can see the empty street, just beyond.

They were looking for me.

I know, because I recognize the man, his wild hair and monkey proportions. He's standing right next to Cooper in the photograph he gave me.

❄

Tonight is the one night I'm grateful they always leave the door unlocked.

It's a matter of principle, apparently.

There's only a few hours until dawn. No reason for them to be awake, or for me to be quiet, but I will anyway.

My heart's starting to go back to normal, and my body's warming up. I might be fine, or I might start to suffer from fatigue or trauma.

Anyone else would, so I need to make my next move fast. Standing in the empty kitchen, watching the single neglected light, still on by the coffee-maker, things start to come into focus. This is my last night in this house. Maybe ever. Hopefully ever.

I've been keeping my things in bags for months, ready to go any time, so that won't be an issue, but there are some loose ends I need to tie up if I don't want this to turn into a missing person case and give the authorities an excuse to come after me.

Not that it seems like they need one.

"Hildy?"

She shuffles into the sudden pool of light behind me. "The hospital was on the news. I called." She's wearing a robe, and holding an empty mug in her hand.

If she's lying, she's made it look convincing. But then, if she is lying to me, she has lots of experience.

"What did the news say?" I ask her.

"It doesn't matter, something about a bomb." She puts her mug down and starts to walk towards me "You okay?"

"I'm fine."

"Did you just get back? You said on the phone that you'd be there all night."

She's close now, and between me and the attic.

"The doctor said the results would be late, because of-" I have no way of knowing how local news is reporting things, and it's probably safer not to guess. "-what happened, so I thought I should just come home."

"Well I'm glad you did, young lady." She puts her hands on her hips, as if pretending to be serious makes her more personable. "We really didn't finish our last conversation, did we?" The stairs are clear, but she'll follow me up.

"No." Don't get the wrong idea, I'm not scared of saying goodbye, but my foster mother's always done her best to accommodate me. Not always easy, I don't want to upset her.

I think I owe her an explanation.

"Well, I for one am glad we got this chance to talk things out while your father's still snoring away," she says. My arms and legs are a little sore, not surprising. My elbows and knees ache more. Again, not surprising. "I know that Truman Academy sounds scary, I mean, it's a long way away, and you have a hard enough time making friends as it is."

I can't help but take inventory of everything I need. It's almost frustrating to know that it's all prepared upstairs, ready to go. I nod along to her pitch. If she stayed up all night, she can only talk for so long. "But the fact is that it's just so much better than what we can afford for you, and they have all sorts of facilities for things like your condition, and you've been on the waiting list for so long that-"

"Waiting list?"

"Your father didn't tell you?" She sighs."Well, I'm not surprised. We both agreed we wouldn't, in case you didn't get in."

"How long was I on this list?" I ask her, mentally counting the steps. Not that I don't already know the number.

"Well, I'm not sure." She stumbles back out into the living room, turning down the volume on the news. I could just go. "It must be years now." It sounds like she chuckles to herself a little. "It was maybe two years ago, yes, I remember," she says. "The agency recommended it to us, called us up, in fact. They were worried about your options for higher education because of the-" She waves her hand back and forth in front of her face. "-you know. I can never say it right."

"Go on." I tell her. She wouldn't tell me this if she were part of it; at least, that's my instinct, but I have no idea what its goals are or what scale it is. Either way, this is useful information.

"There's not much more to it," she sighs. "It's supposed to be an elite private school, for people with disabilities like yours, so-"

I don't have all the information, but it seems like this happened around the same time Cooper left. I can't take the risk that this is all a coincidence.

Even when we still talked, Cooper never said where he was. Once, when I pressed him, he said he wasn't allowed to. I know for a fact he complained about the cold, and he mentioned working by an airstrip more than once after I asked about some engines I heard.

"You said it was in Alaska, right?" I ask her, "can you be more specific?"

"I think so. I could look it up. Why?"

"I-" How much can I tell her? "-I was just looking at the

map, wondering where it was."

"An island, I think. Down the side of Canada," she says. "Don't tell me you've changed your mind? I think it's too late, the deadline for registration was up yesterday."

Have I? It's starting to sound like I should. It's also starting to sound like someone very badly wants me to go there, to the point of dispatching a team of professionals to retrieve me.

I know, I'm jumping to conclusions. They're all I've got.

"Can you call them? Truman."

"Oh, I think so." She sifts through a pile of papers by the phone. "Why?"

"You're right. You convinced me, I should go." She runs a hand down the seam of her robe. She likes to touch things when she doesn't know what to say.

"Well, it might be too late now, it's been-"

"Alaska, right?" I think she's staring, but her hand is near the phone.

"It's supposed to be very private. You're just supposed to get there from an airport on the coast and then-"

I don't like not knowing. You've probably learned that about me already. It's also not in my nature to do what other people tell me to. You probably figured that out as well. I would rather do almost anything rather than not know something, or do what someone else tells me without knowing why.

So that's why I'm going. I didn't like the idea of hitchhiking anyway.

I take her hand, and put it on the phone.

"I thought I was on a list. You want me to go, right?"

"Of course. You'll have to get there-"

"Tomorrow. No time to stop to sleep or eat. I'll be fine."

"But your father-"

"No time to argue, either. I'll get my things." I step up the stairs before she can interrupt. If word about what happened at the hospital gets out she might overreact. They'll probably try to keep it quiet, but I can't take the risk. I need to be gone before then.

I've been planning this for so long, it feels like an anticlimax. Everything I need fits in one gym bag. I pull it out of the closet, swap out some clothes and head back downstairs. I hear the click of the phone landing back in its cradle.

"They were surprised," she says, "but there's a cab on its way. It should be okay as long as you take this." She hands me the scholarship letter. "Should I wake up your father or-"

"No. " I head for the door. I won't have time to eat on the way, so I'll probably be exhausted once I arrive.

"Hildy." Her hand's on my shoulder. "Please don't shut me out. I know-" she chokes. "I know we don't really understand each other, but-"

I know that something needs to be said to comfort her. This is exactly what I wanted to avoid.

"I-" My hand pats my pocket. "I have my phone." She looks down at it. "You can call me. Even on the way." I think it works. She touches me on the wrist and her breathing slows.

"Promise you won't turn it off."

"Yes."

"And promise you'll call when you get there."

"Absolutely." The door opens under my hand. I can hear the hum of an approaching engine.

"All right." She hugs me, pulls back, and faces me. "I'd tell you to stay safe, but you're so much stronger lately. I know you'll be fine."

"Thank you," I say to her. She laughs at me.

"I know you're not great with words, Hildy. Go on, go." The taxi's horn blares.

There are things I want to tell her. I'm grateful for her. I'm sorry I can't trust her.

I'm sure Cooper would think of something to say.

As is, I have to sit and watch her as we pull away. "Airport." I'm going to force this to be worth it.

FILE 2: ATTACHMENT DISORDER

Thursday

LEAVING TODAY.

Coop says it will probably take a while before I like my new house.

Everyone says I should be excited, and how good it is, but I feel bad, and I can say that because this is my diary.

No one will see, but Coop says writing things can make you feel better, even if no one sees. Will definitely write more about parents. They seem nice, but talk to Coop a lot more than me.

I said that to him, and he said they're probably nervous, too. Didn't think of that.

Saw the old man again. I think he's Coop's boss, but he won't tell me. I never get to talk to him but Coop says he helped me get picked. Thanks, old man.

Got to go. Don't want to forget my things.

❄

This isn't what I'd planned, in a lot of ways.

I didn't need you for anything on the way here, but we're getting close.

Don't get the wrong idea, the journey wasn't uneventful. Mom called a few times. I think I got closer to making her feel better. I didn't talk to "dad", and she didn't mention him.

What do you need to know? I suppose anything could be important later. I was just too preoccupied to use you.

I took an airliner for a few hours, another taxi, and ended up over the Canadian border earlier than I thought. No obstacles. I nearly fell asleep in the airport, so I got some coffee.

Regretting it now.

After trying to keep out of the snow and making no progress, I talked to some private pilots. They knew some other pilots who had been paid to fly kids onto an island to the southwest. The Aleutian islands, I think they're called. My destination's right where I thought, technically a part of Alaska.

I showed them my scholarship, and eventually gave one of them some money. I got the impression I could have skipped the first step.

He radioed the island, which doesn't seem to have a name, and after reading out my scholarship letter he got clearance. Whatever that means.

That's where we are now. I've been up for fifteen hours, and I've just woken up from a half-hour nap.

There's not much to see right now. The inside of the plane, maybe. It's one of those small, eggshell white propeller planes. Enough space for maybe four people, a few bags, and an engine. There's occasional turbulence, and more consistent fog. Sometimes I catch a glimpse of water. I suppose it must be the Bering Sea.

I've never given climate much thought before. My old home was temperate, warm during the summer, cold during the winter. Sometimes it snowed near enough to Christmas.

This is clearly very different. At the airport, there were places where the snow was too deep for me to walk. If I were to fall into the water here, I would get hypothermia and die. I have no idea how to avoid this, apart from never going near water or outside. I'd like to assume Truman Academy will have some sort of safety information.

The pilot's saying something. I can hear it clearly enough, but I have no idea what he means. The radio spits for a second, I hear the phrase "permission to land", and feel the descent. The pilot stares straight ahead, I suppose when landing that's the best place for the pilot to stare.

I never found out his name.

I can't say how I feel. It's probably not important, but I expected something more than neutral anticipation.

This is probably the best way to find out what happened to Cooper: I'm not on the run; no one is looking for me, and everything I need to know is probably confined to one island. Still, going exactly where they want me to, whoever "they" are, feels wrong.

I see lights, and snow replaces cloud as the plane cuts down through the air. The first thing I see is the runway, a red glow silhouetting a dark gray stretch of concrete.

It's not small, I can see at least two huge commercial hangars, a few helicopters sitting under heavy tarps, and a mostly dark tower, covered with slowly swinging dishes.

Past the tower there's a forest. I can hear the sigh of swaying trees through the headphones and the airplane's hull.

There's light behind those trees, much brighter than the runway, but the plane's too low now for me to see over them, and they're too thick to see through.

The seat jolts underneath me, and the wheels complain as the descent comes to an end. The lights of the runway flash past, and snow starts to gain purchase on the windows.

Eventually, the plane taxis to a halt.

"You gonna be all right solo?"

I think that's the first thing I've heard him say. I put the headphones in my lap.

"I'll be fine." There are men walking down the runway. Some cradle rough shapes across their chests.

The door opens easily, and I step out onto the runway, squinting slightly into the sudden bite of the cold wind.

Three man-shaped shadows shine a flashlight on me. Two others walk past me.

They're wearing armor. Ballistic vests, maybe. I can't see much more. One of them talks into a radio, attached just below the shoulder. I can't hear it above the wind.

The folded paper in my pocket almost flies away as I hold it out to them.

One of the flashlight beams lingers. Behind me, I can hear a scuffle. The wind carries away the words. One of the men leans forward.

"Checks out." The radio below the shoulder fizzes again. The two others carry a silent pilot past me into the darkness.

One of them holds out a hand.

"Got a phone?" This is a con. Another layer. I don't want to give it up, but trying to keep it might mean giving up my advantage.

"I promised mom I'd call her." The one on the left snatches it out of my hand as I draw it from my pocket.

"Too bad," says another, "this isn't that kind of school." One of the others laughs.

"She's in time for induction, right?" The one with my phone shines his light to the left. On his shoulder is a blank space where his insignia should be.

"Dunno." Their lights go down, and one of them leads me by the shoulder. Something at his waist jostles back and forth in the darkness. A mask, with an air hose like a snake.

❄

They lead me through the snow for a while, past the foot of their air traffic control tower, through a path cleared in the woods, heavy spotlights glaring down on the scarred ground. On the path, the darkness dyes the trees black, stretching their shadows out into the forest.

After a few minutes of silent walking, the woods start to thin. The men, soldiers, I suppose I should call them, hail another pair.

"A straggler, huh?" He holds his watch out under a light. "Little late." There are tents here, low white plastic half-cylinders, like you'd see in a conspiracy theorist's idea of a FEMA camp.

"Doctor's still making rounds, right?"

"Should be." The pair standing guard shine a light into the closest tent. "Let me guess, not your problem?"

One of the men behind me shoves me forward.

"Nope. Have fun."

"They always stick the assholes on the night shift." The new guy, which I'll have to call him since I'm at a loss to tell any of these people apart, takes me by the shoulder and leads me through the clear plastic flap, into the tent.

It's full of cheap metal cots, just thin enough to sit upright on. There are people on most of them, probably around my age. Some of them look normal, like something I might have seen at my high school, but a lot of them have a military look, very short hair, piles of neatly folded clothes, some of them even have knives, maps and compasses.

"Can you follow simple instructions?" The guard looks me in the eye. He's not armed. There's snow all over his uniform.

"Yes."

"Good." He points. "Wait on this cot, I'll go to get a doctor for your medical eval." He waits for a second, and I wonder if I should say something. I suppose he must be waiting for a "yes, sir," but eventually he walks away.

There are a few doctors here already, or at least I assume they're medically trained, they're wearing white coats. Maybe that's shallow of me.

Most of the tests seem superficial, reflex tests, simple eye tests, and a few protruding tongues and coughs.

Students come and go. I didn't really think about what they might be like on my way here, I didn't have time, but they could be a useful source of information.

More likely they'll be a persistent hindrance, but who knows. From what I've seen so far, it looks like there are a few here who really didn't know what they were signing up for, and something tells me trying to leave might not be as simple as asking nicely.

I don't know how to fly a plane. Or a helicopter. Part of me feels like planning an exit strategy this early is giving up.

"I'm sorry, did I keep you waiting?" Someone shuffles up to me, a man in an awkwardly fitting white coat. It's fair, I think, to assume things about this man.

"No."

"I'm Dr. Islet." He holds out his hand. I shake it. "I just

want to make sure the medical records we have here are right, and then-" He pushes back a pair of large, round glasses "-we can make sure you're ready for action."

He's staring down at his clipboard, running a finger over facts and figures. I have to resist the urge to ask what "action" means.

"Okay," I say. A lot of the doctors I've seen seem reluctant to talk to me. Maybe they're afraid of litigious, overprotective parents. Maybe I should tell him not to worry.

"So, Hildegard Pine, correct?" He taps the board. I probably shouldn't be surprised that they already have my medical records.

"Yes."

"You've got quite a history. Lots of symptoms, lots of medications, no diagnosis." Another tap.

"Bad reactions to childhood medications. It doesn't affect me anymore," I tell him. His ID, hanging from his coat pocket reads Dr Halford Islet, head of bacteriology, Truman.

"So all these consultations for insomnia, fatigue-"

"No longer relevant."

"Got it." He rolls up the first page of his clipboard. "We're getting a lot of this sort of thing." He scribbles a note at the head of the page. "So-"

"When you say 'this sort of thing,' what does that mean?" I ask him, scanning over his shoulder for anyone that could overhear.

"Well, it's what Truman's for." He says. "My department's been asked to accommodate a whole host of different conditions. But it seems like you're deceptively functional, so if we're agreed that your untraced symptoms aren't relevant, we've only got one thing left to go."

His lead-in is obvious, but his polite pause gives me a second to think.

I know I'm probably jumping to more conclusions, but this can't be coincidental.

There are people like me here, escapees from foster homes, lured in with scholarships. It sounds like a fair number are off their medication, too. I can't know what this is about yet, but this means there could be others looking to find out.

Whether or not that's a good thing remains to be seen.

Islet's still leaning in, expecting me to finish his question.

"Prosopagnosia."

"Yeah. Now, I'm not a neurologist, but I heard it comes in a few different flavors." He blows air out of his nose, as if a condition coming in "flavors" is supposed to be a joke.

"It's developmental."

"Developmental." I assume he scribbles the same on his clipboard. "Not something I've got a lot of experience with, but you must be pretty sick of people asking you what it's like."

"It's not a disability," I tell him.

"So you'd have no trouble recognizing me?" Dr Islet asks as he draws a small flashlight from his pocket. "Eyes open wide."

"None. Your glasses. Your hair." I point as he shines his light in my other eye. "Even your skin tone. That-" He scribbles something else onto his clipboard. "-and you're wearing an ID card."

"Of course." He glances down, adjusting it against his coat pocket. "I guess it's no big surprise, plus insignia's what you'll be paying more attention to, I'm not a teacher."

"I want to ask you about that." I've never been good at questioning people.

"Well-" His pen taps on the clipboard he set down on the cot next to me. "-I'm not supposed to talk about the curriculum, I mean, I couldn't if I wanted to."

"I don't mean that," I say. Him telling whoever's in charge here that I've been asking questions I shouldn't, is the last thing I want. "I'm just confused. This is Truman Academy, right?"

"We're still on the grounds, technically, but this is it." He sweeps his arm around at the emptying tent. Possibly another joke attempt.

"Your ID says the Truman Institute," I say as I point at it.

"Right, it does." He reaches down to look at it. "They're sort of the same thing, the base was here first, they built the academy on top and repurposed all the staff, like my department. They're just arms of the Beagle Commission, anyway."

"What's that?" The moment I ask, I know I'm being too direct.

"My bosses." He's still looking down at his ID. "It's a QuANGO they set up during the cold war to deal with Soviet biological warfare." He taps the badge. "I head up the bacteriology department." There are guards filtering in, and aside from a few outliers, the doctor and I are the last ones in here. I don't have time for subtlety.

"Does this Beagle Commission work with the government?"

"Not really," he shrugs. "It's mostly "quasi-autonomous" in name only. From what I heard, oversight basically vanished after the 70's."

"Islet!" One of the soldiers shouts, and he jumps upright. "That one ready to go?" He looks back at me for a second. I nod.

"Yeah." He shuffles away, avoiding the guards.

"Then let's go." Another one points me towards another door. "We got a schedule to keep."

They march me back out into the snow, and I watch Dr.

Islet for as long as I can before he disappears behind tents and humming floodlights.

Things obviously aren't held together as tightly as they could be.

Maybe that's wishful thinking, and what he told me isn't important. I have no way to tell for sure. It sounded important.

"Phones!" A group of three soldiers shout, hefting an open crate between them. "Failure to surrender your personal communication devices will result in-" One of them squints down at a piece of paper in his hand "-punitive action!"

I glance at their pile as I pass by. There must be hundreds of phones in there. Mostly small, cellular ones, but there are a few large, brick shaped ones too. Must be satellite phones.

The blare of static down a megaphone disrupts my concentration, and the soldiers shepherding me along break ranks, shoving their way through the crowd, standing around in the snow.

In the center there are crates, piled together to make a podium.

"All right, listen up!" The megaphone screeches as a soldier, standing high above the crowd, flattens a folded piece of paper against his chest. "So-" His eyes skim what must be his script. "-first off, welcome to Truman Academy."

Some tired whoops come up from the crowd. "You've been selected through a combination of merit, achievement, and projections of your future ability." I think he rolls his eyes. "You'll all receive a proper orientation tomorrow. We're about to pass out lesson times, company assignments, and our academy map." Some of the crowd moves as more soldiers, their arms full of papers, walk out amongst the students, handing out piles of paper. "If you receive more than one, please pass your duplicates onto someone without one." I take one, three sheets held together with a single staple, from a guard as they walk past. "While you familiarize yourself with them, I'll go over Truman Academy's ground rules."

The lesson times start at seven in the morning, honestly later than I was expecting, and the topics seem like a mix of practical and theoretical, like survival and combat, usually early in the day, with things like counterterrorism and interrogation into the late afternoon and evening. "First and most important," says the soldier above the crowd, clearing his throat, "are discipline and obedience. That goes for faculty and staff, if-" he squints at the paper in his hands "-if they feel as if they're not being respected, they will let you know." I think I hear a snort of laughter. "Second, all of the following are grounds for expulsion: tardiness, violence directed towards another student not supervised by a member of the faculty, inappropriate sexual conduct, damage to school property, and entry into staff only areas."

"Sounds like everybody worth knowing won't be here long." Somebody behind me chuckles at their own joke as they walk past. I would have to jostle and shove to change position in a crowd like this, it's not difficult to imagine why he doesn't seem to have the same problem as he leans down to whisper to me, eyes still fixed on the rule-reading soldier. "They tell you this was a government school? 'Cus it's not."

I've dealt with his sort before. In my experience, it's best to ignore them.

"No," I say, not looking round. The soldier's still reading rules, and the snow's starting to get heavier.

"There's no way this is legal," he says. Don't get the wrong idea, I'm willing to put up with obnoxious people if they can manage to be useful at the same time.

"Why's that?" I ask him.

"Simple, you saw their uniforms, right?"

"Yeah."

"No patches." The soldiers return from the crowd, their arms empty. "Plus, building a school so close to an airstrip and an oil pipeline? It wouldn't be here if there were any other place they could get away with building it."

"So it's illegal?" I ask, still watching the shifting crowd.

"Can't say yet." He glances down as I glance up. "I'm David."

"Hildegard." He chuckles under his breath as he hears it. I'm used to it.

"Nice. What are you in for?" The crowd starts to disperse, with soldiers leading streams of students in different directions.

"I got a scholarship." It's probably best to stick to the truth as much as possible. David might be useful. He seems skeptical of the situation at least. I can only hope he's not unique.

"Me too." David points to his own chest. "Didn't even realize until a week ago."

"You don't seem very disabled," I tell him. "Or medicated."

"I'm not." He rolls his shoulders as the snow starts to thicken. "Used to have to take this stuff for better focus. Didn't need it."

"So you decided to come here anyway?"

"Didn't decide," he snorts. "Plus, it seemed weird. Thought I'd take a look."

"Weird?" I couldn't stop walking if I wanted to, now. The crowd's too thick, pushing me forward. "Weird how?"

"Well, for a start, I never got a scholarship for anything before," David says, "and my dad was way too intent on me going."

"Your father?" It's going to seem strange to press him now, but I don't have a choice.

"Adopted," he grunts.

Vindication. I now feel slightly less paranoid, and slightly more anxious.

"I'm SAS. You can probably tell," he says. A voice carries over the crowd, something about different companies. The paper in my hand's marked with the words "Charlie Company " so I shove and elbow my way toward the corresponding voice. David has no trouble keeping up, so I try to keep him engaged.

"I thought SAS members kept their identities secret." It's not really a question. A lot of the students are talking, it might look suspicious to stay quiet.

He's fidgeting with something in his pocket. A deck of cards. He holds it out to me.

"Ever seen close-up magic?" I look past the cards, including the obviously extended one in the center, to a face the shape of a roughly oblong potato.

"Don't change the subject." Past the guards, the earth and snow turns green as we step out onto a carpet of fallen pine needles. "Are you even in Charlie Company?" I ask. He holds up his papers.

"I am, and to answer your question-" he looks up at the forest of olive tents ahead. Some wider than others, some longer, and here and there I can see the awkward gray corners of long plastic cabins through the trees. "-that rule doesn't apply to me. I'm the youngest recruit ever admitted to the SAS, and the youngest discharged."

There are five cabins, nestled at random between the tents and trees. I suppose they must be barracks.

"Over here! Remember your quarter number!" Soldiers wave down the students, form them into lines and deal out slips of paper. "Keep your personal possessions limited to the lockers or sacks we give you; failure to do so will result in removal and penal measures!"

David laughs as he peels off into another crowd, and kicks his way through a small drift of snow between two trees.

I slide into the line for the fourth cabin I see, the one pressed against the thickest trees that marks the edge of what must be Charlie Camp, and take a number.

Describing them as "quarters" is generous, but it's better than sleeping on the ground. Inside there are rows of bunk beds, each with a low, narrow mattress, and a single container at the foot with a key resting on top.

Based on the numbering scheme, mine must be the one near the end, but since they're all identical it hardly matters. What I can see outside is more important. Guards talking. Students talking. Groups are forming out there.

Snow starts to settle in the edges of the cabin's doorway.

It's tempting to just stand here and watch how things play out, but that's probably another way to get myself in trouble. If I were in charge here, I would pay the most attention to the kids who stayed apart and watched. Besides, there's more I need to know.

The room itself is cramped and cold, with barely enough space to walk down the middle, between the bunks. The bed itself is hard and narrow. Not all that surprising.

There's more than enough room for important things in the locker, and space for folded clothes on top.

I can see from here that there's already a line forming for the combination of hose and curtains that pass for showers, so that answers that question. The guards are starting to vanish. There are two or three by the base of each cabin, and a few more I can spot on the edge of the slope of rocks and roots with their backs to the forest, but most of them are already gone.

I need to find out where they sleep, where they eat. Where they keep their weapons.

I didn't see anything they could use on my way from the airstrip, and the only things between here and there were medical tents, not something you could spend the night in with this weather.

They looked temporary, they're probably already gone.

There are lights out there. Searchlights beaming into the sky, blinking beacons at the end of antennas, swaying in the wind, even the landing lights of what looks like a helicopter as it cuts over the faraway forest.

"Hi." The landing around the door here is a metal grating. I can hear when people step on it.

"What?" I ask. The offender holds up her hands.

"Uh, I didn't mean to interrupt your brooding, I just thought I'd say hi. I'm saying hi to everyone." She's significantly smaller than I am, and not one of the military types, she has civilian clothes. Despite that, the door to the outside is closed. I left it ajar.

"And now you've done that," I say as I pull the door open again.

"I guess you're right, um-" I've heard that people like this exist, but this is my first time meeting one. "-I like your hair!" she shouts before I close the door on her. I can only hope we're not sharing the same cabin.

There can't be that many things left for me to do. For now, I think I have all the information I'm going to get, and the idea that I have to stay patient makes me want to do something. Anything. I need to stay focused, which in this case, means occupied.

The schedule in my hand says lights-out is in three minutes. No time to shower.

It also has nothing for tomorrow, but that doesn't mean anything.

Maybe part of me thought I could unravel things in a few hours and escape.

I'm really going to stay here.

The cabin is empty for now, so I sit on my new bed. I can hear the wind howling against the door to the outside.

It's not the wind that's the problem, or even the swaying trees, it's the unanswered questions, and the distant roar of helicopter blades. Doing nothing is so much harder than doing something.

I've never been closer, that's what I'll tell myself. Every day I spend here is one more day that I've never been closer to what I want.

I've had nights like this before. Not for the same reasons, but close enough to count as practice. I straighten out, lie flat on my back, and choose to sleep.

FILE 3: SELECTION THEORY

File3: R/K Selection Theory

March 5th

JUST GOT BACK FROM MORE COUNSELING.

I know what you're thinking, I haven't written in a long time, but Cooper brought it up again, and he's probably right.

They keep asking me about "incidents" or "accidents", like it's no one's fault. Trust me, I would be getting violent if I could, then we'd see whose "fault" it was.

It's not like I need school anyway; tons of successful people drop out. The first time I figure out a good way to make some real money, I'll do it, no question.

At least Cooper listens. The closest Mom and Dad get to helping is telling me to make some friends and asking if I've taken my pills.

Shouting. Something breaks. My hands jump for something to grab before my eyes open. There's a man standing over me.

"Outside, five minutes." He stomps off. I can hear more through the walls. Shouts, grunts. Yawns.

It's just my new alarm clock.

My eyes hurt. Actually, most of me hurts. It's probably just the bed. I can hear a lot of running, too. I don't think I have time for a shower, and I don't feel like shoving through a crowd to get there anyway.

Walking, or stumbling, really, into the stream of bodies, I squint into the fresh sunlight.

It's not cold enough to sting, but the air definitely wakes me up.

I'm probably going to need it.

The forest looks different in daylight, with all the industrial lights invisible. There's already a crowd of students gathering. It looks like they're in a hurry, and I don't want to get singled out, so I step out into camp and merge with the crowd.

"Attention, Charlie Company! I am your commanding officer, learn my face! Learn my voice!" More easily said than done. "You'll refer to me as either sir, or commander, your choice!" As more students stumble towards the noise, the crowd thickens, and I lose sight of him.

There's some more shouting, someone shouts back, and the crowd starts moving. Some students near the back with me start glancing back and forth as the pace picks up. A warm-up.

I needed one. This must be the next layer of testing, yesterday basic health, today basic fitness, which means it might be quite far.

I've always had a rocky relationship with fitness; don't get the wrong idea, it's not because I'm lazy. You know by now that I'm not. It's just that being able to run is new to me.

Maybe the novelty will help motivate me, but when it comes to actual physical abilities, I am by no means an athlete.

I might be safe, at least for now, a few of the other students around me at the back of the crowd are starting to stumble and wheeze.

Uphill, the group, or "class" struggle through the twisted roots and boulders as they turn to snow at the top of our small valley. At least the military kids are making a path, otherwise it would be too deep to run. Another shout, I can smell something, too. Food.

"Five minutes!"

The crowd parts as people fall onto benches. There are rows of tables, covered with steaming bowls.

I do the same, I'm much too hungry to run over my usual pre-eating checklist, and by the sound of it, I'm going to need all the food I can get.

It's soup, warm and tasteless, possibly chicken. Nothing to drink, though. Hopefully the soup can keep me hydrated.

There's the squeal of a megaphone; they still haven't learned to use it.

It hasn't been five minutes yet. There's definitely something going on, looking over a sea of bowed heads, I can see some soldiers assembling something, a map, piles of vests. One of the soldiers holds the megaphone out to a gangly, wide-eyed man. He waves it away.

I put my head back down over my soup, sweeping my hair over my shoulders so it doesn't go in my mouth. I have no idea what he'll do if he recognizes me, but I'd rather not be singled out or noticed by anyone.

"Good morning everyone." His voice sounds like the end of an anti-smoking ad. Most kids look up. Some are still too hungry. "You are all very lucky, although some of you might not be feeling that way-" My soup's gone. Is it suspicious to be staring into an empty,bowl? "-so let's discuss why you're all here. Put simply, you are now students of the finest counter-terror academy in the United States. Entirely new, entirely secret." I can hear an engine in the distance. A few of the students whoop. "Along with your curriculum, you'll be undergoing examinations throughout the school year to make sure you're absorbing the syllabus. Today's test will give you a taste of what's to come." The soldiers by the map hail an approaching vehicle, one of those squat, brick-like things as it rolls towards them. I think they're called armored personnel carriers. "Once everyone's eaten you'll divide yourselves into units of three, and I'll brief you on today's exercise."

Groups. A lot of the students are already milling around. Some have even noticed the soldiers around the perimeter. This must be happening all over the island, since the students here all seem like they belong to Charlie Company. Almost all of them are still wearing the civilian clothes they came in. The only person who really stands out is David, he's easily the biggest of the people here, and no one else has such an obvious absence around them. Or a deck of crumpled playing cards.

"David," I say, sitting down next to him. He looks up from his empty bowl. "You're on my team."

"Good choice." He shuffles his cards, all bent edges and tears, into as orderly a pile as he can, and tucks them away. "You're the smartest person here." He grins.

"Before we begin, a word on conduct. We are not the SEALs. When I lead you in drills, I will not shout or scream. If I think you're not Truman material, there will be no second chances. You will be expelled."

"Damn." David rises from his seat. "This guy really likes the sound of his own voice. Too bad we have to listen to it too." Some nearby students stare at him. One of them stifles a laugh.

"Finally, I am a member of a unit called KU Giant. You may call me by one of the three following names; sir, instructor, or Giant 1." He reaches a spidery claw up to touch points on the map. "Here are the objects of our exercise."

He looks different in the daylight, but there's no mistaking his voice or silhouette. This is the man from the ambulance bay, and from Cooper's photo.

"Psst." Someone whispers to me.

"What?" I answer as I watch the crowd. Most of the students have formed groups already. I was hoping to find out what the exercise was.

"Do you need a third person?" The girl from yesterday sits a few feet down the table.

"No!" David shouts. I may have to invest some thought in the best way to control him.

"We do, actually." It's not as if I have my pick of the student body, especially since it seems like all the military-seeming, uniformed students I saw yesterday have ended up in another company.

Being short of collaborators would draw way too much attention.

"Oh, good," she says and jumps to her feet. "I'm Grace."

"You sure about this?" David nudges me. It's more like a shove. I take her hand.

"Hildegard." No need to overthink introductions, but I do need to have some idea of what I'm buying. "Is there a reason you picked us?" I ask her.

"I'm a pretty good judge of character," she says and shrugs. "You seem smart, that's all. And you've got him so-" she starts again, but Giant 1, since that seems to be the closest thing he has to a name, gestures at the map behind him. Hopefully, David and Grace are trading introductions, I don't have enough attention for all of them.

"The object is simple, retrieve these small paper tickets. Since today is your first exercise, the number you bring back is irrelevant." A crowd of soldiers behind him check their weapons. "Everyone that returns here by midday passes as long as they have even a single precious ticket. If you're unable to acquire one by then, it's best you don't come back." He looks into the sky, squinting at the sun, and holds up a stop watch. "Go."

About half the crowd burst into a sprint. The rest mill around in confusion. I think some might still be half asleep.

"It's bad enough I have to team up with two girls, but if you're always this slow-" I grab Grace by the arm. She doesn't need much encouragement. All three of us speed up to a jog.

Two anonymous soldiers throw vests at us as we go by. Probably should have picked those up sooner.

"So-" Grace stutters as she lifts the armor over her head, "-do we have a plan? I mean, it seems pretty simple."

"Did anyone take a map?" I ask. David holds one up. Most of the fitter students are past us already, but the edge of the forest isn't far. It doesn't look that big on the map.

"Right here." Grace holds one up as it flies in the wind.

"Okay, stop." I don't know about the others, but I'm starting to slow down. "We'll take it more cautiously from here." Something tells me putting my hands on my knees might send the wrong impression.

"Maybe you can't tell," David says, "but we need to get in there."

"Why?" Grace asks as she flattens the map against a tree trunk. "We only need one ticket each."

"Yeah, but what if we run out of time?" David taps his wrist "We don't have watches, duh! Doy!"

There's a sharp yell from inside the forest. Then a crack. Maybe gunfire.

Grace points into the trees.

"You really want to go in there?" she asks.

"Yeah," he spits."I live my life in-"

"We are going in." I unfold my own map. "Just not yet."

"Fine by me." Grace sits down against a boulder.

"Are you serious?" David almost shouts."You think there'll even be three spare in there?"

"First-" I still don't know how to handle him. He definitely never gave me the impression of being this competitive before. "-yes, I do. We're not going to wait long, and second-" from the edge of the forest, I can see the ropes of smoke rising from the different camps, the air strip's tower, even the tip of the academy. "-keep your voice down. We don't want anyone to know we're here."

He crosses his arms. "So we're hiding."

"For now, yes."

"There's nothing wrong with hiding." Grace turns a plastic compass over in her hands. I should probably ask her where she got it, but I don't think I have time.

"David-" I start, but Grace cuts in.

"I would've thought you'd be the best at hiding, with all your SAS stealth and wilderness training," Grace says as she folds the map back into her pocket.

"I am." David's arms remain crossed, but his voice isn't quite so loud. "Just because I'm good at it doesn't mean I like it."

"How did you know he was in the SAS?"

"Probably just overheard him," Grace says with a shrug. "He's always talking about it." If I let her go, she's going to annoy him.

"It's time to move." I point into the forest. "We'll head for the closest tickets on the map, get three, and come back as quietly as we can."

"Finally," David huffs. "Staying hidden's not that hard." He taps my shoulder, and points to the ground. I manage not to jump or flinch. "Stay low, no sudden moves, watch your footing. Easy."

The ground's still covered with thick snow. Most of it's already frozen, so other than a soft crunch I don't make too much noise. Grace is fine, but David is much louder than his advice. Hopefully his training counts for something beyond the obvious. We should have agreed on hand signals or something, but it's much too late now; The occasional grunt or cry of pain make it obvious that this exercise counts as "supervision by a staff member," and committing violence against fellow students is perfectly acceptable.

The trees are thicker up ahead, but I can see part of a small hill on the map, so the tickets should be just past it.

Based on the way all the students were acting, they would have rushed for the closest tickets, so I need to accept the possibility that there might be none left; that is, unless most of the students went for the next closest to avoid a fight, but that's probably overthinking things.

The trees ahead open wide, so I get down on my stomach, and inch up on the edge of the rise. Behind me I hear David doing the same.

This is something people do, isn't it? It makes sense to me.

"There's only two," David says as he crawls up beside me. "And tons of tickets left."

He's right. In a small clearing is a metal hanger, like a cross between a radio mast and a clothes line, with small paper slips hanging from its arms.

There are also two students standing by it, with what looks like another two crouched behind trees on the far side.

"You see the other two?" Grace crawls up on my other side.

"Right," David says.

"Why would they stay here?" Grace whispers, "Are they standing guard?"

"Looks like it," I say as I scan the clearing. I can't see any others, but four students, depending on how tough they are, could be bad enough. "If I had to guess, I'd say they're aiming to catch the weaker students, get them expelled earlier."

"Not very fair," Grace says.

David stands up, brushes snow from his shoulders, and walks into the clearing. I almost call for him to come back, but before I can, the first two see him. Grace's hands tense, ready to push her upright. I can't tell whether she plans to help him, or run.

I've never been in a fight before.

For a moment, it looks like David might get away with it. He strolls up to the hanger, and tears off three tickets.

Then the student closest to him throws a punch. It doesn't have much effect. David catches his arm and throws him over his back. The student cries out in pain, and the two hiding behind the trees leap out, both waving heavy sticks like clubs. Apart from the shout, the forest is silent. David bowls over the second student, and before any of them can make a sound, he does the same to the two with sticks. I don't see any blood, but none of them move. He turns one over with his foot.

"Mission accomplished!" he shouts to me as I get to my feet. He walks over to hand me a ticket.

"Time to leave, then," I say. The forest sounds clear for now, but there's no way for me to guarantee that, or how long it'll stay that way.

My eyes jump from him to the students as they stagger to their feet, glance at us, and run off into the trees.

"Wait a second." Grace runs a hand over the tickets still hanging from the metal frame. "Maybe they had the right idea." She holds out a wad of tickets. "Maybe we could get more of an advantage here."

It doesn't take very long to consider the pro and cons. "Turning in all those tickets would draw too much attention."

"I'm not talking about turning them in," Grace says, interrupting. "Just getting rid of them. Fewer kids mean fewer people trying to tackle us in the near future." I glance over at David. No objections.

"Destroy as many as you can," I tell her. "I'll keep watch."

Don't get the wrong idea, it's not that I'm worried about future tests like this, even though I probably should be. The biggest advantage I'm getting here is by indulging both of them.

Finding a place to keep watch isn't hard, so I head for the hollows in the tree the two students tried to use as hiding places, but something stops me.

I can't place it at first, but after a few moments of focused breathing, I recognize the sound of breaking twigs, and the cold air that slides up the back of my neck.

I hear a shout, so I drop to my stomach again, and crawl as low to the ground as I can. The shouting's more like crying now; someone's getting badly beaten, and just over a crest of snow-covered roots, I see them.

The one on the ground must be a student. He's wearing a ballistic vest over what look like normal clothes.

I can't tell because there's a black bag on his head.

As I watch, he falls from his knees to the ground. Three soldiers stand over him with batons. One flicks the remains of a cigarette into the snow.

I've seen enough, so I try to crawl as quietly as I can back to the clearing.

Both of them look up from their piles of torn-up tickets, and I wish for the second time we'd worked on some hand signals. I settle for fast hand motions, and breaking into what I hope is a low, quiet sprint.

By the sound of it, they're following me. Good.

"Ripping up the tickets." One of the soldiers behind us whistles. "That's dirty."

The trees ahead are thick, and the ground's uneven, plenty of hiding places. David starts to pull ahead. My breath's coming faster, making awkward patterns in the air.

"Think they're still around?"

"For sure. These footprints are fresh."

"Then let's go introduce ourselves." There's a hollow ahead, so I try to gesture and hope they follow me as my back slams into place against a tree trunk. Grace is already there. David makes an audible crack as he flattens against the bark.

I can hear the snow growling under heavy, military boots.

"This is stupid," David whispers, "I've seen these guys." His breath washes across my face. Somehow, it smells like fish. "They barely know which end of the knife to use."

"Shut up," Grace hisses.

"You serious?" He turns to face her. "You think these guys can hear us with those earpieces and headphones?" He snorts. Quite a lot louder than I would like. Grace draws breath again, and I hear the clink of equipment as the soldiers in the snow turn and listen.

The two of them get louder each time one replies to the other. In fact, they seem completely focused on trading insults. I might still be able to make it.

I drop two of the tickets in the snow, and tuck the last one into my vest.

David raises his voice again. Really, he's made up my

mind for me, so I rise to a crouch as quietly as I can, and slip away while they argue.

Securing their support isn't worth risking expulsion this early, especially not when it comes with a beating.

The trees are thinner here. I can see the edge of the forest, and the line of tables, seemingly re-stocked with food, that marks the finish line.

I can't say how long I was in the forest, and I don't have time to look at my watch.

It's tempting to break into a sprint. I can see other students already sitting down, eating and talking.

I walk across the snow. When a soldier holds out his hand, I put my ticket in it, and sit down.

I'm not hungry, and according to the medic scuttling past with clipboard and first aid, I'm not hurt either.

There are a lot who are. Most get examined and treated at the tables, or lying in the snow, but some go on stretchers.

The medics themselves are more military than medical, with pouches, vests, and what look like handguns. Watching carefully, there are a few coated, ID card-wearing ones, too.

Probably members of Dr. Islet's staff, but they're heavily outnumbered. Different divisions of the same organization? If so, why do some have IDs, and others don't?

I'm paying so much attention to the medics that I almost don't notice David. He and Grace stagger past the tables and sit, a few rows across from me.

David waves away a medic, and Grace wanders in my direction. As she does, I see Giant 1 climbing his podium out of the corner of my eye.

"Attention, students!" Most look up. Some are in too much pain. "If you're here to listen to me now, congratulations are in order. You have fully earned the right to attend

Truman Academy's class of 2005." Some of them actually cheer.

There's a big group near the northeast edge of the tables that are the loudest. I don't think they were here at the start, they look too fit and well-equipped. "You may have noticed that our exercise today was not entirely as I described it. Get used to it."

Grace winds her way through crowds of students towards me, some of them standing to get a better view. "The gentlemen you encountered in the forest are my direct subordinates. For now, we will call them what they are. baggers." A few in the crowd, mostly the new ones near the edge, actually laugh. "Like me, they are here to ensure you become the best you can be. It may seem obvious to you now, but this does not mean they will encourage you, support you, or otherwise hold your hand." More laughs.

Grace slides into place on the bench beside me. "Be aware, disobeying, disrespecting, harming or even attempting to harm my baggers is a serious violation of academy rules, and should they feel you have violated these rules, my baggers have the full authority to carry out punitive action on an individual basis, grounded in their own personal judgement." No laughs or shouts for that one. "Very good." He claps his hands "Now that we have the dry announcements over with, you may follow your helpful staff onto the Academy grounds where your education can begin." Most of the students still seated get to their feet.

"Remember the tickets?" Grace whispers to me. "You said they were destroying them."

"I remember."

She points into the crowd. The group on the northeast corner. "I overheard them talking about it after coming in," she says. "It wasn't just those four kids, it was a coordinated effort to destroy as many excess tickets as possible. There!" There's a single figure in the center, a girl, I think, with short black hair.

"I see her."

"That's Golf Company," David says, pointing over to them.

"They didn't start out here, did they?" I ask him.

"No way," he says. "Lots of beefy kids, I would've noticed them. I heard their camp's on the other side of the forest, must've come from there."

"Wait, hold on. Either you don't think that's weird,“ Grace says, "or you just didn't feel like mentioning it."

"Mentioning what?" I ask her. The girl in the crowd nods to the students near her, and they set about clearing a path through the crowd.

"You don't see it?" Grace asks. "She looks exactly like you."

Most students have started to move, and as much as I want to see the academy, there's no rush. This might be more important. The trees start to thin, and every few steps I have to blink a flake of snow from my eyes.

"What do you mean?" She hasn't mentioned my abandoning her yet. "Exactly?"

"I mean-" Grace glances to both sides in the moving crowd, "-exactly. Same face. Nothing you want to tell me?"

"Like what? I have a twin I've never met?" Now that I've said it, it doesn't sound impossible.

"Maybe." Grace squints ahead as the streams of students start to thin and part. "Did you see how many tickets she handed in?"

"I didn't." The snow and dirt are gone. Ahead, over the crowd, I can see the front of the academy. I honestly don't know what it was I was expecting, but it looks like an art gallery, a jigsaw puzzle of glass and chrome. Something designed for the front of brochures and not much else.

"The kids working for her handed theirs over," Grace says. "They only kept one each. She got all the others."

"You saw them do this?" There are paths beyond the main entrance to other buildings, with routes cleared to them through the snow. Most aren't as photogenic as the main one. Afterthoughts compared to the main event.

"You don't believe me, is that it?" Grace folds her arms.

"No." I can hear dogs barking, somewhere off in the distance, bouncing off the wall of pine trees, shaking in the wind.

Looking back, the idea that someone would build something so superficial in this wasteland, and be so determined to make it look good, seems wrong. Suspicious.

It's massive. Not sure why it took me so long to realize.

Baggers call for Alpha and Tango companies, and shout out directions, pointing over the shuffling crowds. Smaller groups move off, under escort. The constant motion comes to a stop and we mill around as they decide what to do with us.

"So." Grace nudges me with her elbow. "Got a plan for the rest of the day?" I want to say no, but that probably wouldn't be true.

"Not yet," I tell her. She nods, and before I can tell her anything else, she melts into the crowd.

Fine. She can do whatever she likes for now.

In between shouts, I scan the crowd. Not much else to do. I can see over most of their heads, at least, but nothing important jumps out at me. The short-haired girl is gone, probably already assigned a class, if that's even what's happening.

The only other thing that stands out is the statue, square in the middle of the crowd.

I can't make out the figure over the sea of heads, so I push my way through to the base.

Pressed against it, I have to crane my neck to look at it, but it's nothing special. Just an old man. Jacket with patched elbows, big framed glasses, and what looks like an open book in one hand.

The plaque just reads "X". No name. No date.

The crowd surges forward, and someone shouts for Charlie Company. Time to find out what we'll actually learn here.

❄

There was no time to actually talk.

I imagine it was equal parts exhaustion and fixation, but the day is over now. Topics were self defense theory, survival tactics, and profiling. Basics are intuitive, but in practice surprisingly nuanced, like any discipline.

The staff are monotone, and no scores are given. There were no gaps between lessons. Most were held in the same lecture hall. Baggers are a constant presence.

I am exhausted.

Students are still divided. I saw the short-haired girl a few times. She's definitely in Golf Company, and followed constantly by a group of henchmen.

There's some violence, and like the different companies, it seems based on prior military training. Military kids push around the civilians, which in more practical terms seems to mean that Golf pushes around everyone else.

Most of the students are scared. It's only natural. No one said a word to me all day. Grace fell into bed immediately.

That was a few hours ago. I'm stuck, wandering up and down the mostly empty bunks in our cabin.

My bag's been searched. Everything's still there, but all I brought was a few changes of clothes.

My guess would be a second sweep for phones or weapons, but there's no way to know for sure. Between that and the chorus of sleeping breaths, my bunk doesn't feel safe.

I want some fresh air, but not enough to go out into the cold. Watching the shaking trees and listening to the wind wailing through the slits in the door to the outside is close enough.

"You're still awake," Grace whispers. I've learned her voice, I don't need to look back.

"I am. You just got up?"

"Guilty." She shrugs.

What else did I learn? A lot of the academy is on a slope. There are cliffs on the far side, overlooking a lake, I think it's supposed to be a relic of volcanic activity. It's frozen for most of the year. Apparently, there's a nearby oilfield, too. I have yet to see it.

"I mean, I can't really help it." Grace says. "Something's going on out there."

"Something?" I squint at the line of light cut in the cabin's door, scanning for movement. "Can you be more specific?"

"You didn't hear?" Grace asks.

"No."

"Look." She points to the slit in the door. Over the wind, I can hear more howling.

I step closer, and lower my eye to the gap. There are baggers, winding their way between the tree roots, tents and blackened campfires, heading for one of the cabins.

A line of students stagger out, hands on their heads. There's only three, maybe four. It's hard to tell through the dark and snow. The soldiers draw bags over their heads, and lead them away, towards the academy.

"More dropouts?" I ask her.

"Cabin Two," she whispers, glancing back at the rest of our roommates, still sleeping. "I overheard them, in the profiling lecture. They were planning an escape. One of them said they could fly a plane."

They're gone now. Footprints filled with snow. It's as if nothing even happened, and somehow I get the feeling their absence won't be mentioned tomorrow.

"It looks like other people overheard them, too." Grace nods, steps back from the door. "I think this is what expulsion looks like. Dropouts don't get another shot."

"I don't think they're coming back, either," I say. "Or going home."

She stares at me like I've just spat at her. Maybe I'm jumping to conclusions again, but this time I don't think so.

It's going to take a while for the reality to sink in. It still hasn't really, I only half remember what happened in the hospital. But saying what I just said makes it feel more real. I'm not all the way there yet.

"Look," Grace says, "this isn't really going how I thought it would."

"What's your point?" I ask her. The wind whips the snow into long, white curtains. I glance back, and any trace of the baggers and their victims are gone.

"I just-" Grace stammers "-I think we should stick together, that's all. I want to make sure we stay on the same team." Looking down at her, I'm pretty sure she's afraid. I probably should be, too, but for some reason it's not happening.

Something about this feels right. I should be doing something frightening and dangerous, something proportional to how important Cooper is.

"Yes. Okay."

"Okay?" She squints at me, and draws the blanket around her shoulders tighter.

"Yes. I agree." I can't make things any clearer, but somehow I suspect she's not convinced.

"Fine, well-" Grace backs off, tiptoeing down the rows. "-see you tomorrow, I guess."

It won't be long until dawn.

If things keep up, I won't be able to talk as much as I would like. Don't get the wrong idea, you're still an invaluable cognitive aid, and I'll do my best to keep you updated, but I won't have time to talk during lectures or other lessons. If it's important to finding Cooper, you'll know about it.

But right now, what I need is some sleep. Two or three hours should be more than enough.

❄

May 16th

I actually went to a party today. It's not as if I was invited; it was neighborhood parent thing.

The surprising thing is, I think I got close to having a good time.

Must be the wheelchair, way trendier than crutches.

The thing is, I don't think I actually met anyone I liked. There was nothing wrong with them, they just didn't seem very interesting. One of the parents would always bring the conversation back to her cats. Toxoplasmosis is a horrible condition.

Don't get me wrong, I didn't write just to complain. Cooper drove me there and back, so we talked about it.

He said he's gotten to know a lot of interesting people, and that it's not always a good thing.

Not sure if that includes me.

He says we might start doing some driving lessons next week, if Dad lets him.

❄

"You've all been performing to our high expectations." Giant I claps his hands together.

I've never seen him inside before. He looks bigger against the beige wood walls and chalkboard. More twisted. It's like someone sewed clothes onto a gnarled tree-trunk.

"And since our curriculum has been progressing nicely, I have decided it's time for another exercise." Most of the students either have nothing to say, or have learned to keep quiet.

There are still some groans, some gasps. "There's no need to worry," he says with a grin, "we're expanding our testing to a new skill set. As a result, you'll be taking the rest of the day off. The test begins at dawn tomorrow."

Over the past few days, I've learned that the papers in front of me mean nothing. This isn't the sort of place that values theory, only practice. I honestly think I could have been handing in blanks since the testing began, and only now would I have to start paying attention.

Baggers file in, students file out.

We stream down the halls, and out onto the green that holds the statue. I haven't found anything to tell me who it is, and something tells me the staff don't take questions.

The familiar rows of tables are here, along with the maps, the ballistic vests, even the medical staff, so Dr. Islet might be here somewhere. He might know.

No food, though.

It's not something I'd ever given much thought to before,

but obviously the idea of future scarcity is affecting my priorities.

Students line up outside, and Giant 1 raises his voce again, shouting over the murmur of the crowd as the students organize themselves into groups.

I can't blame them for preparing early, but I don't have the energy.

"Ticket sites have changed, but the object remains the same. Bring back at least one ticket before the exercise ends at sunset, or wash out of the program." The crowd churns as students choose their alliances. "There will be no deception this time around, so in the interests of honesty, know that my baggers will be joining you in the forest, their objective being simply to capture you." Some students cheer. Not sure why. "If they are successful in bringing you back under duress, you will be expelled." All this leaves me wondering, as I shove my way through the crowd, is what new wrinkle they've decided to add.

"Over here!" For a second I see Grace, hopping above the crowd. She seems committed to her idea of a lasting alliance, and if she is, it's something I need to cement. Most students are already heading back to camp.

There's something else rising above the crowd, too, a pile of containers, something like those Giant 1 used, although I can't see him anymore.

"You all know me by now." A tall figure spreads her arms over the darkening sky. "You've seen my troops and my tactics." There are cheers from the crowd surrounding her. Lots of them, there are even fists in the air.

The baggers watch closely, but none of them approach. "What we've been learning here is not just how to lead, because ultimately, we can't all be leaders, can we?" The students around her laugh. They're mostly the big ones, the military academy kids. Golf Company. "Now don't get the wrong idea-" she says. "-there's nothing wrong with being a follower, especially when you're one of mine, and today, I'm going to show you why." The students at her feet wind torn scraps of red cloth around their arms, knotting them at the bicep. Others hold boxes, filled with the same red scraps.

"She's kind of a drama queen," Grace says, "but not in a good way."

"Agreed." The crowd's a little looser now, it's easier to see between shoulders and over arms. "Your offer still stands?" I ask her.

"You make it sound weird," she says, over more cheers, "but yes. We're not dealing drugs, you know."

The red scraps make their way slowly through the crowd. Most people pick them.

"My name is Alanza, and anyone wearing one of my red arm-bands knows the importance of teamwork. They willingly give up their tickets for me, and their fellow students, so that no-matter how we fare in the exercise, every single one of us will pass." Some kids, the quiet ones, surge to the front.

"Have you seen David?" I ask.

"You want him, too?" Grace squints up at the short-haired girl. Alanza.

"No. But I think we might need him," I say, watching Grace scan the crowd. He shouldn't be hard to find.

"I know what the more enterprising among you are thinking," Alanza shouts over the scuffles. There aren't that many bands left. "What if I'm not chosen? Could I just take an arm band?"

"Over there." Grace points. "David!" She just jumps up and down, waving. I'm not really sure what that's going to achieve.

"The answer is simple. If someone wearing one of my arm

bands has it taken from them, by hook or by crook, then they had no right to wear one to begin with!" An enormous cheer bursts from the crowd, so loud that I flinch as I push my way through.

"You again." David scowls down at me.

"And me," Grace says.

"I can see that." He points into the crowd. "You not into this junior fascist rally?"

"I'm not a follower." I can't think of anything else to say. At least it's true.

"So what do you want?"

"Grace and I discussed coordinating. We agreed to work together."

"And?" He snorts "This isn't reality TV. Last time we worked together, you ditched me with-"

"I wouldn't if you'd done what I told you." Complicating things is too much effort. He needs to hear the truth.

"I wouldn't have done that if you two-" he points down at Grace "-hadn't been lying in the snow, giggling to each other about what to do for ten straight minutes!"

"Okay, David-" Grace says, holding out her hands.

"I was not giggling." My voice carries further than I'd like. "Look." I plant my finger in his abdomen. "I don't want you, and I don't need you, but do you really think the opposite is true? That you can survive without us?" His eyes glance upwards for a second. Maybe the idea of a rhetorical question is foreign to him.

"Yes." He folds his arms like the most satisfied man in the world.

"Okay guys-" Grace shoves her way between us "-let's just-" More cheers go up from Alanza's crowd. Some of them look like they're preparing to camp here until tomorrow. Just to prove a point, I suppose.

“You’ve got a plan, right?” David asks.

“I do,” I say. Grace stands back, eyeing the supplies and the baggers, loading weapons and rubber ammunition onto snowmobiles.

“I think you do need me,” he says, “because this plan of yours, whatever it is, needs, uh-” He waves his hands around. One looks like it’s attacking the other. “-action parts. Can you do those?” Grace has a pile of vests, maps and compasses in her hands. At this point, my pride is standing in the way of efficiency.

“Probably not,” I say.

Grace holds out the supplies

“Shall we go back to camp then?” She pats me on the back “You can explain your obviously brilliant plan on the way.”

It would be easy to protest, but something tells me that managing what I say is an important part of “teamwork.”

Most students are already plotting by the time we get there, and without any baggers visibly standing guard, the students spread out into lots of different groups, stooped under tents, crouching under trees, and a few are visible inside the cabins themselves, probably trying as hard as possible to keep their plans secret.

“Crowded,” David grunts.

“Those kids have the right idea.” Grace points in the windows of the first cabin, the one closest to the bottom of the valley. “They’re covered.”

“From what?” David folds his arms. Grace starts to raise her arm.

“Don’t point,” I say. “I see them, too.”

“What?” As much as I don’t want to touch him, I take him by the elbow, and steer him to the edge of Grace and my cabin.

"Baggers in the trees," Grace whispers as we walk behind the building.

"Their equipment's giving them away," I tell Grace. "I wouldn't have seen them at all if it weren't for the shine off their stuff." Our cabin has its windowless back to the forest, and along with the trees, the snow, and the shape of the building, it forms a natural shelter.

"Is this our spot?" Grace asks.

"Should be." I bend down, and run my hand into the ditch under the cabin. "We might be able to hide some things under here." The space is almost wide enough for my forearm, and it could be widened easily. "If there's anyone in the trees, we should be able to see them from here, at least during the day."

"Coming out here at night's suicide, anyway." David sticks his foot in the space. "Might be useful."

"So-" Grace scrapes away a pile of snow, sits down, and unfolds her map "-the exercise?"

"Right." David immediately starts pacing. "You said you had a plan?"

"Not exactly." I don't keep a transcript of exactly what I said, that's your job. Neither of them look impressed. Or pleased.

"So no?" David asks.

"I don't, because before now, I didn't have what I needed." Both of them stare, apparently neither of them willing to entertain the idea that I have nothing. I'm not lying to them, though. "The facts. To know all of them, I need to know what you know."

It doesn't take long to get a portrait of their days, so I won't waste time with details.

David doesn't pay any attention, but whenever he's asked to demonstrate something he doesn't seem to have a problem. I want to believe he pretends to be clueless so his instructors call on him more often, but every time he's forced to resort to hand-signals I become less convinced.

Grace doesn't listen to lectures or participate in demonstrations, in fact it seems from what she says that she invests a lot of effort in achieving the minimum necessary effort to achieve minimum participation. If I was a teacher I'd be disappointed, but in this case I can't really blame her.

What she does do is watch the other students, and even the staff. It seems like she's made an effort to introduce herself to everyone who would spare her a second, and for the people she hasn't met, she has nicknames. At a normal school, she'd be a gossip. Here, she gets to be useful.

"There was a lot we weren't told about the first exercise." They both nod.

"Like they sent armed, prepared adults into a forest after kids." David says.

"Exactly." I point at him. "The first thing we need to think about is what Giant 1 isn't telling us."

"So-" Grace smooths the map flat between her hands "-you want us to predict something we don't know?"

"Yes." It takes a second for me to realize how stupid that sounds. "No. We just need to stay mentally agile, but that shouldn't be our focus, there are other problems to deal with."

"That girl-" David says "-what was her name? Alfonso?"

"Alanza." Grace looks up from her map "Probably going to be our biggest problem." She points to the edge, where whoever made it included a small part of the school. "Most kids aren't allowed over here, but for some reason, when it's her, the baggers look the other way."

"What is that?" I lean in closer.

"The kennels." Grace waves her hand in front of her nose, "I've never been, but I can eavesdrop pretty well, and there's all sorts of things down there, like snowmobiles, definitely some weapons, and dogs, obviously. Huskies, I think." She seems more interested in dogs than weapons.

"What does she do in there?"

"Talk strategy, mostly," Grace answers with a satisfied smile. "And I do mean strategy, the arm band thing? I heard about that days ago, I just didn't understand what she meant, and besides, we know about that now."

"Yeah," David says, "do you know anything actually useful?"

"Uh-" Grace drums her fingers on the map for a moment before something occurs to me.

"How soon after the first day was Alanza going down there," I ask, and the question comes out faster than I expected, "and with who?"

"Now that you mention it," Grace says, "it can't have been more than a week after the first day, and I'm pretty sure it's always been the same core of four or five guys."

"It's with whom," David says, "and I don't see how any of that helps."

"Actually," I straighten up again, "it might. Did you see them?"

"Yep," Grace nods, "all muscle giants, definitely military kids. Definitely Golf. Except for her, of course." She raises a finger. "Are we still not addressing the fact that you look like exactly her apart from your shoe-gaze hair?" There's no reason to shout at her, much as I want to. She's just the sort of person that doesn't think before they speak.

"For the moment, yes." I nod back at her. "Since I have no idea what to do about it, yes, we are ignoring it. But what you just said about her core could be important."

"Okay!" David waves his hand back and forth. "Do you have a plan yet?"

"I do."

The details of the plan are concise, and simple enough to relay.

You don't need to know them. On the day, I'll remember them myself. Besides, it's not what I would call "exciting," although, to be honest, excitement seems like something I'd rather avoid at the moment.

At some point, the subject changes.

It even started to get dark at sometime during our conversation.

"I got a letter, a scholarship offer." Both of them sit squarely in the snow.

"Yeah." Grace draws snow together into a mound. "Same thing. I got the impression something funny was going on. I just wanted to know what it was, that's all."

"I was mostly the same," I say. "Except I think I left it too late, they assumed I wasn't coming, so they came to get me."

"Who came to get you?" She leans in, as if we're telling scary stories around the campfire.

"Baggers. They didn't catch me, but once I saw them, I knew I needed to investigate."

"Wow," Grace says. "You would think it would have had the opposite effect." Something tells me she wouldn't understand that this place is preferable to the alternative.

"Yeah." David leans back against the sides of the cabin. "Did your parents try to get rid of you or what?" Believe it or not, in an adolescent environment people are surprisingly willing to make fun of adoption. I'm used to it.

"I'm adopted."

"Uh-" Grace raises her hands "-let's change the subject. David, how'd you get here?"

"Got kicked out of the SAS. Dad made me go, said it would be good for me."

"Well-" she crosses her arms "-sounds like you've got no

room to be making fun of someone else's parents if your dad straight-up told you to go."

"You can't choose family." David shrugs.

"Not true." They both look at me. "Think about it. We're all made up of genes, but people never tell us we can't choose those, do they?"

"I guess?" Grace honestly looks confused.

"There are genes for being strong, or smart, or fast, but just because someone isn't talented, does it mean they should give up?"

"No way," Grace says.

"Sometimes," says David.

"Whatever." I'm not that invested in proving him wrong. He's probably not. "It's starting to get cold." I hold out my hand to catch a snowflake. "And we need to rest."

❄

It's not snowing. The sky is that big, empty blue that means penetrating cold. I've had some theoretical survival training by now, but based on the wind and water, I'd say hypothermia and even frostbite might be a real possibility.

"Ready?" Grace taps my arm. Her hands are full of the supplies from yesterday. Maps and compasses, complete with the marks I added last night. No coats, though, and no food, either.

The tables have stayed where they stood yesterday, on the exposed slope that leads towards the academy's doors, although today they're lined with food.

I spot Dr. Islet, shuffling among the medical staff.

"Probably not." I look down at her, and she really doesn't seem ready either. There are lines on her face and bags under her eyes.

"I am," David says, wiping the remnants of soup from his mouth.

"We were both pretty sure you would be." Grace pats his arm.

Baggers are tending to snowmobiles on the edge of the table rows, the same ones I saw yesterday, checking skis and loading supplies.

They don't seem too excited. Maybe their spirits will improve once they've had the opportunity to brutalize more defenseless children.

"We're all ready, then." Neither of them need that much encouragement. The camp at the edge of the tables that represent Alanza's' forces seems even louder than yesterday.

"I hope everyone is prepared." Giant 1, atop a stack of empty crates, claps his hands together, breath clouding the air. "I've been asked to re-brief the overnighters, but you all look ready to go."

He hunches forward, leering at the crowd of students, almost as if he has to squint to see them.

"But I don't feel like going to the effort." He sneers, licks his lips, and shouts, "Go!"

The baggers tear off in their snowmobiles, and the red arm-banders burst into a sprint as well.

"Does anyone need to go over the plan again?" I ask.

"Why are you both looking at me?" David says.

"I'll take that as a no." They both look ready. Tired, but ready. If anything, I'm the weak link here. There's no rush, and what we need the most right now is patience.

So, all together, we walk down to the treeline.

"Don't look now," David taps me on the shoulder, "but we've got some followers."

I turn my head. Behind us, staggering through the snow,

are five or six students. Ordinary ones, unarmed and shivering. They look down as I look towards them.

"Have you seen them before?" I whisper to Grace.

"Yeah. Normal kids. I guess they're fans." It's not an army of armband-wearing thugs, but they might be useful, if they survive. I open my map, and run my finger along it to the first marked point.

"We don't have time to take them into account now. The first point's not far."

The students behind us don't have much to say, and as we skirt the edge of the forest closest to the academy, a few of them peel away. I don't have time to tell where they go.

"Now for the hard part." Grace rubs her hands together at the sight of the rising rocks ahead.

"Hard is relative," David says as he claws his way up the first sheer boulders. I can't say I'm looking forward to this, but David easily blazes a trail, and to his credit, he's not slow to reach down and pull Grace up after him.

There are shouts down below. Shots, too. If our hangers-on went into the forest, they're not having a good time inside.

"Shouldn't we-" Grace's foot sends snow and pebbles into my eyes as she climbs. "-do something to help them?"

"Good idea." I have to flatten myself against the edge of a boulder to inch way up to the next slope. "We'll just climb back down again to make sure they're okay." There's a snort above.

"So you do have a sense of humor." David laughs.

"I'm serious," Grace says. I find some solid ground, crouch, and reach down for her. "You saw them turn out for us." I pull her up to my level. "We could probably use more bodies." She steadies herself on the slope, and looks up.

"It's not that much further," I tell her.

"You're ignoring me," she says as we shimmy side by side up the slope.

"Only because we don't want to tell you to shut up," David says, his head poking over the ledge ahead.

"So I'm obviously wrong to everyone but me, is that it?" The path widens into a barren wedge of stone that rises above the treetops.

"I understand." I have to resist the urge to put my hands on my knees. I've heard people go rock-climbing recreationally. "We just don't have time."

"Yeah, plus-" David kicks a pebble off the edge, "-we'd have to baby-sit them."

I can see over the whole forest from here, and all the way up to the academy.

It's strange; looking at it from up here it looks so empty and quiet.

I've tuned them out, but my two assistants are getting ready to argue.

"Grace." I wait for her to look up. "You said the kennels were on the far side."

"Yeah?" I think it worked. David doesn't seem that invested.

"It looks like there's some kind of drop."

"Yeah." Grace sits down, unwrapping an energy bar. "There's a cliff there. The whole school's built on a rise like an old-school castle."

"You haven't been down there, you said?"

"I haven't." She breaks the bar in half and hands one to me. "Lots of ID card swipe doors and cameras, but I've seen it from up above. It's just fenced off snowfields, frozen lake, and then further out there's the pipeline. You think it might be important?"

"I'm certain," I say. "We'll be waiting things out up here for a while. Might as well take advantage of the view."

The nutrition bars Grace brought are like the soup. Not much to say. She just nods while she chews.

I know I should be planning contingencies, but I know if I do I'm bound to lose focus.

It shouldn't be a problem, and I need to concentrate on the passage of time. It won't be long.

It's quiet up here.

Not silent, of course. Sometimes I hear breaking wood, or a shout of pain. But there are better sounds too, sighing clouds and bird calls.

There might even be a waterfall down there somewhere.

"Do you really think this will work?" Grace lies on her back. David stretches. It's tempting to tell her to be quiet. It's not as if we can do anything up here but wait.

"I don't know." I wouldn't blame her for not being convinced.

"You agreed to it." David grunts as he stretches. "Don't second-guess her now."

The silence makes it hard to judge the passage of time, but by now, it's probably time to go.

Not looking forward to more climbing.

In theory, down is easier, but no less dangerous. David gets the idea as I get to my feet and follows me without a word. Maybe Grace isn't a fan of the climbing, either.

I wouldn't blame her for that.

It's not engaging, at least not on an intellectual level, maybe that's the problem; my body and instincts are working, but my mind wanders. Mostly to one place: the students.

The followers. None of them made it up the rise.

Still, it's not that bad. The slopes here are thick with roots. As long as I don't trip, some of them make pretty good hand holds. Since I haven't heard anyone falling, I'm going to assume Grace and David are fine, and stop at the edge of a thick line of trees.

The sound of water is closer, and I can smell spray in the air.

David crouches behind me, and I unfold the map.

"Past this cliff, we should come up behind the tickets-" I tap the grid of black lines "-right here."

"Do we have to climb down that bit as well?" Grace pants.

"There should be a slope," I tell her.

"So you don't know that either." I do my best to ignore the griping and push through the trees. The snow's still heavy here, but there are a few weeds visible at the foot of the trunks.

I feel David's breath on the side of my neck for a second, and my stomach jumps.

The ground gives way, and I fall into a stream of loose, flowing dirt, falling end over end between twigs, leaves and snow, and eventually roll to a stop.

"Second quadrant, second sweep."

"Keep it up, we-"

My instinct is to get to my feet as soon as possible, but I can't help trying to spit the dirty snow and loose hair from my mouth. David definitely landed beside me, but I didn't see Grace.

"You!" Someone screams.

David pulls me to my feet by the back of my vest as he launches himself towards the nearest body, a massive skin-head wearing a red armband.

It's a camp, like the one we just came from, except with actual equipment, tents, binoculars, and even piles of rations.

As David wrestles with a growing crowd, I pull Grace up out of the snow.

"What do we do?" she asks me. I don't think a third "don't know" would be helpful.

"Don't bother with him!" The tall, short-haired girl rises from her seat overlooking the waterfall. "Deal with her!" Alanza. She's pointing right at me, and as she does, some of her henchmen peel off David in my direction.

"Stick to the plan!" I shout it as loud as I can, as there's no time to check if my decision's the right one, and no way for me to know if David can even hear me.

Grace rushes off down the slope behind me, and although I'm not as fast as she is, there's nowhere else to go.

The woods are thick, and I'm tired from climbing, hiding seems like the natural course of action, especially since Grace has just vanished.

We had enough time for a back-up plan. That was my responsibility, and it's my fault this happened, but there's no point in dwelling on it now. Footsteps thunder past me as I flatten myself against a tree, and I count five, maybe six bodies racing out into the forest, all wearing arm bands.

What did I see in that camp I could use?

Alanza was giving orders, that's for sure. She also had lots of supplies. The problem that jumps out at me with that is that I didn't see any tickets.

From what she said about her strategy, she should be collecting as many as possible. I need to be thinking about moving, not sitting here theorizing. Hopefully, the small amount I've learned since I got here will help.

Somehow, the fact that I have no choice makes me feel better. Maybe I'm more afraid of making the wrong decision than getting caught.

"I know you're out there!" The shout rings off the tree bark by my ear, and echoes further into the forest. "Mark my words, the best you and your friends can hope for is expulsion!" It bounces back and forth like a gunshot, and as it fades, I hear a whisper over the roar of the waterfall and the teeming forest. "I know what you are."

It's common sense to wait Alanza and her thugs out, but I don't really have time. Our "meeting place" is just the next landmark on the map, and we definitely didn't discuss what to do once we got there. If Grace and David are together for too long, they'll argue, and probably get caught. So I have to choose between possibly getting caught now, and them almost certainly getting caught later.

Last time I chose wrong, so in the spirit of experimentation, I set off into the forest, low and quiet.

The site itself shouldn't be far. I couldn't make out the waterfall on the map, but I recognize the river, and knowing where it comes from, the landscape makes more sense in my mind.

It was a bad plan.

It's the quiet that makes me realize, along with the wind.

Maybe I'm better under pressure. Maybe I should hang upside down when I come up with the next one.

I made too many assumptions based on what happened last time, even when I knew things would be different. I didn't want to consider things I didn't know or understand.

"She didn't tell me anything!" Grace's shout echoes off the sharp rocks ahead.

"Whatever." David's voice is almost too deep to echo. The most immediate problem here is going to be making my entrance in a way that inspires confidence, so I slow down to a jog before emerging from the trees.

"Now you can ask her." Grace points at me from where she sits. The metal hanger at her back is barren.

"This sucks, look!" David stomps up to me and points into

the clearing. "We've got like-" He holds out a fistful of tickets, lips moving silently as he counts them, "-six!"

"Yes, it's a problem. There are enough for us, at least." I say. Grace starts to pick herself up, and I have more of a chance to scan the environment. "What happened here?"

"Armbands." David scrapes aside a pile of snow with his foot. "The ones I clobbered got picked up by more, going the other way."

"Basically-" Grace says "-based on what we overheard on the way here, Alanza has them all rolling around the forest, clockwise, all at once, like a manhunt."

"How long until they come back around?" Both of them shrug. "We need to get moving then, before they're in between us and the safest way out."

"What about the plan?" David creases the tickets in his hand. As much as I want to, I can't admit it was poorly conceived.

"We'll be lucky to get out of here with enough tickets for ourselves. We need to get going as quickly as possible," I tell them. David marches past me to the treeline.

"For future reference, you can say ASAP," he grunts back.

Grace doesn't have anything to say. Probably too tired. I know I am. It takes a few minutes of digging through the snow before she speaks up.

"Did she come after you?" Grace asks. I don't need to ask who she means.

"I think so." There are distant sounds, impossible to make sense of from so far away, but echoing closer. "She didn't catch me."

"Find out anything useful?"

"She wants to get rid of us." I tell her. "That's all I got."

"Somehow, I think I already knew that," Grace says. Up ahead, David crouches, so we both do the same.

"What is it?" I whisper to him.

"Baggers, I think." The snow's starting to fall again, and I try to resist the urge to shiver as I listen.

"The idea was-" Grace says, as quietly as she can "-to come around from the other side, get to the tickets no one else could reach on time, right?" I nod, without looking back. "Doesn't it seem like Alanza had the same sort of idea? Just with more people."

What was a distant roar becomes louder as three snowmobiles crash through the snow ahead. It's hard to make out through the growing storm, but it looks like some baggers get off and greet the others. Grace and I drop closer to the ground, trying to ignore the cold.

There are students, just a few. Not part of the sweep Grace talked about, but they're definitely wearing armbands. As I watch, Alanza steps out from among them. I can't hear what they're saying, but I don't have to. She points, she shouts, she grabs arms, but ultimately their heads follow her directions.

"What do we do?" Grace asks, mouth partly buried under the snow.

"Just wait."

"I can do this," David whispers. His fists clench in the slowly vanishing dirt.

"David." His head twitches, just enough to know he's listening. "Don't." I don't have enough insight to know how to control him yet. Just asking is a start.

"We want to take her out, right?" Do I? I honestly don't know. Could he do it?

"No," I tell him, and I feel his body tense. "We're taking enough risks as it is, and there are baggers with her."

As we watch, the students and baggers go their separate ways, and Alanza vanishes back into the forest.

Grace is the first to move, and David follows her through the snow.

I know the tree line isn't far, and they're actually moving in the right direction. This is definitely progress.

The snow keeps falling, and we start to rise from our crouches, but David holds up a closed fist. I'm going to assume that means "stop." He points to the hollow of a tree, and a line of footprints leading to it.

Grace steps around the trunk, despite David's frenzied hand signals that I'm almost certain aren't used by any military anywhere.

"Come look at this." I follow Grace to see her standing over three more students, pressed against a tree trunk. "Look familiar?"

"We don't have time for this." David taps the tree as the students stare up at him.

He's right. I can't argue with that. The students don't have anything to say in their defense, but things need to change.

"We need to be more like Alanza." I hold my hand out to David. "Three tickets."

"So you can give them to these dropouts?" he asks.

"Absolutely," I say. "As long as we have enough for ourselves." He hesitates for a moment, before holding out three slips of paper. I drop them into the hands of the silent students. There must be something I can say here to make an impact. Maybe I don't need to.

"Don't waste them." One of them nods. I think I've done what needs to be done. "Come on," I say and wave to Grace and David, "it's not far."

It's true, too. I think some part of me has internalized the map. It's a start.

❄

The soup must be an acquired taste. That or my standards are dropping.

We didn't say a word on the way out. No second-guessing. They both sit on either side of me, David slurping down his soup, and Grace still stirring it. Probably a picky eater.

It's warm; that's the only thing that matters to me.

In the distance, some bagger is reading off names. Whether they're the washouts or the ones that passed, I don't know.

Snowmobiles roar as more students arrive, some bagged, some not, all bruised and scowling. It takes a second of watching the arm bands and the thickness of the crowd to realize Alanza is at the center, without any of her usual composure. She waves away the medics with their blankets and food, and almost spits at the baggers. She doesn't say anything, but I can feel her walking by, doing her best not to stare into the back of my neck.

It's an attitude that takes root. Armband kids storm off back to their camp, baggers shove the medical staff. If everyone wasn't so exhausted, we'd probably be in the middle of a fist fight.

"I just don't have the resources here." The students are almost all completely silent. Most of the medics aren't that vocal. I'm starting to realize they're too scared. "I know about area clearance, but sooner or later one of them's going to end up dead!" I hear an impact, but keep my head down.

"That's the doctor you mentioned, right?" Grace nudges me in the side.

"That's him," I reply. "Dr. Islet."

"He sounds upset," she says. The conflict circles the tables, and comes into view as a few of the students work up the energy to leave. No one steps forward. No leaders.

"He does, actually." One of the baggers shoves Dr. Islet

aside. He gestures to some medics as they prepare stretchers. "Grace, where would he take students he wants to treat?"

"Where?" She looks round at me. "Well, there's definitely no medical bay, at least not for students, so he probably means his office."

"His office?" The doctor runs his hands over piles of bandage rolls. "Been inside?" I ask.

"Nope," Grace says, "it's restricted." She drops the spoon in her bowl "You're not injured, you know, that's the only way you'll get in there." She's right, but security's tightening.

The faculty are adapting and changing how they operate every day. There are double the number of baggers here than last time, most concentrated around the food, probably to stop thieves. Someone has to be coordinating them.

If I want to use this to my advantage, it has to be now. The other problem is that I'm tired, but not actually hurt. I could fake it, but I don't think Dr Islet is more sympathetic to me than he is afraid of the baggers. The second the plan enters my head, I know there's no time to hesitate.

"David."

"Yeah?" He looks up from his empty bowl.

"Break my left arm."

"Okay." Before I have time to flinch he reaches around me, fastens his hands just above my elbow, and I hear a snap.

It doesn't hurt, it just feels strange.

In hindsight, maybe I should have asked him to dislocate it instead. Grace stares at me for a moment before her face comes back into focus.

"Dr Islet!" She yells for him, pulls me up, and waves her arm. I'm not really in a position to object. "Hildegard's arm really hurts!" He rushes over, and runs through the standard questions, I'm focusing too much on not making any embarrassing noises to do anything except nod.

"Your arm's broken," he says. I nod. "I'll have to take a look at it in my office." Grace is obviously suppressing the urge to give me the thumbs up. "Do you think you can walk?" Nod.

"Uh, Doctor." Grace grimaces, and holds her arm. "My arm hurts too."

"All right." He doesn't look back as he rummages through piled supplies. "I'll do what I can for both of you, let's get you both out of the cold."

I almost trip in the snow, and Grace does her best to hold me up. We both stagger off after Dr. Islet, towards the academy.

I look back, just to make sure no baggers might try to interfere. All I see is David's confused squint.

It's almost impossible to focus on the route we take. My arm's starting to hurt. Dr. Islet doesn't say anything, and neither does Grace.

This is definitely a part of the academy I've never seen, somewhere past the lecture theater and the entrance hall, things branch out into a maze of sterile, over lit corridors. On the way a few students shuffle past.

Former patients? They don't look very treated.

"It's just in here, not far." He opens a dingy brown door, and shuffles inside as Grace does her best to pull me through. "Don't mind the mess." He tries to laugh. "It's really not meant for this sort of thing."

It's occurring to me that I'm not very good at dealing with being in pain, or whatever this actually is. It's more like discomfort. The body's internal alarm that something important is wrong. "Set your arm down on my desk." He points to a wooden rectangle, clogged with papers, piles of CDs and crumpled posters."We don't need these," Islet says as he sweeps the more colorful ones into the drawers of his desk.

It's tough not to fall into a chair. "There's going to be a lot more prodding." As Dr. Islet turns his back, opening drawers and sifting through papers, Grace sweeps the room. At least, that's what I assume she's doing. "How does it feel now?" his hands are full of gauze and splints, as if he couldn't find exactly what he needed.

"I don't know," I say as he leans over, running fingers down my arm. "It doesn't hurt that much."

"I think it's a fracture." He goes back to his pile of supplies.

I didn't see Grace move, but she's definitely standing in a different place. "Probably not too serious, but you're not going to be able to use it for a while." He measures a sling against my arm. "There's really not much I can do for you apart from this, apparently," he sighs. "There are no exemptions from lessons here except for expulsion. You could try talking to some of the other staff, but honestly, that's your best option." He fastens the sling around me, and I lift my arm into it.

"Absolutely not." Grace stands behind him, near the desk.

"Well, I can't fault your determination." He walks back to his desk. "If you change your mind, you can come to me, and I'll do the rest. Now," he says and rubs his hands together, trying to smile, "onto the next patient."

"Actually," Grace says, "I'm feeling much better now, I think it was just a bruise."

"What do you mean, the other staff?" The idea's just occurred to me, and the cold running up my arm almost stops me, but Islet's been a good source before. If I don't get anything else out of this I can at least find out more about how things work here.

"Well, you've been working with them," he says, eyeing Grace's extended arm.

"Baggers?" Grace asks.

"Yes, them," he chuckles. "Sort of a silly name. They weren't always called that."

"You said the academy was built on a base," I say. "They came with the school?"

"Exactly." Islet glances up at me. "About two years ago, I think? I've lost track."

At this point, the timing doesn't surprise me. What happened two years ago?

"What were they for?" He looks up again at my question. "Before we were here, I mean."

"Security." He turns, running his hand over the piled papers and empty CD cases on his desk. "And other things. Everything changed when they arrived." He's staring into the distance now, just like in the medical tent. I share a look with Grace. Hopefully, she knows better than to interrupt. "They scare off the more dangerous wildlife, not that we ever had a problem with them," Islet says. "But we started taking on a lot more projects, much higher deadlines, and the baggers would make sure we kept to them." He pauses. "No matter what. I think they resented us, to be honest. Like being here was beneath them. It was always pretty bad between us and them."

"As bad as we have it?" Grace asks, and Islet turns, his eyes refocusing.

"No." He shakes his head, wiping down his white coat.

"Well, that's enough. You're both in the best shape I can get you and I have other patients." Dr. Islet scans his desk for a second, and pats his hands along the length of his coat. "Take good care of your friend." He searches his pockets. "You can find your way back to your dorms, right?"

"Yep." Grace nods her head, and pulls me along by my non-broken arm. Out in the corridor, she sighs. "I think that went well." I can't think of anything to say to her. She's probably right. "You okay?" she asks. Good question.

"I think so," I tell her. "I'll be fine." The papers across his desk, and the medical supplies. His office. It's more than just that, though. As Grace and I leave, we come closer to the academy front. The lights grow brighter, the corridors are straighter.

"Are you super sure?" I stagger a little as we leave the gates. "You're staring."

"I just had an idea."

"A good one?"

"We'll find out."

Most of the students are gone. The staff definitely are, the sun's setting, and it's already much too cold to be comfortable outside.

David spots us as we trudge through the wall of snow that's grown around the academy's front door. He doesn't say anything, but I can see him glance at my sling.

"You didn't actually have to break her arm, you know," Grace says what's on my mind. Not that I agree with her; every moment spent working on the doctor is vital.

"She's fine." David kicks a mound of snow as we wordlessly agree to head for camp. "It's just a hairline." He's probably right, but I'm definitely down an arm. In an ideal world I wouldn't need it, but assuming everything behaves as I assume it will is a fast track to disappointment.

"And you just know how to break someone's arm so that it doesn't actually hurt them?" Grace asks.

"I do." David shrugs. "I think a better question would be why you wanted me to do it in the first place." The head of Charlie Camp's valley comes into sight as I wait for Grace to answer for me.

"I was wondering that too, actually." Grace scans the

students, some of them still sitting outside under the trees or on drifts of snow.

"Not here."

"Usual place?" Grace asks.

"No." I catch a flake of falling snow with my good arm. "Soon it'll be too cold. We'll have to meet inside." I tap the metal around the edge of the cabin's doorframe. It's been sticking during the mornings for the past few days, and the weather's only getting colder.

"We'll be overheard." David leans around the corner, scanning the featureless cabin.

Empty, for now at least.

"Hildegard's right." Grace sweeps open the door, scattering snow along the floor. "We've had so many dropouts the past few days, if we time it right, we could have the whole cabin all to ourselves." David says nothing, so I can only guess that he's satisfied. Grace looks over to me as she takes in the rows of empty bunks. "You said you had an idea, right?"

"I did, although that's not what I meant." I rest my back against the wall, and try to sit as comfortably as I can. "It's more like I've made some important observations." Grace sits as well, but David's obviously not comfortable down here. I can't say I blame him; someone could walk in at any second, but it's this or the cold.

"Like what?" Grace leans back, eyes closed. If I don't get to the point, she might fall asleep.

"Between us, we've seen inside all the buildings that make up the academy, right?"

"Sure," she says, "the lecture halls, definitely, gymnasium, kennels," she lists them off on her fingers.

"I've been to the armory a few times," David says. "Firearms practice. It's where the baggers keep their equipment. Weapons, vehicles, shit rations, basically just a big shed, what's your point?"

"On the cliffs, earlier today, the terrain seemed strange to me, and on our way back from Dr. Islet's office I saw something similar." They're both giving me their best earnest stares. It makes me wonder if I'm the only one here who thinks for themselves.

Don't get the wrong idea, I don't mind, I can't imagine how difficult this would be if they all had their own ideas.

"Obviously," Grace says with a sigh, "we want you to tell us."

"There's something under the academy. Whatever it was, it was probably there first, and that's probably what Dr. Islet, what all the staff were assigned to. They probably still are."

"Why?" David sits forward. I think I've got his attention.

"That's the problem." I roll my arm in the sling, trying to find some way to rest it. "I don't know."

"How-" Grace struggles to stay awake "Why d'you think that?"

"You saw the doors, corridors, all slopes, none of them connecting to classrooms, none of them labeled for classes. Plus the cliff, and," it occurs to me, as I pause for breath, that my affected composure might be breaking down, "it was all underground, and it still is. My point is, we need to know what's down there, that's all, I mean, do you really think eventually we'll just graduate, and they'll place us in military programs or something?"

"They won't," David says.

"Okay, so even if we just assume that's true," says Grace, now fully awake, "what do we do about it?"

"Obvious." David lays his legs out ahead of him, sliding his hands up and down his ankles, gripping them, apparently at random. "We go in," he grunts with effort, "find out what's going on."

"No." Grace waves her hands. "Find out what's happening, sure, but we can't just walk in."

"He might be right, actually," I say, no matter how strange it feels to voice the idea. "Security gets tighter every day."

"No, hold up," Grace says as she stands up, "tomorrow's a 'free day', whatever that means. No classes? Maybe we could look around then."

"Actually, you're right." David points at me. "Right now, the baggers are just as exhausted as we are, we shouldn't just be looking around, tonight's when we go in."

"Okay, you're crazy." She points over to him. "There's cameras, guards, and we have no idea what's down there."

"I've been watching the cameras," I tell them. "They're new, in fact they were one of the first things that seemed off to me."

"So you're an expert in surveillance now?" Grace folds her arms.

"My high school used to get a lot of suicide attempts, so they put cameras in, even in places like the roofs and bathrooms," I tell her. "Here, the spacing's all wrong, we could just walk between them."

"And the guards?" Grace says. "We don't even know their patrols, their equipment-"

"I've seen enough." David stretches his arms. "And I've never seen any posted in the academy anyway."

"That's kind of my point," Grace says and jabs her finger into his chest, "we don't know what's down there. For all we know it could be nothing, or just a restricted area we'll get in trouble for being in!"

"So what's your plan? Graduate? Look," David has to lean

down to look her in the eye, "this is a shitty situation, and we're not going to get anywhere by playing it safe."

Grace looks down at the gray floor, and the flecks of snow still clinging to her shoes.

"I don't take risks without a reason, Grace," I tell her. "I wouldn't ask-"

"Okay, fine!" She almost shouts. "I mean, we're all tired and your arm's broken, but okay, let's go." I don't really know what to say to her, and obviously David doesn't, either.

"Okay." I take in as much air as I can in a single breath. "We'll make it count. I promise." Grace bows her head, and already my mind is working too fast to take in details.

"I hid some coats I found in that hollow you showed us," she says as she straightens up, and I squint against the cold air as she opens the door to the tundra.

The coats come out surprisingly dry, if a little dirty, and I test my arm in one of the sleeves as Grace and David wipe off the dirt and snow.

"We'll take it slow." My arm won't go in, and it's definitely not a good idea to put too much strain on it.

"This way." David points into the woods. "Less chance of being seen." The snow's thick, and following David's lead, I crouch as low as I can.

At night, the academy's lit from below, like a really expensive display house. It looks like one, too. The statue's face is covered with snow, but the eyes feel as if they move every time I look away.

"There and there." I point up to the academy's face at two cameras fixed on the grass.

"Yeah, saw those," Grace whispers, and taps David on the shoulder. "Keep left until we hit the edge."

The snow's still falling, and as I look back, our footprints are already gone. If I wasn't so tired, I'd say this is the perfect night.

"Anything inside we should know about?" Grace is nervous. To be honest, I'm glad. My energy is much too low to be on edge.

The academy's doors are still unlocked. Come to think of it, I've never even seen a guard posted here.

"Corners," I say. "Almost every corner inside has a camera. Every thirty seconds they go from left to right. Probably still on factory settings." The corridors inside are dark, even the classrooms are unlit, full of stacked tables, chairs, and swollen shadows.

Part of me wants to start formulating excuses, in case we just run into someone. All together, we step under a camera, and listen to it whine as we wait for it to turn. It clicks as it stops moving. We step out from underneath.

"This is much easier than I thought it would be," Grace whispers. David chuckles.

She's not wrong.

"This way." They must be wondering where we're headed right now, and I need to be certain nothing shakes their confidence.

The corridors become dirtier as they fall in behind me. Wood becomes concrete, and the tiles along the walls disappear to reveal pipes and wiring.

"This looks like an elevator." Grace runs her hand along a black box, fastened to the wall. "It only has a down button."

"Good. That's the way we're going." David presses the button, and the doors slide open with a hiss.

The inside looks like something you'd see in a mall or a museum, not that I've been in very many. I suppose there must be a factory somewhere that makes elevators.

Stepping inside, I can hear the machinery hidden all around us groan and expand.

"What if we step out, and there's baggers right in front of us?" Grace asks as David strides inside the closing doors. Hopefully, she'll interpret my silence as confidence.

The ride is long. Longer than it should be. I know I'm on edge, but the elevator creaks and squeals for longer than I would like.

I've never been claustrophobic, but something about having no way to know where I'm going, or what's down there is making me tense.

The floor shudders, so I reach out with my bad arm to catch myself, and almost fall as pain shoots through my body.

Grace's arms are almost extended to catch me. The doors hiss open, and David stares at me like an idiot. Whether the idiot is me or him, I'm still not sure.

I step out of the elevator onto a metal grating. Above me, lights swing from metal pegs, driven into stone a few inches above my head. Ahead, at the root of a nest of wires, is a gray, handleless door. The rest is featureless rock.

"For the staff's ID cards." David runs his hands over the small black box, trying to find a purchase on it, as if pulling it off the wall would somehow help.

"I don't think we can get through this, can we?" Grace asks. She scans every corner, but doesn't touch it.

"That depends," I say.

"On what?" She looks back around at me, as if I'd just accused her of something. In a way, I have.

"If you use that ID card you stole from Dr. Islet or not." Her hand jumps to it, and before she can withdraw, David takes it from her and runs it through the reader. It blinks a green light, and the door sighs open.

"How did you," she lowers her voice halfway through the question, "how did you know?"

"There wasn't anything else worth taking in his office," I say, "and I saw him looking for something after we left. Not much of a leap."

"And you just waited until we were down here?" Grace asks.

"If I hadn't," I say as David stands by the open door, holding it open, "you'd've found some excuse earlier, and we wouldn't be down here." Grace glares at me. "Am I wrong?"

"No," she answers, shuffling into the corridor beyond.

Maybe I should call it a tunnel, there's plenty of exposed stone here, wiring too. Instead of a floor there are metal grates bolted to the floor, probably an attempt to provide something like level ground.

"Looks like you were right." David glances back at me with a grin on his face ."This must be one of those restricted areas that'll get us shot."

"Look." Grace points up at something like paper, fastened to the walls with glue or tape. I take hold of one of the lights above, and try to pull it as close as I can.

"Directions?" There are names, numbers, and arrows. Hard to make out in the dim orange light.

"Yeah, look." David shoves me out of the way, and I try not to gasp as he collides with my bad arm "Filing, data entry, culture storage. Hangar maintenance." He reads them out, one by one. "I think we just infiltrated an office building."

"We want filing," I tell them,"records, stuff like that."

"This way, then." David points, and sets off, sliding against the walls. There's air on my face, and the echo of voices. Maybe this place isn't as cramped as it seems.

"I don't threaten people-" The retch-inducing rasp is

unmistakable. Ahead of me, David shrinks as light breaks across his back, and as I follow him I understand why.

The grating below becomes a catwalk leading into a maze of metal stairwells, cables that hang like vines, and blank gray doorways. "-but actions have consequences."

Below me, through the grating, I can see computers and cubicles, arranged in a grid on smoothed earth and stone.

"It's Giant 1," Grace whispers, "and Dr. Islet."

"I know, I know, I mean, I definitely didn't put it down, I don't know what happened!"

"Looks like you got the doctor into trouble," I tell Grace. Giant 1 steps closer, and Dr. Islet rises out of his seat.

"I don't want to hear excuses." As the misshapen solider steps closer, the doctor trips and lands on his back in the dirt. He tries to crawl away, but Giant 1 scoops him up, and presses him against the dirty wall of his cubicle with a single hand. "Just make sure it doesn't happen again." He sighs, wiping the dirt from Dr. Islet's coat.

"We don't have time for this." David taps me on the shoulder, and points down one of the metal stairways. "Filing is this way."

We set off in single file, and below us I can hear the doctor doing the same, trailing his hand along the walls of the dusty corridors until he disappears from sight.

Following the lights beyond the cavern, the terrain's uneven, and some places are too slanted for the gratings, so the floor's littered with loose bolts and wires where the baggers have tried to keep the tunnels lit.

As I keep my head low I notice the rust on the grates, the trickles of water from the ceiling, and the moss growing around it. It's been here for a while.

"Down here." David points, and Grace flattens herself

against the wall. Not fast enough. The beam of a flashlight jumps out across the wall, stretching our shadows.

"You see that?"

Grace's eyes widen as another shadow, tall and studded with pouches and pockets, grows larger on the wall.

"Go check it out."

"What, you think some of the meat found a way down here?"

"Didn't you hear? Islet lost his ID. Plus, what else are we going to do? Stand here for another three hours?" Three hours. There's a shift change at midnight.

"Well?" I prod Grace, frozen against the wall, and the bagger stalks into sight.

There are no pretenses down here, the golden, two-masted ship on his shoulder is plain as day.

"The patch," I whisper to them. They both nod.

"Why'd they hide it?" David asks.

"Don't know," I whisper back.

"Plus, we don't exactly have time to find out right now," Grace says.

A small moral victory, but not much of a revelation at this stage.

Grace reaches up and pulls at one of the cables pinned to the wall. Further down the corridor, in another fork, I can see one of the lights shaking, and the bagger shines his flashlight towards it as it creaks and crashes against the cave wall. David stands up beside her, and with a single tug, he pulls the cable from the wall, shooting a fountain of sparks from the light down the other tunnel.

"Come check this out." A second flashlight clicks on, and a second bagger advances down the tunnel. In the wrong direction.

The others sit still, so I wave my good arm as violently and as quietly as I can, and set off in the fastest crouch I can manage, stepping around the loose rocks and metal pins. I can feel breath on my hair, but don't turn around until I'm past the next sign, and flat against another wall.

"That was pretty good," I whisper to Grace.

"Pretty good?" she whispers back.

"C'mon." David almost drags me by the shoulder down the tunnel. I can hear the mutterings of the baggers behind us, apparently none the wiser, and the sparking of the broken light still spitting into the dark.

"Are we clear?" Grace asks. I glance up and down. There's no sign, but another gray door, and another stairwell of bolts and metal, leading further down into the rock.

"We should be." I point "As long as we can open the door." She slips the stolen ID through the scanner, and the door sighs open.

"All set." Grace almost grins. I move to step into the room, but I can't. The back of my neck shivers, and by now I know better than to ignore it.

I hear the cause before I see it.

Heavy footfalls, and the creaking of metal as it climbs up the stairs below us, almost pulling the bolts from the wall. Before it reaches the top and raises its head I pull at Grace, and all three of us pile inside the filing room.

The door hisses closed, and Grace and I squat to catch our breath. My stomach feels twisted, more than it should be, like it's just recovered from a cramp.

"What was that?" Grace wheezes, almost retching.

"No idea." I'm trying to sound as unfazed as possible. The acid taste in my mouth doesn't make it easy.

"I've seen it before," David says, "first day here, camp was still setting up." He steadies himself on the wall "Bigfoot style. Made me feel sick. Just like now."

"Wait, you saw it?" Grace asks, a little louder than I'd like.

"Yeah," David pants. "Some big thing wearing a diving suit for gimps." He pulls himself up. "On the first day, when they were still unloading stuff. Guess it lives down here now."

"We'll talk about this later," I tell them. "Right now, we have a job to do."

"Hope you're keeping track of all the things we'll talk about 'later', Hildegard," Grace says.

The room is row after row of metal shelves and boxes under narrow swinging lights.

"Let's make this quick, and whatever that is out there won't be a problem. It's got no reason to know we're in here, it'll pass right by." Grace and David scan the shelves. I guess that's enough to convince them to get going.

"We get caught in here and we're dead," Grace says.

"What are we looking for?" David asks as I pick a row at random and start pulling boxes.

"Anything. If I knew what we were looking for-" Grace powers on a computer, squashed on either side by files of beige folders "-we wouldn't need to come down here in the first place."

"Needs a password," Grace says, through a gap in the shelves.

"Can you open it?" I already have a pile of disregarded folders by my side, and boxes more of them at my feet.

"I can try." She turns back to the screen, scanning the keyboard and coffee-stained papers around it.

"Arms inventory." I tap David on the shoulder as he roots through the boxes under me, and hand him the folders full of weapons.

"You think this could be it?" He thumbs through the files. "More than enough here to kill the student body twice over, but I don't think that would surprise most kids." He looks up. "What box was it in?"

"This one." I slide it over to him "No labels. It seems like they threw all their documentation in this room and just ignored it." David sweeps another box off the shelf, and starts to root through it as well.

There's another box, by the very edge of the last shelf, smaller than the others, but it's marked with a black X. Maybe for disposal?

The papers inside are loose, with a few held together by paper clips or clamps, and others marked with attached post-its or small strips of tape.

After a few seconds I find a file, bound with a single staple.

The header is marked with the letters KIA. Casualties?

It's just lists mostly. Names, donors, something called "generation", just a number between one and three, and notes in the margins, all signed "X". Comments on things like arm length, or speed of fingernail growth. Foster families. There's a whole list of them, too, column after column.

I want to find my name, but that's not what matters, so I throw it down and reach for another box.

Cooper isn't mentioned in any of these files.

Maybe something on personnel? I can't find anything about adoption agents or oversight. I don't think the agency itself was run by the Beagle Commission; he must've been a plant, or a contractor or something.

If I hadn't always made things about me when we talked, I could've asked.

That's not a productive thought. He probably wouldn't have told me anyway.

"What was that?" David looks up from his pile of weapons folders.

"It's nothing," I tell him. Neither of them have perspective. It would distract them.

I hear the door rattle. It's not someone coming in, it's more like shaking. It's not an impact, more like a constant rumbling vibration.

"It's still out there." Grace jumps up from the computer, password prompt still flashing. Her hands shake in time with the metal, and the stone walls. The door shakes again.

She turns from the computer, places as many boxes as she can back on the shelves, and gestures at the exit.

"We can't leave yet," I say, without looking up from the latest box.

"What the hell!" she hisses, pointing down to the trail of papers. "They'll know we were in here."

"We've got time." This box is full of ration inventories. I throw it down, and the door handle rattles again.

"It's getting closer," Grace says, ear pressed to the door. I still have Islet's ID card. She set it down when she started working on the computer.

"What the hell is this?" David holds up a fistful of papers, the same ones I threw away. The ones marked KIA. "I'm in this. This has me."

"It's just a student roster," I tell them. There are more boxes than I thought here. Some of them have labels, although most of them are too faded to read.

They haven't been here that long, have they?

"No, it's not." David shifts to hold it better under the light. "Grace, take a look at this." He hands one of the sheets to her.

"Foster parents? Donors?" she says."These are genes, too, look-" Grace runs her finger down the papers "-is this you?" she asks David.

"Yeah."

"And here's me. Espionage-." She pokes herself in the chest. "-and combat." She points at David.

There are personal files down here, in the boxes under the shelves, there are names, hundreds of names. I can't miss a single one. David's shadow falls over me.

"They lied to us."

"So," I hear Grace shifting files, "what does this mean? I'm adopted. I guess you are, too?"

"'Course we are! We all are!" David shouts. "We have to be, but these entries-"

"Okay, okay, but now I think we really need to go," Grace tells him.

"Agreed." David loops his arm around mine, and tries to pull me away from the files still littering the floor. "Time to leave."

"Not yet!" I shake loose and try to gather the papers on the floor. He puts his hand on the shoulder of my broken arm, and pulls me upright. I do my best not to squeak.

"What's your problem?"

"I didn't get what I came for yet." I look him straight in the eye. "I don't care about labs or experiments or whatever, I'm looking for someone."

"Well," David kicks my boxes back under the shelves, "maybe you should care."

"She's not on the big list," Grace adds, "so maybe she's right."

"Not important." David pulls me along. "We're still leaving."

I try to pull his hand off my shoulder without touching my arm, and as I do a tower of boxes topples to the floor. "You really want to fight about it?" he asks. "You won't win."

"Guys, look." Grace pulls a folded sheet from the fallen pile as the rumble outside goes quiet. "Passwords and dates.

It's old, but the rota's fixed, I think, so-" She runs her finger along it "-this one should still be valid." I slide under David's hand as Grace punches in the password, and take over the keyboard. She has the good sense to step aside, shouting something to David while I try to find what I can.

The desktop's full of folders, all labeled with strings of capitals and numbers. I open one at random and scroll over thumbnails of schematics, blueprints, pictures of molecules.

"There's too much."

"We could print it out?" Grace says, but David lifts the lid of a printer, crushed under more beige folders.

"No way," he says. "No ink!"

No personnel files. Nothing about assignments, who was doing what, when or why. The door shakes, files and folders almost rattling off their shelves.

"Hildegard, we have to-"

"Don't bother." Before I can scan another file, something lifts me into the air.

David hauls me over his back, and Grace catches the ID as it falls from my hand. The door slides open, and David kicks the computer's power off as he carries me through the door.

The corridor rushes past, and eventually, David throws me down again. I almost fall, but catch hold of one of the metal railings. The walkway sways.

Underneath us, baggers rush by. The giant figure, whatever it was, is gone.

"Going to behave yourself?" David whispers. Grace sprints past, flattens against the wall, and peeks around the next corner.

"No reason not to," I hiss at him.

"Good." He takes his hand off my shoulder, and heads over to Grace.

"They're all over the place," she whispers to him, pointing down at the rushing baggers below.

"What do you expect?" I say as I catch up. I want to blame them, but I don't think that would help my chances of getting out of this. "We made more noise than we should."

"I think they call this kicking the hive," Grace says, as columns of baggers sprint past, through the corridor from which we'd come.

She turns back to look at me. "What do we do?" Apparently, they're willing to just overlook our disagreement, as long as there's something in it for them. Grace's eyes scan everywhere, from the ceiling above to the crowd below. She's overthinking things.

"Go." I point into the corridor, the second the last bagger disappears. "Now!"

Don't get the wrong idea. I'm not guessing at random. There must be more than one way to get down here.

The baggers that just came through were on guard duty up above. Now they're not.

Of course, neither of them argue, and we all rush up the corridor. David takes the ID from Grace, swipes it, and we all squeeze into the elevator. There's no alarm. Just a soft beep. With the humming of the elevator cables. In fact, it makes me realize I'm in significant danger of passing out.

The door hisses open onto an empty corridor, marked with footprints of broken snow.

"I think we made it." Grace steps out into the school.

Except it's not, is it? It's a display case.

The rest blurs by. The polished floors, the glass, the chrome, the lecture halls. The snow.

The cold almost gets me. I would jog, but I'm just too tired to try.

The camp is silent. No fires tonight. The rest of Charlie

Company have probably moved into the other cabins. There's no one to enforce quarter assignments anyway, so I can't really blame them.

I pull the sheet off my bunk, and wrap it around me as tightly as I can.

"So." Grace sits on the end of my bed. David stands by the doorway. "What was that down there?"

"I think the better question is whether we got away with it." David folds his arms, probably pretending not to be cold.

"We've seen them take students from camp before." Talking warms my mouth. "They have no reason to give us special treatment."

"Agreed." David nods. "Next issue. What in the shit did you think you were doing?"

Both of them turn to me. I can only assume they stare at me.

"I have nothing to say."

"We can't help you if you don't tell us," Grace says.

"I don't need help!" The bunk shakes underneath me as I try to get to my feet. It doesn't quite work.

"Oh really?" David points. "How's your arm?"

"That's not what I mean, I don't need-"

"Just tell us!" Between Grace and I, we might wake up the other students. I think an interruption might almost be welcome. "You wanted to find someone, right?"

"I-" My mouth opens, without waiting for my brain to think of something to say. Both of them wait. It feels absurd to tell them, like a risk with no benefits, but is that actually true?

This is why I made you. Putting this into words, even if there's no one to hear them, puts things in perspective. I've been taking risks since I got here. If anything, this might be the least dangerous one.

All I have to do is something that's against my nature.

"My foster parents." Both of them relax, as if they'd been worried I was about to attack. "They had me taking drugs, they made me weak, and sick all the time, you probably both know what that's like. A few months ago, I figured it out and stopped taking them. You probably did something similar."

"What's that got to do with-" Grace asks leaning forward.

"I'm not finished yet."

"Oh, sorry," she says. David stays quiet. I know he's heard this before.

"My foster parents never trusted me, probably because they had to keep drugging me, I guess, but my adoption agent, he-" I've never told anyone this. It's different, once it's put into words. How do I say this? "He was as close as I ever got to real family, even if he was in on it."

"Something happened to him?" Grace asks.

"Don't know. He disappeared. When they came to get me, I figured Truman was connected. That if there was a way to find out where he went, it'd be here."

"Got it." Grace nods. David stretches his arms.

Is that it? Are they just convinced? Even if they are, I'm not going to push my luck by asking. "If we're gong to find out everything that's going on here, we might as well find out what happened to your dad as well," she says.

"I never called him that. His name was Cooper." Both of them stay quiet for a second. As if they're remembering.

"I never got on with my dad, but I get it." David takes a step back. "Now what about the rest of the shit we found? Guess he's not my dad. Sort of relieved, really."

"Can't we talk about it tomorrow?" Grace sighs. "It's too much to think about tonight."

"No, he's right." I'm not feeling so bad anymore. I think the blanket's starting to do its job. "They know students got in where they weren't supposed to, it'll be much harder to stay secret, so we need to decide where we stand, right now."

"No need," David grunts. "I already know. Even if they made me in a test tube somewhere, I'm not property, fuck that!"

"Yeah! Cuss words!" Grace laughs. "And I saw tons of names of other students on that list, me, you," she points at David, "but no Hildegard." I nod.

"And no Alanza." Both of them stop.

"Yeah, you're right," Grace says. "What does that mean?"

"Don't know." I fall back on the bed.

"Yeah, starting to notice a pattern." I can't see him, obviously. I'm on my back, but I can hear David pound the door-frame. "They all had roles, too. Things they're supposed to do."

"Things they're designed for," Grace adds. "I know you're good at fighting, so being designed for combat's not that surprising-"

"And you're sneaky," David grunts.

"I guess I am," Grace says. "Never really thought about it before."

"That's not all." Both of them stop in their tracks as they leave. "If you both have special abilities, so do all the other students."

"I guess they must." Grace nods. "Could be useful."

"I saw other things, too. In the computer," I say. "Lower levels. Massive tanks, something about bacteria, I think."

"Bacteria, huh?" David grunts.

"And there's a hangar. I saw it in the blueprints."

"What do they need a hangar for?" Grace asks.

"Don't know." I answer. "In the files they called it a "Mobile Silo".

FILE 4: DETERRENCE

September 6th

STILL COMING DOWN FROM THE ENDLESS LECTURE stream. First the principal, then the parents.

For the record, yes, I tried some marijuana. It gave me a headache and made me feel like I'd overdosed on pizza. Not sure how this is a "gateway" to more serious stuff if they're all like this, and again, for the record I didn't do it out of some childish impetus to be "cool", I think the verdict's been delivered on that, I just heard it has its uses as an alternative type of pain relief. That's ALL.

I know I'll probably get him into trouble if it turns out anyone cares enough to read this, but Cooper didn't have a problem with it. I'm pretty sure he's done heavier stuff.

He told me that governments, even small ones, always lose

their perspective on individual people, when actually they're the most important thing of all.

He must have a desk calendar hidden somewhere.

❄

"Mobile Silo?" This isn't my day. I know, because I've had days like it before. Being exhausted from staying up all night and having a broken arm doesn't help.

"You never heard of it?" Grace seems fine. I thought at least what we found would put her off. Maybe she's trying not to think about it. Understandable, and I'm not about to bring it up to her.

"Never." At least we won't be overheard. The murmuring crowd of students shambling towards the end of morning PT is the perfect white-noise cover.

"My dad's this crazy obsessive cold war buff," Grace says. "He would talk about it all the time, I know it had some funky Russian name-" She puts a finger on her chin "-but I can't really remember it."

"And it does what?"

"The name's pretty self-explanatory, don't you think?" Cresting the snow covered hill, there's something by the statue. A podium.

"It is, but there might be more to it." I squint as hard as I can. There are baggers flanking it, forming a line between us and the school. The students stop.

"It's basically this crazy armored truck, I guess it's more like a tank, and it fires a missile, and it has these big magnets to make the missile go faster, and because it drives really fast at the same time, the missile goes really, really far."

"What I saw on the computer didn't look much like a

truck," I say. There's some sort of struggle up ahead. Over the heads of the students I can see Giant 1, climbing his podium.

"It doesn't, really, that's just what it does. My dad has a model on his desk. It has these gnarly arms for picking stuff up, too. I guess it's more like a seal." She mimes clapping her hands together.

"So the question becomes," I try to find a higher spot to stand, to get a better view, "why it was in the computer at all?"

"You think they've got one?" Grace is already standing on the tips of her toes. Craning her neck doesn't help much. A bagger offers Giant 1 a megaphone. He waves it away. Again.

"Good morning, students." The smack of his hands coming together echoes over our heads as the cloud of his breath balloons into the air. "I have good news, and I have bad news."

The crowd makes a noise too muddled for me to read.

"This is because of what we did, isn't it?" Grace elbows me.

"Probably."

"The good news is, we in the faculty are intensely impressed by the progress you've all made!" Some students whoop. Others clap. "The bad news, for you at least, is that we've decided to accelerate the curriculum, to ensure you all get the best placement on graduation." He claps his hands together again, scattering the cloud of his breath. "So we're moving on from theory to practice. I do hope you've been paying attention." Streams of baggers rush past him, out into the snowfields by the edge of the forest, carrying mats between them.

"Uh..." I think it's dawning on Grace what's happening. Not that I'm fond of the idea, either. Hopefully, if groups stay in place we can both rely on David. He's probably grinning like a maniac right now.

"So, let me outline how things will work." Giant 1 hops down from his podium. "Instructors will walk among you, correcting you. You will be assigned opponents at random, changing at random intervals, as my men blow their whistles." Baggers begin leading students down the slope, towards the unfolding grid of blue plastic shock absorbers. "Those of you who meet our standards will eat. Those who do not will be further motivated to improve by hunger."

He stalks into the crowd, as baggers lead more students away. There are few between me and him. This is the closest I've been to him since the hospital. Would it make any difference if he recognizes me as the one that got away? Or did he let me get away?

I lose track of Grace as I walk down the slope, trying not to slip in the snow.

Something tells me I'm not getting out of this by having a broken arm. I shift it in the sling. It's not that bad; in fact, I think it might be in my best interests to pretend it's worse than it really is.

A bagger taps my shoulder, points at a mat, and moves on.

I spot Grace, a few rows along. She waves at me, but her enthusiasm is put on. One of Golf Company, an arm-band wearer, stands across from her, stretching with a grin on his face.

"You should be more concerned with yourself." My head snaps back to see Alanza standing on the other side of the mat. "I told them to go easy on Charlie, but you? No. You're mine."

I don't want to talk to her. Honestly, I don't even want to look at her.

Don't get the wrong idea, I'm not afraid of her, it's just disorienting. It's not that I recognize her, but on some level, I can tell her face is the one I know best.

This is the closest I've ever been to her, and since I'm probably about to take a beating from her, I look her over.

We're definitely the same height, her hair's a lot shorter, but it has the same shape. Her arms have more muscle, not that much, but I don't think that's as important as most people would assume.

She has a scar below her right eye, and maybe another, much older one on her lip.

I'd like to say that I could infer something useful from all this, but I can't.

"I do hope everyone's ready," Giant 1 shouts. "Begin!"

My gut's twisted, and the heat of my breathing almost stings my freezing lips. I expected her to rush me. She doesn't. She just stands there, her breath creeping from the corners of her mouth like a dragon.

There's a chorus around me. Snaps and cracks. Whimpers. There are no shouts, just the soft pads of baggers, strolling back and forth down the rows. Over my enemy's shoulder I can see Grace, fighting to stay on her feet, and to the side I can see David, watching and circling, instead of attacking. One of the guards blows his whistle.

"I should just break you right now." I don't know any fighting styles, or anything about martial arts at all, really, but Alanza's definitely adopted a pre-meditated, well-practiced stance. "I can tell you know nothing, just from the way you stand, but even you should have learned by now to keep your eyes on your opponent."

She won't attack me, of course. She doesn't want to. She wants to talk to me. If I had to guess, I'd say she's more in the dark than I am. Naturally, we just circle each other. I can handle that, even with my arm in the state it is.

She steps forward.

I step back, and she grins at me, like somehow me being afraid of her is an achievement.

She's angry, that's obvious, and whatever's going on here, she thought she was in on it, and recent events have proven her wrong. She might be-

Some part of her makes contact with my face. Not sure what part. Her leg entangles mine, I fall, and I fly far enough that my face is in the snow.

I think I scraped one of my hands, it's warm, and pulses in time with my heartbeat. It's more of an effort to hold back a hiss of pain than it is to get back up. "C'mon!" She kicks some snow in my face as I get my feet "You're embarrassing yourself." The second she comes back into my field of view, she smashes me in the shoulder. It doesn't hurt, but I spin onto my back. I'm definitely glad the mat's here. "On the first few days, people thought you were me, can you believe that?" Her boot comes down next to my face. I move in time, but the movement rips out some hair.

It's not elegant, but I struggle back to my feet before she tries anything else. My instinct is to attack, and she raises her arms, as if she sees it in my eyes.

"You didn't like that," I say, and Alanza's head rises from behind raised arms as I speak.

"So you can talk." She almost laughs. In her mind, getting me to talk must mean she's won. "No, I didn't." She doesn't wait for an answer. Whatever sense of humor or sportsmanship was holding her back is gone.

The first hits are just taps, torso hits to be sure I'm not holding back any sort of fighting ability. I really wish I was, or that I could at least think of a good way to fake it. She's not fooled, and as soon as she throws me off the mat into the snow, she lets loose, and there's no telling where one blows ends and the next begins.

There's really nothing I can do other than what my instincts tell me, so I draw myself into a ball, and wait.

It's not so bad. After a while, my arms go numb.

The time is a blur. I know it can't have taken that long, but it feels like hours until the whistle sounds. The other students switched opponents. I saw them. I guess they forgot to check on me.

My vision's blurry, so there are facts of which I can't be sure. Alanza went somewhere, definitely. Must have gotten tired.

Grace helps me up. I feel like I should be all red, but looking down, my body looks normal.

There are stamps that go on people's hands. I don't get one, and Grace doesn't. David does.

There's food, too. I don't get any of that, either. I think there are tables, set with plastic trays. I don't really know, I'm lying on my back as Dr. Islet looks into my eyes with a flashlight.

I'm reasonably certain there's an argument. I might have been on a stretcher at some point, although I'm not sure who carried it. I also walked, which was surprising.

That's how I got to my bunk. I'm not sure if I slept, but I must have. Why else would the sky be turning red?

Naturally, my whole body hurts. I feel like I have to stretch, so I walk. If nothing else, to check how much time I lost.

Outside, the clouds are turning dark as the sun disappears. The tower near the airfield is just visible as its lights blink red against the ribbons of snow.

"You survived!" David calls up from across the camp. "Nice."

"I'm glad you approve." My jaw hurts. Or maybe it's my tongue. "What happened?" The tents on the way down to him are collapsed under frozen snow, but I still have enough strength to stride through the drifts.

"You got the shit beat out of you." He looks like he's just told a fantastic joke as he meets me in a circle of broken tents.

"I know, I was there," I say. "I'm less clear on what happened after."

"You missed the good bit." There are bruises all over the parts of his chest I can see, and all down his arms. "I'll show you." He leads me along with his hand on my back. "Everyone saw the baggers ignore you. Made a lot of kids mad." I can hear Grace and some other students as David leads me back up the valley, around the back of the cabin towards the hollow I'd found. "I won my fights, so I got food." He shrugs. "More than I needed, really, so I tried to share."

"They wouldn't let you." I want to run my hand along my arm, assess the damage. Almost certainly not a good idea.

"Right." He nods. "There were a lot, and they had guns, but Grace said something pretty smart, we worked together-" Students are clustered around the hole I'd found, backs against the cabin wall, or lying in hollows, dug into the snow.

"What did she say?" I cut him off.

"She asked me what I thought you'd do, if you could." He sits in the snow. "We didn't know if you'd get up again, so we did." Some students look up. Most are too busy eating or trying to keep warm.

"I got the food out." Grace shuffles over to me, without getting up. A crowd of eyes follow her. "It was easy, just like you said." There's something to her grin, or maybe her eyebrows.

Obviously, I didn't tell her to do a thing. "And that stuff you said earlier, about how smart the other students were," she glances over to them, "you were super right. Guess I shouldn't be surprised." She hands me what looks like a cup of soup. I'm in no position to be picky, and it's warm enough.

She wants me to play a character, to be more like her.

At first, it seems completely impossible. This is something I couldn't do if I were in perfect health.

I have to try, though. Grace and David have done their part, and based on what they said, some of the students think of me like a martyr. I have an image to maintain.

I just nod. It could be that I just like the soup, or that I'm grateful. Hopefully, to the students, it's all the proof they need that Grace and David did what they did in the service of my "master plan."

"You talked to Alanza, right?" Grace asks. The students look up. Her and the armband wearers that follow her must be central figures in their daily lives. "Did you find out anything?"

I could just tell her that I didn't, but I should press my advantage, if you can call a small crowd of bruised, freezing children an advantage.

"I did." I take another sip of soup as I try to think of anything I could spin as some kind of revelation. I've heard that when trying to convince someone, you start with the facts, "But it wasn't from Alanza." Some of them sit forward. Perfect. "What they did today was illegal."

"Yeah, of course it was." Grace leans in. "So?"

"So." My brain works faster when it runs at the same time as my mouth. Not sure why. "They took my phone." I point at the students. If nothing else, Grace can't claim I'm not making an effort. "They take yours too?" Most nod. Some grunt. "That means they knew. All along, they planned to do stuff like this. It was never supposed to be a real academy. All we have to do is get a message out."

"Yeah," David says and swallows a cup of soup whole, "but you just said they took the phones, so-"

"The staff have phones," Grace says. "For internal stuff, at least. Not sure if they have a line off the island."

"No good." David inches closer to the fire. "They have an exchange system, like those really old switchboards. That's the only way they can call off the island. I heard them bitching about it."

More stares into the fire.

"The tower by the airfield. They have to communicate with the incoming aircraft. We might be able to raise the mainland on that." A moment of silence. "We'll use that."

"It has guards, I've seen them," Grace says. "Armed ones, and cameras." I swallow the rest of the soup. It's not ideal. I feel wrong the moment I seem them nod.

"I didn't say it would be easy."

The next day is what I've come to expect from Truman. Marching, shouting, complaining. Mostly snow.

I've also developed a slight limp, as I learned the second I crawled out of bed and almost fell. I'm rubbing it in the snow now, trying to keep it warm.

"They want us to go out again in a couple minutes." I haven't learned the names of any of the students I met yesterday. I probably should, but there are better ways to recognize them. This one cracks his knuckles a lot. I think it's a nervous habit.

There's a chorus of groans. At this point we've spent more time outside the academy in the snow than we have inside. I think most of us would kill for an hours long lecture right now.

At the moment my "collaborators" and I are sitting around

the circumference of a shallow pit, just down the hill from the Academy's lawn, watching streams of students marching back and forth into the forest.

Mornings are all like this now, just endless group exercise. It's like a boot camp designed by someone that has no idea what a boot camp's for. Or maybe they just want us too tired to cause trouble.

"Hildegard." Grace sits down beside me, her arms filled with rolls of bandages. "We can't," she pauses for a second, and leans in closer, using her hand to keep things private,"they can't go out again." She glances towards our students, lying spread-eagled in the snow. "It's just too cold, they'll-"

"All right, all right. I wasn't exactly looking forward to it, either." They watch me as I get up, as if somehow I'll fix everything. I guess they don't have anyone else to pin their hopes on. "We need to conserve our strength, after all."

David spots me as I'm halfway down the hill to the tents and stretchers at the edge of the forest, near one of the paths some students have trampled into the snow. Of course, he's not tired.

"Planning something?" he asks.

"Not really." There are armband wearers here, around the edge of the makeshift infirmary, and Dr. Islet does his best to avoid them as he rushes from bed to bed. There are fewer staff than last time. "Just trying to get our new helpers some time off." I raise my hand and call after him "Doctor!" Islet turns from baggers carrying off a motionless student on a stretcher. "We need to talk."

I can hear the snow shuffling as the students I'm about to claim are exhausted slide down the hill after me.

"Okay," he sighs, resting by his arms on the empty bed, "okay. What can I help with? Pine, right?"

"Yes, doctor, these students," I look over my shoulder to see a column of armband wearers closing in, "and me, we just came to ask for leave to rest."

Dr. Islet frowns, as if he's about to shout over me. "I just don't have the authority. You know I don't." He turns away. "I'm sorry."

I think I just realized how much I really didn't want to go back into the forest.

"You can't just say you're sorry!" Knuckle-cracker shouts over my shoulder. The quieter ones with him grunt in agreement, and even some students on stretchers turn to wheeze.

Some baggers on the edge of the camp step forward as Islet's patients slide off stretchers and get to their feet. Some guns are leveled.

"This is just sad!" My head whips around to watch Alanza jog free of the the arriving column towards us, flanked by a crowd of Golf Company students, red armbands flying in the wind. "Trying to get out of PT with a note from your doctor?" For the second she walks past me, our noses almost touch as she glares at me.

"We're cold," one of the students on a stretcher gasps, "we're tired. We can't go on like this!" Empty tears streak down his face. "I can't go out again. We need food, and-"

"Oh, please." Alanza plants her foot on the stump of a tree, looking over an assembling crowd of students. "Do I look like I've just come from a hotel?" She wipes her brow. "Am I enjoying myself, maybe? Do you think marching and fighting endlessly is fun for me?" Students look up at her, completely silent. "We're here for a reason." The wind roars, and the clouds roll past behind her, faster and faster. "Because whether we know it or not, we all have the potential to be the best. Most of you probably don't believe it, some of you might even think it's impossible, but-"

"This is insulting." I'm not going to get anywhere ignoring her, especially when she seems to enjoy winning adoring henchmen so much. Yes, my voice cracks, and I don't have a pile of boxes, but it's better than nothing. "What makes you the judge of someone's potential? Are you a mind reader?" She glares down at me as my voice gets stronger. "Maybe a fortune teller?"

She spends more than a second looking me over. Maybe she wasn't expecting any resistance. Maybe she's considering my argument, or maybe it's that this is the most I've ever said to her.

"I'm not in charge here." Her voice goes back to speaking volume, just loud enough to be heard over the wind. "If I was, do you think I'd be marching and fighting every day?" Some of the armbands laugh on cue. "But that's not the point, the point is, and this might sound strange to some of you," she runs her eyes over Grace, David, and the students that stand next to them, "I have faith in someone greater than me, and at the same time, my driving aspiration is to become someone like that for someone else. I don't ask why, because I haven't earned the right to know," she sneers down at the armbands, "and if I haven't, you definitely haven't." There are a few cheers. Someone near the back shouts something.

'So what you're saying is that we don't deserve to know why we're being treated like criminals," I ask her. Alanza's face, turned into the wind to look over her crowd of supporters, moves back to me.

"You definitely don't," she says. More laughs. "Even I can tell that."

"That's not relevant." I can hear another helicopter in the distance. "We're not soldiers. We haven't been trained to take orders, and I don't see why anyone would want to."

"No," Alanza replies, "you wouldn't. It's an issue of trust,

Hildegard Pine." The blades come closer as the wind dies down.

"So you trust your commander, more than anything, and that makes you better than us?" I ask, and she laughs at me the second I finish.

"No, no. Don't get the wrong idea." Some armbands at her feet chuckle. "It's not trust. It's one of the first things I was taught. It's like you said before, I'm not a mind reader, no one is. When you trust someone, it's never based in reality, it's faith. Comforting, but hollow."

"And what's your alternative?" I say. "Turning your brain off? Becoming a robot? That sounds like the hollow option to me."

"Simple." She smirks down at me. "The solution is never to trust anyone at all." Her henchmen shake their fists in the air. "Cooperation comes from a shared rational self-interest. That's all. Is that too simple for you?"

I walked right into another opportunity for her to make a speech, and I can't say I completely disagree with her, but there's no future in establishing a rapport.

Charlie Company needs to hear a comeback. A strong one.

An engine roars as a jeep crawls through the snow, towards the edge of the stretchers.

"Bullshit!" I have to raise my voice over the engine as baggers step out. "Trusting someone is-" I trail off as I talk. As far as I'm concerned, she's right, but admitting it is exactly the wrong thing to do.

It's probably for the best that the growl of the approaching jeep means the students will have to imagine my counterargument. It's almost certainly better in their heads than anything I could come up with.

The helicopter roars overhead, matte black and unmarked, towards the academy.

Giant 1 clambers out, and stands at the edge of Alanza's crowd of admirers.

"He wants to see you before the address." Giant 1 hisses. She looks him over and parts the crowd. He walks back to his vehicle, holding the door open.

Alanza nods her head with a soft smile, like she's remembering something. She slides into the seat, without another word to her armbands, and the jeep roars back to life. It sprays snow across the stretchers as it crawls towards the academy.

"What was that about?" David stares at the retreating jeep.

"No idea." I say as the armband wearers disperse into groups. The students that stood with us, even the ones in casts and on stretchers, glare at their backs. "But I think," Grace stands by, looking up at me, "I think we made progress."

"Yep," she nods, "good stuff."

"You can't keep doing this sort of thing." Dr. Islet says as he jogs down the stretchers.

"Oh, really?" David takes a step towards him, and Grace puts a hand on his wrist to hold him back.

"We get it, doctor." Grace says as he helps up one of his nurses. "We'll-"

"No, you don't get it." Dr. Islet's glasses fall askew as another tray of bandages falls and unravels in the snow. "This isn't what I signed up for." He stares down at the gauze, an almost invisible stripe over the buried earth. "I'm a microbiologist, my job's to make people better, not-" He hisses, just enough to hold something back. "This isn't why I became a doctor." The medics pull away, and I try as hard as I can to catch David's eye, and hope the shaking of my head is enough to convince him not to say something stupid.

"We can help you," Grace says. "We don't like it here any more than you do."

"No." He shakes his head. "You're just a bunch of kids. As wrong as this is, it would be worse if you tried to escape."

It's the word "escape" that makes things really sink in, and from the way David straightens up, and the students on stretchers turn over, I can tell it has the same effect on them.

Something in the air squeals, and another jeep rolls past, a cluster of loudspeakers blaring from the roof.

"All students will assemble in the main hall at 1200 hours, all students will assemble-"

"I lost my watch." David stares down at his wrist. "How long 'till then?"

"Not long." Grace taps the face of one of the three watches on her wrist. "We should probably go." She lowers her voice. "I think the doctor needs to be alone."

The slope up to the academy is crowded by the time we climb it. I shouldn't be surprised, the call was for all students. Alpha and Tango companies make up less than half of the crowd now. If anything, they look worse than Charlie.

About halfway up the incline starts to be too much for me. Grace isn't in much of a position to help, and asking for assistance from David feels too much like giving up. Ignore it.

There are baggers here, clustered around the statue, and new floodlights up by the academy face.

"Check it out." Grace points and whispers as we blend in with the thickening crowd.

"What?" I follow her finger to the soldiers by the double doors while I catch my breath.

"You don't think they look different?" I follow her finger, and I can see what she means. Their uniforms are pristine, white camouflage, the pattern made up of tiny blocks. Splitter, I think it's called. And they stand at attention, too, with rifles held firmly, and dogs sitting quietly in the snow beside them

"They look new," I say to her as we pass through the doors.

"Yeah," Grace nods, "or," There are more down the corridors, flanking us, like a precessional guard, "they're trying to impress their boss."

"The idea had occurred to me."

The hall is stark, polished wood tiles, with a stage in the middle, and huge, freezing windows down either side.

We've only been in here once before, and at the time I really wasn't in a position to take it in. It's like something from a real estate catalog.

Alanza steps back from the man in the center of the stage, and down into the crowd of students, and her followers rush in to surround her.

There are no soldiers on stage, and I catch just a glimpse of Giant 1, disappearing behind the curtain.

I honestly don't know what I was expecting, but from here, it looks like a man. An old man, slightly bent, wearing a heavy coat over his shoulders, and a wide brimmed hat that he reaches up to remove.

"Good afternoon." The student body goes silent. "I am G." He raises his arm slightly, like someone coming in for a hug from a distance. "The significance is likely lost on you." He continues, adjusting the warped, mirrored glasses on his face with a thick finger. "So to put things in more relatable terms, I am your headmaster." The crowd rumbles with whispers. "Yes, indeed, we like to keep things behind the curtain here at Truman, but rest assured, it was my sincerest wish to greet you when you first arrived, but unfortunately, my debut was delayed by unforeseeable circumstances."

"Gross," Grace whispers. "Serious case of old person

mouth." I can almost see what she means. His mouth seems like a misaligned mess. Everything's there, just discolored, pointing in the wrong directions.

"Of course, I intend to play the role of the beneficent educator. I had done all the research I needed, but on the way here I was informed that many of you are discontent with your cast." Now that Grace's pointed them out, I can't look away. It's not just the teeth, but the pale, sunken jowls, too. His face isn't old, exactly; it just has a quality I've never seen before.

"I don't get it." David leans over me.

"Big surprise." Grace titters under her breath.

"No, look, in my old unit-" He's tall enough that he can talk to Grace over me. "We worked with Scots, Indians, a German. It was a game I used to play, collecting accents."

"So?" she asks as G takes a folded piece of paper from his pocket, and slowly tears it into halves, until it's a shower of shreds.

"So," David hisses past my ear, "I think he's some kind of european."

"Oh, that narrows it down." Grace rolls her eyes.

"Of course, I will be brief." G's shreds fall into the crowd of students. "As I understand it," he turns on his heel, and starts to slowly walk down the stage, "many of you are finding our exercises difficult, painful, exhausting." Some of the baggers shift. Maybe their behavior was under orders, but if it wasn't, they have cause to be nervous. "This is of course the point. You are to be broken down, not just as individuals, but as a unit." He reaches the end of the stage and stares into the crowd for a moment before turning. "Those of you who have been taxed and persevered, you are the ones for whom this academy was founded. You are, right now, in the process of learning how an army is forged, you who are suffering will be the first to learn the truth, the nature of man's greatest strength, and greatest weakness."

"One of the naff countries," David whispers, "like the ones no-one votes for on Eurovision."

"What's Eurovision?" Grace asks.

"Too complicated to explain now."

"It is other men, of course." He sighs. "When we work together, we topple nations, make great works of art, even conquer space, but when we do, we reveal ourselves to our dual natures. You will learn to disregard trust as a fatal weakness, and learn how to take the first step on the long road to actually knowing another. As the curtain rises on our great work together, all I can do beyond shape your curriculum and cultivate your discipline is to wish you the best of luck."

"I'm totally lost." David apparently forgets to whisper.

"I don't think we're supposed to understand this," I tell him. G stops, and takes a few steps towards the edge of the stage, as baggers fan out into the students.

"And, of course," he adds as he steps down from the stage, "in the interest of discipline, those found outside their Company's camp after dark will be shot."

Students were silent for a good while afterwards. I was, too. The march back to camp was slow, and quiet.

This isn't just a case of getting the wrong idea. It would be normal to assume that any student that wanted to escape would be unequipped to deal with the very real violence G threatened us with.

It won't stop me, of course. In fact, after a few empty hours in my bunk last night, I came to the conclusion that I prefer this.

We're past pretending to be students. Now we know what we really are. Prisoners.

The question of why remains, but if someone told me I could leave and take anyone I wanted with me on the condition that I would never find out what happened here-

"Hildegard?" Grace says from the foot of my bunk. "I can tell you're still thinking, but-"

"Our resistance needs some reassurance." It's not in my nature to spell things out like this, but I've learned that Grace's curiosity always outweighs any of her other sensibilities.

"Right," she nods, "if you could-"

There's no need for her to say any more as I follow her down to what's becoming the usual place behind the cabin. It's getting colder every day; we won't be able to gather here forever. Not that we plan to be here for that long, either.

"Well?" It's not David, as much as it sounds like him. The noise comes from one of the students, arms crossed under a blanket, encrusted with frost.

Last night, I put a lot of thought into what I was going to tell them. They're scared, tired, and sore, so as much as I want to tell David to teach him some respect, I know it won't do any good. I'm starting to develop a method to this, as well.

It seems to me that it's crucial I know what people want to hear before I talk, regardless of whether or not I actually say it. These kids want reassurance, they want me to tell them that G's all talk and that he would never have them shot.

There's no question In my mind that he would, and I don't have much confidence in my ability to deceive them, so I'm not going to. There are other ways to reassure them.

"Grace, you remember what I told you to do with the rations?" She nods her head. I still haven't really asked her about how she did it. "We're going to need more. a lot more."

"Copy." She nods.

"David, I need you to get weapons." He nods "You have access to the armory from the firing range, right?"

"Yeah." He jams a thick finger into his nose. "Roger."

"All right, I need three volunteers to follow me after sundown to the edge of the forest so we can get a good idea of the security around the tower." One of the students nods. Two others raise their hands. "Okay, good. There's just one more wrinkle to account for."

"Like what?" David sniffs as he runs his sleeve under his nose.

"It's just a hunch," I say. "But something that Giant 1 mentioned came back to me yesterday." At the very least our meeting here's taken their mind off the cold, and they all stare up at me with their whole attention. "I think there's a possibility that more of his unit arrived with G. If they did, we need to know." Most of them nod or mutter agreement. "I don't have a plan or anything, just keep an eye out. I'm sure I don't have to tell you that a bunch of elite soldiers with no staff responsibilities to take care of could be a problem."

"No shit," David says, his mouth full of gray, flakey rations. "'Specially if they're all freaks like their friend."

The whole thing could take days. Maybe weeks.

Later, away from the other students, I ask both of them, and they seem to agree.

Between that, the approaching cold, the mind-numbing lessons and exhausting exercises, there's almost no time of day when I have enough energy to focus on escape.

It takes a full day for me to realize that this is by design.

I'm lying in my bunk.

There's a pile of snow at the foot of the door to the outside. I think someone asked for a shovel today, to scrape away the ice. It's still there, and sometimes I can feel the wind scratch my heels or the edge of my face.

Later, I see Dr. Islet again. It's not later, actually, since it's morning now. I can tell, because apart from the retreating darkness in the sky, there's a quality to the air. Freshness, maybe.

I say later, because that's how it feels. I think I spent so much energy trying to stay warm last night that I forgot to sleep.

The doctor's doing his usual, trying to make the most of his minuscule staff. Normally, I don't see him out here this early, but there were a lot of collapsing students in this morning's PT.

Going before dawn doesn't help, either. There were times when I almost tripped in the darkness. A few days ago, I might have walked across to him, since the ground here on the edge of the forest is flat. I'm on a stretcher, so at some point, he'll have to get to me. At least I'm sitting up this time.

"I snagged pretty much a whole table's worth of food." Grace is here too. Somehow, the marching doesn't get to her. It might have something to do with her disappearing at the start and reappearing at the finish line. If this keeps up I'll have to ask where her shortcut is.

"Good."

"It'll be cold by the time we get any kids to it, though."

"I don't think they'll care," I tell her, shifting on the stretcher.

"Yeah." She laughs. "Did David say anything to you yet?"

"No." I don't have the energy necessary to express to her how frustrating this is. "I wasn't really expecting him to."

"So what's the plan?" She cranes her neck to get as close to whispering in my ear as she can. "Going to take the volunteer kids and scout out the airfield tonight?" There are layers to her question, but I don't have the energy to consider them.

"No."

"If you don't today-"

"I know. I don't have a choice; if I went in my condition we'd get caught right away."

"Yeah." She nods. "I was getting that impression, look," she flinches as the creak of snow echoes under the field of stretchers, "it'll definitely take a few more days to get all the stuff I need, okay?" I nod to her as Dr. Islet staggers through the piled snow towards me. By the time I glance back, Grace is gone.

"We're sure seeing a lot of each other, aren't we?" Dr. Islet tries to produce a chuckle at his own joke. "So, how's your arm?"

"Getting better." I can't help but rub it with my good hand.

"You've been keeping away from," I can see in his face that everything he told me to avoid recently became mandatory, "you know," he rubs the back of his neck, "overexertion?"

"You know it doesn't work like that."

He nods slowly, looking down at his clipboard.

"You're right," he pushes his round glasses further up his nose, "I'm sorry."

"I bet-" I've never had to fake a laugh before. I try my best, and hope that fatigue and injury makes it seem believable. "I bet no one ever asks you about your job. It's probably just as bad."

He drops his clipboard on the bed beside mine, and reaches out with both arms to steady himself.

"The whole medical staff's been busy since G got here, I mean, look." He points to the beds in the snow "I'm out here by myself. I don't think he trusts me."

"So you knew?" I ask. He's already begun to stare into the distance. I've known a few people like this before. I used to think they were thoughtless or selfish.

"I knew the Beagle Commission's chairman was coming here, and that he had a codename, I didn't think he'd still call himself that once he got here, I mean, what's next, a sign on the academy that says 'no girls allowed'?" It hurts my ribs, but I do laugh, although it sounds more like a wheeze.

He's not selfish, he just doesn't get to talk to a lot of people, that's all. It reminds me of something my foster mother said one day after trying to get me out of my room, something about human contact being a biological need.

"So G trusts your subordinates more?"

"Think so." He nods. "I mean, I hardly know them, we're scientists, after all; but we don't talk that much. I mean," he waves this hand back and forth, "I'm not complaining, under the - I mean in the staff-only parts of the school, it's creepy. They've moved all the cultures-"

"Bacteria cultures?" I ask.

"Yeah." He nods. "That was my job, back when Truman academy was just Truman base. All the tanks with the bacteria I worked on got moved down into the hangar, and now most of my staff are tied up with the Giant Unit."

I think the key here could be not to react with surprise to anything he says, or he might realize he's telling me things he shouldn't.

"Are they," what's the best way to phrase this, "sick?"

"Well, that's the thing, I don't know." He runs his hands through his hair. "There's only supposed to be three of them, but G's got all the medics he reassigned to them working 'round the clock." There are a lot of things I could ask, but since I'm ahead, I don't think I'm going to push my luck, especially since I might get to go inside soon.

"And G doesn't help?"

Dr. Islet shrugs. "He's been working non-stop since he got here, I'm just not cleared to know on what. Lots of running around with sealed suits and geiger counters, definitely not the sort of thing that should be anywhere near very sensitive bacteria."

A shout of "medic!" comes up from the distance. Some baggers carry a stretcher towards us. Not a problem, he's already given me more than I wanted.

"Looks like I'm needed elsewhere," he says, smoothing down his coat, getting ready to move on. "Just," he turns his eyes upward, probably searching for the right words, "I know there's no point telling you and your friends to be careful, or to stay out of trouble," he tells me, "so just be smart, all right?"

I nod, and he hurries off.

At no point was I injured enough to be on this stretcher in the first place, although the opportunity to rest is welcome. Soon I'll have to get up, though. Not really looking forward to that.

Back to power-saving mode.

Not that I need it. The rest of the day is lectures, and it's all I can do to stay awake. Something tells me falling asleep might be bad for my health, if it's not angry baggers, it might be hypothermia, judging by the growing drifts of snow that have crept into the academy.

Come to think of it, Charlie camp's probably the warmest place on the island, and once the thought occurs to me, I can't stop thinking about it.

That's instinct, I suppose.

Once it's over, and I'm stepping through the snow near the edge of camp, it doesn't seem like a long day at all.

It looks deserted. There are no students outside, and I can't see the glint of scopes and binoculars in the trees, either.

What I can see is a thin plume of smoke from behind my cabin. My first instinct is to run to them and stamp it out but after considering it for a while, I think I'd rather take the risk and actually warm up.

No one ever said campfires were forbidden, did they?

"You're back." David hands me a metal cup of soup. There's a tarp now, to keep the snow out, balanced on some cheap metal beams. Any marks they left in the snow getting here have already vanished. Some students shuffle away to make room, and I sit down by the fire.

"Good idea." There's no spoon, so I start pouring the soup down my throat "With the fire."

"Yeah." David nods. "I know." I let the soup settle for a while as I try to absorb some heat.

"No baggers today," I say. Some students nod.

"Must be too cold for them." One of the kids laughs.

Someone else walks through the snow, but looking around would mean moving my face from the fire. The student closest to me shifts, and Grace sits down next to me.

"Get anything from the doctor?" she asks.

"Lots." I tap the edge of the soup cup.

"You want some more?" She takes the cup from me. "The more kids we feed, the more pitch in, I mean, look," she waves her hand around at all the students around the fire, "our crowd's getting bigger every day." Some of them raise their soup. "So," she cups a hand around her mouth, "what did you find out?"

"He's short on personnel. He says most of them are dealing with the unit G brought with him, KU Giant, I think they're called."

"Okay," she nods, "so your hunch was right."

"It sounds like it. He didn't say why, but G has them

working around the clock, and apparently, he's installing something in the school. Something radioactive."

"A bomb?" David sits down on my other side, handing pieces of a torn loaf of bread around the ring of students.

"That's the problem." I've never really thought about food before, but the bread tastes better than it had any right to. "I have no idea."

"We definitely need more information," Grace says "Do you think we should change the plan?"

"No." I shake my head "Absolutely not, as much as I don't like it, it's still our best bet." I dip my bread in Grace's soup and take another bite. "He mentioned something about bacteria, too. He's not happy that they're keeping them in the hangar."

"A hangar?" Grace sips her soup. "If they really do have a Mobile Silo, that's the only place they could keep it. I guess it fits, too, the whole academy's built on a big plateau."

"I don't get why it's such a big deal." David tears a piece of bread with his teeth. "It can move by itself, okay, but if it only shoots one missile, what's the point?"

"Deterrence." Grace sets her empty cup down by the fire as she taps the word with her toe. "My dad was crazy for them, remember? I could never figure out why."

"That doesn't help," David says.

"I'm not sure exactly when it started, but Mobile Silos were distant cousins to the nuclear submarines, the whole thing was always a product of cold war paranoia, and some genius figured it'd be a good idea to have them crawling around on land as well as keeping quiet in the ocean."

"Okay." David gulps down the last of his soup. "So why should I care?"

"Because you can't hijack a nuclear submarine," I say. "It would be maintained and monitored, but a Mobile Silo's a relic, too expensive to buy or renovate for a civilian, but totally unregulated." Grace nods as I go on. "If you did have the resources to find one and fix it up, you could keep it completely secret, and launch without anyone knowing."

"Without anyone knowing?" David rubs his chin, running his hand over his face. "It doesn't change our situation though, does it?"

"No," I say. "It doesn't." Looking up, every single one of the students around the fire stare over, at us. "Calling for help is still our best course of action, we don't know what G wants, and we don't know what he'll do to get it, or even how long it'll take." The fire spits cinders into the cold air.

"You sure you're not," Grace shuffles up to me, leaning in to whisper in my ear, "y'know, mad about your dad? If we do this-"

"I know," I whisper back to her, "I might not ever find out where he went." I watch the students, talking amongst themselves for a while. "If it was just me, I might take the risk and stay for as long as I could, but I'm not responsible for just myself anymore, whether I like it or not."

Grace doesn't say anything, but nods as she draws back.

I hadn't realized that was the case until I said it, and now I don't think there's anything I can do about it.

"If we do call," one of the students says from under a blanket.

"Yeah," says another, "if we just assume that works, who answers?"

"I think you've got a point, there." Grace says to them. "They lured us in by pretending to be a military academy, who says they couldn't do the same thing to deflect an inspection?"

"Plus," David adds, "there's easily enough firepower here to outgun the national guard."

"It's not a perfect plan." They have points, although I wish they'd brought them up earlier. None of them realize the chief flaw, though.

Even if we do call down some superior authority that rescues us, it'll be governmental, and all record of everything that happened here, everything that could tell us why, will be smothered with black ink and folded away in some Pentagon drawer for fifty years.

If I'm lucky, they might be declassified before I die of old age. "But I don't think we have a choice."

"I know everyone wants to go home." Grace jostles the fading fire with a stick. "I mean, this place turned out to be a bit further from five star than I'd like, but we have to be patient." Some of the students grumble. Others get up and leave.

"I'll go get more firewood." David gets to his feet, and I nod as he leaves.

"We'll keep the fire going as long as we can." I point to the supports at the edge of our makeshift camp, and where it attaches to the side of the cabin. "If we work on this, we might be able to keep warmer out here than in the academy." Some students nod, others grunt. Most stay silent.

It sets the tone for the night's work.

Obviously, I'm still in no position to be hauling logs, tearing down cables, or even tying knots, and trying to stay useful, or at least seem like I'm trying, is more complex work than the manual labor I'm useless for.

It doesn't make that much difference, David does most of the lifting anyway.

"What's that?" Grace points up, through one of the small gaps in our canopy.

"More lights," David grunts. "They're putting up towers, too, they must've just turned them on."

"Why?" Grace says. "And why point them straight up?" Staring out into a gap between tarps, I can see a stream of pilot lights.

"Reinforcements." As I point, the roar of a helicopter sweeps overhead, close enough to disturb our makeshift camp.

David gets back to work. Grace watches. The lights and engines don't stop. Some of them I can see, when they pass inside the beam of searchlight, carrying heavy loads lashed to their undercarriage.

I can't sleep. It's not the noise, I don't think. David slumps against a pile of empty suitcases, eyes wide open. Some of the students must have decided to get more use out of them. I think Grace is doing her best to pretend to sleep. Her breathing isn't nearly slow enough.

I can't blame them, something about the atmosphere is suffocating. That's not to say that it's quiet, because comparatively speaking, it isn't. It's not just the helicopters, the wind starts to pick up, and every now and then, a wolf howls.

"Does anyone else hear that?" Grace sits up. There is something, just on the edge of hearing, it's gone now but-

"Is somebody knocking on the door?" David asks, standing up. It starts again.

"They are," I say as I stagger out into the snow and back into the cabin. Of course, the door is still wedged halfway open by a solid drift of snow.

"Oh, hello." The figure turns, and waves a gloved hand at us. "It's me." Dr. Islet looks around the second he removes the hood of his coat and snow goggles. "I was hoping we could talk."

"Not here," I tell him. He follows us back to our makeshift camp, and the students that are still awake look up as he walks through what serves, for the moment, as our front entrance.

"Do they know about," Islet runs his hands through his hair, looking for words, "this?"

"By they, I assume you mean the faculty," I ask him.

"Correct." He nods.

"If they did, you think it would still be here?" Some of the students laugh, as if it were a joke. "Either assignments have changed, or it's just too cold for them out here now. We can talk."

"Well, all right." He puts his snow goggles down, and picks an empty spot close to the fire to sit. "It's warmer in here than in the academy." He laughs, rubbing his hands together.

"Okay, so why are you here?" David folds his arms.

"And," Grace says, "how did you know about this place?"

"Well," he starts, "I'm here just to say that I want to do anything I can to help, whatever's going on under that so-called school, it's," he shakes his head, "it's not what I signed on for. And I didn't know anything about this." He gestures to the camp. "I just guessed that if anyone was putting together some kind of escape plan, it'd be you, I mean, I'm a professional, and I've worked in some pretty bad conditions for the Commission, I can't imagine how bad this must be for you kids."

"Yeah, breaking news," David says, "it sucks here."

"What we need the most right now is information," I tell him.

"I thought you might," Islet nods. "So I did as much snooping around as I could before I came out here."

"The air traffic control tower," I say. "What security does it have?"

"The tower?" He rubs his chin. "I haven't been out there since I flew in, but I think I saw some cameras." Grace sits up. "There are definitely cameras," he says. "Not many, five or six, maybe two on the outside, the rest on the inside, and there are guards, too, armed ones, but it usually runs on a skeleton crew."

"How armed?" David asks, and Dr. Islet shrugs.

"I don't know guns, I heard them complain about it once, though. They said they didn't have enough rifles. I think it's mostly small stuff. Pistols."

"All right." David folds his arms. Grace found a pad and pen somewhere, and is busy taking notes. "What about the Giant unit?"

"I told you earlier," he sighs. "G won't let me near them. I don't think he trusts me."

"What about G himself, then?" Grace asks. "Find out anything about him?"

"No way." Dr. Islet shakes his head. "I've never even seen him take his sunglasses off. He wears them all the time."

"Okay." Grace scribbles onto her pad. "Confirmed facts about our captor: eyewear enthusiast."

"I don't think he likes them, uh, to be honest," Islet says, "he reminds me of a card shark, his face never changes, he's always smiling just a little, you know? It's creepy."

"Added to the list," Grace says, "poker expert."

"We don't need you," David says, pointing, "to tell us G is creepy."

A sound echoes against the canvases. We all jump to our feet.

"Gunfire." I glance over at David, and he shrugs.

"I was still casing the armory, I haven't actually taken any yet," he says.

There are a few more barks, and then a distant wail. After a few seconds, it repeats. A siren.

"Is that the academy alarm?" Grace asks. She doesn't have time to find an answer. With a spray of snow, Dr. Islet leaps to his feet and tries to rip the canvas at the camp's edge aside.

"Stop him!" David runs after him, but falls over the campfire, and students scatter as cinders fly into their faces.

My legs are shaky, so by the time I'm past the canvas I can barely see the doctor, halfway to the treeline. Grace runs past me, and I do my best to keep up with her and David.

I think he has a brick in his hand, and as we enter the trees he throws it. I can't see in the dark, especially with the searchlights dancing across the front of the academy, but I hear a squeal of pain.

Dr. Islet's shadow falls just on the other side of the trees.

David gets to him first, turning him over and checking his pulse.

"Ow."

"He's okay," David calls back to us. There's another flash of light, something more than the searchlights, so I drop as low as possible, trying to find shadows under the trees.

Grace and the students that followed us do the same, and David pulls Dr. Islet down as he tries to get to his feet.

Columns of shadows run past in the snow. baggers.

"What is that?" Grace whispers "A flare?" More gunshots. I can't see much except for flashes from here, but some of the baggers fall into the snow, with their comrades diving down behind snow drifts or fallen trees.

The light passes over the forest. For a second, some of the faces become visible, hovering dots between the trees, vanishing behind the shadows.

"I remember them," Grace says as she growls up to me. "First exercise, remember?" She points. "They wouldn't come up the cliffs."

"I wouldn't know," I tell her.

"They showed up to our camp and everything," she says.

"Yeah." David adds "Some of them were in my firearms training, too."

"When did they stop coming to camp?" I ask them.

"The night we all agreed on the control tower plan, I think." Grace says. "Guess they figured they could do it better."

"Yeah." David points as some of them appear, running against the snow. "Except something tells me they're not going to get that far."

"He's right." Grace turns to me, half her face glowing in the light of the flare "We have to help them."

Dr. Islet struggles quietly in David's arms. A personnel carrier, like the ones the baggers ride around in, crashes down the slope and drifts to a stop. The instant it does, a ringing sound echoes from the opening hatch. A layer of snow falls from the trees above, and I raise my arms to shield my face.

"Absolutely not." I reach out to catch Grace, already half standing, and my grip almost pulls her back down.

"Why?"

A group of shadows emerge, one wide and squat, another hunched, and a third one, taller and broader than any normal person. In an instant, one of them launches off its feet, onto to the top of the vehicle, shaking it, and leaps into the air. One hurries after it, hefting a weapon. Another, the enormous man, just walks through the snow, taking the squealing hum with him. I un-grit my teeth.

"Giants," I answer, forcing down the unnatural nausea.

"We can't just leave them, though!" Grace shouts. There's another flash of light, and in it I see the faces of everyone who followed me here. Watching and waiting.

"We have no weapons. No plan." I think David's the first to agree. "The only choice is us and them, or just them."

"We can't just-" Grace starts, but can't finish.

"We're staying here until it's over. Everyone keep as still and quiet as you can. Once they're gone," I tell them, "we let the doctor go, and head back to camp." Dr. Islet's stopped struggling. A nod travels around the crowd.

It doesn't take long. The shadows merge with the swaying forest as the flare above fades away. There are a few more gunshots. Not many, and then something like a roll of thunder.

The personnel carrier grunts, groans, and begins to grind away into the fresh darkness.

"Go." I point back to Charlie camp, and the students around me rush, staying as low and quiet as they can in the forest. It's not that hard, and by the time we reach the edge of the valley's slope we're all sprinting.

I can only hope that whatever students are left at Truman that haven't joined us didn't see anything. For all I know, that might've been the last stand of Alpha or Tango.

I was expecting someone to say something once we reached the campfire.

But no one does. Even Dr. Islet stands motionless once the students release him. Some are catching their breath. Most are trying to get warm again.

"We should have helped them." The words hang in the air, like a dead cow on a hook. They're probably waiting for me to argue.

"Yes, we should have."

"So," David turns me from the fire to face him by force and I try not to wince at his hand on my shoulder, "why didn't we?"

"Can I, uh, go now?" Islet asks.

"Wait an hour or two," I tell him. "They're probably still on alert."

"Don't change the subject." David says.

The students around us are exhausted, of course, but they are listening. " I - we couldn't have helped them, and don't pretend," I say and jab him in the chest with my finger, "that without any equipment of any kind we could've fought off baggers and the Giant Unit, all right? Because if you ever actually do fool yourself into believing that you might as well just shoot yourself."

The camp is silent. David has nothing to say, which I would guess means he agrees.

Nobody wants to talk about what this means for our plan.

After what feels like an hour or two, the fire burns down.

Once dawn starts to glow through the curtains, Dr. Islet leaves.

I haven't slept, obviously.

To be honest, I haven't been able to take my eyes off the campfire.

It's just a rope of smoke now, turning in the soft wind, catching the occasional snowflake as it twists.

Some students have started coming and going. Mostly going. A few come back with more firewood. David's still here, although I have no way of telling if he's really asleep. Grace has disappeared again. Maybe out looking for more food. I don't think I've eaten.

There's a bang, and the crack of ice. Something crashes against the side of our cabin, and a student outside the camp shouts for a second before going quiet.

David jumps to his feet, fighting to tear the blanket from his chest as a steady stream of baggers erupt through either side of the camp's curtains.

Before he can stand he's surrounded by a crowd of them, rifle butts aimed down in a constant stream of blows.

I don't have the energy to get up. I hear Grace scream.

The students sleeping by the fire barely have the time to wake up before there are bags on their heads.

Someone grabs me from behind by the hair, and my vision goes blank as a bag is pulled over my eyes.

I have a pretty good idea of where I am, sort of defeating the purpose of the bag.

I'm not quite being dragged. I think I have just enough energy to stay upright as they shove me along.

First it was cold. Then there was a slope. Now it's a little warmer and I'm walking on wood. Polished wood, based on the squeaking it makes.

There are a lot of others, too. I'd guess they're rounding up the entire student body, with a few notable exceptions, which means that whatever they're upset about they've either caught the culprit, or they have no leads whatsoever.

I should be worried about what's going to happen next, but I definitely don't have the energy for that.

Sounds open into a dull roar of moving equipment, boots and voices. A bagger, or what I assume is a bagger, shoves me to the floor, and I can hear him raise a gun.

There are rows of others, I realize. Probably all bagged, most of them breathing quickly, some even crying quietly.

"Anyone attempting to stand will be shot!" A voice rings out from the what must be the stage of the huge lecture hall. "Anyone attempting to remove their bags will be shot!" There are some cries, some gasps, a few retches. "Anyone resisting quest-"

"That's quite enough, colonel." This routine doesn't fool me for a second. My foster parents used to do this all the time. "I think it's best you bow out for now."

G's voice grows closer as I listen to his shoes tapping across the brittle, polished wood. Someone whispers.

"All positively identified, sir. They're all here." The

bagger's voice is raised just enough for me to hear it through the bag on my head, but G's still too far away.

"Yes, sir." Another voice answers. "Last we checked, she's still in bed, sir." The hall is quiet, apart from the occasional shift of a bagger's foot.

"Now." G raises his voice. "I imagine the majority of you are confused. Perhaps frightened. This is understandable. This is not a training exercise or a test of any kind. Last night certain members of the student body committed a serious infraction, and have since been expelled, but not without consequence. Two men are dead, and although I did not know them, I am certain they will be missed." His voice comes in and out, so he's probably walking back and forth down rows of kneeling students, just like he did on the stage. "Naturally, it's in everyone's best interests to ensure a similar tragedy is avoided, and since I, as your school's administrator am taking responsibility for your education, I will be questioning you all personally, but there's no need for nerves. If you have nothing to hide from me, than you have nothing to fear from me." I hear a subtle sigh of cloth, and then a few coughs.

"I didn't do anything," someone hisses.

"I can see that, young man. Are you in a firearms course?"

"Yeah, so?"

"Can you tell me what this is?" Rustling. I think he reaches into his coat.

"Dunno." The student answers. "Some old gun."

"Old?" G sighs, and I can hear him turning it over in his hand. "I suppose it is. This is a Makarov. By most accounts, an unremarkable handgun. Reliable in its simplicity, semi-automatic. Nothing special. Ideal qualities for a leading man, wouldn't you say?" I can tell the student, whoever he is, bites back something angry.

"I don't know," is all he says.

"No. You wouldn't, America is all about war, isn't it? No time for the arts." The student shifts. "What's this?" G asks. "Ah, yes, the armbands. Alanza does enjoy cultivating her crowd of admirers. Tell me, what do you think of her?"

"Think of her? I guess-"

"You have romantic feelings towards her?"

"Wha-" He shifts a little, like he's trying to back away on his knees "-No-"

There's a snap, like a breaking twig, and something heavy falls to the floor. A few pairs of boots pound past, lift the body, and take it away.

"You." Another slip, another bag removed. "Are you, or anyone you know, connected to last night's curfew break?"

"No, no, please believ-"

"I believe you," G says, "not cast from a military mold, are you?"

"Uh, no, no sir."

"So what qualified you for my academy?" I can hear moving hairs. He can't be more than a row from me.

"Sports, sir. Football. Scholarship."

"American football." G doesn't laugh, exactly. It's more like an audible smile. "What would X say if he'd lived to hear that." There's a metallic tap. "What is this?" G asks. "An earring? Not quite playing the all-American hero, are you?"

"Uh, it's just-"

"Why did you get it?" G taps it again. I'd guess from the sound he uses the tip of his gun.

"Why? I guess-" The student, whoever he is, doesn't seem like he knows. "My friend got-"

Another snap. Another fall. More pairs of boots.

"You." Further away this time. "Are you, or anyone you know connected to last night's curfew break?"

"I guess I am." It's Grace's voice. "I knew some of them."

"Really?" G says. "They didn't include you in their plan?"

"Nope." G paces around her. She's doing her best to project confidence, but I can hear the shaking in her voice, and if I can, G can.

"A little small for the part, aren't you?"

"What part?" Grace answers. There's a small struggle, a cloth running over cloth. The bag goes back on her head.

"I imagine you can guess my question?" Another bag comes off.

"No," David says, "I wasn't listening."

"The curfew break," G says. "Did you know anyone connected to it?"

"What's a curfew?" I can hear David shrug from here. Some baggers beside him shift. There's a thump, and David chuckles.

"No," G says. and the boots on the wood retreat. "There's potential here. Leave him be." The footfalls get louder, and the occasional squeak on the floor gets higher and higher. Something catches on my head, and I wince at the light.

Up close, G is much worse. He smells like fresh mud, and his head looks like an egg, just fished from a sewer.

It's not that he's burned or scarred, it's like his skin's sunken, as if he were ancient. Maybe he is, but he doesn't move like it.

For the moment he draws breath to speak. I see his teeth, black and jagged.

He removes his glasses, and I look into the soft skin around his eyes as they tighten. He swallows, hisses, and straightens up.

"We're done. Take them back to their dorms. Lessons resume in one hour!" he shouts, and all at once we're hauled to our feet.

Bags come off at random as they throw us out into the snow. Mine goes on again about halfway back to camp.

There's no time to rest, or if there is, it doesn't register to me. Physical Training starts up again as drill instructors jog through the snow, shouting, except now they're flanked by baggers at all times.

The route doesn't go through the forest, only around the academy.

The students are silent, apart from the ones that cry, give up, or just collapse. Even Alanza's armband wearers, when I see them, are silent, although she's nowhere to be seen.

It's at this point that I'm glad you're here. the marching gives me time to think.

Comparatively, the route isn't that long or hard, since we're just going in circles, and as tired, hungry and cold as I am, I think I'm starting to get used to this.

This is the challenge at the gate of the thing I want most in life.

I think, for a while I lost sight of that. It's supposed to be hard.

I pull away from the staggering students behind me, into an empty snowfield all my own.

It's not much, but it helps.

Don't get the wrong idea, things aren't lining up to be knocked down.

The baggers call the column of students to a halt, and soldiers arrange the students into pairs as cars and personnel carriers growl down the slope, to the foot of the Academy's plateau.

There are no matts, and no tables of rations. Just baggers in a row between us and the school, and a shouted order to fight.

There isn't a fight, of course.

I'd like to say that all at the same time, students rushed, grabbed the baggers' guns, and wrestled them to the ground.

They didn't. My opponent, a scrawny boy barely filling his fatigues, just leaps towards me. He grabs, tears, twists. It's not hard to hit him, and he can't do anything but fall to the snow, curling into a ball and going still, like a poisoned spider.

Baggers pull him up, throw him on a stretcher, and the next opponent approaches. Another desperate, starving person. If nothing else, it's good practice for the parts of close-combat I've managed to retain. Most go quiet the moment I hit them. Others growl and crawl around in the snow, trying to get up. For now, at least, I'm past pain and exhaustion, but I know I won't stay that way. Sooner or later, I'm getting to hit another wall.

My winning streak lasts until I stumble. Baggers try to lift me onto a stretcher, but I walk back up the hill, where Islet's medical staff have gathered around a pile of quiet students.

There's no food, but I snatch up a foam cup of warm coffee before any else claims it, and roll my left arm. It doesn't hurt as much as it did, so I slip the sling off to test it.

"You really shouldn't, you know." Islet taps me on the shoulder. "I mean, the arm, not the coffee, you can have that." I roll my shoulder to throw off his finger, and focus on savoring the warmth.

Grace and David are talking, over there. It's not a row of stretchers so much as it is a crowd. "Listen, we need to talk about what happened," Islet says, "I can't keep putting myself in danger, if I get caught, the injured students-"

"Fine," I tell him. "Can't say I'm surprised." Among the things I'm too exhausted to do is persuade Islet to do anything useful. It's not necessarily that it would be hard, I just don't like his attitude, and the fact that he's obviously never gone hungry for a day in his life.

"You're still alive," David says. There's a bandage around his bicep, and dark bloodstains underneath.

"Yeah, for now," I tell him. Grace snorts at me.

"Maybe trade action movie tough-guy-isms later?" she says. It's not the tone I'm used to.

"This is the part where you two ask me if I've got a plan," I say.

"Yeah." David stares down at the students still fighting.

"Against my better judgement." Grace turns a roll of bandages back and forth. "I assume that means you have one?"

"I have a better idea of the facts, now." I tell them, following David's eyes down to the fighting students.

A bagger tosses his knife between two of them, and soldiers gather around. I suppose that's where David's wound must have come from. "Things are going to keep getting worse." David nods along with me, but Grace still has a skeptical squint. "So we stick to the plan, and accelerate our schedule."

"If we do that-" Grace raises her voice, but I cut her off.

"I know, we all know exactly how bad this can go."

"So," Grace says, "as far as you're concerned we have no chance, sticking it out here?"

"We don't." David nods. "Most of us, anyway. She's right there." Grace stays quiet.

"Save your energy," I tell them. "Tonight, we'll meet, so bring as much stuff as you can find that might be useful. We'll plan out the details, and-"

"And what?" Grace asks, "just rush in and telephone for help?"

"Yeah," David says, "police, coast guard, whatever you have here. Cowboys. The sheriff."

"It's not perfect," I say, "I know for a fact that we can't do it unless we all agree."

"Yeah, all right," Grace grunts, "I'll scrape together as much food as I can, David-"

"Yeah," David says, "I can get my hands on a few guns, maybe some body armor, should be better than nothing."

"We're agreed?" They both nod. "Then for better or worse, we move tonight."

❄

"No rifles?" one of the students asks.

"No rifles," David says. "This is the star of the show." He lays a weapon down in the snow by the fire. "Some German sub-machine gun piece of shit. Four full clips."

I should be nervous, but mostly what I feel is relief. There are more students here than I thought there would be. Having some hot food helps, too. It's probably why we've drawn such a crowd. Grace has really outdone herself.

"Is that it?"

"No." David points into the crowd. "And shut up. I got these, too." A collection of guns fall into the snow. "Five pistols. Nothing special. Between them, eight clips, and here," he empties another sack into the snow, "five ballistic vests."

"Are we ready to talk?" Grace asks.

"Not just yet," David says, "I also found these." Four hand grenades roll into the snow. "I called dibs when I found them," he grins, "just so everybody knows."

"Okay, we'll divide up the equipment later." Grace takes up the sacks, weapons, armor, and lays them out in rows. "So, now Hildegard's going to lay out the plan."

Based on her pacing, I'd say she wants me to get up, but as

she walks back and forth she reminds me of G, walking up and down the stage, and I can't stomach the idea.

"Our core objective is simple," I start, "seize control of the air traffic control tower, and use its radio to contact any and all authorities, tell them what's going on here, and have them come in to assist us." I think a lot of them want to hear the word "rescue." I don't, and I'm the one giving the speech. "They key is going to be speed if we're going to survive long enough for help to actually arrive. Our plan's divided into three phases." Grace starts sketching things in the snow, and students lean in to watch. Of course, I didn't tell her to do it, and visual aids aren't necessary here, but I trust her instinct when it comes to dealing with people. "First is the approach," I tell them. "And the most important thing will be avoiding detection for as long as possible. From there, we eliminate the academy staff in the tower and enter the second phase, which is our takeover. We post guards, and prepare to hold the tower for as long as we can while trying to make contact." They're following me so far.

Now for the bad news. Grace probably hasn't mentioned it to them, since it only just occurred to me.

"The third and most dangerous phase begins once we actually make contact. We just hold the tower until help arrives. The problem is that we'll be broadcasting on radio frequencies the academy staff have probably got someone keeping an eye on."

A nod shakes across the assembled students. Hopefully, the idea that this won't be easy is sinking in. "Best case scenario is a single bagger listening in, and if we're really lucky he'll be asleep. But we can't assume that, so most likely we'll have to deal with armed aggressors within a few minutes."

They're all silent as they glance back and forth. Grace stares into the campfire.

"Should we assign equipment?" she asks. Some of the students stand up.

"Yes. David, you take the sub-machine gun, a pistol and some body armor."

"I'll take the guns," he says and looks over at the crowd, "but they need as much armor as they can get."

"Before we actually decide who has what," I say to the students with their arms outstretched, "we need to consider individual roles." I take one of the ballistic vests. "David takes point, and I'll be going in with him to appraise the situation as quickly as possible. Grace, do you think you'll need one?"

"I'm going to be trying my best to not get shot, but-"

"Real surprising," one of the students speaks up, "keep all the equipment for your friends. Guess it doesn't matter if we get killed."

"It's not a question of friends." Now's the time, so I get to my feet. "I don't know you. I have no idea what skills you have, if any."

"Oh, so I might as well leave, is that it? I'll take my friends-"

"You know them better than I do," I tell him, "take the leftover stuff and divide it out however you want. We're leaving in ten minutes. Be done by then." I leave the camp. I don't have anything to do out there, and the truth is I can't focus at all. So I stare out into the night, trying not to look at the lights of the tower, just over the forest.

Soon it'll be over, one way or the other.

"We're really going for it?" Grace asks, stepping out into the dark.

"Shouldn't you be supervising?"

"David's got them under control. That's not why I came out here."

"If you want to say something," I tell her, "just do it."

"Okay then." She sighs. "I know we all want to get out of here and find out what's going on, and I know I shouldn't say this without presenting some sort of alternative, but I don't think this will work."

"I know how you feel," I tell her.

"Oh, good, I-"

"But we got this far by trying things we thought would be impossible, didn't we?"

"Yeah, true," Grace says.

"And it's not just us, Grace. We need to consider the other students. They haven't had as easy a time as we have." It takes a while for Grace to say anything after that, long enough for me to watch the lights on the tower blink in and out behind the swaying trees.

"You still want to go, that's fine, but don't pretend you're doing it for someone else," she says.

"This has nothing to do with me. There's no other option," I tell her. "I came here for something that I probably can't get if this works, and if it doesn't we're all dead, so call it stupid if you want," I turn to watch her expression, "but it's not selfish."

David leans out through the camp's improvised entrance and calls us back in. The moment before we do, Grace taps me on the shoulder, just enough to get my attention. "I don't know if maybe I just don't get you, or if you're fooling yourself, but you know how wrong this can go."

"I do," I say to her, and Grace nods, stepping back into the light. I stay in the night for a few seconds more. I'm not going to consider what she said. I don't have room for doubt right now.

"Time's up." David steps out towards me.

In the dark, holding a weapon, something about him looks very different. The students we've "chosen" stumble after him, looking exactly the same. Grace tosses a ballistic vest to me, and I slide it on over my head.

"Do we need to go over hand signals?" I ask them. "Or are we okay with the ones they taught us?" Nods travel round the crowd.

"I think we're good." Grace scans the students. "Right?" More nods. "Looks like we're as ready as we're going to get," she says.

"Just one more thing." I tear the extra pistol off David's waist. "This is mine." I roll it in my hand. It's heavier than I thought, and colder, too.

I've never actually fired a gun, for whatever reason. I'm not in any firearms classes, but if I have to use it, I'm not really doing my job, am I? Hopefully, it's just for show.

"All right. Just like last night, stay low in the trees until we hit the base of the tower." I have to fight the instinct to stick around, waiting for a start signal.

I suppose it's not that complicated, really, all I have to do is start walking. So I do.

The other cabins around camp are dark and silent. The tents are empty. No fires are lit.

Except for where we step, the snow is featureless. The sound of distant engines is in the air, along with howling wolves and wind. It's just like any other night.

A twig snaps as I drop to my knees on the edge of the forest. The treetops shake as a helicopter roars right overhead.

"More deliveries," Grace whispers by my shoulder.

I give the signal for quiet, hoping she'll get the message, and point ahead. It's practically a straight line through the trees, but I take things as slowly as I can.

Inching through the snow, only stepping when I have absolute silence. Not everyone puts as much effort in, but even David's improved. Or he's actually trying this time.

Something catches on my foot. A metal peg. Looking around, this must be where the medical tents from the first day stood. It's looks completely different, all covered in snow.

It doesn't take long for the lights in the night to silhouette something more concrete.

First the trees thin out. Then the snow gives way to tracks, and eventually, to gray.

I signal a stop.

It's no more than twenty feet to the foot of the tower, and the snow-covered ramp that leads up to the door inside.

Another helicopter passes overhead. Or maybe it's the same one, already on its way back. There's also a man, standing alone in a pool of light.

I signal, and someone taps my shoulder. I turn back, to watch Grace rubbing her hands together, trying to keep warm. She doesn't meet my eye, and neither do the others.

Before I can turn, I see David, shuffling as quickly as he can out of the snow. Grace hisses, and I hear some muffled swearing.

The man, the guard, I guess, stands with his back to us, clouding the air with his breath. I can't tell if he's a bagger or just a staff member. He doesn't have a mask, and he's only armed with a small pistol at his waist.

David wraps his right arm around the man's neck, and grasps his own wrist. He drops into a crouch, flattens against the side of the tower, and motions to us with his head.

I check to the left and right, like I'm crossing the road, run as fast as I can across the concrete, and flatten against the same wall.

"I thought," David says as the man in his grip struggles, "I thought," he continues, tightening his grip, "you were going to keep me waiting."

"So did I." I catch my breath for a second. Now that I'm here, I can see it wasn't that far.

Grace is about to make the run when a spotlight sweeps into the space between us, and the students flinch at the sound of another helicopter's engine.

"I think," David says, "I found the weak link in the plan."

Students cross, as low as they can, one by one.

"I'm trying not to think about it." I tell him. They pass by me, backs to the wall, and file towards the door.

"So," David says, rising again and pulling the silent, still-struggling man with him. "Why are they here?" I can't answer him, not where they can hear. Any blow to morale, and the whole thing could fall apart.

"You know we can't do this alone," I tell him. He doesn't reply.

It doesn't matter if it's true, even if it probably is.

Grace draws level with a gun in her hand and a nervous smile on her face.

"No going back now," she whispers. A few students eye the door, but before they can try, I turn the ice-cold handle, and duck away from the opening. Grace aims into it.

"Clear,." she says.

"All right." I look into the corridor. "Camera in the corner. Stay against the left wall."

We shuffle in line down the corridor, heads craning upwards at the camera.

"Go!" Grace whispers, and students push past me, almost into the camera's sight, and I strain my throat trying not to shout at them.

I pick my way up the stairs after them, David behind me, and crouch in the corner of the stairwell. Nothing. No alarms.

I can hear people up ahead, so I step as quietly as I can around the line of students pressed against the stairwell's wall.

Grace gets down on her stomach to scale the final flight of stairs.

The landing at the top has no cameras, so I pass her and crouch by the entrance to the control room. She stares for a moment, and then slides the small mirror in her hand across the floor to me.

Why she didn't use it herself I don't know, but I turn it slowly in the light, and see four men. Three crouched over control panels, wearing fatigues and headsets, and another one by the windows that look out over the airstrip. He's the only one visibly armed. Tilting up, there's a camera inside, in the upper north corner near the window.

I signal down to them, although I'm not sure how to tell them that only some of the men seem armed. They crawl across to me, Grace on my side, and we rise to a crouch, flattened against both sides of the doorway.

"Three count?" Grace asks.

The men inside go about their business. David crawls upwards, struggling soldier still in his grip. I shake my head at her.

"Focus on the camera," I say, and Grace nods. "Everyone ready?" My question's louder than I'd like, but everyone gives the okay, so I give the signal as quick as I can. Before things get too complicated.

David goes first, machine gun raised in his right hand, captive held out in front, and I flinch the second his gun starts screaming.

It doesn't last long, and the quiet after is almost louder. I jump to my feet and rush into the room, smashing against the other students as they slide and roll under desks and computers.

It's not a question of choice, the second I hear another crack of gunfire, I fall behind a pillar to the left, too narrow to really cover me. Another shot. The remains of a camera fall to the floor, scattering sparks across the shattered glass.

The gun in my hand feels like it's pulling my arm off, and bullets ping against the freezing metal at my back. I lean out, more by instinct than by choice, and see a single helmet hang above an overturned desk for a moment, before retreating behind another flashing shower.

I try to feel my way across, the gun in my hand, not taking my eyes off the solitary, overturned desk.

Trigger, hammer, safety, everything's there. My position's perfect, too.

I step out from the column, flinching at another snap of gunfire from the students, and pull back the safety.

The helmet comes up again, and a gun comes with it. I don't fall, exactly, but seeing the gaping barrel I almost collapse to the ground, and find cover under the side of another broken desk, shattered computer tower at my feet.

Another hail of gunfire. A cry of pain and a gasp, and then another shot.

The windows, all at once, shatter and fall to the ground.

"Got him!"

"Everyone okay?" Students start to rise at Grace's question.

"I'm hit," one of them gasps. "Went right through me." I straighten up, and flick the safety back on.

"Grace," I say. She looks up from the injured student, clutching a bleeding shoulder.

"This is the part where you tell me not to bother helping her, right?" she asks.

"Just keep the plan in mind," I tell her. She goes back to winding bandages around the blood.

"Anyone else?" I ask. A few raise their hands with cuts or bruises.

"Yeah, actually." David drops the soldier to the ground. "Could've been worse, he took most of the hit for me." A bloodstain spreads across the top of his former captive's chest.

"David!" Grace rushes across to him, and starts to tear open his fatigues.

If there was a time to abort, this is it. The students around me are tired, and a few are injured. More than I expected.

"Is he going to be okay?" I ask, shifting debris from the radio controls.

"I think so," Grace answers. "But his arm's kind of wrecked, and I really don't have the tools to get the bullet out."

"Relax." David tosses his weapon to his left hand. "I can handle it." It falls to the floor. He reaches out with his left, and takes it as slowly as he can, trying not to grit his teeth against the pain.

The students with their eyes on him seem unfazed, so I finish clearing the desk of mugs and pens.

There are lights outside, some headlights, even a few flashlight beams.

I lean over the radio, twisting the knobs, getting a feel for the range, and turn back to the students as Grace takes over.

"Hello? We're being held prisoner in Truman academy, we need help," she says into the microphone. Nothing but static. She looks up at me.

"Keep going," I tell her. "Cover as many frequencies as you can. Every second counts." I turn back to the others as they scan the ruined room. "The hard part starts now. baggers could be here within minutes," I tell them. "We take and hold the tower for as long as we can. Balaclavas, everyone." Grace slips hers on. I tie up my hair and do the same. "Once we make contact, even if we can't hold the tower, we still have a chance as long as we keep our faces hidden." The students' faces vanish behind black masks.

"Sure this a good idea?" David struggles to put his on, testing the weight of the weapon in his left hand. "If they can't ID us they might just bump off the whole student body."

"I don't think they will," I tell him. "And they can't treat us any worse, so it's a risk I'm willing to take."

I pull the headset on, and Grace rushes up, scanning a list of frequencies taped to the side of the console.

For now, things are holding together.

"This one looks good." She points. "Oh, and this one."

"You researched radio frequencies?" I ask her.

"Yeah." She nods. "Well, no, it's just that sometimes baggers write them down or tape them to their walkie-talkies or shoulder radios." She points down at the list. "So these are all inside the Academy, but ones with higher digits-"

"Okay, just keep it up." Grace sends her message again as I push her forward, and grab my gun off the desk.

The activity down near the runway's getting more intense. More lights, more shadows.

It's the middle of the night, and they have no reason to suspect anything. Even if they had been monitoring their radio they shouldn't be reacting this quickly.

Is it possible baggers at a nearby post heard the gunfire? There were other students that knew about the plan, too. Would they have a reason to turn on us?

"Getting nervous?" David laughs, trying to find a comfortable spot against the upturned desks.

Students all turn at once to look at me. "I'm thinking on the fly, here, we know that we can't pass ourselves off as personnel, we didn't have time to get codes or anything like that." A searchlight shines through the window. "You." I almost point at them with the end of my gun. "They'll see you!" The student, short brown hair and dark skin, rolls and flattens herself against the wall. "We need some people at the top of the stairwell, too." They just blink at me. "Volunteers?" I ask. Three of them get to their feet, sharing glances as they tiptoe across the room.

"How would they know we're here?" I ask.

"Dunno." David shrugs. "Maybe our guys here missed a check-in. Maybe we missed someone, or maybe," he leans around the edge of his cover as another beam of light sweeps the room, "maybe you're just being paranoid."

"I think I've got something," Grace says. "Hello, hello? We need help, we're-"

"Hold on, slow down, kid what's your-"

Glass shatters, metal tubes roll into the room, hissing, leaking smoke. There's a crack, a shower of sparks, and Grace cries out as she falls.

"Cover!" David shouts. More shots cut through the smoke. Grace lies still under the ruins of the radio.

I do my best to crawl across to her, leaping between the empty spaces that flood with light.

"Ow." Grace pulls a bloodstained hand down from her forehead, and looks over at me, face half held in her other hand. "We're in trouble, aren't we?"

"Can you move?" I ask her over the gunfire and roaring wind.

"Yeah, probably." The sounds of the storm outside clear as another light blinds me, and before I can cover my eyes, the roar of a helicopter's engines sends snow and broken glass flying into my face.

"Hah," David says, firing his gun through the broken window towards the aircraft. "I think they want us to give up." A line of golden lights spread through the control room, rushing through the air and bursting into sparks in the ceiling. The flash darkens my eyes, and by the time I can see again, a few more students are motionless.

I know one. The short haired, dark skinned girl, lying next to the post I gave her. In the next flash, I can see how much of her is gone. She died where I told her to.

"We can't do this."

"What?" Grace asks over the helicopter's blades.

"I thought-" David dives to the side as another wave of bullets tear the desk he'd hidden behind into splinters. "I didn't think they would just shoot at us, I thought-"

"You thought wrong!" David shouts from the stairwell. The helicopter draws level with the tower, and the searchlight washes across me as I kneel over Grace.

"Come on." I do my best to lift her, and she rises into an awkward hop. "We're leaving."

"And then what?" David asks as we look down the stairwell.

"We still have masks." Looking back around, the other students, shaking and bloodstained, fix on me. "If we can get somewhere secret, split up, make it back to camp, we might-"

"Somewhere with no cameras?" David flinches from another gunshot. "We really didn't think this through, did we?" I know he means me, as if I have to think of everything.

"We could use the academy tunnels. No cameras down there, remember? Must be the only place on the island," Grace says, as one of the students fire down the stairwell. "Then we can split up, sneak back to camp."

"It could work, if we can make it all the way there." I nod, raising my weapon. "The woods'll be full of baggers, we need to be quick if we want to make it."

"This is the best we've got, huh?" David limps down the stairs, machine gun swinging from his good hand.

A pile of snow's fallen around the open door, and swarms of reflected flashlights run up and down the metal.

"Once we get out there-" Every eye is fixed on the door, but I'm hoping they're listening anyway. "-you'll want to run, I know I do, but if we break ranks, they'll just-" Weapons steady. I can hear breathing from the other side of the door. "-just don't."

Only a few shots are fired. Three or four, David bursts through the door, and the column of baggers fall back into the snow.

"Go! Go!" I lead the students sprinting into the snow, running as fast as we can for the tree line where at least we'll have some cover.

Between the shadow of the trees I have enough time to look back.

Grace follows the closest, and David staggers as fast as he can at the back, between them there must be maybe fifteen students, most unarmed and injured.

We've left the helicopter behind, but the forest is full of shouts, barks, wandering flashlight beams and roaring engines.

"Stop, stop." I hold out my arm, and Grace tries to crouch beside me. She almost falls. "Look."

On the edge of the academy's slope, Giant 1 stands in the middle of an improvised camp, baggers pulling down lights and supplies as they pile into the forest.

"Looks like they don't expect us to run further inland." Grace whispers. "We just wait here 'till they're done?"

"Not sure," I say, looking back into the forest. "We might not have time."

"Don't forget," she says. "He might seem like a creepy uncle, but if Giant 1's part of a special unit, there's probably a good reason." She pats me on the shoulder. "While we're taking a break, I'll go check on the kids."

Something's happening down there, but the baggers' disappearing lamps don't shed enough light for my brain to understand what my eyes are seeing.

I squint, trying to make out as much of the moving snow as I can, when a harsh ringing stings my ears.

In the second my eyes close against the sudden pain, a man appears in the snow.

Just, appears, no footprints, nothing, he's just standing behind Giant 1, who barely looks up at him. He's tall, broad, and wearing some bizarre body armor, like a cross between a SWAT officer and fighter pilot. The same man I caught a glimpse of under the school.

"What is that thing?" Grace crawls level with me.

"My guess would be another Giant," I tell her.

"The nausea guy?" Grace asks.

"Looks like it." The two Giants watch a personnel carrier grind up the slope, around the back of the academy. The big one, wearing the strange suit, nods his head and blurs, as if he'd suddenly gone out of focus, and disappears.

"Oh," Grace says. "That's probably not good."

"What's the holdup?" David grunts.

"Nothing," I say. "Giant 1's moving off." The camp comes apart, and the twisted soldier leaps into a jeep that roars towards the airstrip. "Go!"

There's no need to scare them with something we can't do anything about.

I run as fast as I can up the slope, sounds of the bagger-filled forest retreating behind me.

"You remember the way, right?" Grace asks between breaths.

"Yeah." I push open the academy doors trying to catch my breath by supporting my weight on the handles for a second. "Don't forget about the cameras!" I shout over my shoulder.

We rush in, and the doors slam closed against a flurry of snow. A few students stop to catch their breath.

"Come on!" David grabs one of them by the collar, pulling him along as we set off again. "We're looking for the elevator, right?"

"Yeah." I point. "Should be this way." The corridor starts to slope down. "There!" I point.

From the end of a long stairwell, I can hear the echo of an elevator's gentle ping.

The crowd stops to breathe, bent over with hands on knees, some peeling off half of their masks to take long, hitching breaths. I try my best not to do the same, but my own heavy breathing echoes through my head as a shiver crawls up my neck.

The second it does, my ears refocus, stinging in the cold as they strain for any sound.

At first, all I hear are heavy footfalls, the swaying of rubber tubes slapping against metal, and the smell. An indescribable, stinging stench.

David raises his gun.

"What the fuck is that?" Grace shouts. An inhuman shadow steps away from the elevator's light.

"Well, well." The figure heaves itself up the stairs, gently tapping a long, thin hose against the palm of a heavy, gloved hand. "What have we here? Seems my hunch wasn't so far-fetched after all."

David fires, and for once, my eyes don't close. The bullets smash into glass, sending showers of sparks scattering against the dark, peeling walls. Eventually, the harsh crack of gunfire gives way to soft clicks, and low laughter.

"Who are you?" I raise my pistol, not that it seems like it'll do any good. The face behind the glass, pale and hairless, stretches into a smile. Skin flakes scatter into the water around him like fish food.

"I'm Giant 4. Nice to meet you." He levels the thin black hose towards us, and pulls back on the trigger.

My feet are already moving, and I pull Grace along with me. There's a hiss, for the second before my head turns back to the academy's twisting corridors, I see a cloud of pale mist burst and fill the corridor, entangling the students, boring down their throats.

I run as fast as I can. It's not very fast, but it's better than nothing. David follows, firing into the mist, aiming towards the desperate choking and manic laughter.

"Where now?" Grace gasps.

"Don't know." I choose turns at random, trying to find another slope, another stairwell.

"I'm out!" one of the students yells. I hear another one trip and fall.

"There!" Grace points, and I turn as quickly as I can, down toward another set of dingy stairs.

"Incoming!" another student shouts, shooting into the receding fingers of mist as the heavy, figure of Giant 4 advances through it. The hose rises, and another cloud of mist rushes forward.

"Just go!" I push Grace down the steps, and she calls for the other students as she hammers the call button. Running to her, a finger of mist licks my ankle. I don't stop. It hurts, but only in a theoretical sense, like I'm reading it off a medical chart.

The doors open, so David and I flank them, shooting into the pale cloud as the elevator fills. The second the doors close, David pulls the pins from three grenades, and throws them towards the hissing cloud.

"Going down." He grins, as the flashes slice the fog.

The maze of mist is replaced by a simple, well-lit box. A few students collapse. I'm seriously considering it myself.

"What now?" Grace slides to the ground against the walls of the elevator.

"We stick to the plan," I say. "Escape through the tunnels."

"Is this the part we figure out what went wrong?" David asks. "Because I have a pretty good idea." He takes a step towards me. The elevator shakes, and avoiding his eye, I see the mist seeping through the elevator's roof.

"Run!" I pull Grace out just in time as the vapor swells and bursts. David leaps free, but a few more are caught in the vapor. For a moment, all I can do is watch them, shaking and turning red, and then Giant 4 falls, crushing them under his weight.

We run out into the tunnel's lights, casting narrow shadows as we run to the sound of the massive swaying tank on Giant 4's back, scraping back and forth against the cave roof.

"How do we lose this guy?" David shouts. "I've got one clip left, and one grenade, not that they seem all that useful." The tunnel expands into a cave, equipment, search lights and empty metal tanks lying scattered on the floor. There are openings, staircases, scaffolds and ladders.

If we'd followed the route from before, I might at least have an idea of the layout, but now I'm completely lost.

A figure stands on one of the walkways above us. Before I can raise my gun, it falls, raising a cloud of earth and dust where it lands.

"You made it." Giant 4, emerges from the tunnel and stumbles to a stop.

He lowers his hose. "Thought you were still in bed, Three."

I've had enough. I raise my arm, aim, bend my elbow, inhale, and fire three shots.

My arms and ears sting. The figure, Giant 3, rises slowly into a twisted hunch, long dirty toenails gripping the dirt.

There are holes in his uniform where I shot him, and more down the back, where his fatigues have split to accommodate what looks like a heavy, deformed spine.

He pulls a long, black strand of hair from his face with a dirty claw.

"G says we're not to hurt you." Something moves, wriggling under his skin from the top of his lips to edge of his eyeball. "So lay down your arms." He coughs, and a cloud of what looks like dirt muddies the air. "We'll escort you to the brig."

"Come on.," Giant 4 says. "What makes this lot more important than the rest of the human shields?"

"I know how this goes," I say as I tap David with my elbow, and he slides the sub-machine gun, last full clip attached, into my hands. "If it's all the same to you two, we'd rather not." I start running for the closest opening, and the hiss of Giant 4's hose spreads after us.

"Are we just making things up now?" David asks. "This whole thing's starting to feel like a fever dream."

"No." I turn, and fire a burst into the mist. "Look. I'm the reason we're in this situation-"

"Hildegard," Grace leans on a wall, catching her breath, "I don't think it would've made much difference what plan we had."

"That's not the point," I say. "I think most of us can still make it."

"Most of us?" David reaches a fork, and chooses the left path, and I reach out to stop him.

"During the assembly, G reacted when he saw me. I don't

know how, but I think if they know who I am, they won't hurt me."

"You're going to draw them away?" Grace asks. "That's a pretty big risk, if you're wrong-"

"I know." I look down at my hand, perfectly steady, holding the gun. "But I've been asking the same thing of all you." It feels like it should be shaking, I'm freezing, and bruised, and it still aches where I got the fracture. "We can still do this, head back to camp," I say and fire into the approaching mist, "I'll draw them off."

Grace opens her mouth to say something, but David pulls her away, up the slope to the right, and the students go with her.

I fire at the mist again, and run down the left tunnel, the one filled with wiring and metal plates. By myself, it feels better to run.

I don't have to check over my shoulder or stop to let someone catch up.

Alone, I can hear Giant 4's footsteps, smashing into the rock.

If I have a choice, I'd rather not go to any sort of brig, so I weave, looking for signs, but mostly taking turns as quickly as I can, my eyes snapping back and forth across the stone walls, looking for directions, or at least some clue as to where I'm going.

There's no question that I'm faster and more agile than a man wearing a fishbowl on his head, but I can't say if that holds true for the other one, wherever he's gone.

It's a maze down here, and I know nothing about my surroundings, but wherever everyone is supposed to be, they aren't here now.

There are piles of papers, empty styrofoam cups, but no fog. No fishbowl man, and no hunchback.

Eventually, I stop to catch my breath against a cave wall, trying to hear something over the occasional spurt of badly wired lanterns and dripping water. There might be voices, a long way off, but there's no way I can make out what they're saying. They might be far away, I might even be safe by now, but if I stop now I won't be able to start moving again.

I have to pick a direction. Left? Right? I guess I shouldn't limit myself, I could choose up or down, too.

Up, is probably my best bet.

Not that there are a lot of paths that lead up. I can see one that goes down, just a dirt slope, and another metal walkway that leads out over some empty cavern. I don't like the openness, so I choose down. I should've figured out a way to stay in touch.

For all I know, the Giants followed Grace and David, totally forgetting about me. Or maybe they got as lost as I am. They only just arrived, right? They can't know these caverns that well.

There are doors down here, lots of them. No more catwalks or high ceilings, though.

I look inside, as quickly and quietly as I can. Bunks. Rows and rows of them.

There are people in them, too.

This is where they sleep.

As I watch, one of them turns over.

A drop of water falls from the ceiling into a bucket on the floor.

There are more archways, too, some of them hung with curtains, just pieces of tarpaulin cut from supply crates or troop trucks.

Down the way, there's a bigger room, completely tiled, and still lit. Rows of benches and a counter, covered with empty pans and plates. A cafeteria. Empty.

I want to lash out, attack, break something, hurt someone. I don't care if it's a bagger, or a Giant, or G. But I can't. There's no one here.

So, naturally, I keep walking.

I know this feeling. I should, I've lived with it my whole life, but it stings all the more now that it's back.

Was I too tired to feel it, or was something else staving it off for me?

There are a lot of crates here, piles and piles of them. Most stand open and empty in corners or on the edge of doorways.

I hear footfalls, and twitch into the first hiding place I see, the other side of a door to my left.

It's just a metal sheet bolted into the rock, but it's opaque, so it's better than nothing.

I watch from between the hinge and wall. A few stretched shadows stagger down the rows, from one door to the other.

They're taking their time, and checking the rooms, too. My eyes wander to the room I've hidden in.

It's bright in here. I would move to turn off the lights to avoid casting a shadow, but they're too close now. There are IV stands, and a stretcher, stained with blood. Lots of mechanical parts too, round glass shapes, like Giant 4's fishbowl helmet.

Something rings in my ears, the telltale sign of actual quiet. Occasionally, one of the oblong lights, built into the wall, flickers, and the buzz is the only sound I can make out.

From here, I can see beds, with curtains drawn around them and crowds of carts by their sides.

I can hear the baggers coming closer, so I step out from behind the door as quietly as I can, scanning the room for somewhere to hide.

I check under the bed, but something between the

curtains catches my eye, so I pull them back.

Bloody bandages. Burst casts, too, sitting in an empty bed.

Counting the others in the room, this bed makes three in total.

More footsteps, and this time I can hear equipment, too, so I duck further into the room, trying to clear a path without disturbing the bed or the carts.

There's a space under a table in the corner, strewn with personal effects, so I hide under it, and watch the flashlights advance down the walls.

A bagger, goggled and masked, pokes his head inside, shines his light, and just as quickly walks past.

"Clear?" A voice further down the corridor asks.

"Yeah, clear, what, you think any of the kids are smart enough to make it down here?"

There's no answer as the second bagger passes by.

Don't get the wrong idea about this place; it's dark, out of the way, and it should be safe for now, but I can't stay down here.

As quietly as I can, I pull out from under the desk. The baggers walk back to what must be their quarters.

If this keeps up, I might not get out before dawn. Obviously, that would be bad.

I don't know how many rounds I have left in my gun, for all I know it might be zero, and I have no idea how to check, so I scan the room for something I can use as a weapon.

There are IV stands, but those are awkward and probably too heavy. I could use a syringe, but I'd have to get closer than I'd like to use it, and I don't see anything to use it with, just empty containers.

Air bubbles are lethal, aren't they? Does it need anything in it to work?

The desk I hid under is covered with things. A dented

bullet. Some kind of necklace. A faded photograph.

I start to search the rest of the room, but my head turns back to the photograph. I turn on the lamp at the side of the desk.

It's a photograph of me.

Obviously, it can't be me, but I'm one of the few people I've ever recognized. I make an extra effort, every morning in the mirror, or at least, I used to, long after they told me it wasn't something you could practice.

There are others in the picture, too.

In fact, it's a whole crowd, wearing uniforms in varying states of damage and neglect. They're squatting in front of a jungle.

My eye goes to the man in the corner. He's definitely younger than the man I know, but I can't mistake Cooper.

He sits the same way, and the tilt of his head over the gun cradled in his arms is just as distinctive. I always thought it made him look wise, but here he barely looks old enough to enlist.

I run my eyes over the rest of the crowd. There's a man in huge body armor, like an old diving suit, a twisted hunchback, and a man like a spider monkey, grinning into the camera with too many teeth.

They're all standing around me. I have a knife in my hand.

It could just be the lights flickering again, but this room doesn't seem as safe as it used to, so I rush out into the corridor as fast as I can and start back up the hallway.

I want to say that things make more sense now. Maybe they do.

These people, whoever they really are, think I'm something or someone that I'm not.

And they have a plan for me.

FILE 5: SEPARATION

File5: SEPARATION

February 1st

STILL ADJUSTING.

It's not as if Cooper's gone, but calling him's not the same. I mean, he has a job, all I keep doing is interrupting him. What if he gets in trouble with his boss because he takes my call?

So I haven't called him all week. It's not so bad, but I got pretty close to breaking down and giving in a few times today.

He would never snitch on me, but I always got the feeling that he thought he knew what was best for me. Not that I didn't believe him, but he's not here anymore. He can't stop me from doing whatever I want, even if it is stupid.

I guess we'll see.

❄

I shouldn't have, but I ran. I took the photograph.

To be honest, I don't remember exactly what happened. I know I wandered around under the school for a long time, and I know I hated the walk in the snow.

One thing stood out. The sunrise, in the snow, past the forest. Halfway back to camp, I stop and watch. It's quiet. No marching. No engines.

I almost didn't start again.

The campfire's burned out. The camp behind the cabin is abandoned, and the valley is silent.

No question whether I'll sleep in my bunk now.

The next thing I see is sunlight, and a shadow.

Someone passes by the door of the cabin, running a baton down the walls. Walls of awakened students follow him.

I step outside, and watch as they file down into the usual marching order.

Another column sets off from the cabins further down. Below, a bagger starts to call out attendance. I didn't know there were this many students left.

Some of the voices that answer are ones I recognize.

Rushing would look suspicious, so I move towards the assembly as naturally as I can.

Not that I could rush, even if I wanted to.

"Present!" I shout from the back of the crowd. Faces turn to see me. Quite a lot of them.

I catch a glimpse of Grace and David ahead, but the man at the head of the column calls out again, and the students set off at a pace I struggle to keep.

I won't fall behind though, because now I know that this place has what I need. All I have to do is survive until combat, beat some exhausted kids, then I can eat.

The march is short, like it's been for the last few days, and we don't go anywhere near the forest.

I don't see any increased security. If anything, there are fewer soldiers out here than there have been for the last few days. The weather is clear, too.

Come to think of it, it's been ages since I heard the wind without having to filter out the whine of an engine.

Not something I'd ever thought about before, but it helps me run.

On the approach to the snowfield, I can see the usual set-up, stretchers at the ready, with tables covered in steaming bowls of soup.

No mats anymore. Not enough baggers to watch, either, just poles thrust into the ground, marked with red tape that flutters in the wind.

"Five minutes! Get ready for combat drills!"

Most students sit, or lie in the snow. Some of them, especially in the arm-band heavy columns that have just arrived, start stretching.

"Grace." I call over to her as I see her sitting near the top of the slope.

"You're okay, then," she says. "I'm actually not really surprised." I sit down next to her as another line of marching students comes to a stop in the field of poles.

"Did everyone else-"

"Yeah." She kicks the snow. "Your brilliant plan was a total success."

"What's that supposed to mean?" I ask her.

"I've done this before." Grace doesn't take her eyes off the snow. "I used to try and play with my brothers all the time. It doesn't matter how smart we are, you can't always beat someone who's strong just because you're smarter."

"That's not helpful," I tell her. "Did you lose anyone on the way out?"

"Nope." She shifts a small drift with the end of her shoe.

"If anything, we got more. Kids have been asking me about what happened all day."

"Any idea where all the baggers went?"

"No." Grace shakes her head. "They didn't take off after we wrecked the airstrip, so they're probably still around."

"Break's over! Line up!"

Students stagger for a moment, and I pull Grace to her feet. She's in no state to talk about the photo.

To be honest, I'm not either.

The actual combat is what I would expect. Every student I can recognize from last night seems more capable, almost a match for the arm-bands. Being fed and having somewhere warm to sleep is turning into a bigger and bigger advantage.

My first opponent is tall, thin, and shivering. He draws breath to speak, and I shove him over.

Like I thought, he doesn't have the strength to get back up. A lone bagger pulls him away.

Things go like that for a while, and it's almost a relief from the marching. Even Grace does well.

It's barely worth watching David.

"I finally get to take another crack at you." I'd been watching the baggers, a small column of them running alongside a jeep crawling up from the foot of the academy's plateau. "I know what you did. Both times, I knew." Alanza cracks her knuckles. A few arm-bands, already enjoying some soup, cheer. "I hope you're re-"

"Are we related?" I ask her.

"What?" She drops her readied hands.

"It's a simple question."

"I-"

"That's fine," I tell her, "I just wanted to make sure you didn't know."

Mine is not a complex punch. My thinking was that I

don't really have the time to perfect a refined technique, so I chose early on to stick with the basics. I think this is what's called a "sucker-punch". I feel her nose give way under my knuckles. She falls backwards into the snow, coloring it red.

"You-" She tries to jump to her feet, so I kick her in the ribs.

"Don't get the wrong idea," I tell her. "A lot of my-" the word 'friends' sticks in my throat. "-my allies hate you." She rolls backwards onto her feet. Of course, I don't stand any real chance against her, but I've already got what I wanted. "But personally, I have nothing against you."

The first hit is right in the chest, and immediately it feels familiar. I stay on my feet.

"Bullshit." Alanza spits the blood streaming from her nose into the snow. "All you've ever tried to do is undermine me." Her fist jumps forward again, but it hits my forearm, and I slide under it. This would be a good time to hit her, but by the time I've thought it, her arm's already back in, and swinging her elbow towards me. It hurts.

"You don't know why you're here, the same way I don't," I hiss.

"Wrong," Alanza spits again. "I know why I'm here." She steps back, her blood leaving a pattern in the snow after her. "Because I'm the best, that's all there is to it."

"Why am I here, then?"

"You?" She leaps forward again. "You're just a mistake." I don't see whatever it is she does with my arms, but my face lands in the snow.

"Something tells me-" My jaw aches, but the cold helps. "-you might change your mind before we're done." Alanza stalks back as I try to lift my body, and plants her foot on the side of my head, forcing me down again.

"That's enough." Two baggers force her off, one with a

raised gun, and another pulls me to my feet. For a moment, all I can do is watch my bruised, blood-streaked face reflected in his goggles.

"Move." They lower their weapons, and push me up the slope.

At the top is a jeep, engine running, surrounded by baggers. It's the most I've seen all day.

"Wait!" I hear Alanza call after me. "I won!" she shouts. "I beat her!"

One of the soldiers opens the door of the jeep, pushes me inside, and closes the door on me, cutting off Alanza's shouts.

The other gets into the driving seat.

"Pine, isn't it?" G grasps his wide hat, and places it softly in his lap. "You're proving to be quite the puck."

The engine growls into life, and the car starts to move, the interior gasping and rattling as it rolls over the rough snow.

My first move should be to find out the stakes and why he's here. He has to have a reason to watch the students doing something they do every day.

"I'm not really into theatre," I say.

G leans back, arms wide and his head tilted up.

"Really? I've heard you have an affinity for masks."

"Have I broken school rules?" Once I ask, his head drops down again.

"What is a rule, really?" He pushes his strange glasses back up his nose. "If it's your grade you're concerned about, you needn't be. By all accounts your performance has been excellent."

The car jumps as snow gives way to something rougher.

"Good." I can't tell past his glasses, but the slant of his head makes it look as if he's watching me. "Are we going somewhere?"

"No, not really." He pulls back the plastic cover from the

window behind his head, glances out at the snow, and replaces it. "But I find a moving backdrop a valuable aid to conversation."

"So this isn't about my performance?" I can't find a right way to sit, and the pouches and bags fastened to the door behind me press into my back. "It really seems like Alanza should be here instead of me."

My instinct is to assume that G knows exactly what I've been doing. Probably Grace and David, too. He knows. He has to know.

"Noticed her, have you? It would be a challenge not to." His hands meet. "She has a tendency to cast herself as the lead without asking anyone else. Still, I'd hate for you to get the wrong idea about her."

"All right, fine." I cross my arms. "Why am I here? What do you want?"

"Giving in already?" G's face peels into a smile like a slit. Something you watch an eclipse through. "It was always her or you, and besides, aren't perverse old men known for their propensity towards abducting teenage girls?"

Alanza is part of this, no question. She might not know anything, but she's obviously an important piece of the puzzle.

I was hoping experience would help, but lying to my foster parents and teachers barely registers as practice. I have to change my approach.

"You're not answering my question," I say.

"Can't you at least appreciate being out of the cold?" he says. "No, I shouldn't be surprised, it's almost ironic that you're so convinced that I want something from you, when in fact the reason I took some time away from overseeing my program today is to find out what you," he points at me, "want."

I can't answer him truthfully, at least, not at first. It's just common sense. And there's the matter of principle to consider. Something tells me he'd respect me less if I was more honest with him.

My mind feels clearer now that I'm warmer.

Maybe he wants a fair fight.

"You mean the reason I'm here?" I ask, and he nods. "You sent out a letter, remember? And a scholarship, too. Made it seem a lot nicer than it turned out to be."

"Really?" He falls back. "You don't appreciate our facilities? Where else can you learn to lead your own insurgency?"

It's not even necessarily a lie, but he knows the answer I gave him isn't the one he wanted. I think he gets more direct when he's getting what he wants.

"I think your curriculum's been lost on some of the students," I tell him. "Mostly the ones you killed."

"So," G pauses as the car jumps over a bump in the road, "you didn't come here looking for anyone?" It doesn't come as much of a surprise, but I still feel it deep in my stomach.

He knows Cooper. He might know where he is. What happened to him.

"I don't see what difference it makes," I say.

"Naturally, you wouldn't." G leans back again, running his fingers over the wide-brimmed hat that sits next to him. "But that's only because I haven't told you yet. It might seem odd to you." He rubs his chin. "But we two play the same role. We both want the same thing. The Truth."

There are a lot of things I could say to this. I might even get an advantage from keeping the conversation going for as long as possible. He clearly adores the sound of his own voice, and if nothing else I can keep warm in here.

"Bullshit." Unfortunately my brain had already sent an earnest response to my mouth.

"Of course." He laughs, I think. It sounds more like a wheeze. "I don't blame you. We are, of course, looking at metaphorical pictures of vastly differing sizes." I can feel the car slowing. If he planned ahead, and he probably did, this is my end of the line.

Except I'm not finished yet.

"So, you know everything there is to know about me." I sit back as far as I can while he nods along. "You have all the information, and there's no way for me to know what you're planning."

"I'd like to think so." He nods again as another, wider grins spreads across his face. "But a lifetime in intelligence work has taught me that knowing everything about a person is unbelievably difficult."

He focused on me, and just ignored my comment about his "plan". My guess is it means one of two things: either it's a deliberate misdirection, or his words reflect his priorities. Come to think of it, he hasn't mentioned any other students except for Alanza, and the academy has barely come up.

"You don't blame me," I nod, mostly to myself as the car comes to a stop. "But that's what this is, all of it." Anything I might have to trip him up is gone. I'm reduced to thinking out loud. Slightly embarrassing, but the speed is what I need. "This is all bullshit, the scholarships, the academy, the companies, all the competition, we're just-" I can't find the word, and the jeep rolls to a stop. The door behind me opens onto the cold.

"Sir?" A bagger calls in.

"One moment." G raises his hand.

"Distractions," I say, "or human shields." G leans forward, further than he's ever done before, until we're as close as we were during the assembly. He smells like cigarettes and oil. "Or just food for the dogs?"

"You've never had any illusions about the fate of the expelled." His grin widens. "No, that's no surprise. If your contemporaries prove too weak or too troublesome, they are permanently disposed of. Is that what you wanted to know?"

"No," I say, "I already knew that. I want to know why."

"Yet you chose to compete against them. You're so much like her," he whispers. His knees are bent, as if about to get up, and his arm is raised, just slightly, as if he's just decided not to touch me.

"I'm guessing you mean the woman from the photograph?" I ask him. He falls back into his seat, and gestures to the bagger outside.

He's right about the others. I'm the reason a lot of them have been expelled. Killed.

Wouldn't someone else have done it anyway? Would G have ever let anyone leave?

More useless thoughts, I push them down.

After a few seconds of silence, the engine underneath me growls to life again. G taps the screen between passenger and driver.

"Back to the Academy."

"Let's just be frank with each other," I tell him. "It'll make a nice change of pace for you. It seems like you know what I want to know, so-"

"My unit," G interrupts, "KU Giant. It's technically a CIA designation. It's the only photograph you could be talking about."

"I don't care about your unit, I-"

"No, of course." G sighs as the car leaps over another bump. "It's your father you're concerned with. He is that, isn't he? A father figure? Are we still being frank?"

"You know who he is," I say, as clearly as I can against the gravel raking the floor. "You probably know where he is."

"Were you anyone else, I might be impressed." G says. "Have you really gone through all this to recuse one perfectly innocent, unremarkable adoption agent?"

I want to just tell him that I did, but it wasn't just that.

"Partly," I say, "I think I would also like to stop your plan, and maybe if there's time, ruin your life."

G draws back, coughing with laughter as the car shakes to a stop.

"Well," he says, "you wouldn't be the first." I hear a door open, and boots crunching through the snow. "I respect your goal. Noble," he says, wiping a sliver of spittle from his mouth. "Some might say, selfless." He nods. "Yes, in fact you could say that I'm somewhat specially cast to appreciate your ambition." G points, though the covered window behind me. "You've seen the statue." I keep my eyes fixed on him as I listen to the baggers outside.

"Yeah, I've seen it."

"My father died, when I was very young," G says. "That man became my true father. In many ways, bonds like that are stronger than ones of blood, wouldn't you say?"

"I wouldn't know," I tell him as the door swings open.

"It's been illuminating, Ms. Pine," G says as I step down into the snow. "I look forward to your attempts at ruining my life."

I trudge down the slope without looking back, listening to the heavyset jeep roar away into the forest.

There are still students here, although all the fights are over. I take a cup and gulp it down, even if it's cold, smudging the winner's stamp on my wrist.

"Hildegard!" Grace shouts as she runs through the surviving students, arms full of emptied soup cups. "Somebody wake David up!" she calls out.

"Did something happen?" I ask her as she hands me another half-empty cup. It's better than nothing.

"Nothing we weren't expecting," David grunts as he gets to his feet. "I noticed there were no baggers." He points down to the now-empty snowfield where a few splashes of red still mark the spot where the fights were. "And I saw things weren't going well. Kids giving up. So, I picked my opponents. Lots of soup. "

"You got lots of easy fights," Grace says. "And I admit I was feeling pretty down about-"

"I know." I try to steer them away from talking about the previous night.

"But then, everyone saw you fight Alanza," Grace says. "Including me. Especially me. After that, I started getting food together like normal. Much easier with less supervision."

"Not much of an improvement," David says. "But damage control definitely achieved."

"Yeah." Grace nods "And we weren't expecting G to just appear, what did he say? Did you find out anything good?"

"No," I say. "I only found out things that are bad."

"What's that supposed to mean?" David asks.

"It means," this doesn't seem right. "No."

"No?" Grace squints.

"I was going to just try to ignore what happened, but I shouldn't. I had a lot of things wrong, and-"

"Okay, okay." Grace holds out her hands. "Don't burst a blood vessel." David crosses his arms.

"There's no pretending that everything's all right, or that what we did didn't have consequences," he says. "But we're definitely not giving up."

"All right, then." I roll my bad arm, feeling the pain of the fracture shoot up into my shoulder and tumble down my wrist. "We'll need at least what we had last night. As much as we can get."

"Sounds like you have a plan," Grace says as the students around her start to rouse.

"No, not yet. Has anyone seen Islet?"

"He was skulking around earlier." David points to the rows of empty stretchers, sitting unattended. A few have fallen into the snow. "Haven't seen him since."

"Don't sell him short." Grace says. "I'm pretty sure I saw him spike some arm-bander soup."

"Then I think it's safe to say he's still on board."

"We really have to put up with him again?" David asks. "Can't we just kidnap him?"

"I've got it covered." Grace says. "I'll talk to some of the other medics when they turn up to clean up the stretchers, the question is when and where."

"He knows the camp." I scan the crowd of watching students, and raise my voice slightly so they can all hear me. "Tell him to meet us in the same place, a little earlier, if possible."

"And what are we going to do until then?" David grunts. "Stand around?"

"I'll need you to carry as much food as you can back to camp," I tell him. "Once we're there we'll work on repairing it until Islet arrives."

"Okay, so when?" David asks.

"Right now, let's go." I'm not really looking forward to the walk back or trying to renovate the camp, but if I want to attract more students after yesterday, food and heat are a necessity.

"You really think people will buy what we're selling?" David asks as he jogs alongside me.

"Don't know," I tell him. Of course, he just expects me to talk while running. "We might be the only option."

"Good point, " he grunts.

"I'll find firewood." I point into the valley, now totally abandoned. "You work on the tarps." I take a freezing breath. "Clear as much snow as you can."

"Got it." David puts on speed and sprints past the door, still frozen open. He kept pace with me, instead of sprinting past like he obviously could have.

I keep going past the camp, and into the forest. Not too far, just enough to catch my breath pulling fallen wood from snow drifts.

I walk back with my arms full

"How is it?" I ask David as I drop the wood into the blackened pile.

"Basically as we left it," he says as he knots some tarp around the second floor railings. "Could be better." He glances down. "Ever started a fire before?"

"No," I say. The old sticks Grace used are still here, she's bored a hole through the center of one. "Anything I should know?"

"For you," the tarp tightens as it expands, and a few more feet enter our camp, "probably be patient."

Making a fire isn't hard, but trying over and over is obviously frustrating.

As students start to file in I'm glad I'm not having to do this while actually freezing to death.

"That's a spark," Grace points, "keep it up!"

"Don't patronize me," I say, and she laughs as she pats me on the back. "Did you send your message?" I ask her.

"Yep." She sets down her armful of loose sack, full of food, and starts to count them out. "Medics seem like they don't know what to do with themselves."

"Not surprising." A spark catches, and a tiny finger of smoke climbs the narrow wood in my hands. I place it as carefully as I can in the middle of the fire. "They're not in the loop. I'm surprised G isn't kicking them all out here with us."

"Why doesn't he?" David sits down by the fire as cinders start to rise.

"Dunno," Grace says as she watches more students sweep aside the tarp curtain. "I mean, why are we here?" She turns to me. "G didn't shed any light on that did he?"

"Not intentionally," I say, watching the fire grow.

"That doesn't really help," Grace says.

"Can't say I'm surprised." David stamps a tent peg down into the earth. "We found those files, right? Some government project," he snorts. "And to think I was worried about being treated like property. Seems like all they're trying to do is get rid of us."

Grace hands me a metal cup of soup and a finger of bread.

"Do we know when Islet's coming?" I ask her.

"Nope," she says. "He might not come at all."

"I'd better make this last then." I dip my bread in the soup, and try to take the smallest bites humanly possible.

I don't taste it, of course. I can't stop thinking about things I could do, or things I could have done. I know dwelling on them probably isn't a good idea, but I can't stop, either. It's not as if I can change the past.

Sooner or later, there won't be room to push things down anymore.

I don't know what happens then.

The sun set maybe half an hour ago. There's still some blue in the sky. The fire is high, though, so the cold on my back doesn't matter that much.

The tarp rustles, and Dr. Islet stumbles in. David steps

up and catches him as he almost falls. The crowds of students jump to their feet, and Grace hands the doctor a cup of soup.

He sits down across from me, bruises covering the left side of his face.

“What happened?” Grace asks.

“Looks recent,” David says. Islet nods as he gulps down a cup of soup.

“On the way here,” he gasps.

“They caught you?” Grace hands him some bread.

“No,” he says “Just some bored baggers, I guess.” He laughs, pulling his glasses down off his face. “They let me take them off, can you believe that?”

“Yeah, actually,” Grace says. “We can.”

“So this is your new plan, right?” He looks across at me. “I know you’re trying your best, but-”

“We don’t have a plan yet,” I tell him. “We need your information on what’s happening under the academy.”

“I guess I should stop being surprised at you,” he says. “Let me guess, you know all about what’s going on down there?”

“We don’t have the whole picture,” I tell him. “That’s why you’re here.”

“The whole picture?” Islet sighs. “I don’t have that either. All my staff are getting locked out, we barely get to eat. Now that we’ve sequenced the bacteria it seems like they don’t give a damn what we do.”

“Bacteria again,” David says. “A biological weapon?”

“I don’t know.” Islet slurps the last of his soup. “I only sequenced part of it, and they keep the different teams apart.”

“Is that what they’re going to launch from the Silo?” Grace asks.

“You knew?” Islet asks.

"We found out about the Mobile Silo a while ago," I say. "We saw blueprints for it, orders for parts, too."

"Well, that's what they've been doing for days now," Dr. Islet says. "Hauling down the tanks of bacteria, assembling missiles."

"They're going to launch." Grace stands up as she says it.

"Right," I say. "There's not going to be any placement in special forces. Or graduation."

A few students stand up, like Grace. A few gasp. Most don't seem surprised. "If I had to guess, I'd say that once they launch, they won't need us. It'll be a massacre."

"You think so?" Islet pushes his glasses back up his nose. "It could be, we've been getting weapon shipments with the missile parts and replacement components for the Mobile Silo."

"Stop saying we," David grunts. "Unless you're with them."

"No, no, I'm not." Islet waves his hands back and forth. "You're right."

"We have to stop them," Grace says. I can't help but tally up the numbers. At the very least the baggers outnumber the students two to one. Almost certainly more, not counting KU Giant. Then there's the equipment discrepancy, and the differences in energy from eating and sleeping. I know there are vehicles, too, I've seen plenty of personnel carriers and jeeps with mounted guns, as well as the helicopters that are always coming and going.

"Uh, Hildegard," Grace says. "We were sort of hoping you'd come up with something."

I only wanted to find out what happened to Cooper. To be honest, I think I might already have lost my chance. It can't be my priority anymore. By the sound of it, it's not just the students that are in danger.

“There’s only one way we can get enough supplies, weapons, and bodies to stop the launch.”

“Okay,” Grace says. “What’s that?”

“This should be good.” David leans back on the walls of the cabin. All the students stare at me.

“We have to take over the school.”

FILE 6: INSURRECTION

March 15th

I'm writing because you're the only place I can get thoughts out of my head. Cooper was right. It helps.

I got caught. The pain got too much in the night, and I caved. The pills were easy to get rid of, but they found them. Lectures don't affect me at this point, there are more important things to consider.

I told Cooper, and he lied to me.

I told him that I stopped taking them, and all he could talk about is how important they were. How much better I'm getting. He know's it's not true.

Nothing's changed, I just have a clearer picture.

I know, because the moment I got away from mom and dad, all I could think about is a better way to get out of taking the pills.

Down the toilet?

I don't care if they read this and find out. I almost want them to, then they'll know that I'll never give up.

I expected the normal bullshit from everyone else, but not from Cooper.

I will find out why.

"I..." Grace stares around the silent students. David laughs.

"Nicc." He claps his hands together. "I like it. Let's do it."

"I really don't see-" Islet runs his hands through his hair. "I mean, I really, really don't see how we could accomplish that, we don't have numbers or-"

"He's right," Grace says. "Even assuming we weren't all exhausted and starving-"

"We can't." I throw some escaped twigs back into the fire. "This isn't a question of what we can get away with. It has to be all of us, or none of us."

"So what, we have to recruit everyone who's left?" Grace asks.

"Absolutely," I say. "It's the only way this could ever work, the question is how to actually achieve that."

"As usual." David points as Grace passes around more food. "You sound like you have an idea."

"Not a complete one," I tell him, "but with those files we found-"

"The ones marked KIA, right?" Grace says as students take pots of soup from her arms.

"Exactly, if we can prove we were all brought here under false pretenses, or created in some government program-"

"Wait, wait." Dr. Islet rises to his feet. "You've actually

seen inside the KIA folders? All they told my staff was to stay away from them."

"Yeah." David leans back against the side of the cabin. "We did that a while ago, no big deal."

"Yes." Islet looks down into the fire. "Yes, that might work, if that's what's really in them, but-" Whispers run across the students, some of them get to their feet. It's only fair they want to know what we mean, but there's no time to explain it to them right now.

"What?" I ask him.

"Well, you remember what I told you about the staff cleaning house?" he says. "That included destroying all their documentation. Shredding, burning, even."

David swears under his breath, and Grace, looking over the angry students, turns to the doctor.

"Maybe you could tell us what you know about KIA," Grace says. "For those of us who don't know."

"Well, I don't know that much myself, I mean, I'm a microbiologist," Islet begins, but David interrupts him.

"I thought you said you altered genomes," he says.

"Well, yes." Throughout the crowd, more students are rising, and David takes a step forward. Islet's a useful ally, but not as valuable as the drive hating him could give us.

That, and while everyone's distracted I can take the time to think of another solution.

"Which is it?" David asks.

"You're absolutely right, I work on the genes of bacteria and viruses, but that's nothing compared to the human genome!"

"So?" David says. "Spill the beans."

"Okay, okay." Islet holds up his hands. "I don't have the whole picture, but I think the whole thing's a late Cold War artifact. As far as I know, some generals in the late seventies read this paper about domino theory, and the idea that the whole thing hinged on exceptional people a nation could turn into a figurehead It was a way to win without escalating the amount of actual force involved. Soft deterrence."

"Pick up the pace, nerd." David steps closer again. "What's that got to do with us?"

"Right, right, I'm getting to it, it's pretty simple." Islet straightens his tie. "Basically, a lot of people were into the idea, so the Beagle Commission started working on designer soldiers under NATO supervision."

"Designer soldiers?" David asks.

"Yeah." Islet nods. "I know it sounds crazy, but they were so far ahead of their time they could sequence for physical traits, and even aspects of personalities. The idea was to distribute them, uh, I mean you," Islet shrugs, "and oversee your adoptions into influential families, at least, that was the plan. The actual adoptees don't really seem to match up with the Commissions original criteria." Based on the reactions from the students, some of them aren't taking it well. I can't say I blame them.

David steps between the doctor and the crowd. They have valid questions. Things like "are we clones?" and "why do we exist?" If everything goes well, we might still get some answers.

"Wait, wait!" David shouts them down. "We can just use the doctor to convince them, can't we? All the other students need to hear this."

"I don't think so." The way everyone stares makes it seem like they all forgot I'm here. "He's more useful on the inside," I say. "And besides, not everyone will take him at his word." Students step back. "Something he said made me think. You remember when we split up?"

"Yeah." David says. Grace nods.

"I saw an old photograph down there." There's no need to tell them the details. "It was somewhere I've never been, but I was in it." They keep staring. "My point is, when we first discovered the KIA files, I couldn't find my name. How familiar were you with the files, Islet?"

"Pretty familiar," he says. "It was fascinating stuff, but you're right, I didn't see your name, and it's pretty hard to miss."

"What does that mean?" Grace asks. I draw the photo from my fatigues, and she leans in to stare.

"I don't know."

"You're a clone," David says. "Of whoever that is." He points down at the monochrome jungle.

As soon as he says it, I know it's what I'd been thinking, I just wasn't willing to consider the idea, or its implications.

My instinct is always to hold back how I feel about something. To ignore it until it becomes useful or relevant.

Right now, it's not useful, since there's nothing I can do about it, but it might be relevant.

There's no benefit to feeling anything about it. Maybe later, once we're out of this, I can work it out, but there's no precedent set for being cloned from another person.

Is it like finding out you're related to someone? Like being diagnosed with some sort of disease?

"We're not in the picture." Grace says.

"You wouldn't be." Islet leans in as well. "I've never seen this before, but the assumption seems sound. The rest of the student body wouldn't bear so much physical resemblance to another person, but-"

"Wait," I say. Maybe the cold is getting to me. That or hunger's slowing me down. "That can't be. If I'm a clone-" Saying it out loud doesn't feel right. It probably won't ever feel right. "-then Alanza must be a clone of the same person."

Being related to someone never seemed that important to me. Probably something to do with being adopted, but I can't say I'm enjoying the idea of telling everyone we're twins.

"There's no way we can trust her," Grace says.

"So?" says David.

"So," I tell him, "she doesn't know about anything happening under the school, we talked about it before."

"Before she handed you your ass?" David laughs.

"Yes," I say. "Both times."

"I think you did pretty well the second time," Grace says.

"She's bought into every lie we've been told here. She really thinks she and her henchmen are competing for special forces placement or something."

"Yeah," David says, "because she's a psycho."

I've never been an expert in untangling feelings, but it doesn't feel right to talk about her like that. "I guess I can't really blame you for seeing her that way," I say. "But did you see how upset she was when G wanted to speak to me instead of her?" They all stay quiet. "Whatever, the point is, she's the key. If we convince her, tap into her followers and resources, we'd have a real chance."

"How are we going to do that?" Grace asks. "It's not as if we're all best friends."

"We're not," I say, "and I can't guarantee I'll be able to convince her, even with the photograph, but I don't really see a choice."

"So what?" David points into our crowd. "We just all head over to Golf Company camp and tell them to let us in?"

"The baggers are mostly gone," I say. "And the faculty trust Golf, they won't be guarding the camp, but if I tell Alanza I want to talk, I'm confident she'll at least listen to me."

"So," David says, "the answer's yes?"

"Looks like it." I get to my feet and tuck the photograph away. "But we need to be ready to move the second I convince her."

"Assuming you can do that," Grace points out.

"Correct," I nod. "I can't think of any other way to win, so future plans are going to proceed under the assumption that I'll succeed."

"Fair enough," David laughs.

"We need to go as fast as we can." I pull a pack from the ground, testing its weight.

"Wait, wait," Islet says. "What do I do?"

"We need a way to signal you," I tell him

"I still have my beeper." Islet points down at his belt. "I thought you knew."

"That was just me," Grace says. "I saw the number in your office."

"All right." I swing the pack onto my back. "We'll contact you when we need you to make a move, the rest of you," I point past David and Grace, "we need as many bodies as we can get, and since we might not come back here, take everything you might need, food, weapons-"

"Wait. Once I get the signal," Islet asks, "then what?"

"We don't have time for the details," I say as I stamp out the fire. "Attract some attention. Disrupt operation. Keep as many soldiers occupied for as long as you can, recruit some of your staff if you can."

"O-okay." He nods as we file past him into the snow. "I'll do my best."

"Do you actually know the way to Golf Company's camp?" Grace whispers to me as I settle into pace at the head of the column.

"I think so," I whisper back, "but I prefer not to guess."

"Just follow me, I've been over there a few times." Grace

steps just a fraction ahead of me. It's simple to keep pace with her while still looking like I know where I'm going.

"So." I look down at her. "That's where all the food came from?"

"Mostly." She shrugs. "They've always had more than enough."

The idea behind what I'd said to the students is starting to sink in.

We're probably never coming back to Charlie camp. I should be pleased about that, really, but I can't shake the feeling that part of the reason will be because some of us, maybe all of us, will be too dead to make the return trip.

There are questions I should ask Grace. Somehow, it seems wrong. They're not exactly essential, I just want something to occupy my mind on the quiet journey into the snow.

"Is it going to be a long way?" David asks as he draws level. "'Cause some of the kids at the back are very much not up for another long walk."

"Nope." Grace points to plumes of smoke rising from the woods on the slope away from the academy. "Right there."

"No wonder they did so well in those early ticket grabs," I say to no one in particular. "It was on their home turf."

"Do we have an actual plan?" David asks.

"Enough of one," I tell him. "Just follow my lead as closely as you can."

"Right," he sighs. "Because you're always so transparent."

The trees on the edge of the forest loom like prison bars. Luckily, more than wide enough to step between. After a few more minutes, I can see the fires. Out here on what must be the edge of the camp there are stripes of black plastic and olive green under the snow.

Collapsed tents, still shivering in the wind.

"Is this it?" David's question echoes across the tree trunks.

"This used to be where the hangers-on camped out." Grace says. "Golf camp is just past here, in this little outpost, just a few concrete rooms in a hill, not that I've seen all of it," she laughs. "Can you believe they used to post guards out here?"

"That's perfect," I say. "David, shout out something suitably inflammatory."

"Well." He rubs his chin. "I don't know that much about Alanza." He draws a deep breath "Come out, bitch! We come in fucking peace!"

I wince at the sheer volume, and I can hear some of the students behind me moan.

"I think that'll probably get her attention." Grace kicks the snow. "Now for the hard part."

There are a few distant shouts. The sound of something heavy turning over. Some rolling shadows, and after a few minutes, a crowd of students emerge. Most of them look tired, injured, or both, and the number of arm-bands seems pretty thin.

"We came to talk," I shout towards them. "By now you must have figured out that the people who brought you here lied to you!"

"This again." Alanza steps down the frosted slope, through the crowd of staggering students and broken tents. "But now we've moved on from excuses to conspiracy theories."

"Has anyone here-" My voice really isn't used to being raised above a certain level. Not that a sore throat would be at the top of my current list of injuries. "-actually learned anything?"

Students look around at each other.

"About discipline and sacrifice?" Alanza asks. "Definitely." She steps closer, and so do I.

"I know you're sincere," I say. "So ask yourself, why would I come here If I didn't think I would convince you?" Alanza whispers something to a student at her shoulder, and he sets off at a jog.

"Obviously you think you can, although I'm really not clear on what you're trying to convince me of in the first place."

"This isn't a military academy," I shout. "This-"

"What is it then?" Alanza shouts back. I don't know if I can really say.

"I don't know." Some of the armband-wearers laugh. "I've tried my best to find out the truth about this place, but I still don't have the whole picture." I run my finger along the photograph, hidden in my palm.

"Ever heard of Occam's Razor?" Alanza turns her back on me, speaking to her followers. "I guess the idea of inadequacy just drives some people crazy."

"So everything about Truman's completely as it appears, then?" I ask her, and she turns back towards me.

"Of course it is!" She steps forward again, until we're both apart from our crowds. "Why wouldn't it be?"

"I spent a long time trying to figure out why you thought that," I say. We're close enough to speak normally now.

"Maybe because I'm rational? It's special training," she says. "It's supposed to be hard."

"You know G, don't you?" There's no question in my voice. "From before you came here." The Golf Company students shift over her shoulder.

"What does it matter?"

"Humor me."

"Fine." She glances over her shoulder. "I've known him all my life. He's a friend of my father, and a mentor." Whispers travel around the crowd.

"And you trust him?" I ask.

"We've been over this," she sighs. Don't get the wrong idea, I'm useless with faces, but I can hear the way her tone changes. Somewhere along the line, the idea he might not be everything he said he was had entered her mind.

"You have prosopagnosia, right?" I ask, and she flinches at the word. "But I'm guessing at some point, your henchmen pointed me out." She narrows her eyes at me. "Am I still right?"

"We've been over this," she hisses. "What's your point?" I extend my arm and open my hand.

"I found this under the school, in the bagger quarters." She takes it from me.

All I have to do is wait. Both crowds go silent.

"What the fuck is this?" She holds it back out to me.

"Haven't you been listening?" I look her in the eye, as much as she'll let me. "I still don't know." I take the photograph back, and tuck it away.

"So you came here to show me an old photograph with a look-alike in it?" Honestly, she's being more stubborn than I thought she'd be.

"I came here for your help." Arm-band wears aren't laughing anymore. "G's getting ready to do whatever it is he's going to do."

"And you want us to do what? Storm the school? Mutiny?" The skin around her face is starting to redden.

"You still trust G? Look around!" I point into the forest. "The baggers are gone! How long has it been since you had a real lesson? Now that everything's ready they're abandoning their disguise and leaving us out here to freeze to death!" My shout carries past her to bounce around the forest.

Alanza glances down at the hand that held the photograph, rubbing her index finger and thumb together.

"Just because someone doesn't tell you everything, that doesn't make them your enemy." Her eyes are unfocused. Remembering something.

She won't surrender, not to me.

Time to switch gears.

"So you're content to leave all these people that have supported you and fought for you out in the cold?" A few shouts come up from behind her, and she turns to the Golf company crowd.

"Are you serious?" She glances back at me as she shouts. "You want to quit and buy into this conspiracy theory just because things are getting tough?" More yells, closer to the front.

"She's got a point!"

"What's with that photo?"

"I haven't seen any staff since yesterday!"

"We're all hungry!"

"Training doesn't just stop!"

I cross my arms.

"Sounds like you need to make a choice," I tell her. "Keep making excuses, or solve the real problem."

"Golf Company doesn't need to know!" she shrieks at the crowd."We're not afraid of cold or hunger or pain!" All I have to do now is keep my cool. She might make it harder than it sounds, but if I can pull it off, she'll beat herself. "We're at the top of this school for a reason! We were all chosen to be here, that's why we have food and shelter and warmth!" She points back at my crowd, still quiet. "They've never had a win over us, even without the staff supporting us, they might as well not exist!"

A gasp travels around the crowd, and Alanza stops in her tracks.

"Well." I have a comfortable window to come up with

something suitably withering. "I'm guessing the rest of Golf didn't know about your special arrangement with the staff." I opt against comedy in favor of pragmatism.

"Of course they did!" Alanza points into Golf. "You knew, don't pretend you didn't! You can't come to me, begging for food, and then act as if somehow you didn't want their help, they always knew we were the only ones who deserved it!"

Golf Company stays quiet.

"Looks like a vote of no confidence." I glance past her. "Golf Company!" I shout across to them. "I already have a plan in motion to stop whatever G's doing, but we have to combine our forces to stand a chance." They stare silently back at me, shifting back and forth like the trees. I need a little something extra. A gamble. "Or you could just go back on whatever medication they had you on."

"You can't just order them!" Alanza shouts. "They won't turn on me just because you're offering them an easy way out; we stand up for more than just-"

"Somebody shut her up!" I shout, and the clearing erupts into chaos.

Looks like I didn't win over all of them, but it should be more than enough.

"You!" Alanza starts to sprint in my direction, but David rushes past me.

I don't have to move an inch.

Alanza slides under his fists and throws blows of her own. There's plenty of space to back up, but moving away now might send the wrong impression, especially to Golf Company, so I do my best to stay put as an arm in the throat sends David rolling into the snow.

Before Alanza can take another step, someone puts their arm on her from behind. She catches their wrist and snaps it without looking towards her attacker, but another Golf student breaks from the crowd, and another.

After a minute or two, Alanza vanishes behind a wall of camouflage and falling fists.

"We need to take inventory." I point Grace towards the camp as the brawl subsides. "David, get all the able-bodied students together and equipped with any weapons you can find." He nods, rubbing his throat.

"What should we do with her?" A student, almost as big as David, points to Alanza, arms bound around a tree trunk, snow falling on her closed eyes. "Leave her?"

"We can't abandon her out here," I say. "She'll freeze to death, and she might still be useful." The big student slowly slides the armband from his bicep, and drops it in the snow. "You think she'll be a problem?" I ask him as he looks down on me, and then back to Alanza.

"No clue." He wipes his brow. "I never got her, but twenty, thirty of us, just one of her and she still gave us a run for our money." He looks past the trees to the light of the academy. "Yeah. You ask me, we should get rid of her right now."

She's clearly still conscious. I can see her eyes move every time someone steps past her.

"You're probably right, but we might be able to bargain with her."

"I took attendance," Grace says as she taps me on the shoulder. "Golf Company's still pretty huge, and it seems like most of them like the idea of actually throwing down with the baggers, plus, look!" She leads me further into the camp, and the fog gives way to concrete doorways in mounds of earth and improvised tents. "They have rifles, explosives, armored vests."

"Everything we need," I say to David as he strips a handgun.

"We need to get word to any other students left in the other companies," I tell Grace. "Can you do that?"

"Yep," she nods. "One of the kids that helped smuggle food works Golf's radio."

"Perfect. We'll assemble them, arm them, and brief them as fast as we can."

"On it." Grace jogs off. David watches her go.

"You think this'll work?" David asks as he follows me through the concrete archway into the bunker at the center of camp.

"We've been through this." I tell him in the sudden silence.

"All right," he says, arms full of loaded clips. "You're the boss."

I'm not certain I'll ever get used to that feeling. The idea that someone more powerful than me just implicitly trusts me. That's what got Alanza into trouble.

"We'll need you for the takeover," I tell his back. "But if you get the chance, keep an eye on Alanza."

"Yeah, she'll be out the first chance she gets," he says.

"It's not just that." He stops at the edge of the olive green tarpaulin that hangs in the doorway. "Don't let them hurt her."

"Going soft, huh?" He laughs as the ragged tarp falls behind him.

What follows takes longer than I would like.

First the students, armed and armored, assemble in one place.

It's more than I expected. Next, the leftovers from the other Companies arrive. They don't ask what's happening or why. Most understand, those that don't are swept along by momentum and the promise of food.

“We have everything we need?” I whisper to Grace as she runs between the ranks.

“Almost.” She hands out a pair of armored vests.

“Do we have radios?”

“Should do,” she nods.

“All right, then.” Grace catches me as I step up the improvised podium.

“No pressure,” she says.

“We all know why we’re here.” My throat’s still a little sore, but my newly discovered volume carries well enough. The crowd stops whispering. Most of them get to their feet. There’s no point in pushing them for discipline.

“To kick some ass!” someone yells.

“Yeah, fuck this place!” Another person I’ve never heard before shouts. Alpha and Tango. If they’ve come this far they must be doing something right, and if anything they have more reason to be motivated than Golf.

In theory, at least. The crowd doesn’t paint much of an encouraging picture.

Their attitude’s understandable, but not necessarily helpful. “Well, you’re not wrong, but we don’t have a lot of time.” I can see the setting sun through the trees. “So I’ll lay out our plan as quickly as I can, everyone following?” The crowd nods or shouts, raising their weapons. “Most importantly, we’ll be splitting into two groups, one of which will be going underground with me to stop G. The others will stay on the surface to hold the academy. The most important thing right now is for the right person to find the right group.” I point into the snow. “Underground group to my right.” Several Golf Company students step up immediately. “Everyone should know that going under the academy will be much, much more dangerous. Anyone who doesn’t volunteer will stay on the surface.” More of Golf Company step forward, but the rest of the crowd seem unsure. I watch the group as it grows, until I hold up my hand. "That's enough, we need some of Golf Company to stay on the surface and work with the rest of the Alpha, Charlie and Tango."

"Yeah!" David shouts "And we don't want to hear about any measuring contests when we get back!" Some kids near the back laugh. "I will personally beat the piss out of anyone who isn't being a team player!"

"Okay, underground group. If any of you don't have any weapons, grab them now, and make sure you have radios as well." Some of them peel off into tents or open crates as Grace jogs between them, arms full. "Academy group." I point to the much larger crowd. "The majority of G's forces are underground, where we'll be going. But odds are once they know what's happening they'll try to regain control, Your job is to make sure they don't. Sweep the school interior, find every underground entry point you can, and turn them into choke points." I can see a few nodding heads, but most stare down at the snow, or at the guns in their hands. "Before we move out, are there any questions?" The attitude of the students I've left on the surface makes me want to leave Grace or David with them, but I'm just as sure that I'll need them both under the school. If they do what I tell them, they should be fine.

The crowd is quiet, apart from the rubbing of hands, and the crunch of feet going up and down in the snow.

"I think we're good to go," Grace says from the edge of the crowd.

"Well, let's go then." I hop down from the podium, and Grace passes me a handgun. Some of the crowd, mostly Golf Company, cheer.

The snowfields turn amber in the dropping sunlight, and the wind is still.

Out of the forest, things are quiet, except for the sound of marching feet. Ahead, the academy is silent and still.

"Grace," I whisper, and she runs to my side. "Tell the surface group to wait here, and move in to sweep for the choke points in five minutes."

"Got it." She scurries off. My instinct is to make one last check on morale and equipment, but I don't think we really have time. I can't see anything through the windows, no silhouettes, no giveaway glints of metal. Nothing.

"Everything's good on their end." Grace jogs back. "We heading out?"

"Yes we are." I scan the distance for a second, and sprint up the slope to the academy, staying as low as I can, the rustle of cloth and clink of metal following me.

At the entrance, I glance back at the students I'd left. Some check their weapons. Most just sit in the snow.

David forces open the door, and we file in.

I point out cameras, still whirring in the same positions, and head the column as I lead them to the door I'd used to escape, weaving between corridors, stairways, and the entrances of classrooms, all empty. Some probably never used.

A shadow paints the wall ahead, and I come to a stop as quickly as I can.

Before I get a good view, it vanishes. I check corners, and spot the door I used. Dirty and gray, like something you'd only see on the darkest end of an alley.

Whatever it was is gone now.

"Clear," I whisper. Golf Company probably has hand signals, but I don't know them.

"Clear," comes from the end of the line, so we file down towards the door, and Grace runs her hand over the panel.

"Is this one different?" she asks.

"Don't think so," I say. "It was fine when I used it."

"I'll do it." David claws at the panel, almost ripping it out of the wall.

"How long is this going to take?" I ask him.

"Dunno," he says. "Not an electrician."

"Let me look at it." Grace elbows her way to the panel. Or tries to, at least.

My eyes are fixed on the students at the end of the line, flattened against the wall, and turning their head to the corridor every twenty or so seconds. I pace up to them as quietly as I can.

"Seen anything?" I ask him.

"Nothing." I can't tell through the snow goggles, but he doesn't look attentive. I slide past him, and stare into the growing twilight. A flashlight runs over the wall by me. Before I can duck back into cover, someone shouts.

I leap back, and the student by me raises his gun, and fires into the shadows. Bullets fly back and forth as I run back to Grace and David.

"I think they might have found us," Grace says.

"The panel?" As I point at it, the elevator's doors slide open and students start to organize.

"Wait, wait," Grace says. "If they've radioed in, they'll know we're coming."

"So we should abort?" I ask her. "No, no going back now." The students arrange themselves in the elevator as David raises his gun, and the shadows of advancing baggers loom on the far wall. "Plus, this can only help the others," I say as the doors close on me. "Okay." I raise my voice again. "Our objective is the hangar Islet told us about." My voice bounces around the elevator as it creaks and groans. "Speed is essential, don't stop to engage unless you need to clear a path." I can just hear the affirmatives over the sound of student reloading and checking weapons, jostling for room in the elevator.

I didn't have to check. I shouldn't have checked.

"Plus," Grace says, "baggers will be coming in behind us."

The doors let out a gentle ping as they open, and we all burst into a sprint.

First are the cavernous offices. The footing's uneven, and the air's full of dust, and as we roll down metal stairs, batter down plastic cubicles walls and piles of shredded documents, I hear the elevator rising again.

"This way." I point down into a familiar tunnel, at a girder I marked with a scratch.

Something cracks above me, and shards of glass rain down. It's the hanging lanterns, shattered by gunfire.

"No alarms," Grace shouts over her shoulder. "They know we're here, what gives?"

I wipe the broken glass from my shoulders as Golf company rushes past, pausing to crouch into firing positions.

"Simple," David says. "They don't want reinforcements." He shoves open a door in the blackened rock, and it breaks from its hinges, tumbling down a gray stairway. "They were spoiling for a fight."

We crash down the stairs, and into squat, metal corridors. Somewhere down here is where I found the photograph, so the baggers' barracks can't be far off.

"Where now?" Grace asks.

"Now I'm not sure." I point to the furthest door. "But we know to head down." Golf Company storms ahead as David covers the rear, sometimes squeezing off shots that spark against the metal floors.

Wires on the floor grow thick like tree roots in a ruin, and at some point, the halogen lights give way to a deep red.

I've never been this deep.

"This looks like down." David points to a panel, fastened to metal railing that runs around the edge of a square platform. It's covered with black and yellow safety patterns, and sitting at the top of what looks like a deep, dark shaft.

"Nowhere else to go." Grace flips up every switch she can find, and the platform groans as red lights flash. There's a screech of metal, and it starts to move.

We pile on, and crouch under the railings as the sprinting baggers stop at the precipice and shoot down at us.

"Surface group's probably fighting by now," Grace says.

"Let's hope so," I reply.

"You don't think they will?" she asks as David fires over her.

"I think they'll try, I'm just worried about whether or not they'll succeed."

Eventually the baggers are out of sight, and there's about a minute of silence, except for the heavy breathing of an exhausted crowd.

"So far so good," Grace says out loud. The platform creaks as it crashes to a stop. the red lights around the edge go dead for a second, and start flashing again as the platform begins to grind upward.

"Everybody off!" I shout "They're calling it back!" We step off as the platform goes, and I watch it move for a second up into the darkness.

"Let's keep moving, we've got a head start," David says, and the students raise their weapons again. "Still got everything we need?" Some of the Golf students pat the explosives on their belts.

The corridors are longer, and less well-lit. I have no idea what we'll find down here, and I can't help but be reminded of the communications tower. I didn't question myself then; maybe the fact that I am now is a good sign.

That, or it's just the benefit of experience, and I'm still just as wrong.

"Is this what Islet was talking about?" Grace shifts a radiation suit, slumped to the floor, with her foot.

"Looks like he was telling the truth about conditions down here." I point to the holes in the red material.

"Damn," David says. "This guy got fired." He points at the bullet holes. "See, because-"

"Still got Islet's contact?" I ask Grace.

"Yep," she answers.

I nod. "Now's the time."

Grace presses a single button on the beeper at her waist.

"I'm a little worried," she says. "I mean, we still don't know what's down here, but I think it might be-"

"Spit it out," David says.

"Nuclear," she says, pointing down another red-lit corridor, branded with black three-pointed suns inside yellow circles. "Like, dirty nuclear."

"Why?" I ask. "The layout's too narrow to transport a warhead big enough to fire from the Silo."

"Dunno," Grace says. "Maybe it's for when they're done here."

"What do you mean?" I ask, scanning the darkness.

"Can you think of a better way to get rid of the evidence of what happened here?" Grace asks. "No traces, just a big ol' crater."

The cry of motors echo down the slope, and I set off again, scanning the shadowed walls for any sign of where we should be going. My hands were shaking on the way down. They're still now.

"Over here." David slaps his hand against a rainbow of

arrows, and we follow the wall down more stairs, stepping over jet-black cables that sprawl across the floor.

"More medical staff." Grace points at piles of men and women wearing white, piled against the walls in lines.

"They've been executed," I say, trying to not to dwell on them.

"You think Islet's okay?" Grace asks.

"We can't rely on his support anymore," I tell her. "That's all that matters."

"This looks important." David points down at a narrow staircase "Maintenance entrance." He says, tapping the sign at the top. The steps are clear of debris and lit better than the rest.

"Agreed." I point down at the squat door. More like a hatch, too low to stand up in. "This is probably our best bet." I look back over the students. Grace seems shaken, and I can't say I blame her. I probably do too.

David's unreadable, as usual, but the students past him, for the first time, are shaped like people instead of baggers in different uniforms. All of them look at me.

"Equipment check," David whispers, and hands fly over guns, belts, and satchels of explosives.

"Our only role here is to destroy the Mobile Silo. If everything's gone like we planned, baggers should all be rushing upstairs by now." They all nod. "Once we're done here, we head up, and catch them all between us." I glance at the door. "There's probably still some security, so we stay low and quiet, and get this done as fast as we can." More nods.

"Who's going first?" Grace asks. My hand 's still steady.

"I am," I say, pointing to the satchel. "Divide up the charges, once we're in, we'll split into groups."

No more time to think. I open the hatch as quietly as I can, and slip through it in a crouch.

On the other side are gray cylinders, resting on their head. Taller and wider than a person, with cables like vines running between them.

Past the cylinders I can see railings against a distant wall. A bagger, just one, shifts from foot to foot. There's a shape past him and the railings, something massive and metal, much too large for me to see from here.

"I think we got lucky." David taps me on the shoulder, points to a far-off door, and the metal gate at the end of what must be the Silo's hangar. "They probably don't use this maintenance entrance much anymore." He passes me a handful of gray lumps, each one embedded with a little black box.

"Remember to put them somewhere out of sight." I hiss to him as he crawls away.

I squeeze between the cylinders, and if I push between them there's just enough space to fit between the rows. There are serial numbers on them, and taps, too. I think these must be the tanks for Islet's bacteria.

Beside me, Grace slips her plastic explosive onto the underside of another bacteria tank.

"No question, that's the Mobile Silo," she says. I follow her, past the tanks, and stand beside her. We emerge from the rows of tanks and lean over the railing, watching the lone bagger's retreating back.

"I thought it would be-" I don't really know what I thought. "-less ugly?"

"Dad would love this," Grace says as she stares at the empty missile cradle.

It doesn't look much more sophisticated than a truck, covered in ugly patches of tundra camouflage, and with caterpillar treads instead of wheels. The car's different, though. It looks more like the top half of a battle tank, covered with hatches, mismatched, lumpy modules, and arms the width of highways, resting quietly on the hangar floor. Enough to stay independent, armed, informed, and to coordinate a strategic launch. Nothing else.

Something about the cockpit draws my eye. Like it's a sleeping animal, like the random angles of metal know that no matter how misshapen, harmless or ugly it seems now, it's a machine designed to either prevent, or cause, the end of the world.

"Look out!" Grace pulls me back into the cylinders as footsteps grow louder. Through the grating above us, I can see more baggers. They're not spreading out, and their weapons aren't raised, but the sound of their boots just feet from my head makes them seem dangerous enough.

"As we speak, sir." Something in the hangar groans. I can't see from between the tanks, but it looks like a crane is lowering something into place. A long silver cylinder. A missile.

"Everyone ready to move?" The rasp couldn't be anyone but Giant 1. "We'll only have a few hours after launch to make ourselves scarce." The footsteps retreat, and start approaching again. A staircase to our left. He's coming this way.

"Yes, sir. our insurance policy is primed and ready."

"I assume our fearless leader is holding onto the detonator?"

"He didn't say, sir."

"Naturally."

The tone of his voice is relaxed. My guess would be the idea that students could be down here, organized and in force, had never occurred to him. It might be the only reason we haven't been discovered. The baggers upstairs must be too busy to report in.

"What about Islet?"

"Being held topside sir, per your orders."

"Dismissed." His footsteps come closer and closer, until his warped silhouette is visible between the tanks. Grace and I edge around them, until our backs are against the other side of the tank. We share a glance, but not for long enough to know what it means.

Islet's safety can't be a concern right now.

I can hear something, like a small ringing, like someone's tinkering with something small and metallic. I lean to the left, take a chance, and glance towards him.

Giant 1 stands against the tank, his fingers unwinding a cap halfway down its length. As it opens, he slides in a small silver tube. A few drops drip into it. He looks up, and straight into my eyes.

He sees me, I know he sees me.

It takes everything I have to not shout, or jump towards him, or roll back into cover. He winds the cap closed, all while staring at me. He closes his silver tube, tucks it into his uniform, and turns away.

I listen to his slowly retreating footsteps as I catch my breath.

Grace extends a shaking thumbs up to me.

"What was that about?" she asks.

'No idea," I say. "And there's no time to figure it out now, let's go." We both wind our way back between the bacteria tanks, checking the blinking lights of the explosives underneath.

"We got all the ones here for sure." Grace taps the underside of a tank while I listen to the buzz of my radio.

"How's everything on your end?" I ask. For a second all I hear is static hiss.

"-all good. Not enough explosive, but we spread out.

Should get them all, over," David spits. Probably way too close to the receiver.

"Good. As long as everyone's accounted for-" I glance out through the gaps between the tanks to watch more baggers disappearing upstairs. "-we should start getting ready for the second step." I refuse to say "over".

"Got it, over." David replies.

The hand on my gun is still. At any time, I could fire through the tanks at the baggers. Even Giant 1, if he's still around. It's probably smart to get out of range of the explosives first, though, so I make that my priority.

I tap Grace on the shoulder, point, and lead her through the maze of cylinders.

As I do, the room shakes and resonates with a slow mechanical groan.

Across the room I can see David and the rest of the students, sheltered behind another forest of tanks. David gives me a quick "OK" signal.

Above them, the baggers and Giant 1 stop, turn, and watch.

Something about the light's changing, and it takes me a second to realize that the enormous gate at the end of the hangar is opening, and starlight's flooding in.

I have to crane my neck to see, but there are two figures coming in from the cold. As they ride an elevator up towards us, a gentle gust of snow starts to settle on the Mobile Silo's massive loading arms.

"Should we, I dunno, do something?" Grace asks. "Or just stay put and wait?"

"Sir." Giant 1 and his men salute as G and the other draw level with them. I can just hear the echo above the wind.

"Is the missile loaded?" G asks.

"Yes sir, one hundred percent on schedule." The figure by

him, the massive man with the hidden face, is clear for the first time, but waves of fuzz travel up his body, as if something inside were shaking. Across his body, tubes warp and expand, and every now and then a burst of smoke shoots from dials fastened to his chest.

"Did you see that?" Grace taps me on the shoulder.

"What?" I whisper.

"He's signaling." She points to G's hands. She's right, and the instant I see it, I can hear something above me. baggers, moving into position. I turn and raise my weapon, right down the nose of three rifles, pointing straight at me.

I hear Grace at my back, dropping her weapon.

"You next," one of the baggers says. Another gestures with his gun.

"We'll get nowhere if you get shot," Grace whispers. I raise my hands as slowly as I can, and drop my gun to the floor.

"Kick it here," one of them says, and I slide it to them with my foot. "Now move." With our hands up, Grace and I walk backwards, out of the bacteria tanks.

I can still pull this out. There's no going back now.

I turn to face G, running my hand over the pocket that holds my detonator, hoping the move will hide where my hand goes. It's still there, and my fingers tighten around it.

"It's only natural," G says. "Players without a part try to disrupt our final act."

"You're Golf Company," Giant 1 says as his men disarm David and the other students. "Somehow I expected more discipline from you," he says, clapping his hands together. "I can't say I didn't expect this, or something like it." He turns to G. "With your permission, sir, I'd like to check on the rest of the student body, make sure they aren't cooking up more surprises for us."

"Go," G nods. "They've played their part. If they make trouble, kill them."

"Yes, sir." Giant 1 points. "You, you, and you, with me."

He leaves with a detachment of baggers, weapons at the ready. If the students upstairs know what they're doing, this shouldn't be a problem. Maybe I should have left them all up there, and done this myself.

"So," G sighs. "What are we to do with the rebellious Ms. Pine?" He takes a single step, probably working up to another pacing session. "I suppose this is the double-edged sword of our Kids In America, without initiative of their own. Apart, even with their exceptional genetic skills, they pose little threat to a coordinated body." His eyes flit across Grace and David. "They're easy prey for demagogues, however. Once united, their terrible efficacy is realized. Part of me is pleased to see them at work. Still-" He stops to rub his gray, pitted chin. "-that leaves us with the question of punishment."

"My recommendation?" For a second, he was looking at the leaving soldiers, not me. It was long enough to palm the detonator. I hold it up to him, "Explode."

For a second, all I hear is the sound of baggers raising their weapons, and the massive, silent man hissing his smoke into the air.

G lurches, wheezes, and retches as he stumbles and splutters. A shower of spittle coats the floor as he rests his hands on his knees, face shaking.

It takes a few seconds to understand that he's laughing.

G wipes away a string of drool with his sleeve, and run his tongue over his teeth.

"Do it." Faster than I can react he closes his hand around mine, and raises his thumb above the button. I wrestle for a moment, pull it away from him, and it flies out of my hand

and rolls across the floor, clattering between the bacteria tanks.

He points with his chin, and baggers retrieve it, pulling the explosives from the undersides of the tanks. I still don't have enough breath to speak.

"You-"

"It's not your fault." He runs his hand through my hair, rubbing my face with the strands he's pulled loose. "You wouldn't have done it anyway."

"You don't know that," I say. He's still wearing his glasses, the opaque kind that cover everything, but I stay fixed on where his eyes must be.

"No, I really do." He draws back, winding my hairs around one of his fingers, twisting it and tugging at it. "You know why my codename is, and always has been, G?" He looks up as the baggers shift from foot to foot behind him.

I glance over to David and the crowd of Golf Company students, standing straight up with their hands in the air, motionless at rifle point. One of the baggers holds up my detonator.

"Got it, sir!"

G ignores him. He reaches up, and removes his glasses. What's underneath isn't much of a surprise, just cracked, gray wrinkles and engorged, bloodshot veins. Like he hasn't slept for years. He steps closer, staring into my eyes. His are black, too dark to tell iris from pupil.

"You couldn't identify me," he says, "if you saw a photograph of me with different clothes, you'd have no idea who I was, would you?"

"I think the smell would give you away." I've been reaching for ideas since he captured us. I'm not sure there are any left.

"You know why?" he asks.

"It's a neurological condition," I say. "Developmental. It's always been that way."

"True. Correct. But that's not why." He steps back, wipes his bare eyes with a sleeve, and pushes his glasses back into place. "Did you know Alanza suffers from the same thing?"

"Yeah," I answer.

There aren't even that many baggers in here. If the students got close enough, maybe we could overpower them, but G, and the shaking man, they're unknown quantities. All I can do for now is keep him talking.

"You and your sister are that way, because that's how I made you." He turns away, marches across to David, and scans the face of the Golf Company students for a while. "G stands for gamma." He shouts into the hangar. "As in-" He turns back to the students, running a hand over the massive man's torso, and pouches fastened around his waist. "-the gamma brainwave." He points at Golf Company. "Can anyone tell me what that is?"

"Just a guess," David says, "is it the first letter for go fuck yourself in greek?"

"I like that." G nods, over and over. "Unscripted, very sincere. But no. It's something I was also born with." He stalks back over to me, arms folded behind his back. "I have been told it's rather like the sensory organs of a shark. It started with gamma, but I have learned to distinguish between different kinds, different brainwaves." I don't think it would be a good idea to move, not even enough to look, but I can hear Grace doing something behind me. Probably using my body to hide it from the baggers.

"So that's how you knew we were here," I say. Not a question.

"There were other signs," G says, running his hands along the railings, staring down on the Mobile Silo. "It would have been harder to ignore you. The non-stop buzzing." He rubs the bridge of his nose. "I hate the feeling of people trying not to be found." He rests his head for a second against the railing. "Hate it, but-" He stumbles back in our direction. "-I very much enjoy the feeling of a liar. No one has ever lied to me."

"So-" I take another breath, without thinking of what I'll say. Whatever Grace was doing, she's stopped. Is there something else I can ask him? "-no wonder you froze Islet out."

"Yes." He nods. "It was you he chose to collaborate with? Unfortunately the doctor was an open book, but his state of mind did provide an invaluable review of your performance." He shakes his head. "And here I was worried he was leaking this to," he pulls himself back. "Well, let's not discuss this now."

"What are you going to do with us?" Grace steps from behind me as she asks. She passes something to me as she does it. A cold, heavy oval, covered in rough edges. A grenade.

"I honestly hadn't considered it," G says. "Originally I'd planned on recruiting any members of the student body to survive, but now-" He turns, and stares back over the Mobile Silo. "Maybe that was overoptimistic. I think I will have to execute you all."

His head snaps to the side as an alarm screeches into the hangar.

Lights flash, and baggers spin in place as revolving orange lights cover the ceiling of the hangar.

"Find out what's happening!" he shouts to the nearest solider. I extend my hand, showing David the grenade, pull out the pin, and throw it.

Along with Grace, I dive back into the bacteria, ducking gunfire as I weave in between the tanks.

"What was that?" I ask Grace.

"Morse code." She taps her radio. "Tapped on and off. I told them to give us a distraction, and they did."

"How'd you know they'd understand?" I ask.

"I really didn't," she says. "Thought it was worth a try." The explosion stings my ears as I turn away from the black, billowing cloud.

I sweep the floor and grab the first gun-shaped object I can find. My hand already aches from the cold, so the recoil isn't a concern. I fire into the smoke as fast as I can, watching the flashes from David and Golf Company doing the same.

"He didn't know."

"Huh?" Grace asks.

"What was going on up upstairs," I say. "Either G's lie detector doesn't travel through solid rock, or it doesn't go very far."

"So?" Grace ducks under a fountain of flying sparks.

"He experiences it as a physical sensation," I say. "Remember, he mentioned a buzzing?"

"He has to notice it," Grace nods. "If he's distracted-"

The cloud's full of falling shadows, but it's impossible to tell friend from foe.

"We need to get over there." I pull Grace by the shoulder as we sprint through the open space between bacteria tank forests. There must be a few baggers left, because some of them fire at us, but most don't even come close.

"I think they're in trouble," Grace says as we plant our backs to the tanks next to David.

"What's happening?" he shouts to us from the row across. A bullet pings off the metal by his face.

"They're morseing back," Grace points to her radio, "SOS."

"Everyone!" I shout, or at least try to shout, over the gunfire. "Head upstairs! We're almost done here."

The air shakes and whines like a burst speaker. I almost fall from my feet as the tanks we'd just fled from flash into roaring flames.

The students by me duck and flinch as burning shrapnel rains down on them, and I narrow my eyes against the cloud of scalding smoke.

G and a huddle of baggers run through the flames, stopping for a second to place a hand on Giant 2, the shaking man. I can see their lips move, but there's no way to tell what they say to each other.

"What's-"

"It's that thing again!" David shouts over the others, pointing into the fire.

"Focus on G!" I yell as loudly as I can over the fire. "He's heading for the entrance we came in through, the hatch!" My hand's long since gone numb, so shooting at him while I talk doesn't rate as a problem. "We kill him and this is all over!"

The lines of fire tighten, but G's already vanished into the expanding cloud of darkness.

Giant 2 steps out of the fire.

Where the bullets meet his body, they flash, spark, and disappear into a cloud, like we're shooting into a sandbag.

"We can still get out the way they came in, right?" Grace asks, ducking out of cover to scan the room. "There," she points, " the actual entrance." Another sound is rising above the gunfire and flames. It's like tinnitus, which I probably have by now, a subtle ringing, but from the way the students bow their heads, I know they all feel it too.

"Yeah, I see it," David shouts.

"Move up! Everyone. Move up!" I shuffle down the rows of tanks, trying to keep low, making sure everyone can hear. "Move down the row, and when you're on the end, run for the exit!"

"What about us?" Grace asks as she fires another shot towards the remaining baggers, crowded with smoke.

"Don't get the wrong idea." I'm talking to Grace, but this applies to everyone. "We're not retreating."

"Right," David says. "We're advancing!" A bullet flashes past the metal by my foot. "Towards future victory!"

Giant 2 holds up his hand, looking down through the heavy lenses at it like he's never seen it before. Students push past me as they move down the row, returning fire.

Just out of curiosity, I squeeze a single shot off towards the Giant, getting nothing but another cloud of dust. There aren't even holes in his suit. The only wear and tear is the black of burns, and he doesn't even seem to have noticed them.

"Uh-" The sound leaves my mouth before I understand what I'm seeing. A vibration's traveling up his arm, waves shaking two at a time, like a heartbeat. His hand's hardly visible. It looks like it's shaking. "We should move." The familiar nausea in my stomach vanishes.

"We are moving," Grace says.

"No, I mean, really move!" The giant's hand closes into a fist. "Everybody move! Run!" I grab Grace by the back of her neck and sprint as fast as I can for the stairs. Not everyone heard me, but they all see me run. The crowd follows as I listen to the whine behind me burst into a roar. Something picks me off my feet and pitches me through the air.

I can feel something in my face break as I slide across the floor. Through my shaking vision I grab Grace by the wrist and pull her to her feet as all around me students do the same, clawing for footing and weapons as the smoke cloud swallows us.

"Over here!" someone shouts. "The door!"

"I'm fine, I'm fine," Grace pants as she shakes me off and runs through the cloud.

"Everybody okay?" David asks at the doorway.

Somewhere in the explosion I lost my weapon. No time to look for it now.

"We're all still good." Grace says. The rest of her words disappear under the rising wail. Through the smoke I can see the luminous lenses that pass for Giant 2's eyes as he climbs the steps towards us. "Shit," says Grace.

We all stand still for a second as the smoke trails past us in uneven ropes, sucked upwards into the tunnel at our backs.

"We can't lead him towards the other students," I say. One of the others raises her weapon, and I catch her arm. "Save your ammunition."

"Do we have anything on this guy?" Grace asks. "He's in the photo, right?"

"I think so," I say. "The suit was different, but-"

"Fuck this!" David yells. "He's not so tough, he's like, what, six eight? Three hundred fifty pounds?" I follow his eyes, to the sea of flame, to the edge of the hangar, to the empty expanse of the night sky beyond.

"David." I can't really think of anything to say. It's not as if I'll actually be able to control him.

I never did make any headway on that.

"Relax." He turns to look at me. Just for a second. Just long enough to see the blood on his chattering teeth. "I can do this."

Giant 2 raises a hand again, and the same shivering heartbeat crawls its way up his arm.

"Come on!" I point up the corridor to the elevator. "We're leaving, we can still win this if we go now!" The moment heads turn in the direction I point, I hear David break into a sprint.

The most important thing is to project confidence. I don't

feel anything. It's too early for that, so I run as fast I can, not checking whether anyone is following me.

I hear the the crash of two bodies colliding, and then the groan and breaking of the hangar's railings. A thud of something heavy landing on concrete, far below.

Grace appears next to me, keeping pace, as more and more students appear in my peripheral vision.

The growl of flames and the scream of sirens retreats behind us.

On my chest, the radio buzzes and roars, spitting fragments of David's voice back and forth down the tunnel. Half a shout, the end of a cry of pain. Then nothing.

It might not work, but he's given us a head start. It could make all the difference.

Grace claws up the stairs, pulling herself along at the head of our exhausted column, crawling up the tunnel in the deep crimson light.

There are too many straight-ahead stares.

"Weapons check," I say, and hands start running along barrels, clasping clips of ammunition and wiping away blood.

A lot of grunts and no words. I can't get the smell of smoke out of my nose.

"What's your status?" I tuck the radio under my chin as I speak into it. "Anyone?"

"Yeah, we're-" A burst of static runs down the line. "-not so good." There are a couple of shouts in the background. Gunshots.

"What's your location?" I ask as the red lights thin out. Students don't have to be encouraged to keep moving, at least, and I set as fast a pace as I can, trying to avoid the bodies of the medical team with their overturned stretchers and piles of useless, bloodstained equipment. "Hello?" No response.

"This way!" Grace points to a line of bullet holes. "Right here."

"He's dead," a voice down the line whispers. "Um..."

"Your location," I say again. "We can't help you if we don't know where you are."

"We're-" Another burst of static. More gunfire. "-second floor stairwell, east wing," he whispers. "We were moving patients to the principal's office."

The floor slopes up, and we follow the trail of burns and bootprints through the dust into the caverns. The radio keeps spitting into the silence.

"We went around that freight platform, I guess," Grace croaks. "Elevator should be just up here, c'mon." We step around the remains of smashed cubicle walls and battered metal tiles, flinching at the slightest sound. The tunnels haven't changed, and at the end of a passage, silver doors glow softly.

The doors of the elevator close the second I step through them, and looking around the faces, their eyes are up. They have an objective.

"There could be baggers on the other side of the doors," I remind them. "Don't let your guard down." They only nod.

"That," Grace gasps, "that sounded like Islet. On the radio," she says.

She's right, but I don't have time to say so. The doors ping, and slide softly open.

The wall ahead is riddled with bullet holes. I still don't have a gun.

"Second floor stairwell, east side, right?" Grace whispers, dropping low with the rest of the students.

"Right," I say.

"We're not far." She points "There's the stairs down to the

kennels, so we're in the west wing, but it should be almost a straight line from here."

I set off without confirming. I really shouldn't be first, but after what just happened, I need to take risks to keep them all focused.

"Cover!" A bullet flies past me and tears a hole in the wall.

Starting to get sick of bullets. I flatten against the wall and three Golf Company students crouch in the corridor, sending a wall of fire down towards fleeing baggers. Some fire back. Most collapse.

"Looks like we caught them running." Grace puts her hands on her knees, and kneels down to catch some breath.

"No time to waste," I tell her.

"Yeah." She waves her hand, sucks in a breath, and stands upright again.

"Hey!" one of the students shouts. "Most of these guys were pretty beat already." The stairwell's in sight.

"You think," Grace takes another big breath, "you think B-team actually pulled it off?"

"Maybe," I say. "And don't call them that."

I take the first step, and the moment I do another bullet flies past me. It could be that I'm getting used to this, or it could be that I'm just too exhausted to flinch.

"It's us!" I shout up the stairs. I'm not sure why, but I've never been comfortable announcing myself, or even saying my own name.

"Yeah!" Grace yells. "So don't shoot us!"

Two dirty, bloodstained faces peek around the corner.

"Oh shit!" one of them shouts. "You actually made it!"

We climb the stairs, scanning the blue carpets on the upper floor, now marked with scorch marks and bullet holes.

"C'mon." Another B-teamer waves. "We all holed up in the principal's office."

"Wait," Grace says, halfway along the corridor, near a dismembered fern. "We heard from Islet, is he okay?"

The door to the office sways ajar, and a crowd of students sit around, while others pass through them, applying bandages and examining injuries.

"Hildegard!" Islet shouts from inside the office. "I wasn't sure if you could hear me." He hands off a tray filled with blood and extracted bullets to what looks like another member of his medical team.

"We heard you," Grace says. "We're just surprised. G said he took you prisoner."

"He did," the doctor nods. "But after he started killing off the medical staff, I think he forgot, that," he draws a slow breath, "or he just didn't care anymore."

"Why'd you come up here?" I ask, as Golf Company mingles with the other students.

His eyes wander. "I can't lie, not now. I just wanted to get as far away from this as I could, but I managed to take some of the others with me, and we've been helping the students, so-"

"It worked out for the best," Grace says, raising her voice. "We successfully destroyed all the bacteria under the school-"

Islet's eyes widen for a second.

"-and-" Grace pauses to swallow, "-they're down one Giant."

"We need a status report," I tell them, trying to keep my voice as even as possible. "How much of the school's under control?"

"Uh..." Islet sits down in the chair, behind the now-overturned desk. "By the time we got here it wasn't a question of control."

"Doctor!" A student rushes in, holding a smoking walkie-talkie, and supporting a friend, limping on a bleeding leg. Islet jumps to his feet again, setting the injured student on the ground, elevating the leg, and shining a small flashlight across it.

"What happened?" I ask them.

"It's G," he says, never taking his eyes from Islet's treatment. "We overheard the baggers, they formed up around him, somewhere near their comm room, and called in a chopper." I scan the ground and snatch up a weapon.

"That's where they had all the phones, right?" Grace says. "The one outgoing line."

"Trashed." The student groans. "By the time we got in it was just broken glass and charcoal."

"If G escapes, we're all as good as dead," I tell the room. "And he has a lot to answer for." They all look up. "So who's coming with me to bring him in?" Some stand. Others raise their hands. "Grace." I tap her on the shoulder. "Take two minutes to organize them, make sure they're all healthy and armed."

"Got it," she nods. "He's going to get what's coming to him."

"Islet." I drag him aside. "We need to talk."

"Uh, okay," he nods. "What is it?" I listen to the murmur of voices and the clatter of equipment.

"I saw the medical staff." He nods, making a show of listening. "Radiation suits." His eyes roll down to his feet.

"You saw the bomb?" he asks.

"I saw enough to guess," I say. "We all did."

"I didn't want to," he gasps. "We were forced, we installed it at gunpoint, I hate-"

"I don't care how you feel about it," I say and shove him against the wall, "I need to know how big it is, what kind of detonator it has, and if it can be disarmed."

"Well," he gulps, "it's tactical grade, I remember they said that, just enough to-"

"Get rid of the evidence," I say.

"That was the idea." He nods. "Even if we take the academy, they might-"

"They won't," I tell him. "G wouldn't trust anyone else with the detonator, so we won't give him the chance to get far enough away. Don't get the wrong idea, Islet, I need to know if it can be moved."

"Moved?" He flinches again. "You want to use it?"

FILE 7: OCCUPATION

December 22nd

We got rid of the chair. Apparently, other people need it.

I would have paid money to see it go into a car crusher. Crutches at least I can hit people with.

Either way it doesn't make much difference, I've been taking this medication for years, and as far as I can see, all it does is keep me alive. Highly overrated.

Cooper says the way I feel is normal. I don't think he really understands how awful that seems, but at least he was trying. He gave a speech about how precious and gifted I am. He hasn't pulled that out in a while. I stayed quiet, like I usually do, but it's always the same, lists of things I've never even come close to doing or saying.

Like he's talking about some other person.

❄

"How are they?" I ask.

"Well," Grace says, tilting her hand from side to side "There's good news and bad news." She fastens fresh armor on. "They're all ready to go, we have plenty of able-bodied students, and now we have more than enough plundered weapons."

"Okay?" I strap a vest on, and take a handgun. Starting to develop a dislike for larger weapons. "Bad news?"

"They saw Giants with G, number one, and the diving suit guy."

"Fine." I fasten a grenade to my thigh. "We'll crack open his suit with explosives." I raise my voice. "Everyone bring as many explosives as you can carry!"

"Oh, and Alanza escaped," Grace says as quickly as she can. "And no one knows where she went."

"That could be a problem." I examine the students, freshly armed and armored. Most are Golf company, but there are smaller, hungrier-looking ones among them. "We don't have time to plan around it, though." I raise my voice again. "All right, let's go!" Most grunt. The smaller ones almost cheer.

"What did you say to Islet?" Grace asks, as we descend the stairs, weapons raised.

"Working with him on a contingency plan," I say, tapping my radio. "Are you receiving me, Islet?"

'Yep. Loud and clear." He clicks it off.

"Sounds like he doesn't really want to talk to you." Grace lowers her voice to a whisper as the students ahead signal the all-clear. "You know we need him."

"I do." My hands fly up and down, checking my equipment as my eyes stare straight ahead. "It doesn't mean I have to like it."

"He's scared," Grace snorts. "Not everyone's like you."

It doesn't sound like a compliment.

I glance down at her, but her eyes are fixed ahead. I know what she means, I want to tell her how I feel, lay out my regrets, but now is definitely not the time.

I'm not that good with words, either. It would take too long.

"Is that a helicopter?" Grace whispers. A shadow rushes through the frosted glass of the academy's front, and a searchlight, tilted upwards by neglect, shines off the metal. The churn of flying blades is unmistakable.

"Stay low, we need surprise if we want to stand a chance." Everyone crouches, nods, and crawls through the shattered glass where the academy's double doors used to be.

Clustered in a pool of light are baggers, all facing outwards, signaling as their fellows pull equipment and vehicles up from the camps.

"Looks like they're cutting their losses," Grace says. "Grabbing what they can salvage before they leave."

"Just like us," I tell her.

I can't see them very well without sticking my head out of hiding more than I'm comfortable with, so I crawl across to Grace, point to an concrete barrier, overturned in the snow, then point to the other students, and start working my way through the cold on my stomach.

I wait until they draw level with me, and try to slide my head around the side, holding my breath so the cloud doesn't give me away.

I can definitely hear a helicopter, and the baggers are working to clear the snow by the statue, holding his golden book up to the night sky.

Giant 1's definitely present. He's at least a head taller than the ordinary baggers, even with his unhealthy slouch. I can see the man in the diving suit, Giant 4, standing by the shattered glass of the academy door. At the base of the statue is the strange, dirty hunchback, too, arms so low to the ground that he almost crawls, steam rising from the parts of his spine that have broken his uniform.

They're definitely talking, but at this distance I can't make out the words. The voice is a different story; it's not hard to identify G as he's almost carried by a tight-knit group of soldiers from wreckage of the academy out into the snowfield.

No time for plans or signals. He's covered from every angle. I can barely see his dirty coat, but every now and then there's an opening. Is there a rhythm to it?

A limp. Every second step.

It's not the baggers. They spread out to give him some space. Is he hurt? It doesn't matter, I slide my hand through the snow, looking along the barrel as well as I can while lying freezing in the snow, and try to time my breaths along with his steps.

Step. Breathe in. Step. Breathe out. Step. Breathe. Stumble. Shoot.

"No!" someone screams, and gunshots fly in every direction for a second before the students return fire.

I pull myself back behind the fallen barrier, listening to the beat of the shots. The bark of the mounted guns on the jeeps. The roar of grenades. The hiss of Giant 4's mist-spewing hose.

"Did anyone see if I hit G?" I ask into the radio.

"Nope."

"Negative visual."

"No."

"Couldn't see."

In this position, all I can do is lie in the snow and watch the forest sway in the night wind. The students by me do the same, waiting for the fire to thin. There are lights above the tree, and the helicopter we heard hovers closer.

"You bitch!" someone screams over the thunder. "I know you're there!" Something whistles through the air and flattens a pit in the snow by my hand with a crunch. The students jump to their feet and sprint away, diving, and falling through the snow as blood and steam fountains from their chests.

I grab the top of the barrier and vault. The snow's dirty with red and black, but there's something ahead, so I dive for it as the grenade I'd left behind blows the concrete barrier to bits.

It's a snowmobile, lying sideways in the snow, with a still body next to it. Not enough to crouch behind, but better than nothing.

More shots bounce across it as gunfire sends one of the skis flying, and I get a clear view of Alanza, holding out a gun with one hand, the other covering a waterfall of blood that runs from her shoulder. She's trying to steady herself against the base of X's statue.

The hunchback leaps past her, over my head and down into cover, and then away again, cackling as bullets vanish in the trail of vapors he leaves behind him.

I try to free my hand, find some way around the snowmobile to fire, but Alanza shoots down at it as she glances at G, huddling behind the baggers, and throws a flare down onto the ground that explodes into light and writhing red smoke.

"Three!" Alanza points, and the hunchback vaults a burning jeep into the midst of a group of students, running for cover. He doesn't have a gun, just long, dirty nails. They disappear behind another vehicle, moving towards us as it fires until the tires hiss and melt in a carpet of Giant 4's burning mist.

My hair starts to whip in the wind as the helicopter stabilizes itself overhead, and Alanza's shouted orders are drowned out by the drone of rotors.

It doesn't really matter at this point. Maybe if we'd had time to plan, or if there were more students.

No. It's not a question of numbers or weapons. From here I can see it's a rout, even Golf Company are on the verge of breaking. It's the Giants, the psychological advantage.

I take another look around the burning wreck of the snowmobile. Their numbers are dwindling, and all but one of the jeep-mounted guns is quiet. The students are pinned down, but not running.

"Islet." I flip onto my back and pull the shoulder radio to my ear.

"Hildegard?"

"I need everything useful you know about KU Giant." Another bullet passes by.

"Well, I wasn't allowed to treat them," Islet stutters.

"I know!" I have to shout over the helicopter. Glancing under the cover of the snowmobile, I can see the mist creeping closer. "It's the diving suit man, and the jumping hunchback, you know them, right?"

"Both at once?" he gasps. " That's four and three, I think." I hear something fall, and the flipping of papers."Uh, which one first?"

"Definitely diving suit," I say as I watch him spray mist over a concrete barrier. The students behind it scatter and run, but some them aren't fast enough.

"Okay, let's see, Portuguese, mid-forties-"

"How do I kill him!" I shout down the line.

"Okay, okay, right here." Islet says. "He has a skin condition, he, uh," he reads for a second. "Seems like instead of oils his skin secretes some sort of acid, so if-" He pauses "-if he's not in water he burns himself! Break his suit!"

"Easier said than done," I tell him. "Anything else?"

"I think it's some sort of chemical reaction with water," Islet says. "If he runs low on water he won't be able to use it as a weapon, or he won't have enough in his suit."

I have to move, so I jump to my feet, start running, and roll as more bullets come my way. The radio's receiver falls from my hands, and lands upright in the snow.

The baggers have pulled down the slope following the helicopter, away from the statue, so I run straight forward, scanning for Alanza and G as I flatten against the square plinth.

The others are still by the academy doors, some of them even taking cover inside.

The ones I can see all have their eyes fixed on me, but they don't move.

This isn't something I know how to do.

I have no plan, no resources, and any chance of success I had is probably in the snow with my lifeline to Islet.

But losing here isn't an option, so I need to change my approach.

What would David do?

"She's still up there!" I hear Alanza shout. "Get rid of her!" I crouch and turn my head to watch the helicopter touching down, probably no more than twenty feet from my hiding place. Giant 3 leaps up to the helicopter, and reaches out his hand for G as it hovers down towards him.

At this point it's pretty obvious what David would do, so I lean out from behind the base of the statue and empty my gun in every direction.

The way the rotors whip the snow into my face makes

aiming impossible, but that's not the point. I keep firing until the gun is empty.

I don't have any more ammo, so as I watch Giant 4 advance through the snow, I throw my gun at him.

It spins through the air, cracks against his glass dome, and he crushes it underfoot, sending a spray of mist towards me.

I flatten against the statue again, and watch the mist caught in the wind rush past me.

They aren't still watching.

Grace is first, she comes charging past the overturned jeeps, almost trips in the snow, and crashes into the statue beside me.

"You're crazy," she says.

"I hope you brought a gun," I tell her, and she looks up at me for a second.

"I think that's the first time you've even come close to making a joke," she says. "You're one of those Chuck Jaeger adrenaline junkies, aren't you?" She holds out a rifle, and I swing it around the base of the statue without looking, empty the magazine.

"I hadn't considered it before," I say, as I watch more students follow Grace, vaulting over debris and rolling under bullets. "You might be right."

"What made you think this was a good idea?" Grace asks.

"I never thought it was a good idea." More students join us at the base of the statue, and others crawl through the snow, or push an overturned jeep forward as bullets ping off it. "I just asked myself what David would do."

Grace bows her head, and nods.

"You're probably right," she laughs. "So you don't really have a plan?" One of the students pushing the jeep cries out as a window shatters, and it comes to a stop as Giant 4 stomps closer.

"Not exactly." I lean out of cover again, and watch Giant 3 pull G and Alanza into the helicopter. The hunchback steps away from them, and the two of them hug.

"We've got a clear shot," Grace says. "In theory, at least." Another student cries out in pain as Giant 4's mist seeps under the jeep they'd used as cover. Most of them are lying in the snow, and the jeep's come to a stop.

"Take a few and break left," I tell her. "Get the shot if you can."

"What about you?"

I grab the handgun holstered on her thigh and sprint as quickly as I can, running towards the jeep, unloading into the glass dome on Giant 4's head. There's no time to look back to see if Grace hesitates.

"You again." The peeling, underlit face behind the glass turns towards me as fast as his massive suit allows. "I've been looking for you." I squeeze off a few more shots, just to make sure I'm keeping his attention, and tense as he raises his hose.

I can still hear the helicopter. I inch down the slope, around him, and into the wind.

I can hear gunfire, too, but as I twitch I see the helicopter out of the corner of my eye, rising up and away in the night.

"Don't tell me you've dried up," I say, and he narrows his eyes. He probably hasn't, but I've still got plenty of space to run.

His hose hisses, but a bullet flashes from his helmet as the students under the jeep crawl through the snow to fire at him. He turns and starts to spray, so I fire what's probably the last of my ammo towards his hose and it splits open in his hand, gushing hissing liquid across his helmet.

"Yes!" I can hear Grace shout. "Nice shot!" I have no idea if I'm the one that actually hit him, or if she's even talking to me.

The giant takes the hose in his hands, rips it from his backpack, and throw it towards the student under the jeep. Most escape, but the ones on the ground get drenched and start screaming.

He lurches towards me, drawing a handgun from a compartment on his leg, and growls as the water around his lips bubbles and froths. He raises the gun, and there's nowhere for me to go except back, so I start running.

I roll into the snow, hoping it'll throw him off, and I hear a gunshot go over my head as I listen to him staggering towards me, ignoring the gunfire from the other students.

I try to find a place to hide behind the statue as I watch Grace and the others that went with her run back up towards us.

I'm almost there when something catches me from behind and knocks me to the ground.

Giant 4's arm doesn't hurt that much, or it could be the cold and the adrenaline have made me completely numb, but it is heavy.

If I go under his boots, he'll crush me for sure.

"Just die!" Grace shouts. Her gunfire doesn't even spread cracks across the glass.

In the distance, I can hear something over the thud of approaching footsteps.

A buzzing motor.

Giant 4 turns his head, and I do the same, watching the plume of snow explode from the forest and crash towards us. The Giant raises his gun to fire, so I jump to a crouch, and leap out of the thing's path.

Giant 4 tries to do the same, but before he can the rogue snowmobile slams into him, crashing into the base of the statue and tumbling into the snow, sputtering and smoking.

"You okay?" Grace pulls me to my feet as Giant 4 starts to

rise. "Guess not." She brings up her gun, but I hold out my hand to stop her and the others with her.

The man in the diving suit staggers to his feet as the plinth cracks, and with a slow creak, the statue topples, smashing him into the snow.

A chorus of shouts go up from the students as the glass dome cracks, and the hissing water flows out into the snow, burning into a widening puddle.

"Ow." A figure rises from the snow, streaked with blood and soot.

"Woah!" Grace shouts. "David?" She rushes over to him.

"Kept you waiting, huh?" He groans as students lower him into a sitting position. against the broken plinth. I push my way through the crowd, staring and staggering, to stand over him.

"What happened?" I ask.

"Simple," he says. "The concrete broke my fall." Some of them laugh, but I think most are too tired.

"That's it?" Grace says. "You were just fine this whole time?"

"I don't know about fine," he says, and raises his left arm. "This is super broken. I just touched him for a second, but by the feel of it-" He clenches and unclenches his pale, shaking hand. "-the second I did all the bones in there fucking exploded. Might not be fixable."

If they think their best fighter's gone for good, they'll lose morale, and the boost from his reappearance is too much to throw away. I have to distract them.

"So by the process of elimination, the one you killed must have been Giant 2," I say, as loud as I can. Obvious, but effective.

"Yeah." Grace runs her hand over David's reddening arm. "That's something."

"I didn't kill him," David says. "I don't know what happened. We landed, we fought a little, he fucked me up hardcore, and then he just disappeared."

"Disappeared?" Grace says. "He was winning, and he ran away? Maybe if G ordered him-"

"No." David interrupts. "I mean literally disappeared. One second he was staring down at me, then he started buzzing, and then nothing. I thought you'd need backup, so I grabbed a snowmobile outside the hangar on the edge of the lake, and you saw what happened next."

"You decided to ram the first thing you saw," I say.

"Yeah," he nods. "Anyone complaining?"

I hear a groan, like someone holding back a scream.

"Give me your gun," I say, and Grace hands me another pistol. I walk over to the edge of the boiling puddle around Giant 4, and hold it over him. He holds in his breath, and his eyes bulge as he looks up at me. The skin around them starts to bleed into the hissing water.

"This is the part-" He winces, and more skin flakes off into the water. "-the part-" he gasps. "-where you say you'll make it quick if I tell you-" He coughs blood into the water. "-everything?"

"I was considering it." I pull back the hammer.

"We should probably just shoot him," Grace says.

"Not yet," I tell her. "He must know something we can use."

"Oh, I do," he rasps. "You're all dead."

"We already know that," I say. "Anything else?"

"I can't believe this." He turns in the hissing puddle, staring up at the sky. "Killed by a bunch of kids, I've seen-" He splutters and snorts of bubbles of blood. "I've done-" A carpet of red foam flows down his chin. "-there are worse ways." He slurs. "I can see the stars, at least."

"Talk!" I jab the pistol at him.

"My only regret," he shakes upright, twitching and writhing, "is that I won't get to see what he does to you!" He shivers, retches, and falls back into the puddle, motionless.

The night is quiet, apart from the quick breaths of the students.

No alarms. No gunshots. No helicopters. Not even wind.

"What now?" Grace whispers.

It's a fair question. There's a lot to consider before making my next move, but if I want it to be the winning one, I need maximum cooperation.

Most of us are alive, and David's still here, but there's no time to relax or be grateful.

"All right." I turn to the crowd. "This isn't a victory, but we haven't lost yet, either." Most of them stare past me. They're probably not capable of absorbing complex instruction right now. "Everyone inside, Grace." I point. "You're in charge of finding food, drink, and thermal blankets."

"Right." She nods.

"Round up the students you trust," I say, "and make sure everyone who needs it gets some rest, and David-" He looks up from the side of hissing puddle.

"Yeah?" He aims a soft kick at the broken glass globe.

"Make a small squad, of the four or five you've observed to be the most capable." He nods. "Make sure Grace's team has everything they need, and then meet me in the principal's office."

"Right, just one thing," he says.

"What?" Students have already started filing past under Grace's supervision, stumbling and shivering as the wind picks up.

"Does that make you the principal now?" He grins.

"Yes, it does."

Of course, it doesn't take long for everyone to run inside. Don't get the wrong idea, it's cold, but not as cold as it's been for days. It might be warming up.

"Islet." He looks up the moment I enter my new office.

"Did you get him?" he squeaks.

"Not yet. We're going to need your help downstairs, there are a lot of injured students-"

"I can't, I just don't have the resources, bandages, antiseptic-" He rifles through open drawers and bags that line the ground.

"Improvise." I point the gun at him. It's empty, of course.

"Look." He raises his hands. The students still in here don't seem all that upset. "There's no need for threats, you know I want to help."

"Do you?" I ask, "because it seems like every time we rely on you, you find a way to provide the bare minimum."

"I do my best." He lowers his hands towards me. "I'm not like you, like any of you. I wasn't-"

"Wasn't what?"

The students on stretchers sit up, or roll to face us. "Grown in a lab? Designed for murder? Pieces of equipment?" Islet gulps, but says nothing. "We're past the point where you can compromise, doctor. G will be back, and he knows you collaborated with us. You won't get a chance to talk to him. He'll have some faceless enforcer blow your head off the first chance he gets."

"You're right," Islet nods. "You're right, I just-"

"I understand you're afraid." I lower the gun. "But we need everyone to give their all, or we're all dead. Simple." His hands drop to his side, still shaking. "Now," I ask. "Are you going to help Grace or not?"

"I'll-" His eyes search the room as he fills his arms with half-empty bags and first-aid satchels. "I'll do what I can."

"Good." I point with my chin. "Now get out of my office." Students rise with the doctor, and within a few minutes, the room is empty.

The door sits ajar.

I walk, as quietly as I can, and softly click it closed.

I think this is the first time I've been alone for days.

It feels like it. My breath comes faster and faster, and my arms tense and cramp up.

I stride ahead, grab the desk, and sweep everything onto the floor with a shout, stamping my foot into the sparking computer, breaking the spines of the books and the hood of the lamp into a smoking mess on the floor.

I massage my aching throat, and sit down in the high-backed, red leather chair behind the toppled desk.

I close my eyes for a moment.

It's not heavy, so I pull it upright.

Running my hands over the drawers, I test the knobs for weight.

The second on the left holds the public address microphone. I withdraw it, and place it on the desk in front of me. It's still plugged in. I depress the button. I haven't really thought of what I'm going to say.

"Attention, everyone. This is Hildegard Pine, your new-" My first instinct is to say "ruler", or maybe "overlord". "-principal, and right now I'm going to address your concerns and make clear what our next steps are." I release the button for a second. Make sure everyone's listening. "Our first and most obvious problem is G. We can be certain he'll return soon with more men, weapons and equipment. Since we can't be sure when this will be, our first priority is the security and fortification of the academy. The specifics will come later, but for now I'm calling on all able-bodied but unassigned students to take stock of entryways, lines of sight and strong positions, make sure David, who I'm sure you all know, is aware of them. We need absolute knowledge of the academy's layout." I release the button again.

Obviously, I can't tell them all my actual plan.

Or how I think this will actually play out.

That, and Alanza might have sympathizers in the student body, and she'll almost certainly return with G's attack force, whether he wants her to or not. "Our close second priority is the Mobile Silo hangar's contents, and the Mobile Silo itself." No sound of despair or protest through the floorboards, just the echo of my voice. "I will personally lead a team with the aim of holding hostage the sensitive materials and equipment down there, but it's possible there are still baggers present, so until we're ready, I have to ask everyone to stay out. I'll be working on the next steps with Grace and David soon," I say, "so consider them second in command. Until then, stay determined." I release my finger for a second, and change my mind. "We still have a chance to make it out of this."

I lean back in my enormous chair, listening to the wind beyond the walls, the sound of footsteps and muffled speech.

❄

There's a knock on the door, and David sweeps it open. Not sure how long I've been sitting here.

Did I sleep? Probably not for long.

"Done rallying the troops?"

"For now," I answer.

"You wanted to talk?" he asks, and I get up. It wasn't a comfortable chair anyway.

"I did." I walk past him, and close the door on the five or six muscle-bound Golf Company students outside.

"Secret stuff?" he asks.

"Absolutely, look." I sit back down. David glances at the pile of debris I left at the foot of the desk. "G's not going to leave us alone. He could be here by tomorrow, and he won't leave anything to chance." David nods. He doesn't need convincing. "Any preparations we make are only going to slow him down, and from the way his Beagle Commission operates in public we know he has the influence to turn other authorities on us."

"So?" David folds his arms.

"So even if we stop his plan, even if we kill him, if the Beagle Commission remains active, we can't go home." David closes his eyes, and nods again.

"Right." he says. "Obvious when you think about it, but I can see why you wouldn't want to announce it."

"We might still be able to work something out with him," I say. "The next order of business is going downstairs to see what we can use for leverage, but-"

"But you don't think he'll settle for that." David says. "What's your point?"

"My point is that we can't stay here after G's beaten, and once we escape, the Commission will brand us as terrorists. That's how everyone will see us until we destroy the whole organization."

"You're leading me on." He paces. "Usually that means you want me to do something, but you're not sure I'll agree, right? You don't think I'll like it."

"Correct." Obviously I'm not giving him enough credit. "I'll get straight to the point, then. We need that bomb downstairs."

"The one you said was," I can just see him narrowing his eyes, "Nuclear?"

"Well, if we're going to be terrorists-" I don't have to finish.

"I get it. The mother of all bargaining chips." David nods. "I'll get my guys on it." He makes for the door.

"I don't think I even have to say this." He pauses with his hand on the knob. "But don't tell anyone. Especially Grace."

"Understood." He nods.

I lean back into the chair as the door closes under its own weight.

The next few hours are slow, awkward chaos.

Most of the students are exhausted, so only the most disciplined and physically conditioned are able to continue carrying out my orders.

What this means, really, is that things happen slowly, partly because of physical exhaustion, and partly because sleeping bodies make excellent speed-bumps.

I sincerely wish I could do the same. In fact, I spend a fair bit of the time it takes me to find my way from my office down to the school's underbelly estimating time windows, guessing at whether I could fit rests within them.

"There are five or six." David points to the rows of black, twisted wrecks. "Dubstep man must've missed them when he dropped the bass on me."

"Enough to hold hostage?" I ask him, as his squad hauls the tanks into a stack in the corner.

"Dunno." David shrugs. "It's more than none."

"True. We have no idea how much G actually needs." My eyes scan the students, crawling across the metal monster in the pit below. "Make any progress with the Mobile Silo?"

"Not a chance." He crosses his arms. "Maybe if we had some serious tools, like torches, drills or saws." A fountain of sparks scatters across the hull's white camouflage. "It's looking like this thing was made to just sit in place for months, maybe years without opening, so-"

A shout echoes from below as a student loses his grip on the metal and falls to the ground. Some others rush to help.

"I think I get the picture," I say.

David leans over the railing. "He'll be fine," he says. "It wasn't that far. Big baby."

"The bomb?" I step back from the railing.

"I've got my boys working on it." David points to the maintenance entrance, the one we crawled through earlier. "They're drawing straws now."

"What for?" I ask.

"Well, the place is plastered with radiation warnings," he says. "I told them they're being paranoid, but-"

"Understandable," I say. "But we're on a time limit. Let's go motivate them."

The corridors between are still dim and dirty, although at some point, someone tidied away the bodies.

I can't help but wonder if this whole place is irradiated. G wouldn't have come down here if it was, would he? Of course he wouldn't, but the idea stays with me until red lights and radiation symbols are all I see.

Even if the whole school was irradiated, it wouldn't make it any more dangerous, would it? Worst case scenario: we all get cancer in a few years. It's better than being shot and having G throw our bodies to the wolves.

"Hey boss." David's "boys" salute me, reminding me of another reason to lose sleep. Alanza is still out there. If nothing else, I can count on G to be practical. Not her.

"You still pissing around out here?" David asks. "Scared of a little radiation poisoning?"

They're stood in a circle, red rubber radiation suits half donned, plastic faceplates dangling around shoulders or behind backs.

"They would be stupid if they weren't." I say. "Personally, I'm glad they show enough creativity to procrastinate."

"We weren't just putting it off," one of them raises his hand, empty rubber sleeve dangling above the ground. "That doctor came through a few minutes ago, really freaking out about something, so we-"

"About what?" I interrupt and take a step closer.

"Dunno," another one says. "He said he had to prove a theory?"

"David." I point at him. "Make sure this gets done-" There's an acronym I remember people like this being in love with. More than military types usually love acronyms, at least. "-ASAP."

They all nod. I have learned their language. "If Islet's upset about something, it's probably very important." David starts squeezing into a radiation suit, and I point at the talkative student "Which way did the doctor go?" He points wordlessly down the corridor.

"One of the data entry farms," he says. "I think."

The corridors stretch as I stride over cables and bloodstains. Obviously, I don't have a map of the place, but I remember seeing windows into beige hells of cubicles and box computers. I almost wish I hadn't said what I did to them, because the reality of the idea's stuck with me. Islet's not the bravest, but he's rational. He's disturbed for a reason.

"They actually did it." The muttering derails my train of thought. "They really did it!" I follow the sound of breaking office equipment to Islet, standing with his hands planted firmly on a desk, his body shaking, dripping sweat and tears into a broken keyboard.

"Islet!" He arches his back, turns, and places broken glasses back on his face as I call out his name. "They said you found something."

"I ran out of supplies, so I came down here." His hand shakes. "I was just doing what you told me, to find out what the warheads were really for, and-" He falls into an office chair.

"And?" I ask.

"And I did," he says.

"So what is it?" I step closer, scanning the screen, trying to make sense of what looks like a web of words.

Some are painted different colors, and there's some sort of medical readout near the top of the screen, flatlined. "Some kind of designer epidemic? A biological weapon?" Islet shakes his head.

"It's not a weapon at all."

"What is it, then?" I stand closer, and ask again.

"I found the missing link." Islet holds a floppy disk between his thumb and forefinger. On it is a peeling label with "program" written on it in faded blue ink. "I found what the programmers were working on."

"You're not answering my question." I tell him. "I need to know everything there is to know if we're going to get out of this."

"All right." He runs his hands through sweat-flattened hair. "Let me see if I can explain it." He touches the screen, and runs a finger over the dancing words that run down the side. "I was on the bacteria side of the project, and you got your information from me, so it's only natural that we assumed the cultures were the be all and end all, especially when they were turned into warheads."

"There's more to it?" I ask.

"Like I said." He nods. "It's not a weapon, as far as I can tell, it's a surveillance system, the ultimate privacy invasion." Watching his finger. I start to see patterns. Words highlighted in bright red, things like bomb, hate, panic, guns, bomb. Government.

"What are these words?" I point at the screen, hoping a proper explanation can fight off the dread that's swelling in my stomach.

"Here's my understanding," Islet says. "First, you're infected by my bacteria." He points down at a folder on the desktop, labeled "vectors". "He's harmless, and totally asymptomatic, so you'd have no way of knowing, but he makes his way to the brain, and once he sets up shop there he starts to learn your brain patterns, and then he'll squeeze off little bursts of radiation," he taps the screen, "something totally harmless, I think, I'm not a physicist. That was as far as my part in the project went," he says. "Not that teaching him to give off the type of radiation they told me to was easy, I had to-"

"Focus, doctor," I say, and push his chair closer to the screen.

"Okay, right, that was all I knew until today." He pulls up another folder from the desktop. "The first thing I found was this."

The file balloons into a schematic, something like a squat, metal mushroom. "These things are years past what the top physics labs have, in terms of-"

"Radiation detectors," I say. He nods. "The same type of radiation emitted by your bacteria." Islet nods again. "So what, it's an untraceable tagging system?"

"That's what I thought at first," Islet says. "An untraceable way for a government to keep track of its citizens would be bad enough, and these detectors have massive ranges, but that's not all." He holds up the disk again. "Then the program comes in."

This is all starting to sound familiar. I think I can guess what comes next.

"Along with the detector, it distinguishes what part of the brain the bacteria emit from, right? It broadcasts brainwaves." I take the disc from him and set it down on the desk.

'How-" He turns in his chair. "I mean, there's more to the program. It detects down to the keyword. You can set bookmarks in chains of thought, even flag concepts to cause alerts on an individual or national scale, but how did you-"

"It's G," I say. "He explained it to us when he took us prisoner in the hangar earlier." Islet stares up at me. "He says he can detect brainwaves, like a shark or something. He's used the Beagle Commission's resources to recreate it for use on a massive scale."

"Yeah." Islet nods. "What do we do?"

The walkie-talkie at my waist hisses and spits.

"Hildegard?" Grace asks through it. "Come in, fearless leader." I raise it to my ear.

"I'm here."

"I've got something up here you should probably see," Grace says. "Not sure how to describe it apart from gross."

"Is it a problem?" I ask her as I watch Islet's face.

"Don't think so," she says. "Not yet, at least."

"All right, Where are you?"

"Kennels," she says. "Bring a coat."

"Write this up as well as you can," I tell Islet. "Keep it simple. And start working on a potential counter." He nods, and I set off again.

"Hey!" David calls out as I pass by. "Going somewhere?" he asks. "What was going on with Islet?"

"Long story," I tell him. "Grace has something she says I need to see." Behind him, the crowd of students stand far apart. Two in the middle hold a long, silver cylinder between them. "Is that it?"

"Yeah." He nods. "Heavier than it looks."

"All right." My eyes run over it for a second. No marking or handholds. A metal grille, a few protruding wires. Even a dent where they probably dropped it. Nothing to give away the monster inside. "Have them take it to our ammo stockpile under the school, guard it twenty four seven." He nods and salutes. I wonder if he even knows he did it. "Once that's done, find me on the way to the kennels."

I make my way back up through the elevators, and retrace my steps through the upper level, checking my memory with every step so that if worst comes to worst, I can still find that bomb.

The stairway's near the back of the school. It must be set against the far side of the plateau.

"Package is squared away," David says as he falls in beside me.

"Is that what we're calling it now?" I ask him as I pry open the metal door.

"What else would we call it?" he says as I scan the snow-lined stone steps. "Big fucking bomb?"

"Can't argue with that." I pick my way down them, tracing the smaller footsteps in the snow. The cold grows until my breath appears, and I can hear the wind howling between the stones. Through squat square windows I can see the frozen lake, and the shadows of what might be the oilfield beyond.

"Hey." Grace points a flashlight up towards us. Two other students stand around, behind chain links or over empty metal bowls. It smells awful. "You brought David."

"I was between jobs," David says. "What's such a big deal?"

"Well." Grace runs her flashlight over rows of metal pens. "You remember we used to hear them howling."

"Yeah," David says, stepping closer to the first pen.

"But not for a couple of days, right?" she says.

"What's your point?" I ask.

"They're dead." Grace's light settles on the face of a dog. Some kind of working dog, probably for guard duty, but up here it might've been used for pulling sleighs as well. "Poisoned, we think." As she lingers on them, I can see the streams of blood that've run from their eyes and mouth. "No sign of struggle. We don't think they suffered."

"baggers wouldn't poison their own dogs," I say.

"No clue what happened, but it's probably something to do with him." Grace points over to a larger cage. Five or so bowls sit overturned, something misshapen between them. As Grace illuminates it, I can tell it's a person. Or it was.

"Fuck, that's nasty." David opens the cage and stands over it. "Were they eating him?"

"As near as we can figure, yeah." Grace says. "Good way to get rid of a body."

"Looks like he didn't agree with them." David turns the figure over with his foot, and suddenly everything that was strange and warped about the body makes sense.

"You didn't identify him?" I ask Grace.

"Not really." she says. "I mean, most of the face is-"

I step into the cage, and set my foot against the body's arm, measuring. "This is Giant 1," I say. "Look at the arm length and the crooked back."

"No way." Grace steps forward outside the cage.

"She's right." David kneels over him, patting what's left of his bagger uniform. His arms run over the neck, and tap the dark stains underneath. "His throat's cut, but-"

"But-" Grace says "-he's been down here for days. Maybe more than a week, which means-"

"Whoever we saw by the bacteria tanks wasn't Giant 1," I say. "And if he's been dead for more than a week, whoever replaced him's been overseeing training-"

"Yeah, okay-" David interrupts me "-who's that?"

"And when we saw him take some bacteria," Grace says as she turns to me, "he practically winked at us!"

"He did." The memory's faded behind a haze of adrenaline and borderline panic, but I know he made eye contact. He saw us. Now I know why he didn't risk raising the alarm. He was getting ready to make a getaway with the bacteria. Our mutiny might even have blown his cover. "And knowing what we know about the bacteria, he might already have it somewhere he can replicate it."

"Wait." Grace shines her flashlight in my face. "What do we know about the bacteria?"

"Yeah, spill it," David says. "What did Islet say?"

I glance around to each of them, and the students with flashlights, still lingering on the mangled body.

"Not here," I tell them. "Make sure everything's in order and meet in my office."

❄

On my way up, I can see the sky turning blue over the shoulders of students piling ammo and weapons. I have to resist the temptation to check on the bomb, and think over the facts. There's really only one conclusion I can make from these disconnected facts, and it's not the sort of idea I should assume. I'll discuss it with them. If I'm lucky, they'll be able to prove me wrong.

The chair's still stiff and quiet. It might be a while until

Grace and David are ready, so, as quietly as I can, I pick up and replace everything I'd thrown on the floor.

The gray phone sits, watching me as I do it. The only thing I hadn't thrown to the ground.

"Ready for us?" Grace taps on the door as she pushes it open.

"I'm ready," I say, so David enters with Grace.

"Why do I get the feeling I'm not going to like this?" David asks. Grace pulls a chair from the edge of the room and sits in it.

"Are you going to pace again?" she asks.

"Absolutely," I say. "I've just learned one very important fact, and Grace's discovery of Giant 1's body heavily suggests something I've suspected for a while now."

"Okay," Grace says. "Let's start with what you know." She glances at David. "The bacteria, right?"

"The bacteria," I nod. "Islet worked out what it does, I started him working on countermeasures but-"

"Hold up-" Grace raises her hand. "What does it do?"

"It's an undetectable infection," I tell her. "When it reaches the brain it attaches to neurons and releases harmless radiation, which is then detected by specialized equipment, and interpreted by a computer program." Grace nods. David stares straight ahead. "It seems like G's developed a mass surveillance tool based on his unique sixth sense."

"Still not convinced he wasn't making that up," David says. "People can't read minds."

"Maybe not." Grace looks down at her feet. "But it explains everything he's done. He's a spy. He wants to know everything." She laughs. "And people call me nosy!"

"What's next?" David says. "The thing that's got you worked up?"

"The body," I say, and they both nod again. "It explains

the secrecy of what should be a government agency, the KU Giant unit, even the idea of a fake military academy, and a nuclear bomb to wipe out the evidence."

"AKA us," David says.

"So?" Grace asks. "Does this go all the way to the top, or what?"

"Interesting choice of words." I run my hand over the desk. "I started with the assumption that we were dealing with a massive government conspiracy, some kind of invisible wing of the military industrial complex, but it's not that simple."

"How is it not that simple?" David says. "Let's face it, they made us, we found paperwork, and it explains a lot, so-"

"Those papers were old," Grace says. "Really old."

"Exactly." I turn from the desk and face them. "If they made us, why kill us off? It bothered me every time I saw the baggers execute someone."

"So maybe they didn't?" Grace asks.

"No, they did." I rub the particles of dust from the desk between my thumb and forefinger. "But we have to be more specific when we say "they". What we mean is the Beagle Commission, but they've changed since then."

"They changed their minds?" David folds his arms.

"I don't think so," I say. "I think we're in the middle of a civil war between two of the Commission's factions."

"What?" Grace asks.

"Remember Islet's office? When he told us about when things changed at the base that used to be here?" Grace nods. "Two years ago," I say. "That's when it must've happened."

"This is getting too complicated for me," David says.

"It's not as complex as it sounds," I tell them. "First, they made us, for whatever reason, I still don't have the whole picture, and they supervised our adoptions." The words remind me of Cooper. He never seemed that paranoid, just safe. "Obviously they watch us, but at some point there's a split, and G leads a rebellion. He gets away with plenty of money, men and connections, enough to get what he wants, but not enough to fight off the loyalists. So he builds a fake military academy and gives all the KIA scholarships so we'll come, but in reality-"

"We're human shields," Grace says. "Or hostages, or something."

"He uses us to camouflage his assembly of a relic from the sixties, something no one would expect him to use," I tell them. "Launches while the loyalists are still working out where we are, and how to extract us safely, and then wipes us out afterwards as a slap in the face."

"Guess we must have been expensive," David says.

"Yeah." Grace nods her head. "They must have been on the same team once because Alanza-"

"G's own personal clone," I say as I watch them take it in. "The rest of the Commission didn't do what G expected them to, though." I pull out the photograph of KU Giant, squatting triumphantly in the jungle. "They sent someone to infiltrate his scheme by impersonating one of the few people he actually trusts."

"The person disguised as Giant 1," David says. "He left with G."

"Right." Grace nods again. "And a sample of this mind-reading bacteria. He probably stole info on how all the other bits work, too. Is that all they wanted?"

"If the Commission's loyalists have a plan to stop G, I haven't seen any evidence of it," I tell them. "G misread them. They don't care that we're here. It's still up to us."

"But even if we do stop him," David says, "there's these other fuckers who think they own us."

"Exactly." I pace around the desk. "Even if we win here, we can't go home, or if we can, it won't be like it was before."

Both of them go quiet. I don't blame them. "Somehow," I continue, "we'll have to break the idea to the rest of the students."

"You want to take down this whole thing, don't you?" Grace asks. "Some of us have families we like, you know."

"I don't." David raises his hand. "Plus." He turns to Grace. "No one says you can't talk to them."

"You're right." Both of them turn back to me. "I do want to destroy the Commission. Expose them."

"Yeah." Grace rubs her hands together. "But telling all the students they can't go back to their families, for a lot of them that's the only thing that's kept them going. Couldn't we, I dunno-" She runs her hands through her tangled hair. "-work something out with the Commission? I mean, if they don't like G they can't be that bad. And they've never directly tried to kill us."

"I won't rule it out," I tell them. "They could all be idealistic philanthropists, but what kind of person sends a spy to murder and steal, and puts us in danger to cover for them?"

"Right." Grace nods. "They have the bacteria."

"And," David says, "they don't want anyone to know they have it."

"True, but it's more than that." I turn the chair under my hand, and it swivels slowly in random directions. "They think they own us. I don't know about you, but I'm not property. I'm not an object."

Grace opens her mouth to speak, but the second she does, the phone on the desk rings.

For a moment, all we can do is stare at it.

It rings again, so I pick it up.

"Hello?"

"Hildegard. I might've known you'd take to my office." The lip licking is unmistakable.

"Is there something I can help you with, G?" I aim my stare at David and Grace. They both sit up at attention. "I'm in the middle of a meeting." He laughs at me for a few seconds, and takes a short detour into a cough.

"That makes two of us," he says. "I'm just calling to makes sure you understand our last conflict was just a rehearsal. My full force will be something-"

"Bullshit." I spit down the phone. "How many men do you really have to spare? One less Giant, that's for sure." David silently pumps his fist. Grace holds out a thumbs up.

"You killed Four?" G asks, the frenetic rhythm gone from his voice.

"I don't see why I should tell you," I say. "Not unless you're willing to make a deal with us." The words don't feel right, but I'm not speaking for myself anymore.

"A deal? You want to negotiate?" he asks. I must be right about something. If he had enough men to be certain he could take the Mobile Silo and the bacteria from us, he would've hung up by now. "All right," G says. "Tell me your terms."

To be honest, I haven't thought of any.

"Amnesty," I say. "Agreement to let any student who wants to go home, for you and the rest of the Beagle Commission to leave them alone."

"Done," G says. "Next?" I shouldn't have lead with that. I won't get it, but at least Grace and David heard me say it. That might help morale later.

"Disarm and dismantle the Mobile Silo," I tell him. "Kill all the bacteria."

"You know I would never agree to that," G says. "What are you planning? Don't tell me," he chuckles. "You have an audience."

"I don't see what difference that makes," I say, and he laughs at me again.

"I understand, you have to make them think you're all on the same side," he says. "But inside, you're spoiling for a fight. It's in your blood. You enjoy it all, don't you? You weren't alive before I brought you here."

"Sounds like you're sticking to your usual nonsense," I tell him. I have to say something to keep him talking.

I could mention the imposter that's almost certainly in his ranks, but it might be more of an advantage not to tip him off. The spy could disrupt his operation, or even assassinate him.

"You think if you take me alive I'll tell you what happened to Cooper?" My hand goes limp for a moment, and I have to clench my fist as hard as I can to prevent myself from dropping the phone. "Yes," he hisses, "obviously the time for backstage dealings is ended, so let me be completely transparent with you. If you keep getting in my way, you'll never find him. Your only option is total submission. Turn over the Mobile Silo and what remains of the bacteria undamaged. These are my terms. Then, and only then, will I tell you what you want to know."

I put the phone down.

"What did he say?" Grace asks, jumping to her feet.

"He's on his way," I tell them. "Probably with every man and gun he has left. He was willing to negotiate, so he must be desperate."

"So what?" she says. "Time to get ready?"

"Finally." David grins. "Let's get this over with."

"Go and brief everyone," I tell them, and tap my walkie-talkie. "Keep me appraised of any defensive measure you come up with. We're going to need everything we've got."

"Wait." Grace hesitates on her way through the door. "Even if we get everything we want, we beat all the baggers and Giants and Alanza and we somehow convince G to tell us everything, what then?" I push the door wide open.

"Don't worry," I tell her. "I've been working on it."

Short amber rays are filtering through the concrete and broken glass as we step down the stairs. Golf Company are resting, but the rest of the students stir.

The air's warm. It's not dawn yet, but I can see the glow of the sun over the edge of the forest.

"I'll go with Golf and check our armory," David says. "And we'll draw up an inventory."

"Good." I nod at him. "Grace, track down Islet and work with him to make sure as many kids as possible are awake and able."

"Understood!" She salutes and runs off.

Now comes the hardest part.

It's one of the reasons you're here with me. The waiting.

I'm not going back to the office. Not when the phone could ring again, so I wind my way out to the front.

One of the lecture halls has been battered in by one of the bagger's APCs.

Must've happened sometime last night.

There's no door anymore, just a big hole that leads out to the broken glass of the academy's mouth.

I was wondering if I'd have to wake anyone, but most are already upright and mobile. Some even run their hands over wounds or weapons. Preparing. Tying bandages as tight as they can, counting rounds, whispering to each other.

They don't need any help from me. Not yet, anyway.

I walk through the broken face of the school into the scorched snow and stand by the toppled statue. There's equipment out here, among the fallen baggers, so I scan the drifts, staying well clear of the still-hissing diving suit.

My route's almost a circuit, around the plinth, down the

slope, where the helicopter swept the snow away, and back up again.

I'm almost tempted to check on the old camp when my toe catches something hard in the snow. A pair of upturned binoculars, still reflecting what's left of the starlight.

I wipe the snow off them and look through. They're still functional, but nothing special.

The cold's already getting to me, so I start back towards the academy, but stop by the statue. From this direction, he's facing me. His legs are snapped off just below the knee, but other than that he sits untouched, angled into the snow.

I remember looking it over on my first day, but not really taking it in.

"X."

He's not all that tall. His posture's proud, but not triumphant. His outstretched hand is holding a book. Not up in the air, just close enough to read. Come to think of it, now I can see better, those might be reading glasses around his neck.

"Hildegard?" My walkie-talkie buzzes.

"Speaking." I raise it to my mouth.

"Me and David think we've got something," Grace says. "Meet us in the busted lecture hall?"

"On my way."

The walk back's nothing special. The academy's awake now.

They know what's coming, they don't have to be told.

"There you are." Grace points as I kick past some of the rubble that leads into the former amphitheater. "What were you out in the snow for?" There's a crowd with her, and another around David.

"You've found a following," I say as I climb the steps towards her.

"Yep." Grace nods. "We've been talking defense, and

along with David," she glances towards him, "we're actually feeling pretty confident."

"Good." Grace's crowd is diverse for the most part, but women and rifles are heavily represented. "I assume there's a focus on sharpshooting."

"Boy is there," Grace says, and some of the girls behind her laugh and raise their rifles. "Yeah, I knew a few of them from my food-smuggling days, I got together with them, they called their friends-"

"What's your plan?" I ask her.

"Well," she says, "the Bitches and I were eyeing the-"

"Excuse me." My hand comes up. "The what?"

"Oh." Grace turns back to her friends. "That's our secret unit codename. The Night Bitches. We figured it wasn't fair, since the Giants get a cool codename and we don't it would level the-"

My first instinct is to tell her to conduct herself like a sensible adult. But a sensible adult would probably have given up by this point. They're clearly enjoying it, too. Maybe I should mandate codenames if they're this good for morale.

"Your plan?" I remind her.

"Right, we were exploring the upper floors." Grace points straight upwards. "There's lots of little holes up there where the glass fixtures and beams are open to the sky, like they didn't even bother finishing the roof, so we thought we'd all pile in there."

"Sounds practical," I tell her. "Just make sure you have a way to retreat quickly under the school. If we're overrun up here, we can hold out longer down there." Grace nods at me, and the rest of the Night Bitches do the same. "And what about you?" I turn to David. He's fidgeting.

"Look what I found." David holds out a squat, heavy gun with an enormous round magazine. A grenade launcher. "Me and the Golfs went on a scavenger hunt, and we turned up a lot of shit like this in the bagger barracks. They kept all the good stuff underground." Students behind him lift sacks of grenades, a missile launcher, and crates of what look like rocket-propelled grenades.

"Fine." His crowd's restless. They should be exhausted. I don't think I've seen a single one of them sleep. "Do you actually have a plan to use them?"

"Yeah, all right, get this." He holds his hand out in front of him, as if he's trying to mime a globe. "According to the guys," he says and points back at the Golf Company students with him, "their camp was right by an old base, nothing huge, basically just a flak cannon and some fences. We thought it was useless, until-" He points again, and one of the students holds up a chain of shells the size of a forearm. "-we found some ammo for it!" They all cheer. "So while Grace picks them off, we'll man the gun, and shoot them down while they try to land, and blow them up if they try to get close." Another cheer. Hopefully, their enthusiasm will be infectious.

"That sounds good." Morale is good, but I don't want to encourage them too much.

I'm sure I don't have to remind you of David's history of recklessness. "But don't die on that gun. Like I said earlier, if you're overwhelmed, head for the school, and we'll keep the doors open as long as we can." David nods, but someone behind him shouts.

"Fuckateers don't run!" David's head snaps around to look back into the crowd.

"I'm going to ignore the lack of discipline on display here," I say. "And assume-"

"Uh," David looks back to me, "the boys heard Grace had a codename, so they decided we should have one too."

"And?" I ask.

"We're the Four Fuckateers," he says. "It was a group decision."

"Only four?" If I keep him on the hook longer, maybe he'll think twice about this sort of thing in future. If there is one.

"Yeah." He nods. "Psychological warfare." David taps his temple.

At the base of the amphitheater, the still-injured students are crowding around Dr. Islet and what's left of his staff.

"Get into position now," I tell both of them. "Just make sure your communications are working." Both of them nod, stand, and begin to file out. We're past the point where my reassurances would make any difference. They've found their own ways of coping.

"Islet," I say as I step down towards him.

"Yes!" He snaps upward from examining a bandaged leg.

"It's not long now," I tell him. "I want you and your staff to take charge of anyone injured." Islet nods at me. "Set boundaries for a hospice, and equip some volunteers with basic knowledge and supplies to act as medics if you can." He nods again. "And get ready to move underground."

"You don't think we'll hold them off?" he asks.

Obviously I can't say that.

"We don't want to get caught by something unexpected." I say. "G's unpredictable. We have to be ready to adapt." He nods. If anyone could use a morale boost, it's the doctor, but coming up with some sort of exciting name for him is beyond me.

Watching the last of David's and Grace's groups leave through the broken wall, I know I should've defined more of a role for myself. As it is, I'm almost dead weight, so I wander back towards the office with its fake ferns and imitation hotel carpets. There are windows here, wide enough for me to watch the snowfield through my binoculars.

"Test."

"Test!"

"I'm receiving you."

The black oblong buzzes a few more times. Messages, taunts.

As I watch the dawn break through my binoculars, I'm starting to realize what makes G a threat. I still don't know how credible his claim of mind-reading is, but I'm starting to realize he had a better read on me than I thought.

What he said about Cooper's sticking in my mind. Even if I take him, he won't tell me.

If I fight and win, I'll never get what I came here for in the first place.

Don't get the wrong idea, I'm not even considering giving up. Somehow, I don't think that was what he had in mind anyway.

He just wants the idea of giving up to weigh me down.

I might still find out. Assuming about half of the students stick with me after this is all over, and we take the fight to the Beagle Commission and expose them. He'll probably be dead by then.

Admitting he might die hurts, but it feels right. Like beating constipation.

Sorry. I couldn't think a better analogy. Like pulling out a bullet? Somehow, I still haven't actually been shot.

"We've got something." My radio cracks. "On a hunch," Grace says, "I sent two kids to the air traffic control tower, it's mostly trashed, but-"

"The radar." I hold it closer to my ear. "Good thinking. They got something."

"Yup. Big blobs, lots of them," she says.

"Aircraft. You getting this, David?" I ask.

"Yeah." I can hear some distant cheering behind him. "Ready to roll, just say the word."

"All ready up here, too." Grace adds.

There are no students up here in the corridor. I think I'm glad. If they all just stopped and stared I wouldn't know what to do.

As is, it's obvious.

I settle behind G's desk, and pull the public address microphone towards me.

"Attention, everyone." I do my best not to overthink my first words. "I've just received reports that we've detected the enemy's approach on radar. They can be no more than a few minutes off." That's not really true. I could ask, but I suspect the students Grace sent have no idea how to tell distance on a half-destroyed radar display. "Everyone here has made it this far alive, so you all have my total confidence." Mostly true. Islet has good intentions, but I don't trust him not to run off into the tundra first chance he gets. "But bear in mind that underestimating our former captors will almost certainly mean defeat. We do not have the numbers or resources for a drawn-out fight, so it's essential that when I give the signal, everyone retreat underneath the school, where we'll have much better defensive options." Completely true. If we're forced underground, our best options are probably to renegotiate.

Ideal scenario: we ransom away the warheads and the Mobile Silo for our freedom, sabotage them, and somehow blow the whole thing sky high after we leave. Probably not realistic.

"Hildegard," Grace fizzes down the walkie-talkie. "The scouts in the tower see them. One big cargo plane. Lots of attack helicopters. Lots of the big fat ones with two rotors, more little ones."

"Pull them out of the tower," I tell her. "David, open fire."

"Roger." Another round of cheers is followed by the first half of an earsplitting crack as the radio cuts him off.

"As of this moment," I tell the academy, "we have made contact, and are opening fire." I'm already on my feet, trying to see around the door and out the window. I can't leave this unfinished though. "We-" I still don't know what to tell them. How could I? There are crowds of them, all from different backgrounds. Some are probably cursing me right now.

"We're going to do our best," I say, "And the only chance we have at staying free today, is if you do too."

I pull myself away from the desk and down the corridor to the windows.

I don't need my binoculars, I can see the shells rising from the forest with my naked eyes.

Black, spinning wrecks tumble into the airfield, and I think one of them crushes a hangar. If David can block the runway with burning wrecks we might be in a very strong position.

It won't be safe up here much longer, so I take the steps as quickly as I can, listening to the rhythm of the gun outside firing into the dawn's gathering clouds.

"Islet!" I point at him the second I see him. To his credit, the heavy gunfire hasn't rendered him catatonic.

"What?" he asks, as if I'm accusing him of something.

"Do we have any pilots?" I ask him. "Someone who can fly a cargo plane?"

"No!" he shouts up the stairs towards me. "No one like that. I mean, I've flown private planes, but they're-"

"Good enough." I stride past, glance into the ruined lecture hall, down the corridor to the academy face, and into the dingy passages that hide the elevators. Everything's as ready as-

"We missed a few!" David shouts down the radio. "Too much smoke. They've got boots on the ground!"

"Stick to your plan," I tell him, raised voice echoing through the silent school.

"Oh, we will," he says. "I was afraid I wouldn't get to use this stuff, should be-"

Something cuts him off, and all that comes through the radio is a hiss.

I test the button a few times. Nothing.

"Grace, did you hear that?" I ask her.

"Yeah," she says, voice perfectly steady. "Some kind of explosion. I'm seeing some smoke from the forest. No gun. baggers are all over."

"Are they in your range?" I ask her, listening to the new silence.

"They're all over the forest," she says. "They're rappelling down from choppers, completely ignoring David's position." I can hear her take a deep breath. "Yeah, they're in range."

"They knew." I say, mostly to myself. "Fire at will, Grace." The hall's quiet, and the battle's visible now through the gaping hole in the wall.

I can almost make out the baggers, sprinting through the snow like stick figures, diving to the ground in time with the gunfire from above.

"Boss?"

"David?" I snatch the radio back up to my ear. "Are you-" It might have been better to stay in G's office. "-what's your status?"

"Not-" He gasps in what sounds like pain. "-not great."

"What happened?" My eyes are fixed on the smoke plume now, and the two bloated helicopters that swoop over it.

Without that gun they could land on our doorstep.

"We were reloading," David says. "It was one of the rounds. Somebody fucked with it, I didn't-" Another gasp "-didn't see it in time."

"All right." There's no question Alanza is responsible. She would've known about the gun and how powerful it would be in repelling attackers. She shared what she did with G, and he briefed his soldiers accordingly. "Can you move?"

"Yeah," David says. "Not very fast."

"Your men?" I ask.

"We're still here," he says. "Most of us, anyway."

"Okay, here's the situation." I watch one of the black figures fall in the snow. They aren't falling fast enough. "The gun was sabotaged by Alanza, the baggers expected you to all die in the explosion, so they've already written you off."

"That-" he coughs, "-that could be a good thing."

"It is," I tell him, and toggle the channel on my radio. "Grace, focus your fire around David's position. Give him as much space as you can."

"Got it," she answers.

"David." The channel changes back. "Blast your way through them and get back in here."

"We're retreating already?" he asks. "C'mon, I've still got most of my body parts left."

"Grace is going to cover you." It's probably best to ignore jokes about his injuries. I have no way of knowing how badly hurt he really is. "But you can put a big hole in their line on your way here."

"All right, all right." There's a crack of gunfire. "On my way." It takes a few second for me to realize it wasn't over David's radio. There's a small hole in the concrete on the left side of the gaping hole, and Islet shoves past me. A student holds her hand to her chest as her palm turns red.

"You." I point towards a student on a stretcher, cradling a

weapon. "Give me your gun." He hands it up to me without a word, and I test the weight as I step up to the opening.

My arm still aches where David broke it, and I've never handled something this size.

Everyone else is doing it. How hard can it be? Turning it over, the clip's half empty. Still better than nothing.

"Taking them on all by yourself?" Islet asks as he pulls the injured student away from the gunfire.

"I don't know." I raise the rifle I've been carrying, brace it against my shoulder, and stare down the sight.

I've never really considered the quality of my eyesight before. It's never been important before now. It must be quite good, because the second I focus, the stick figures widen into the black masked uniforms I'm so familiar with. "Is anyone going to come up here to help me?"

The last part is louder, obviously.

I'm not going to fire yet. The forest is still quiet, and most baggers are crawling forwards on their stomachs. My hand tests the wall to my right, the stability of the concrete step underneath, and I crouch, trying to keep my weapon as level as possible.

Around me armed and injured students rush into every open space.

A helicopter over the forest explodes, and all at once the trees are alive with flashes and howls as the baggers on their stomach are tossed into the air.

It's still too far to make out identities, but I can see figures rush from the trees, sprinting towards us.

"Don't fire until I do." I keep my eyes fastened to the sight of my gun. "Your priority is to clear a path for David." None of them answer. Hopefully that means that we have a perfect understanding, rather than them all being paralyzed with fear.

Another helicopter soars overhead, and a rocket leaps from the group and smashes into the underside. A black wreck falls into the snow. It's not far now.

David's almost at the statue, but the line of baggers swells again. Probably from landing further back. G's cargo plane might even have touched down by now.

Bullets cut into David's path, and dark helicopters wheel overhead, hovering above him as he and his men dive between the rocks and wrecks in the snow. There's nothing I can do about those, but baggers are closing in around him.

I draw in a breath, concentrate, focus on a target, and release a shot.

There was nothing different about him. He falls into the snow silently.

The crowd around me explodes as gunfire tears past my ear into the snowfield.

David and his men weave through it all, under the attack helicopters and through the exploding snowdrifts as they sprint towards us.

He bursts through the gap, coated in equal parts blood, dirt and snow, and Islet rushes towards him.

"Him," David pants, "he needs you." He points back into the line as half of them collapse, carrying a blood-soaked student between three of them. Islet strides over and begins to examine him as I step down from the hole.

"You intact?" I ask David.

"Mostly." He holds a dark red dyed hand. "Lost my pinky, but who needs it, right?"

"You should have Islet look at it." I tell him. "It could get infect-"

"It's fine." He says, fastening a bandage around his hand with his teeth. "We've got bigger problems, right?"

"True." I can't help but nod. "Could you tell anything

about their equipment?" Gunfire again. Sounds like Grace is working overtime. "Their tactics?"

"Nope." David shakes his head. "Too busy dodging the helicopters. Check this out." He holds out a deck of cards, bound by elastic and burnt almost all the way through the middle. "Magic saved my life."

"All right." I turn my head back to the opening and watch the thickening line of baggers closing in. Grace just doesn't have enough guns. "You still have some weapons left."

"Should do." David nods. "Not many but-"

"Pass them out!" I call over the sounds of battle. "RPGs'll be a liability underground, so we might as well use them up now." David's group passes their weapons around, and the first one shrieks through the opening to blast a crater in the snow.

"Is that it, then?" David asks. "We're giving up on the surface?"

"Without anti-aircraft ability we don't have a choice." I grab the radio and pull it to my ear. "Grace. We're getting ready to evacuate underground."

"Understood," she says. Another shot echoes through the roof overhead.

"You and I are going to be the last ones in. Start making your way down to us now."

Grace says nothing, but she clicks her button once.

"So I'm an invalid now?" David asks.

"You're with me, business as usual." I tell him, and hand over the rifle I'd been using. "Islet, start moving the injured." He nods, and his staff of volunteers begin to carry the immobile in a line from the lecture hall. "Everyone else!" I shout "We're covering Islet! We meet Grace at the elevators. Anyone who doesn't think they can fight any more go first. The escorts stay up here for as long as we can."

"Here," David says. "We'll trade." He passes me a handgun. "Not much ammo left, but-"

"It's fine," I say. "Let's go!"

The students by the hole let one last rocket fly and then pour down towards me as Islet's train of injured and volunteer medics march out into the halls.

The gunfire stops, and once I go further inside the wailing wind quiets down. All I can hear is the murmur of the students. I'm almost leading a school trip.

It doesn't last.

First comes the sound of glass breaking, and then more gunshots. I can see their silhouettes down the hall, breaking down the barricades, fighting the wind and rubble to aim for us.

It's all the encouragement they need, Islet's parade of injured and willing surge down into the darkness. I try to point them in the right direction as quickly as I can, gun-arm going stiff as I push limping bodies and stretchers along.

Turning corner after corner, the shadow of the baggers are never gone for long, and once we reach an elevator, there's nowhere left for us to go.

The doors chime as they open, and Islet's the first inside, bodies choking the machine as it shuts. This might be the first elevator we ever used, hard to tell.

"This is going to take, what?" David scans the group. "Five trips? Eight?"

"That's really not important right now." What's left of the students who fought with me in the lecture hall mingle with David's bloodied Golf Company converts. "All right!" I shout to them. "If I have to tell you what to do by now, you're not going to make it!"

Honestly, my mind is blank.

Injury, physical exhaustion and lack of sleep are

catching up with me. What happens next is not what I expect. They fan out, check their weapons, find cover. But they laugh.

Some of them laugh a lot. It echoes down the halls, where the baggers will hear it.

Before I can think anymore about it, a storm of plaster explodes down the hallways towards me, and I crouch lower as David leans over me to fire.

This is the first time I've really noticed, but all these gunshots are starting to make my ears really hurt.

The elevator returns, and I listen to the frightened shouts as the injured pour in.

Would they have been better off if I'd stayed in my doll-house town? If I'd just never come here?

Knowing what I know now, G wouldn't have left me there.

He might have come looking for me himself, although I'm still not certain why.

For the purposes of our hypothetical, we have to ignore that fact. If I'd somehow managed to avoid coming to Truman, how would things be different?

It doesn't feel fair to all these students to say that G would have succeeded. Just because I'm here doesn't make them any less brave or strong.

A shot parts the wooden beam inches from my nose.

I can't afford to navel gaze for much longer, so I stretch my arms as far as they'll go, fire a few shots around the corner, and pull back.

I can't see what happens. Not like before. It's much easier to avoid thinking about the lives the people I've shot used to have.

The elevator chimes again. Another rush of frightened feet.

"Grace is supposed to be here, right?" David shouts from above me.

"In theory," I say.

Naturally, he doesn't reply. No one wants to consider the idea that Grace is gone. She probably isn't. In fact, if I hadn't come here, Grace probably would've unraveled the whole thing herself. She definitely would've had more fun.

Did the students only follow me because she did?

It's not a productive question, especially since it's impossible to answer.

I could ask the same thing about David. There was nothing superficial to convince them, and I definitely didn't persuade them. They chose to follow me.

This can't end the way G wants it to. I can't think of how to stop him, just clinging to my ransom ploy won't work.

I still don't know, but I owe it to them all to find a way.

One of the shadows in the corridor falls, and a hail of shots shatter wood and plaster. For a moment, the corridor is quiet, and Grace sprints down at the head of a column.

"Just in time," she pants. "Right?"

David pulls her in, and her group flows into place, filling the holes left in our line.

"Are we winning?" Grace asks. The elevator calls again, and the crowd thins as more pile in.

"I think we are, actually." I say, looking over my shoulder at the huddled students.

I stop the second I look back to them. David pulls Grace towards him, leaning down as far as he can. Her arms circle around his neck as his hand slides down her back.

They kiss. Quickly, gently.

"Two more trips in the elevator." I tell them, turning back to the shuffling crowd. "Maybe three."

"What?" David asks, almost dropping her. "You jealous?"

"Great," Grace says, still red-faced. "Sorry about that," she pants. "Then what?"

"In theory," I tell her, "we'll be underground in a powerful defensive position with access to all the stockpiled weapons, all the baggers rations, and obviously the Mobile Silo. We outlast them until G gets desperate enough to deal."

"Simple enough." Grace replies to the sound of rushing boots and swaying equipment. "We do have a plan for stopping them from following us, right?"

"The hangar," I tell her, as more baggers fall into cover down the corridor. "We can block the main door, rely on the maintenance entrance, and still keep access to all our supplies."

"Okay, I get it," Grace says. "They'll have to cut through what's probably a lot of inches of steel, or go around the other way and come in over the lake and into the other end of the hangar-"

"Where we'll have an easy time shooting down at them." I finish for her as a fresh gunshot breaks the corridor's quiet.

"Are we shooting back?" David asks, "or what?" The elevator opens again and this time there's plenty of free space.

"This is the hard part," I say. "It can't fit us all at once."

"I'm not going." David doesn't move an inch.

"Me neither," Grace says. The remnants of both their groups press themselves into the elevator, supporting the last of Islet's patients as the door closes behind them.

A few moments of silence follow. A lot of shuffling, no shots.

"They waiting for something?" David whispers.

"Dunno," Grace say back. "Not complaining."

Things haven't fallen apart yet. My plan's not as cohesive as I made it seem, and it's possible that the students who haven't heard it or didn't understand have chosen to do something else that'll get them killed. There could be other problems, too.

As I listen for the sound of the elevator returning through the wall, I'm reminded.

Heavy footfalls, and the panicked shuffling of smaller bodies. The subtle screeching, like a broken modem that's fallen down a mountain chasm.

A sudden cramp in my stomach. It's not enough to distract me anymore.

The elevator behind us opens for the last time.

"Go!" I point, and Grace, David, the others who stayed fill the small square space.

The doors close without a glimpse of him or the figure, but he has to be out there.

"That was one of the Giants, wasn't it?" Grace asks. "What did you call him? Two?" She turns to David.

"Doesn't matter what he's called," David says. "He's a problem."

"If he's here, I think we can safely assume-" The elevator doors open onto the narrow caverns of G's netherworld, "-the other Giants aren't far behind."

"Aren't there just two now?" Grace asks as we pick our way down the tunnels towards the sounds of students.

"Hopefully. The impostor's probably gone," I tell her. "It's just the big one, and the hunchback."

"Yeah." David nods. "We're not far from where we first met him."

The injured students have gathered in the caverns. I don't have time for a headcount, but the size of the crowd looks right.

"Do we know where we're going?" Islet asks, much louder than I'd like.

"This way." I point him into the tunnels that led us up out

of our escape from the hangar. It seems like a long time ago, but it can't have been more than a day.

Flashlights play over the cavern's ceiling, converging from different directions.

"Pick up the pace!" David hisses as he pushes Islet along.

The convoy isn't as slow I thought it would be, but I raise my weapon anyway as I stand at the rear, just in case the baggers above spot us and start taking potshots.

The caverns, dim corridors, and dingy passageways blur past.

If I miss something, anything, it could be fatal, but to be honest, a lot of my attention and energy goes towards staying upright.

Who knows, maybe a fresh gunfight would do me some good.

We make it to the bagger's quarters without firing a shot, students scooping up anything they think might be useful from the bagger's barracks as we go. The air turns heavy as we reach the red-lit hallways, ringing with the sounds of pursuit from above.

The huge hallway is obvious, and we rush into the hangar the way we'd left the day before.

"Find the maintenance entrance!" I shout as we pour out into the cold air of the Mobile Silo's lair. "Barricade it, seal it shut, make sure nobody can get through." David jumps down and takes charge while Grace scans the door controls.

Within seconds sirens are spinning as the enormous steel doors we'd just come through glide together. With a heavy yawn of stretching metal, they lock into place.

"Okay," Grace says. "For now at least, we're good."

"Find a way to block them if you can," I tell her. "Or turn them off, or something, we don't want G to use some sort of remote control to open them again."

Students spread out, finding places to lie or sit. Islet and assistants carry the stretchers to the web of scorch marks where most of the bacteria tanks used to stand.

"While everyone is making themselves at home," I say, too hoarse to really shout. "See if you can find the controls for the hangar doors. We don't want the cold coming in on us." I'm not sure if anyone actually hears me, and I'm too tired to check.

I sit by the steps as students stagger up and down, lean back, and rest my head against the wall.

With my eyes closed, the rhythm of the sounds is regular. Predictable. Footsteps. Growling machinery. Low talking.

"Found the hangar control!" someone shouts. Somebody else shouts back, and I can feel the enormous metal doors grind towards each others as they close against the snow and swelling sunlight.

Someone cheers, and it travels around the hangar for a few seconds.

I'm not going to discourage them with reality.

My body's not un-tensing. I've never found relaxing easy, but this is a problem.

I need rest if I'm going to figure a way out of this.

If I could just get some sleep, or even just some rest, I know our chances would improve.

❄

My head shoots up as I hear something against the door. Just a gentle impact. Not that I should be able to hear anything "gentle" through that much steel.

As soon as the thought appears I'm on my feet.

Everyone else goes about their business. Probably for the best if it turns out to be a false alarm. It's still quiet as I approach, but the moment I flatten my ear to the door I hear a mechanical sound. Grinding. Sawing.

It's muffled, but it's there.

My first instinct is to ignore them, although I don't know if that's a desire to preserve morale and keep the students rested, or just my personal exhaustion.

But G knows the school. He had it built, he wouldn't order his men to try and break the door unless he knew it was possible. That, or he's more desperate than I thought, and I really can't take the risk.

Above me, one of the silver rows of lights shakes. It flickers, and falls to the floor in a flash of sparks. It doesn't hit anyone, and everyone nearby jumps away, but it comes with a shower of dirt and chunks of concrete.

It makes clear what I should have known. There's no escaping from this.

"What happened?"

"Busted lamp, I guess."

"Boss?" David taps me on the shoulder.

"Get everybody who can stand armed," I tell him. "We need-" The sounds behind the door gets louder.

"Got it." He runs down into the rest of hangar, and most students answer with shouting and sprinting.

"This can't be happening!" My eyes are still fixed on the door, but I can hear Islet shouting among the injured. "I thought we were done!" He's coming closer. "You said we were done, that we could hold out here, that we-" Someone holds him back at the foot of the stairs. "-we can't hold them off again, we'll-" The more he talks, the more pairs of feet come to a stop.

I turn around, and his hands are on his knees, hyperventilating.

He's reached his limit, and in the past threatening him or

belittling him was only ever a band-aid. I don't think I really understand him well enough to make him feel better.

"Quit being a pussy, Islet!" Someone shouts at him. The doctor doesn't have a reply. He's gone quiet, but I can see the tears in his eyes, and the students who have stopped to watch him.

"Doctor." I walk down towards him as I hear another shock travel through the ceiling and into the floor. "No," I say. "This applies to everyone." They've stopped watching Islet and started watching me. I have no idea what I'm going to say, but I'm grateful for the adrenaline shot the situation's given me.

"What should we do?" someone asks. I've been staring into space too long.

"Islet's been doing his best," I say. I don't have time to focus on him, but for the second I did he looked surprised. Better than nothing. "And so have we. You've all given everything I've asked, and probably a lot more, and I can tell you now, for those of you thinking of giving up, G won't take you back."

Everyone's stopped. I'd rather they be preparing, but it's better than having them panic.

"I understand you all want this to stop. To go home if you can, and there's no shame in that, but-" This is the point where I need to pivot. Something surprising. "-I know it doesn't seem like it, but we're so close to winning this."

The reaction's about right. They're not going to cheer, not so soon after being robbed of such a badly needed rest. "G's desperate, panicking. And I know-" They need something more from me. Not David or Grace, I get the feeling I could say anything to them. "-not all of us see eye to eye. I haven't been much of a help to most of you, and I'm sorry for every time you've been hurt or left behind, but-"

I don't know if this is what they wanted to hear, but it almost feels good to thumb through the memories of running through forests and bleeding into the snow and know I didn't enjoy hurting the other students.

G was wrong about me.

The door behind me shakes. "Look, you remember what I said about going home?" Some of them nod. David definitely does. Weapons are being passed around. "I always-" The floor shakes again. "I never liked my home, or my foster family. Some of the things I did when I first came here were products of that, my actions, directly or indirectly, lead to a lot of you getting hurt, or even killed." More dust rains down on us from above, and students start to move around the hangar, hunting for cover.

It doesn't matter if they're hearing me or not anymore. I think this is just something I have to say. "It was just because I'd never really known-"

My ears sting for a second, and a wave of thunder smashes through my stomach as silence crashes down on me. Pieces of broken metal fly past my head, and I claw for something to pull me to my feet.

"I thought they were still cutting through?" David shouts. I can't see from here – .

"That's Giant 2, right?" Grace says. I can barely hear her over the rush of booted feet. My stomach's so twisted I want to scream, and, sprinting through the murk, I fire at anything tall and gray. They disappear before I know what I've done to them.

"Over here!" A line of muzzle flashes burst through the cloud, and I run towards David and Grace, crouched at the foot of the stairs, broken pieces of the massive metal door still spinning at their feet.

"David, you remember where you got that snowmobile?" I

ask him as I duck under a spray of bullets.

"Yeah," he says. "There are ten, maybe fifteen, I didn't count."

"Not enough for everyone," Grace adds.

"All right." The dust's settling, but not fast enough. I don't see Islet, or anyone else, in fact. I can hear Giant 2's footsteps up above, as slow as always. He's in no hurry, and the absence of shouted orders make it unlikely that G's here too. That means he's not certain he'll win, so even if it doesn't seem that way, it means there's still a chance.

"You look like you're thinking." David says. "Really hope you are."

"I have a fallback." I tell him. "But we'll have to split up."

"Mind running it by us first?" Grace asks. "You know-" Sparks spit past her ear. "-for old times sake."

"We can't save everyone," I tell them. "So we choose a number of students to escape towards the oilfield on David's snowmobiles, and hope G goes easy on the rest."

"What, just run away?" Grace spits as she raises her gun again.

"We need to destroy what's left of the bacteria." I turn to face David. "You've got the detonator?"

"Left it where I was sitting," he says.

"Now we know who's doing what," I tell them. "David, get the detonator, choose the most able students, and destroy as much of the bacteria as you can, including the warhead still loaded on the Silo." He nods again. "Grace, you're with me, we'll go through the maintenance entrance we barricaded and grab the bomb from the stockpile."

"Hold it!" She has to shout as the cloud that muffled the gunfire fades. "What bomb?" She squints at me. "You mean the one we passed by earlier? The nuclear one?"

"Obviously," I say as I scan the path to our new exit. The

scorched and twisted remains of the bacteria tanks won't give us much cover anymore, but there's no alternative.

We'll probably have to run and hope for the best.

"So you just decided not to mention it to me?" Grace asks as David rolls from cover, shouting orders.

"You were opposed to it," I tell her. "But it's essential. I thought that if everything went well we wouldn't-"

Grace pulls me around by the sleeve, forcing me to look her in the eye. "G won't back down to threats, you know he won't!" Grace shouts. "And there's no way, at least, I hope there's no way you would ever use it anyway!"

"Do you trust me?" I ask her.

"I wouldn't be here if I didn't," she sighs.

"Then let's go." I count the seconds and run as fast as I can, diving the last few feet between the empty hangar balcony and the twisted tanks at the perimeter.

Weaving through them, I find the barricade and start to peel it apart, sending barrels, tarps and empty weapons flying. Grace joins in a few seconds later, and the rough hatch is almost open. Another burst of sounds erupts behind us, followed by the ring of metal crashing into metal.

"Lucky we didn't get much of a chance to build it!" Grace shouts over the gunfire.

"There you are!" Islet crashes into cover next to us. "David sent me!" he pants.

"What for?" I ask as the stray pipe tumbles away.

"You ran through all that?" Grace says.

"He says you need biometrics to arm it," Islet wheezes at me. "And the bomb's no good as a threat without it and I should still be in the system, so-"

"All right." I pull open the hatch. "You first." And push him through.

The corridors beyond are virtually untouched. For whatever reason, the baggers haven't come this way.

With Giant 2 as their can-opener there's no reason for them to.

"Do you think-" Islet stumbles. "-think that David can hold them off for long enough?"

"That's up to us," I tell him. "Not David."

"Sure we know where we're going?" Grace says as we turn a corner.

"Just past here," I say. The red light and radiation warnings are unmistakable. "This is the ammunition stockpile I told David to stow it in."

"Did he leave any guards?" Grace asks. "Because if he did, where did they go?"

"We did at first." I push the doors open onto a long, shadow-filled room.

It's filled with emptied cargo containers, swaying wires and flickering lights. "He must have pulled them out to help defend the school."

The ammunition and weapons are piled high in the center, with a long silver cylinder leaning against the mess of barrels and belts.

"I really thought it would be bigger," Grace says.

"So what do we do?" Islet asks. "Just pick it up and carry it?"

"Right." I wind my hand around the handle. "One person on each end, we'll-"

My eye twitches as it catches the glint of something metal above us.

The second before it happens, I push Grace down as hard as I can. We both fall to the floor and wind our way around piles of crates. The bullet mark is obvious.

"I didn't see-" Grace whispers before I slash my hand across my throat at her.

"Unexpected." Someone smacks their hands together. "He said you'd be here. I didn't believe him." There's a series of metal bangs, like someone hopping awkwardly down slopes of hollow steel. "But that's why G's in charge, and I'm stuck babysitting."

I can hear Islet moaning in pain. Too quiet to be exaggerated, but from this angle I can't risk checking on him. The stretched shadow of Giant 1, or the person impersonating him, is just visible around the edge of the crate I'm using as cover.

"We know that's not him, right?" Grace whispers. "So-"

"Right now it doesn't make much difference," I tell her. "He's still a man with a gun. Probably trying to take this opportunity to get rid of us, just in case we give him away."

"So what do we do?" Grace asks.

"Top priority is our bargaining chip," I say while scanning my surroundings.

There are plenty of spaces between the unevenly stacked containers, and more than enough piles to get some height, so I point to one. "I'll keep him distracted if I can, you outflank him."

"What about Islet?" she asks. "We can't just leave him."

From where I'm crouching, I can just make out the end of Islet's leg as Giant 1 sets him into a sitting position against rough red metal. He's left a trail of blood, and his trousers have turned dark.

"We'll get him if we can." I say. "For now-"

"Got it." Grace disappears between two containers, while I crane my neck out as much as I dare. There's a single bootprint in Islet's blood, but beyond that, nothing.

This could be good. A chance to answer some question I'd thought I'd have to give up on.

But only if I can get him to give something away.

"There's something I've been curious about," I shout into the room as I check my weapon. "Your numbers, are they for seniority?" My ears strain for something that might give him away. The first thing I hear is Islet's whimpering, then the electrical hum of the lights, and awkward groans of metal. "Are they just to distinguish you from the others, or do they indicate in what order you were inducted?" There's no way he doesn't know what I'm trying to do, but I really can't think of a better way to do it.

Something moves up in the corner of the room, and I raise my gun as Grace flies into view, thrown against the side of another open container.

She doesn't look hurt, just winded, and the moment Giant 1 strides towards her I know I have an opening, so I sprint forward as fast as I can towards the piled ammunition in the middle of the room, firing off as many shots as I can.

I step over Islet, and try to carry the bomb one-handed. It's much too heavy, but I manage to drag it along the ground. I motion to Islet, and he crouches into an awkward limp.

Above me I hear the crash of warping metal as Grace crashes down towards us, so I drop the bomb and catch her.

"You okay?" A trickle of blood runs from her mouth, but her eyes are still moving and her breathing is regular.

"Fine," Grace says. "Just pissed he got the drop on me."

"I should kill you." Giant 1 stands above us on the edge of the closest crate, pistol raised.

"Do you think you can shoot us all?" I ask him. "Without any of us hitting you?"

"You're probably right," he shrugs. "I'm not much of a marksman anyway. Not that it matters." He glances down at his watch. "My men'll be here soon. They're all good shots. Trained them myself."

I know what he's saying isn't true, and he must know we

know that, so why stay in character?

"Are you allowed to kill us?" I ask him.

Grace wipes the blood from her face. He hops down from his container and draws a knife from a sheath below his shoulder.

"Maybe not." He advances on us. "I don't think my boss really said." I should probably be scared. It's tough when you're this tired.

"Before you do, then," I say, "tell me something." Grace is close enough that I can tap the back of her hand. I have no real way of signaling her, so hopefully she knows me well enough to understand the plans I make up on the spot.

"Why should I?" He's never stood this close before. There are many reasons beyond the obvious that make it uncomfortable, but the smell stands out. Old blood.

"I think you'll find it enlightening," I say. "You're a professional, right? Dedicated to self improvement."

"Of course," he replies. "I'm glad you understand."

"Wouldn't you like to know why you missed me in the hospital?"

Don't get the wrong idea. I'm not confused, or even testing him. There's no way that this Giant 1 is the same one that led the attempt to capture me. That man is the one we found half-eaten by dogs.

"An inexplicable blot on my record," he says. "Tell me what you did, and I might be persuaded to turn you over to G."

I have experience with liars. Not that I know or have known a lot of them, it's just something everybody does. Of course, I can't watch a person's face to tell if they're being truthful, but I like to think it's a skill I've succeeded in developing.

I know he's lying. It's a fact, but his reply is perfectly

paced.

Is it possible he really believes it?

"You mishandled something very simple," I say, and tap the open palm of Grace's hand. "Light levels."

"Light levels?" He leans in closer. I think I can hear approaching footsteps, too. Lots of them.

I can't risk even glancing over at Grace to guess if she's understood. "You didn't escape in the dark."

"At first I didn't think I'd escaped at all," I tell him. "I was certain you saw me."

"Maybe I did." He leans in even closer. "Did you ever think of that?" That would definitely confuse things, but there's no way. He's bluffing.

"What was I wearing?" I ask him. He takes a step back, and with my peripheral vision I glance at Grace.

"You really think I-" He takes another step back, and Grace raises her gun.

Giant 1's arms come up by instinct to snatch it away, but she steps backwards, aims past me, and hits the electrical box we'd run past near the entrance. The lights above us spark and die, and the second they do, Grace bowls into him.

I grab his other arm as she aims punches into his midsection, but it's like holding onto a tree branch, too narrow to really gain a purchase, so we struggle for a moment until a flash breaks through the darkness, and Giant 1 topples over, hissing with pain.

"Grab the bomb!" I shout as Grace and I fumble through the darkness for the single red point of light that shines through its metal shell.

We both grab one end, and try to pull Islet to his feet.

"You-" Giant 1 hisses, and Grace rushes over to kick his gun away into the shadows. "-you really-" I can't really see, but it sounds as if Grace kicks him in the jaw.

"Work with me, Islet," I say as I try to pull him upright.

"I really can't feel my leg," he says. "I can't walk. I can't." I can hear him gasping for air like a fish.

"Okay, ready to go." Grace hefts one end of the bomb in her hand, and tries to pass it to me, but with Islet on my back, I can barely grasp it.

The lights above flicker, disappear, and start to glow a deep red.

"Kind of slow for backup power," Grace says, "we-" Shouts echo down the corridor from outside.

"No more time," I tell her, "let's go." I shift Islet's weight on my back, and try to jog as quickly as I can.

"Wait." Grace stops at the edge of the room.

"What?"

"Where'd he go?" She points with her one free hand.

"Hopefully back to wherever he came from," I say. There's a trail of blood with a handprint in it. The room's empty.

"Freeze!" someone shouts down the corridor.

"What are we, cops?" another bagger shouts. "Just shoot them!"

We both break into a sprint, and I try not to think about how easy it would be for just one of them to get lucky and hit us. Any kind of wound would make us too slow to escape.

"How did you know?" Grace pants as we wind round corners and through doors. "The lights?"

"When they came to kidnap me the first time." A bullet pings from exposed concrete by my shoulder. "Giant 1, the real one, he saw me in the dark."

"So?" Grace stumbles as the difference between our heights cases the bomb to shake.

"So all the Giants have some sort of specialty," I say. "So this impostor would pretend he could see in the dark, but-"

Something scratches my shin. I almost fall, and as I steady myself, the bomb falls out of my hand. It pulls Grace's arm, and crashes to the floor.

She dives for it, but the baggers are advancing too quickly, and as I stumble under the gunfire, Islet falls to the ground.

The scene plays out silently in my head.

The bomb is supposed to be our only hope. Leverage. I know that I tried the same thing before, I thought G might be shaken, or that if I knew more about what was happening my resolve might be enough to convince him I'd do it, but watching the weapon roll towards the baggers, David is absolutely right.

Grace reaches for it, and I pull her back.

"Help me carry Islet!" I shout over the gunfire, and she hefts him over my shoulder.

"Are we giving up?" she asks as the baggers stop to retrieve the bomb. I could shoot at them, they've just stopped dead in the middle of the corridor, but that's all I've ever done. It won't actually change anything.

I can see more of them pouring down the corridor. Too many to fight.

"No." I brace against Islet's weight, and run as fast as I can, passing my gun to Grace so I can steady the doctor with two hands.

"Are we going to-" Grace asks again.

"We'll find somewhere safe," I tell her. "Make sure Islet's not dying, then we'll head back to David."

"And then what?" Grace pants "Fight them all off?" I'm starting to slow down. Can't feel my feet.

"I don't see an alternative."

The baggers don't chase us, although they probably have more than enough manpower.

"Help me get him down." Grace pulls Islet to the ground

and runs her flashlight over his leg wound.

"In my professional medical opinion," he says. "I'll probably be fine." He laughs. "Y'know, for maybe the next ten minutes."

"Can you walk?" I ask him, crouching down to meet his eyes. His knee shifts, and winces in pain.

"Unlikely, look-" He rests his head against the soot-stained wall we laid him on. "-if you're going to get away, there's no way you'll make it if you try to bring me."

"We're not going to leave you," Grace says. "Plus, you can ride a snowmobile with one leg, right?" He turns his head, sweat glowing in the dull red light.

Everybody's leaving it to me to make the hard decisions. It's probably my fault that they've started to depend on me.

If I'd taken the long view I would've delegated occasionally.

Obviously, I'm procrastinating, and there's no time for that, and it's not because I don't want to make this decision. I already have.

"I don't know about either of you," I say. "But I'm getting tired of settling. As of now, it's all or nothing." I grab Islet by his stained white coat and pull him to his feet. He hobbles in place, and we set off again. "Besides," I tell him, "I traded a nuclear weapon for you."

"It's just past here, right?" Grace points down the corridor.

"As long as no one's barricaded it again," I say.

"So," Islet wheezes as he picks his way along, arm around my shoulder, "is there anything I should know?"

"No," I tell him. "There is no plan."

"Oh, good." He pants as Grace lifts the hangar's maintenance entrance as quietly as she can.

"We might still be able to make something work," she says.

"Just because we don't really have a bomb, doesn't mean we can't threaten them with it," she whispers. "That's deterrence, right? As long as we keep you away from G."

"How are we going to do that?" I ask. "The baggers already have the bomb. There's no way they didn't report it."

"Yeah," Grace says, "I forgot about that, maybe-"

From what I can see through the hatch, the hangar seems quiet. There's something in the air, too, like ash or snow. There are still gunshots, but the only ones visible on this level are baggers, the massive shape of Giant 2, and what are probably the bare, clawed feet of the twisted-over Giant 3.

"Is that coughing?" Grace whispers to me. "Not too many shots, either, and look." She points into the hangar. "The tanks, sans charges." Baggers are rolling the round cylinders into a rough pyramid.

G stands by them, silently watching, as fire is exchanged over the balcony to the lower level, just feet from him. Every few seconds, he points without looking.

"I don't think that's all of them," I tell her.

"Not that it matters," Grace says.

"It might do," I say."If they don't have them all, it means David's probably still alive."

"Deterrence is outdated anyway," Islet sighs as he slides to the floor against the nearest wall.

"What?" Grace asks while I scan the hangar.

"What you were saying earlier," Islet replies. "It's still in fashion, sure, most people are still comfortable with the idea, but the alternative ideology is the reason you're both here in the first place."

More gunfire. A bagger hands G a gas mask, and he presses it to his face as he runs his hands over the bacteria.

"What's that supposed to mean?" Grace asks. There's no harm in letting them talk for now.

I need time to come up with something.

"This might all be over your head," Islet tells Grace, "but you know about the Cuban missile crisis?" She nods, and Islet goes on. "After that, there were a lot of people who had their faith in deterrence shaken, it was too close a call, they said. I remember, my dad was one of them." He sits further up the wall, trying to get comfortable. "I guess I can see where they were coming from. Anyway, maybe ten or fifteen years after, "super soldier theory" started to get really trendy. Superhero comics were just starting to really explode, so-"

"Yeah," Grace nods. "I remember my dad showing me some from, like, World War Two."

"There was a thesis that started the trend." Islet nods. "It's been a while since I read it, but I remember it saying that the idea of heroes and war were inextricably linked. It's when you need heroes most, I guess."

"How's that an alternative?" Grace asks, shuffling closer to me to get a better view into the hangar. She's probably just humoring him.

"The paper talks about this Finnish guy, a sniper who fought in a war against Russia in the thirties, or maybe forties. Most kills ever by one person. Basically, the idea was that-"

I can see some of the students now, it looks like some of them have climbed around the side of the Mobile Silo and are using its armor as cover, but every time one of them pops up to take a shot they either cover their mouths, or they start to choke.

"I think I get it," Grace says by my ear. "It wasn't deterrence they had an issue with, just the nuclear part. If you make people the deterrent-"

"Right," Islet says. "I'm pretty sure the idea of mythologized super soldiers is what led to-" He stops, searching for the right words. He must be feeling better.

"Us," Grace says.

"It wouldn't work," I say, watching G pace. "You can't beat a nuclear explosion in hand-to-hand combat."

"But people wouldn't hesitate," Grace says. "There'd be no mutually assured destruction, so-"

"The paper addresses all the issues I could think of," Islet says, "deploying in secret, using propaganda. It seemed right to me, like a logical counterpart. It asks the question of who's stronger, the weapon, or the solider that holds it."

"Does it seriously say that?" Grace asks. "Sounds like a pretty pretentious paper."

"I'm paraphrasing." Islet winces in pain as he shifts his leg.

"We exist," I tell them, "because someone wanted to prove it was the soldier." I turn around to look at him. "Is that right?"

"Don't ask me," he says, "it wasn't my idea."

"Do you have anything yet?" Grace asks as she taps me on the shoulder.

The truth is I don't. That doesn't usually stop me, but everything I can think of involves somehow bluffing the human lie-detector.

"Not yet," I tell her. "We can't reach David or anyone else from up here, we can't reach the bacteria without going through what looks like all the remaining baggers and both Giants, so-"

A black-clad solider jogs through the ruins of the door, fastening a mask around his face. He's giving some kind of report.

"Uh..." Grace squints at him.

"What are you doing?" I ask her.

"Trying to read his lips," she says. "The plastic's kind of thick. At least I can see G's." The quiet passes by. The stuff in the air, whatever it is, is muffling sound. I tear up a strip of bandage from one of my pouches, and try to work it into a simple mask.

"Anything?" I ask as the bagger joins his comrades.

"I think," Grace says, "he just reported us and Giant 1 as MIA. G says he wants to launch within the hour. Apparently they're running out of time."

"That could be good," I tell them both. "Do we know what sort of time limit they're under?"

"I might," Islet says. "I only sequenced the interaction with neurons. We weren't allowed to talk about our role in the project, but I remember someone complaining about life-span." He puts his head back, rubbing his temples "I think, it was something like a measure to prevent there being large wild populations, to stop them from mutating outside our control, yes that's right." He snaps his fingers louder than I would like. "The bacteria can't survive for long outside a human host, that's why growing so much of it was so difficult."

"We don't have to blow the tanks," I say. "We just have to puncture them."

"Not as easy as it sounds," Islet says. "They're tough and-"

I tune him out. As I watch, G slaps the shoulders and hisses in the ears of his men. I think I might be onto something. Would that make this my third wind? "Oh." I can't help saying it. It probably makes me sound like an idiot.

"What?" Grace asks. "What is it?"

"We have them exactly where we want them," I say. "They might as well be standing on a big red X."

"All right," she says "You're going to have to explain-"

"Islet," I ask. "This stuff in the air, it belongs to Giant 3, right?"

"I think so," he says "Airborne carnivorous spores. Nasty. He would't let me look at it."

"Grace," I ask her. "How far do you think you can get before they spot you?"

"Pretty far," she says. "Maybe all the way down to the lower level if I can make it to the stairs, Just be honest, am I some kind of bait?"

"Only a little bit," I tell her. "Run downstairs, and tell them to open up when they see the signal."

"Okay," she says. "What if I don't make it?"

"I'll go early," I tell her, holding up my last grenade.

"Don't breathe in," Islet says, pointing at the falling flakes inside the hangar. "You don't want that stuff in your lungs."

"Okay, yeah." Grace nods to herself as she makes a second mask from the scraps of bandage I hand her. "Run for your life, don't breathe in, got it. Easy."

My hands run over my gun, testing the weight and the sight. Probably around six shots left. More than enough.

"I'm not going to tell you when to go," I whisper to her. "It's your-"

"Actually, I think it would help," she says.

"All right." I push her on the back as she crouches down. "Go!"

Grace explodes from the hatch and weaves through the wrecked bacteria tanks. As I watch, I balance the grenade in my hand, scan the scene, and pull the pin.

Bullets fly first, then shouts. Grace rolls under them as she sprints around the far side, and G stands, watching, throwing soldiers into position with pushes, or wrenching them by the arm or the shoulder.

He's standing next to the tanks, so if my throw lands on them or near them, G will easily deflect it, and as much as I'd like to hook my grenade so it just blows his head off, I don't have the timing or the experience.

Grace is gone, or at least I don't see her, but the gunshots from around the Silo redouble. I have to assume she made it, so I emerge from the hatch, aim between the scorched empty tanks, and throw as hard as I can.

G doesn't notice at first. I can't make out what he's saying, but he's too busy screaming orders and pointing. The sharp metal note the grenade makes when it hits the tanks reaches his ears a second too late, I watch him turn, gasp, and stumble as the explosive spins, and falls behind the piled cylinders.

The metal bursts, and G's thrown to the floor by the exploding tanks. Giant 2 leans over him, reaching out to help him up, but G bats him off, running a hand over his blood-streaked face.

That's not what's important, though. My eyes are fixed on the polluted air.

For a second nothing changes, but then the flakes spin, stir, and plunge down towards the dirty puddle that leaks from the destroyed tanks.

That's supposed to be the signal.

The second the air clears I can see David and Grace emerge from either side of the Mobile Silo's cockpit, and the baggers, focused on the explosion, all shake and fall as the students explode from their hiding places.

I raise my weapon to fire at Giant 3, but someone in the chaos beats me to it, and the twisted hunchback throws out his arms as a fountain of brown blood flows down his chest.

Giant 2 pulls G away by the shoulder as baggers fall and students climb towards them, rushing by the rows of blasted tanks.

"We actually thought we were in trouble for a while there!" David shouts as he fires towards the retreating line of baggers. "What was that anyway?"

"Islet said the spores in the air were carnivorous!" I have to shout over the celebrating students. "Giant 3 knew about the bacteria in the tanks, and so did his parasites. They went in there looking for food, and-"

A roar of wind shatters what was left of the metal and glass as thunder rushes through the ground.

I push my way out of the hatch, weapon raised and ready.

"What do we do about this guy?" Grace shouts, unloading her weapon towards the retreating baggers that surround G and Giant 2. "He doesn't seem to care about bullets!"

"Doesn't matter!" I shout above the chaos. "He's not getting away this time!"

I bound up the stairs towards G as he retreats, back towards the shattered doorway, and students follow me in a wave of shouts and gunshots.

"You've got nowhere to go, fucker!" David roars as he unloads towards the baggers. "It's rematch time!" He charges forward, throws his gun to the ground, and wraps his arms around the Giant's waist, bowling him over with a tackle.

G screams over the gunfire, taking soldiers by the arm to show them their targets or pulling them along at the collar.

"You!" I point down the stairs at a group of students sweeping through the broken bacteria tanks. "Head through the hatch and come into the hangar from the other side!" They all nod, raise their weapons, and sprint through the opening.

I can't know if they were trying to avoid the fighting, but at least this way they'll cut off G's retreat.

"Is it me?" Grace gasps as she steps into the cover of the stairwell behind me. "Or is this working?"

"Don't jinx it," I tell her, listening to the furious crashes and pulsing thunder of David and Giant 2's wrestling match.

"Should we help him?" Grace asks, peering out of cover.

"No time," I say, thinking out loud. "We need to hold G down until the kids I sent can flank him." She raises her weapons and fires towards the line of baggers, hiding behind scraps of broken metal, glass, and twisted steel. "I know what you're thinking, Grace, but if anyone can take care of themselves, it's him."

"You're probably right." Grace grunts as the gun kicks against her as she fires. "So what do we do here, just keep going?" I flatten against the steel, feeling the cool metal through my hair, listening.

"He's limiting himself," I say, listening to G's shouts of directions and targets. "And he's not leaving them any room for initiative."

"So?" Grace asks. "How-"

"Two fronts," I say, pointing up the stairs. "Take some people, go around, take the route through the control room up to the entrance. I'll stay here, and we'll advance at the same time."

She nods, sprints across the gap in a moment not filled with gunfire, and speaks to the students beyond.

While I'm watching her, I listen to the fight. It's winding down now, and the next push is going to be the last.

If we time this right, G'll be running for his life right into my flanking force. David's still in action, too. I can't make out the words, but somewhere among the ruins of what used to be a control room, they're still struggling.

Grace'll probably get a good look as she runs past them.

"This doesn't end how you think it does!" G calls from across what's left of the room. My eyes are still fixed on the gray walls on the other side of the hangar. If he thinks he's going to lure me out of cover by shouting, he really hasn't been paying attention.

Another crash from inside the control room, almost certainly a sign that Grace's team is in position. My hand tightens around the gun in my hand.

"Go! Go!" Grace yells over the hum of silence, and muzzle flashes cut the darkness of the broken bulbs.

I spin around the sheet of metal I'm hidden behind, and the students around me do the same, picking our way across the dented floor as G stands silently behind his wall of baggers.

I hear David cry out in pain, and as I scan the narrow shadows behind Grace's advance, one of them stretches longer than the others.

Someone unloads into the back of Grace's charge, shattering glass with the sounds of thunder as student after student falls to the ground.

I keep up my fire, but there's not a lot I can do with just the students I have.

G kneels behind a broken piece of the hangar's door, where my shots can't reach him.

"Let's be honest," someone shouts. "What did you all think was going to happen?"

Grace stumbles through the debris, an enormous rifle thrust into the small of her back, Alanza's arm around her throat.

"Very nicely done." G claps as he steps out from behind his cover. 'You can come out now!" He shouts across the room. I slam back into cover, and try to steady my breathing.

The flanking force just changed from a necessity to a liability.

Is David still fighting? I can't hear him anymore.

I can't risk moving from this spot, but there's broken glass on the floor, enough to make some guesses. I see the reflections of Alanza, and other students, too, with red armbands tied around their arms. Re-tied.

Maybe if I'd taken a better account of everyone I might

have spotted the signs. They must be the ones that sabotaged David's anti-aircraft gun.

The students across the gap meet my eye, hands shaking.

"You really should come out," Alanza says. "Your friend-" She grunts. "-she's too good at trying to escape to keep her for long."

"You." G hisses. "Go up into the tunnels, round up the rest that's waiting in the wings. They might still have some use."

I'm drawing a blank, but I'm not going to give up. That probably goes without saying by now.

'Okay, all right." David grunts. It sounds like someone pushes him along, so he can't be counted on for a sudden reversal.

I put my gun on the floor, try to give the students still in cover a look that instills confidence, raise my hands, and walk into the open.

"Five stars," G says, stepping closer, brushing dust from his coat. "You've absolutely exceeded my expectations." Somewhere along the line he lost his hat, and there are bloodstains on his sleeve, but he doesn't look injured.

Behind him, Alanza holds Grace at gunpoint, along with five of her arm-band wearing cultists. "Someone find Islet," G says, "he needs to be made accountable."

David's being walked along in what looks like a headlock, Giant 2's massive arm fastened around his neck, shards of glass embedded in his face.

"So you waited until the last minute?" I ask Alanza. "And had your-" I'm not sure what to call them. Losing my cool here feels like a bad idea. "-loyalists just gun us down from behind." I can see the bodies from here, smeared with dust and lying in piles on the floor.

"Obviously," Alanza says, kicking Grace to the

ground,"you had the wrong idea about us." She hands her rifle off to one of her henchmen. "I think it's better this way, actually," she says. "Now I know who to trust, and who can be turned by one shallow speech."

Students are walked together, hands on heads, and stand in line at gunpoint.

Alanza's soldiers do the same, leading Grace and I back down the stairs.

"It wasn't my-" Islet gulps down a yelp of fear as G motions to have him dropped to his knees.

"I believe you," he says. "You haven't stopped me, but the only remaining missile is the one already loaded on the Silo. You came very close, and so I applaud you," he smirks. "Not literally, of course, and don't expect an encore."

Giant 2 pushes an exhausted, bloodstained David down the stairs towards us, staggering as he pushes through the bodies and wreckage.

"Why?" Islet sobs. "Why do all this? You might have made them, but they're just kids."

"This isn't about them," G says. "It never was, and in hindsight, using them as cover like this may have been a mistake."

"A mistake?" Alanza asks. "How were we a mistake? I've done everything-"

"Not you." G turns and puts his hands on her shoulders. "You've achieved everything I'd ever hoped you would in this crucible, but the rest-" He glances back at me for a second.

He's learned his lesson from last time. She responded badly when compared unfavorably to me, and somehow I get the impression that being placated by simple praise is the opposite of what he wanted in a daughter. "They've multiplied the scale of our schedule. With only one missile-" He sighs as the baggers below crawl across the Silo's hull, unfastening and opening. "We'll have to throw caution to the wind, aim for maximum exposure."

"Does she even know what they're for?" I take my hands off my head, and the baggers around me raise their guns. "The missiles?"

"What are you doing?" Grace hisses from the side of her mouth. I step forward and the baggers raise their weapons again to club me, but G holds them back with a gesture.

"We're past the point when you can drive a wedge between me and my leading lady," he says. "The tenacity is appreciated, but your role is now over." G steps down towards the nearest ladder, the one that leads to the ground floor of the hangar.

Below us, I can hear the mechanical roar of an engine bursting to life.

There are only two baggers to the row of disarmed students. The rest are probably out sweeping the academy for stragglers.

I might be able to grab a gun, but with Giant 2 and Alanza so close my chances probably aren't good.

"Is it time yet?" she calls down to G as the cockpit doors hiss open.

"Not yet!" he shouts up. "Soon!" Her grip tightens on the hand rails, and the doors close behind G with a metal growl.

Alanza doesn't mean the launch. She's been promised something.

I'm taking in everything. The sound of shifting weapons, the overpowering smell of oil and ozone. The feeling of electricity in the atmosphere. The frightened breaths that cloud the air. Something about the cold reminds me of one of my first days here, when Grace spotted lenses in the trees.

There was power in that. Seeing them didn't change anything, but knowing they were there made us stronger.

I've made speeches before, changed people's minds, right?

It's not much, but it's all I've got.

"You don't have to do this." I turn my head, looking down the line. "You're not like the others, and no one can force you to do anything. I can't count the times you could have killed us."

Giant 2 stands motionless, apart from the humming waves that shake up and down his body. The head, or what passes for one under a mess of scopes and tubes, tilts.

Barely visible, but good enough for me. "But you didn't. You're a soldier, I understand that, but you have to know that everything being done here is wrong." He doesn't move.

"Don't waste your time." Alanza walks down the line of captive students, lackeys in tow. "I've known him for years, and he's never said a word. I don't think he can."

"You don't even know why you're doing this, do you?" I ask her. "All for some abstract promise of truth, right? That's what he told me."

"I'm not a brat like you." Alanza tilts her nose into the air. "I don't need a reason to do as I'm told."

"I probably know more than you, then," I tell her. "I had Islet analyze the bacteria. I know what he's planning."

"If I needed to know," she says, "he would've told me." The shaking waves that run across Giant 2's body are softening. At least, I think that's what they're doing.

"And if your job was to guard a prison camp of children, would you do that without questioning it?" She stands as straight as she can, staring into my eyes. "What would he have to order you to do before you question him?"

"Anything," she says. "He could order me to do anything. That's loyalty. If you're trying to paint me as some sort of mindless-"

"No, you had your chance. This isn't about you."

"You really think-" I tune Alanza out, and watch the waves travel along Giant 2.

They widen and fizz until they cover his whole body. He bows his head, and with a rumble like the aftermath of thunder, he vanishes from sight.

There's a moment of stillness.

I aim a punch into Alanza's face as David leaps into action.

Obviously, she hits me back, and it hurts a lot, but pain's no longer a factor. By the time she's done it, Grace hits her in the midsection, and my students are wrestling with her armbanders, grappling with them on the floor or throwing them over the railings.

David, stolen gun in his hands, clubs Alanza in the face, and students explode across the hangar as baggers fall.

"This is too much fun for me," Grace smiles. "Let's wrap this up, okay?"

David topples an armband wearer, burying a fist in his gut. Alanza rolls across the floor and rights herself by the railing, scanning the floor for a weapon.

I pull a handgun from a fallen bagger, but before I can aim it the whole hangar shakes.

I drop to my knees for balance as I raise my arms against an enormous bright light.

"Nice." David's silhouetted against the light of the Mobile Silo's cockpit, rising from the hangar below. "I never got to fuck up a giant robot before."

"Dear children." G's voice echoes across the hangar, carried over hissing speakers. "The final curtain is calling us." The railings shatter and break as the machine rears up, loading arms smashing where the stairways and ladders used to be and fastening like claws on the concrete we stand on.

"You don't deserve any of these people!" I shout the first

thing that comes into my head. "Alanza, even the baggers, at least they fought us!" David sprays fire against the cockpit, but it slides across the camouflaged metal like drizzle. "You're just an old, toothless coward!" I shout. "You've killed so many people here, and for what?!" More shots are fired. None of them make an impact.

We're free now, the baggers and Giants are all gone. Not that it matters anymore. "Surveillance? Intelligence? You'd do all this just to invade people's privacy?" My throat hurts, but it's been like that for days.

"As you grow older, your perspective widens," G rumbles across the hangar. "You learn your role better. You're all at a great advantage in this area." His machine shakes with internal motion. "Your parts in this world are very well-defined. I should know, I chose them."

"You sequenced our genes together," I shout up at the metal monster's face, "that doesn't mean you get to say who we are!" The students around me shout as well, until the air's filled with threats and taunts.

"It would be comforting to think so, wouldn't it?" The hangar shakes with G's question. "But you must realize by now that this isn't true. Especially for you, Hildegard."

"I wasn't on the list of sequences." I'm shouting towards G, but the students need to hear this as well. "And Alanza-"

"Yes, Alanza." The Mobile Silo groans as G angles his cockpit down towards her. "You are sisters. Twins." She stays quiet, staring up at him. "For you two, my principle holds more than true. I oversaw the sequencing and growth stages for every one of the director's Kids In America, but neither of you two can hope to outrun your mother's looming shadow."

"So, I am a copy." Alanza says to the leering machine.

"More than I knew your codes, I knew her. Your mother." G closes in. "You two," he pans his lights across us both, "you're defined by the role she played. I know every thought that could ever enter your mind. Every action or plan you could ever conceive of. Everything you could or would ever do. It's already been scripted for you."

"I don't care," I say and point my gun up at him. "If I'm a clone," I look over at Alanza, still staring up into the light, "if she's a clone. It doesn't make any difference. Just look how different we are! You can't control us just by knowing what pieces we're made of!"

It hadn't occurred to me before I shouted it out loud, but doesn't that prove it?

He knew her, whoever she was. That gave him an advantage at first, that's probably how he knew about the airfield takeover.

But, even assuming he's right, and he really could predict everything Alanza and I could do, we've both changed since we got here.

I don't know about her, but I've met new people, had my ideas challenged and tempered, and probably found out more about myself than anyone would actually want to know.

No wonder things have been spiraling out of G's control. The more I changed, the less he knew me.

The cockpit cranes back with a metal squeal as the students shout their agreement, firing wildly into the Mobile Silo's hissing joints and sparking against its armor plates.

"How sad, but hardly unexpected," G rumbles. "You've refused your script. A sure recipe for embarrassment."

There's no version of this scenario where we talk him down. I need something. Anything.

"Is that it?" I ask. "More theatrical metaphors to cover up how catastrophically wrong you've been about everything so far?"

"You'll learn exactly how right I am after the launch," G

says, mechanisms across the back of the Silo hissing and extending. That'll do.

"Grace." I turn to look down at her, gun swaying in her hand.

"Please tell me there's something we can do," she says as the hangar doors sigh, and begin to grind open.

"David!" I point. "Find the door controls, keep him in here for as long as you can!" He nods, and sprints up the stairs for the ruins of the control room. "Grace." I point into the middle of the hangar at the long yellow crane they'd used to load the missiles. "Use the crane to break off the firing mechanism."

She stares at me for a second as David runs. "Got it!" Grace sets off at a sprint.

"Defiant to the end." G's loading arms raise sparks from the crushed railings. "What a waste." One of the arms rises up, and the mechanisms on the end ball into a massive metal fist. "It's almost as if I knew all along that it would come to this." It crashes down faster than my eyes can follow, shattering the concrete and leaving an expanding cloud of dust.

Everyone around me opens fire as one

"Aim for the joints if you can!" I shout. "Try to find spaces between the armor!" I run to the railing as fast as I can, past Alanza, and search for David in the dust, but by now the hangar doors are almost open wide enough for G to escape.

I can't see David, and I don't have the time to look for him as G swings around, searching for Grace at the base of the crane. "Grenades! Explosives!" I shout, and a few go flying past me, splashing puddles of fire across the Mobile Silo's side.

Another explosion rocks the side as David emerges from the smoke, grenade belt in hand.

"Control's busted!" He shouts across to me. "He's going to get away!"

"Get away?" Alanza says as the Silo rears up, and students scatter as G aims another giant punch into the hangar walls.

As my head turns back, Alanza has already vaulted the rails. She grabs hold of one of the Silo's loading arms, and above us the crane groans as the ceiling starts to give way to showers of dust and chunks of concrete.

Another explosion hammers the side of the Silo, and as it rears back again, the crane hook suddenly falls towards it.

"Yes!" I hear Grace shout. "My claw machine days are paying off!" The hook clangs across the Silo's armor, catches underneath one of the long metal rails by the side of the missile, and with a mechanical squeal, it starts to pull.

"I'm caught on something!" G voice's echoes over me as the metal strains and sparks. The Silo falls back to ground level with a crash, and in a shower of sparks the rails are ripped free as the crane tears in half.

The hangar fills with whoops and cheers as David throws the last of his grenades down on the smoking Silo.

"What did we actually do?" he shouts.

"He can't launch!" Islet shouts from down below. "He can't do it! The missile won't get enough speed without the rails to accelerate them!" The shouts of triumph burst into crazed cheers.

"Did I do it?" Grace asks over the gap. "I think I did it!"

The Mobile Silo's treads snarl as they raise sparks from the hangar floor, and the machine turns to face the frozen lake, shining in the morning sun.

Vents along the back yawn open and hiss steam into the cold.

"No." Islet stares down as he runs up to meet me in what's left of the control room. "Look." He points up to the roof of the hangar at some mechanisms, still only just holding onto the pitted concrete.

Shouts of victory fade as metal arms unfold downwards towards the Mobile Silo as it growls across the hangar.

"What's he doing?" I ask Islet as he scans what's left of the hangar.

"Replacement parts." Islet sets off at a sprint, taking the steps up to the remains of the control room two at a time. "Backups in case the old parts failed." The hangar flashes with gunfire again as students scatter in every direction, looking for a line of fire.

Alanza is still down there, holding on as tightly as she can, climbing towards the cockpit. I doubt anyone's trying too hard not to hit her.

"Is there anything we can do?" David asks.

The question flies over Islet's head as he ducks and throws a curtain of rubble from one of the control room's still-lit consoles. "I can't tell," he says. "The whole interface might be destroyed, but I've been working with this computer for a long time." The unfolding machinery jumps and sparks as flashing cables fall from the ceiling and swing across the empty space. "I think this will do it." Islet says. "But look-" He wipes away a layer of dirt and sweat from his face as he looks up at me. "-I'm no good with words, but I'm sorry. There's so much more I could've done or said." A groan of breaking metal echoes across the hangar, and the unfolding arms snap into pieces, and clatter across the Mobile Silo's back in a shower of sparks.

Alanza nearly loses her grip as a piece falls past her, tearing ugly gray scars in the Silo's hide.

"Islet." Looking him in the eyes, I've never realized how afraid he must be. It's not something I've got much experience with, but I think I must be in the minority.

He needs to hear something. If not inspiring, then at least encouraging.

"I'm sorry, too. There were times when we mistreated you

or took advantage of you, I shouldn't-"

"Almost, almost." G's filtered laugh just carries over the mechanical roar of the Silo's whirling treads. "I still have the boosters, if I use the airstrip by the oilfield-" Flaps across the Silo flare and warp as holes open, spurting fire across the rear treads. "-yes, that'll do, I can still get enough range to hit a major city."

Everyone rushes towards the railings, firing down on the Silo as Alanza crawls up the arm towards the cockpit.

G's not going to wait for me to find the right words. It's almost a relief.

Why do I get the feeling I won't have the chance later?

"Islet!" I pull him towards me. "If I don't come back, here's what I need you to do-"

"From where, I don't-"

"Don't talk!" I say as the Silo's engines shriek. "Just listen! The real Commission will be here soon. If they find you, or anyone else, they'll probably kill you. Take all the students, find the bomb, and escape on the cargo jet G brought."

"All right, understood," he says as I back off. "Where do we go? What do we do when-"

"I haven't thought that far ahead, hopefully it'll be better than nothing." I test my weight, scan the distance, jump over what's left of the railing and catch one of the swaying cables.

I hear Grace gasp and David yell as I skin my palm, and the breath erupts from my chest as I grab the end of the missile cradle and pull myself up onto the back of the Silo.

It shakes as it speeds up, and my eyes are stung as it leaps out into the open air, thundering across the frozen lake and leaving the hangar behind.

Hopefully, they'll forgive me for being selfish one last time.

I still have to find the truth.

FILE 8: THE CURSE

File8: THE CURSE

January 1st

Happy New Year and fuck you.

Cooper's leaving. Were things getting better? No. Now he's giving up on me.

He said things were changing, maybe not for the better.

No shit.

❄

The metal slices my palm as I pull myself onto the missile, crawling along against the wind and trying to push my hair out of my eyes.

Ahead, at the end of the rocket is the swell of the Silo's

mechanical torso, and above that, the hatch that leads to the cockpit.

In the distance, the outline of the oilfield is growing.

I pick my way along the missile, grasping at loose panels with my nails and keeping as low as I can against the howling wind and thrashing snow.

Something metal groans, and a jagged piece shoots past me, cutting my eyebrow as it flies into the Mobile Silo's wake.

"Do you think I didn't know?" Alanza shouts down the missile to me from where she clings to one of the missile's fins. "I knew!" She stalks down the length of the cradle, grabbing handfuls of antenna and cable to steady herself. Her hands are empty, but there are grenades at her belt.

They worked before. If I can get my hands on one I might be able to breach the cockpit, so I follow the metal wire with my hand, pull myself upright, and brace against the missile's fastenings.

"You didn't!" I shout back. "And you never will! Because you'll never cross him to find out, and he'll never tell you!"

"What would you know?" She steps closer again, almost within reach. "You've never been me!" Still closer. "You've never been forced to live with strangers who claimed that they knew you!"

"There's no convincing you." Maybe something about the situation made me think I could talk to her. Maybe some part of me likes the idea of having a sister. She stares me down, and silently raises her hands.

"All right." I nod, and sweep my hair away from my eyes. "Let's settle this."

I reach out to snatch away her belt, but she catches my hand, twisting it away, and smashes a foot into my knee. She probably expects me to flinch or step back.

I head butt her, and she falls backwards and slides down

the missile, catching one of the flaps behind me, shouting something against the wind.

I step closer to grab the grenades still swaying from her belt but she claws at my ankle, and I fall, smashing my chin into the metal as my arms reach out to catch her.

Pulling at her uniform, I claw at her as she tries to turn and aim a punch into my face, but the machine rumbles over something, and Alanza's face collides with a piece of harness.

I reach out while blood streaks down her face and pull away the grenade.

Nowhere to put it. I'll just have to hold on to it, and climb back up with one hand. Yeah, that'll work.

There's the familiar crack of a gunshot, and my shoulder shakes. I can't see very well through the water clouding my eyes, but it looks red. I don't feel a thing.

"I could have guessed you might try something so dramatic!" G shouts over the wind as he stands in the toothy hatchway of the cockpit, holding his glasses in place with one hand, the other on his gun.

Another bullet shrieks over me, so against any kind of judgement I clench the grenade between my teeth and try to pull myself up again, but another shot raises sparks from the metal by my hands.

"You!" Alanza shouts. "You said you'd tell me about my mother!" My hand keeps slipping. It's covered in blood and starting to lose feeling.

G's gun drops, just a fraction of an inch.

"I made a promise," he says, "but not only to you." He fires twice, ripping holes in the missile by Alanza's hands. She isn't hit, but screams like she is.

"We had a deal! I trusted you!"

"I taught you better!" G shouts as he draws back into the hatch to reload. This is my only chance, so while he takes the extra second to check his chamber I pull the pin, and aim my throw down, under the blurring treads.

For a moment, nothing happens. G aims across the missile again, swaying between me and Alanza, but then the Silo rumbles.

I turn my head to see the back end crash into the air, broken treads thrashing the snow as the enormous machine seems like it's about to roll end over end.

I can't think of anything to do but hold tight as darkness and disorientation roll over me.

All I can do is listen to metal screeching as the white snow flashes over and over again against the gray sky.

❄

I smell burning.

The moment after, I realize how much my hand hurts, and smoke rushes in with my gasp of pain.

The motion of my coughing forces me to my feet.

I can't see much. Wreckage. Treads. One of the Silo's loading arms, half sunken in a pool of burning oil.

"You!" Alanza throws off a piece of debris into the ash dirtied snow. "You did this!" All around us black pillars stretch up to the sky, and broken metal hangs like dead skin over what used to be the oilfield. She coughs as she shouts, spitting cinders and flakes of oil onto the ground as she runs towards me.

I catch her tackle with my arms and try to push her back as she claws at my neck, but her arms fold around me and knock me to the ground. She aims punches at my face, so I roll to the ground, but stop at the very edge of a pool of oil and wind my arms around hers.

She steps over the pool, and her foots hits G as he crawls

from the wreckage, tossing his burning coat down onto the black stained ice.

I go for her gut in the second she's distracted looking down at him, and follow up with my slashed palm and bleeding shoulder. They're numb, so I don't feel the recoil, and it paints her soot-black face blood red.

It doesn't stop her, and she tries to grab me again. I lever her weight against me and throw her off onto a bed of broken concrete. She lands with a crack.

"You-" The second I speak I realize how hot the air is, so close to the burning oil. "-have no idea what you're doing." Alanza spits a soup of snow, blood, and oil onto the ground, pulling herself up onto the remains of a rusted beam. "That's why I beat you. He would never tell you, and-" She stumbles, as if her legs are numb.

"Like it matters." Alanza grimaces as she raises G's gun. She must've grabbed it from him as he was crawling away.

There's no cover, nothing I could dive behind, just a broken machine and a waterfall of oil running from a mountain of broken drums. "I'm not going to shoot you," she says, tears streaking her face,"you broke me." She aims down at an unbroken barrel at her feet. "I'm going to do something worse. I'm going to curse you. Every time you think you've done something good, you'll remember this," she spits. "Everything you've taken from me will follow you. Forever!"

I'd like to say I tried to stop her. There's too much space between us, and too many obstacles.

The barrel bursts into a fountain of fire, swallowing her in light and smoke.

After my eyes adjust, I watch the black figure inside, standing motionless for a moment.

It falls back into a pool of oil that lights with a shriek of burning air.

Behind me the Mobile Silo groans, and the missile rolls from its harness into the pool of oil around it.

Alanza's fire crawls towards it along the ground, creeping closer with every second.

I stop and listen to the burning for a second.

Not enough strength to do much else. On the edge of my vision, broken concrete is scattering as G crawls along the ground, pawing at broken chunks too high for him to scale.

"Where do you think you're going?" I ask as I pull him back by his collar. Somewhere in the crash he's lost his glasses, and for a moment, all I can do is stare into his strange, sunken pits. I plant my foot on his neck, and watch him squirm for a while.

"The bacteria," he gurgles through blood as the oil around the missile lights.

I push him back down with my boot.

"Don't you have something you were going to tell me?" One of his eyes is full of blood, and the other is vacant, staring off at nothing. Was he hurt in the crash, or were they always like that?

"Your adoption agent," he wheezes as tears run down his face, "your real father. He was one of our agents, assigned to oversee your upbringing. I vetted him myself."

"Keep going," I say as I take my boot off his neck. "Where is he now?"

"Dead," he sighs, trying to sniff the tears, snot and flecks of oil from his face. "Killed."

I should feel something.

I will later. Somehow, I knew.

"Who?" Behind me the missile bursts into flames and I feel the heat on my back.

"The same thing that always kills people like us." G closes

his eyes against the growing light. "People who work in danger, or in secret, soldiers and spies-"

"The simple version." I press my boot into his neck again.

"Simply put-" he coughs "-your so-called father took his own life during interrogation, rather than give up your location. We-" he coughs again, spilling blood down the front of his shirt "-we found you anyway." I step back, away from G and the coating of ash and snow that's settling on him. "He trusted you!" he screams at me. "Trusted in you! That's why he's dead!"

"You-" He's talking. He has information I need, I just can't focus. Cooper wouldn't do that, not if there was any other option. "-you said you vetted him!" I have to shout, it's the only alternative to shutting down. "You assigned him! So why-"

"He worked for the Commission." G shifts in place. "After the split, he stayed loyal. Even with X gone, he wouldn't give you up." He coughs again. "I had to do something, I-"

"So you killed my father and all these children that you helped create just so you could spy on people?" I ask as I step closer. Feeling's starting to come back as I scan the ground for weapons.

"Spying. Surveillance." He laughs with what's left of his face. "Privacy's already becoming a comforting fantasy. That's why I did it."

I want to interrupt him. Smash in his head with a twisted pipe, but I have to hear this.

"Once the infection was too large to control, I was going to-" G wheezes as his chest suddenly falls. "-going to open source the software, and the schematics for the detectors. No more privacy, not for anyone. Equal surveillance for everyone. Then-" He sputters, and a fountain of blood leaps into the air.

"Open source?" It feels bizarre to talk, feeling like this, as if something ordinary has become completely insane.

"Yes." He nods. "We could finally kill the spy's worst enemy. Trust would disappear." His eyes turn upwards, at the dark sky, tears reflecting the firelight. "We wouldn't need it anymore, we'd live in a world of perfect honesty."

I understand what he's saying. No, more than that, I know why he wanted it. "You are like me, aren't you? If you'd told me all this before I came here, I might have helped you. You really have never trusted anyone."

"You understand?" He turns his head towards me as much as he can. "It wasn't easy, but at least-" He hisses in pain. "-at least it's over now." G holds out his gun for me to take. "You're active now. The Commission knows you."

"I've made plans." I say as I take the gun from him.

"You think you're better than me." He coughs as I stand over him. "Just because you relied on someone else?" I don't answer him. "You'll see, eventually. My way was the only way." He nods to himself, over and over. "Then you'll be down here, with someone else standing over you."

I pull the trigger, and his head snaps back.

❄

"Sure we have enough?" Grace asks.

"Enough for now," David answers as he shepherds the line of students on board. As they file past me into the hold they lay supplies down in small piles. Bandages. Ammunition. Weapons.

My voice cracks as I croak at him. " You've made sure the bomb's secure?"

"As secure as we can make it," David says. Grace holds a radio up to her ear.

"Five minutes left!" she announces to the cabin. "Then we're fueled up and ready to go."

I can't see the school from here, just the ropes of smoke that rise from where it used to stand. Now and then someone glances at me as they stumble past, but no one questions me.

"This really isn't necessary," Islet says as some ex-Golf Company students lead him inside the plane's gaping mouth. "I can be a mouthpiece, talk to the Commission!"

"Islet." I stand up to face him. "We need you more here."

"You can't just take me along." He opens his arms. "I have a house. A cat!"

"We'll get your cat," Grace says.

"You sure you want to be standing up?" David asks me, looking as if he's getting ready to catch my unconscious body.

"Just a little longer," I tell him.

"Whoever you're a clone of must be a beast." He laughs, and a few other students chuckle along with him.

"That's what this is all about, really," I tell them. "That shouldn't matter." Students look up, and before I know it I'm raising my voice. "Our genes don't determine who we are, how we act or what we do. They don't control us, or who we connect with. We won here, stopped G from forcing his idea of a utopia on everyone, but fighting for freedom will be just as hard."

They need to hear from me, this can't feel like a defeat. "Today, I found out that my father, the reason I came here, killed himself to stop G from finding me."

"That sucks," says David interrupting as more students file past him.

"Yes, actually," I continue without looking at him,"but it made me realize something important. When I found out, I knew that I couldn't have felt any worse if he were my biological father. On the way back here, I thought about how Alanza is-" The burning shadow flashes across my mind. "-was my twin. It didn't mean anything. Genes don't mean anything." More nods, grunts of agreement. "It's more than that." I look around at all the dirty, blood-streaked, smiling faces. "We're family now, and we don't have to be related to be that way. Nobody does." They laugh and whoop. Some of them clap, like I've just given a commencement speech. For the first time, though, I don't mind.

I didn't know it until I said it, but I believe it.

No, more than that. It's true.

"Checklist complete!" Grace shouts into the cabin. "We'll be taking off in less than two minutes. Keep my seat warm!" She points to the space next to David as they share a glance.

Staring out into what's left of the forest, I feel an itch, somewhere along my neck, a twitch, a shiver.

"Shit!" David dives past me, grabbing a gun from the pile as the hull of the cargo plane shakes.

The shimmering body of Giant 2 slowly stalks up the ramp from the runway, hissing as it passes in and out of focus. The figure's arms rise, and palms open.

The students fan out, surrounding the Giant as his hands rise to his head and pull off the gray machinery covering his face. The goggles and tubes fall to the floor.

"I'm sorry. Truly, I am," he says. The vibration is gone, his body's standing perfectly still.

"You can talk?" Grace asks.

"I can. Often, I choose not to. I've worked all my life with my unit, with G, but you-" He raises his hands towards me. "Hildegard. You were right. What I was doing, what I had done, were both wrong."

"What do you want?" I ask him.

"To help you," the Giant says. "To join you." David's gun

is still leveled at him. "We're alike. Neither one of us has a place in this world."

"If we're going to go," Grace says, "it's now or never." She holds out her radio. "Islet says he's all ready to go, we just need to close the cargo doors."

"Don't get the wrong idea," I tell him. "It won't be easy." He steps inside, and David lowers his gun as the cargo doors begin to grind closed and the engines outside begin to whir.

"All right then," Grace says, "Everyone settle in." Giant 2 settles next to some students who immediately edge away from him.

"Got a name?" David asks as he sits down across from him.

"It's-" his eyes flicker, as if he has to try to remember. "-Frederick."

"Nice to meet you." David holds out his hand.

"Likewise."

They shake hands as Grace and the others stare. The doors close, and the cabin lights flicker on.

"Who taught you how to wrestle?" David asks him.

"I could give lessons," Frederick says, glancing around at the students that surround him.

The hum through the sides of the plane transforms into a roar.

"We'll probably need them," I say as I lean back. My stomach lifts, and my head rolls back and forth.

How long will it take me to fall aslee-

FILE 9: FINAL REPORT

TIME: Null

DATE: Null

CLEARANCE: SAE

THE I THAT WAS ME IS GONE.

I left it behind on that island where the children were.

It's not always that easy to leave an I behind, but this was a special case.

It's said that the bigger they are, the harder they fall, so it follows logically that a Giant falls very hard.

I'm between I's now, and that's always a discomfort. I could wear some of my warmer noses and ears, but it feels dishonest. Ironic. A costume without an actor, G would say.

Luckily, the weather is freezing, and I can cover up without arousing any suspicion.

I've chosen a pay phone near a main road, at the center of

a small town. Only an hours journey from that awful school. No one else is around, and even if there were, they're all covered up, like me.

I pick up the phone, and input this month's number.

It belches opera in my ear. Unmistakably Handel.

"One," I whisper into the phone. It clicks, to confirm. "Two." Another click. "Six." Another. "Seven, eight." The final two clicks.

"JD," the other voice sniffs. "It's a sad fact of our relationship that I cannot call your level of efficiency exceptional. The sample?"

"On it's way to you." I hate the sound of my unchanged voice. It barely comes above a whisper.

"Very good." There's the sound of a china teacup being set down. "And can you confirm our reports that dear G has met his end?"

"I can. Shall I recover the body?" I ask.

"Don't bother, JD. Come in at once, you must be at your absolute limit, impersonating such a thug in those horrendous conditions."

"Thank you, Director. will there be anything else?"

"No." The sound of a creaking armchair. "I suppose not."

"Very good, sir."

"And be sure to upload what you have when you come in," he says. "Tell me, the girl, you made observation of her?"

"I did, sir."

"Did she have any idea she was infected?"

"No, sir. Her sample will come in along with mine." The wind whips across my face. "You'll be reading her thought logs by morning."

"No more need for questions, then." I can hear the smile in his voice. "I assume the bacteria activated correctly, without her medication?"

"Yes, sir, it should give us a window to a week or so before her arrival, as well as a smattering of earlier memories."

"I'm still stunned, I suppose." The creak of the director leaning back in his chair "I had no idea G would prove resourceful enough to mass produce that bacteria of his, or that he would believe it so important he would make an attempt on my life."

"You see the best in everyone, sir," I tell him. "I was only shocked that reports of your death affected him so severely."

"Yes." I know him. He's nodding to himself. "It feels wrong to have deluded him into thinking he'd become so accomplished as to split my commission in two, but one can hardly argue with the results. No one but him could have modified our bacteria for mass production. Dismissed."

I set the phone down, and step in place, testing the new length of my legs. The airport is a long walk, but I have no other options.

I crane my head to look into the sky at the lights of an enormous plane flying by overhead. I stand still and squint through the snow, capturing the roaring engines and dark gray hull.

From the author

Thanks for reading. I hope you enjoyed K.I.A. and I hope you'll consider writing a review for Goodreads or Amazon.

If you didn't enjoy K.I.A. I want to know that, too. You can always contact me through my website or my FaceBook page.

If you'd like to know more about K.I.A., the story world, the characters and the writing process behind the book, you'll find bonus materials on my website.

Once again, thanks for reading.

Web: AlexanderCharalambides.com

FB: facebook.com/ajcharalambides/

ACKNOWLEDGMENTS

This book wouldn't have been possible without help from a lot of people. I'd like to thank everyone who read and commented on early drafts and especially my sister, the talented Mina Chara who designs my covers and enthusiastically lets me know when I have a dumb idea.

To all those who've competed for copies of my book in Facebook events, thanks for taking the time. Your enthusiasm helps to keep me motivated.

Everybody who bothered to like and comment on my various pages on the website and on Facebook, I may not always have time to reply, but I appreciate every one.

To Diane and Jenny of BookRhythm, whose tireless marketing efforts have allowed this book to find readers, what would I do without you? You've introduced me to a whole new world and I will always be grateful.

I've never met my Aunt Elspeth, but I see her 'likes' and hearts and comments everywhere I go online. I'm sure I don't deserve such loyal support, but I really appreciate it.

ALSO BY ALEXANDER CHARALAMBIDES

Black Blade

Lance knows that at heart he's a knight, so when the sword Excalibur turns up in a museum toilet, he does what any red blooded teenage hero would do. Grabbing the sword, he takes on the quest and never asks unimportant questions like 'why?'

While Megan, his loyal sidekick, tries to keep Lance grounded, three strangers, claiming to be wizards, come to guide him on his quest. The prize? The Holy Grail.

What is the Grail? What will happen if Lance fails? If you are truly chosen, do you need to ask?

"All in all, this is an eminently well-written and intricately plotted read that will entertain you for hours as the teen twosome try to navigate the treacherous magical underworld into which they've been thrust. And the bickering wizards add a sometimes comic and often obscene layer of sophisticated characterization rarely found in YA fiction." Publishers Daily Reviews

Would you take up the Black Blade?

95702464R00207

Made in the USA
Lexington, KY
11 August 2018